LET C

The desperate Ro ring at Thessalonica's wa gate had slammed shut the people on the city the gate that George hadn't managed to get in with the others, those shouts did no good whatever. The gate didn't open again, and what looked to George like all the Slavs in the world were bearing down on him.

George ran for his life, slashing at a Slavic archer as he sprinted. The barbarian fell back with a howl of pain. He was in among the Slav archers now. If they closed with him, he was dead, and he knew it. But he was still swinging his sword, and they were armed with nothing better than bows and belt knives. That left them unenthusiastic about closing.

Breath sobbing, heart thudding as if it would burst at any moment, he ran into the brush. His boots scrunched on dry, fallen leaves. He groaned—how could he hope to go anywhere without giving himself away with every step he took? He wondered if the barbarians had let him get into the woods just to give themselves the pleasure of hunting him down. He'd watched cats playing with mice. Let the little creature think it can break free? Why not, especially when it's blocked off from its hole?

"Sometimes the mouse *does* get away," he panted, dodging between tree trunks. "Sometimes the cat ends up with a stupid look on its face." Most of the time, the mouse got eaten, he knew, trying not to think about it.

From right beside him, a voice spoke in Greek: "Sometimes mouse gets help." He had all he could do not to scream. He turned his head.

A satyr looked back at him, its amber eyes wide and amused. "Come," it said.

Baen Books by Harry Turtledove

The Case of the Toxic Spell Dump
Agent of Byzantium
Werenight
Prince of the North
A Different Flesh
King of the North
Thessalonica

HARRY TURTLEDOVE

THESSALONICA

This is a work of fiction. All the characters and events portrayed in this book are fictional, and any resemblance to real people or incidents is purely coincidental.

A Baen Books Original

Baen Publishing Enterprises
P.O. Box 1403
Riverdale, NY 10471

ISBN: 0-671-87761-5

Cover art by Darrell K. Sweet

First printing, January 1997

Distributed by Simon & Schuster
1230 Avenue of the Americas
New York, NY 10020

Printed in the United States of America

I

George was hunting rabbits in the hills not far from Thessalonica when he spied the satyr. His first thought, when its brown eyes peered out of the ugly, snub-nosed face and met his, was to make the sign of the cross and frighten it away.

He didn't act on his first thought. He was the kind of man who commonly thought three times before he did anything. His build matched his character: he was stocky and strong, thick through the shoulders, by no means someone who moved quickly, but hard to stop once he did get moving.

Instead of crossing himself, he raised his right hand and rubbed his chin. Whiskers rasped under his fingers. He should have shaved yesterday, or maybe the day before. He thought about growing a beard. They were coming back into fashion, though many Romans, perhaps most, still plied their razors as they had since the days of Constantine the Great.

When he didn't drive it off, the satyr cautiously came toward him, picking its way along the rocky ground with surprisingly delicate, graceful strides. He supposed getting a rock in its hoof would cause it as much trouble as that would for a horse, which the satyr resembled from the waist down.

It was certainly hung like a horse, its phallus juttingly erect. The old stories said satyrs were hard all the time. Till now, George had never had a chance to put the old stories to the test. Satyrs were rare these days, almost six hundred years after the Son of God came down and was made flesh.

What a trophy to bring back to town, George thought. Bishop Eusebius would probably bless him from the ambo of the basilica of St. Demetrius. He could all but hear the bishop going on about another turn being given to the winding sheet Christianity was wrapping around the corpse of paganism: Eusebius was a good man, but one who sometimes had a distinctly mortuary cast of mind.

He didn't pluck an arrow from his quiver and set it to his bow, any more than he had signed himself. He stood quiet and let the satyr approach. Up in an oak tree, a blackbird trilled. The breeze sighed through the leaves of the tree. The satyr made no sound at all. Maybe, being a creature of wood and forest, that was its way. And maybe, being more than an ordinary creature, it had ways on which Christian men were wiser not to speculate, for the sake of their souls.

It paused almost within arm's length of him. Nervously, it stroked its erection with one hand, as a flighty woman might have played with a lock of hair while hardly noticing she was doing it. Then, as if making up its mind, the satyr pointed to the skin George carried on his belt.

"Wine?" it asked, its voice a plaintive baritone. It spoke in Greek, of course, being native to this soil. George had grown up with Latin his birth speech, but, like most Thessalonicans, he was fluent in both tongues.

"Yes, it's wine," he answered. Water up here in the hills was mostly good, but still, who would drink water by choice?

"Drink some, please?" The satyr's syntax was rusty, as if it wasn't used to speaking with men. It probably wasn't.

These days—these centuries—few would welcome it, or even tolerate it as George was doing.

As was George's way, he hesitated before replying. Drunken satyrs were supposed to do all sorts of appalling things. But the wineskin he carried wasn't that large to begin with, and he'd already drunk from it. The satyr could hardly get drunk on what was left. Besides, it sounded so sad.

He unfastened the skin from his belt and handed it to the satyr. The creature's homely features became almost beautiful for a moment as joy lit them. It fumbled with the cord that held the skin closed; obviously, it wasn't used to dealing with any man-made things, even ones as simple as that. But it managed, and sighed with ecstasy as it poured wine into its open mouth.

Considering the quality of the wine, George was glad he'd given it to the satyr, which was taking far more pleasure from it than he ever could have. He would have been miffed, though, had the creature guzzled the skin dry. He was about to say so, in no uncertain terms, when the satyr figured that out without his help. After wiping its mouth on its hairy arm, it held the skin out to him.

"Thanks," he said, and swigged from it himself. The wine tasted better than it had; maybe being touched by the satyr had improved it.

Being touched by wine had certainly improved the satyr. It seemed bigger, stronger, younger, and even more ithyphallic than before. It had lost its hangdog air: its eyes flashed. Its large nostrils dilated, as if to taste the wind. "That good," it said, almost crooningly.

"Glad you like it," George answered, polite as if he were talking to a monk. He cocked his head to one side, studying the satyr. "Didn't know your kind came so close to Thessalonica anymore," he remarked, looking back over his shoulder towards the city.

"Not like to come so close," the satyr answered. A moment later, it added, "Hard to come so close. Saints almost everywhere to keep me away."

George nodded, half matter-of-factly, half sympathetically. As Christianity's hold on the land tightened, the old creatures found it harder and harder to approach holy men or holy places. The satyr hadn't had any trouble approaching *him*. He shrugged. He was just a man, just a sinner. He knew it.

"Where have you been living?" he asked.

"Up in rough country." The satyr pointed off to the north and east: rough country sure enough, well away from the Via Egnatia that still—tenuously—linked Thessalonica with the Adriatic and Italy on the one hand and with Constantinople on the other. The satyr went on, "Villages not so bad. Not so much—" Being what he was, he couldn't make the sign of the cross, but George got the idea.

He nodded to show the satyr he followed. Bishop Eusebius was always talking about doing a better job of evangelizing the little upcountry villages. It wasn't only satyrs that hung around them. Bacchus still came around in the fall, when the grapes were being crushed for wine. Up in the hills, Pan had a festival, too, though even there some said he was dead.

"Why didn't you stay up in the rough country, if it was easier there?" George asked.

The satyr's eyes got wide. It stroked itself again, as if for reassurance. Breathing wine fumes into George's face, it answered, "Not easier there. Not so good, no. People all right, even if some—" Again, he would have crossed himself if he could. "But new *things* in woods."

"What kind of *things*?" George tried to put the same kind of dread into the word as the satyr had, but knew he didn't come close.

"Lots new things in the woods." The satyr looked back toward the northeast, as if expecting those things, whatever they were, to burst from the woods and tear it to pieces. Up and down, up and down went that hand. After a moment, it added, "Wolves worst. Yes, wolves." It nodded to itself; it might have been comparing the wolves to something else almost as dreadful.

George scratched his head. For one thing, you heard wolves howling outside the walls of Thessalonica every winter. For another— "I wouldn't think ordinary wolves would be the sort of things to worry you," he remarked. Satyrs weren't what they had been, back in the days before Christianity came to this land. They were a long way from diminishing to mere flesh and blood, though.

"Not ordinary wolves," the satyr said. "Not *ordinary*, no." It seemed grateful to George for having given it the word to describe the wolves, even if only in the negative.

"Ah," George said. "New sorts of powers trying to come down here: is that what you mean?" The satyr nodded, head moving in rhythm with its hand. George shrugged. "I expect the priests will drive them away."

The satyr made a noise like none he'd ever heard before. After a moment, he realized it was half moan, half giggle. "I watch priest go out to wolves," the satyr said. "He not see me, or he" —once more, it indicated the sign of the cross without actually making it— "and I have to run away. But he not see. He find wolf. He go up to it. He do that thing, thing make me run."

"Yes?" George said when the satyr didn't go on. "What happened then?"

Again, that strange mixture of mirth and terror burst from the satyr's throat. It was an appalling sound, one that made the little hairs on George's arms and at the back of his neck stand up as if he were a wolf himself. "Priest do that thing," the satyr repeated. "He do it not at me, so I see safe. And wolf—eat him up."

"Really?" George said. It was, he realized, a foolish response. He consoled himself with the thought that it was better than making the sign of the cross, which would have routed the satyr. It had been a long time—a lot longer than he'd been alive—since powers that could stand up against Christianity's most potent symbol had come into this part of the world. He nodded slowly to himself, fitting puzzle pieces together like mosaic tesserae in the church of St. Demetrius. "They must belong to the Slavs."

"Slavs." The satyr spoke the word as if it had never heard of the people so named. "Who—what—are Slavs?"

George's nose was long and beaky, admirably made for exasperated exhalations. "They and the Avars have only been raiding the Roman provinces south of the Danube for the past generation," he said, his tone perfectly matching the irritated sniff.

"Ah, only one generation," the satyr said in some relief. "No wonder I not know."

"Only one . . ." George fell silent. He studied the satyr. He'd shot that *only one generation* as if from a catapult, propelled by sarcasm rather than twisted cords. The satyr, though, had taken him literally. And why not? he realized. What was a generation to a being essentially immortal? The satyr was speaking with him now. It might have spoken with St. Peter when he traveled through Greece not long after the Incarnation, had it so chosen and had the saint not driven it from his presence by overwhelming holiness. It might have spoken with Alexander the Great. George shivered. It might have spoken with Achilles before he sailed for Troy. No wonder it took mere generations lightly.

"This wolf thing eat up priest," the satyr repeated. It ran a tongue as long and red as its phallus around its mouth, imitating a wolf licking its chops. "Then it look over to where I am. It not blind and stupid like priest—it see me. It think about eat me up, too. I see it think. Then it decide, *I full*. I see that, too. Wolf get up, go away."

George wanted to say *Kyrie eleison* or *Christe eleison*, but didn't, for fear the holy words would make the satyr flee. He looked at it with an emotion he'd never expected to feel toward its kind: sympathy. "You're in a hard spot, aren't you? If you come down to places like this, the priests and holy men will get you. If you stay where you have been staying, though, the wolves will do the same."

"Not wolves only," the satyr said. "Other things, new things, never-seen things. Frightening things."

Frightening because they're new or frightening because they're frightening? George wondered. To an immortal that had grown used to the ways of its part of the world, change of any sort had to seem like the end of that world. What must the Olympians have thought when Christ overcame them? The satyr hadn't been so strong as all that—but the other side of the coin was, lesser threats were dangerous to it.

"What I do?" it mourned now. "What I do?" Its eyes bored into George's as if it was sure he had the answer.

He wished he did. But he was a Christian himself. Some—many—would have said he'd already shown too much tolerance for this creature of the old dispensation. As far as he was concerned, though, the Good Samaritan made a better model than the Pharisee who went out of his way not to help lest he be defiled. And, in purely pragmatic terms, what he'd learned was worth knowing, not only for his sake but for Thessalonica's.

None of that did the satyr any good. It made another strange noise, this one full of despair, and started for the trees. "Wine sweet," it said, as if suddenly remembering, and then it was gone.

George strode into Thessalonica through the northwestern gate close to St. Catherine's church. He carried a couple of hares and a couple of partridges: not a great day's hunting, but not bad, either. He and his family would eat well tonight, and tomorrow, too.

Calm washed out of Catherine's as he walked past it. Unlike Demetrius, she was not a warrior saint: very much the reverse. She had been martyred in Alexandria after besting several pagans in debate; when her head was struck off for her temerity, milk flowed from the wound instead of blood.

Feeling her holy influence eased George's worries . . . for a little while. With such spiritual strength behind it—to say nothing of the imperial soldiers and the popular militia to which he belonged—Thessalonica could surely stand up against anything the Slavs and Avars might do, whether with their soldiers or with their gods and demons.

Most men would have let the rationalization satisfy them. In spite of Catherine's calm, George could not make himself forget the satyr had said a Slavic wolf had devoured a priest who tried to banish it. *You should pray more*, he told himself, *and think less*. He'd been telling himself the same thing for a good many years. He did pray, frequently and sincerely. He never had been able to make himself stop thinking, though.

He brought the game he had killed into the shoemaker's shop where he hadn't worked that day, having gone hunting instead. That did not mean the shop had stood idle. With his wife Irene, his daughter Sophia, and his son Theodore to help with the work, things got done whether he was there or not. He sometimes suspected things got done better when he wasn't there. He'd never voiced that suspicion aloud, for fear Irene would confirm it.

She looked up from the undyed leather boots she was making for Peter the miller, who lived down the street. Her eyes brightened when she saw the game George had brought home. She had a few years fewer than his thirty-five—he wasn't sure how many, but then, he wasn't sure whether he might not be thirty-four or thirty-six himself—and looked younger still: her hair was still dark, her skin unlined, and, despite three pregnancies, she had almost all of her teeth.

She said, "You did well there—probably better than if you'd stayed here." Like him, she made such calculations almost as second nature. Their parents had arranged the marriage, of course, but it had proved good not just because of the properties and families it joined. They thought alike, which made them enjoy each other's company.

"Shall we stew them with cabbage and leeks, Mother?" Sophia suggested. She was fifteen now—George was sure of that, because she'd been born in the year Maurice became Roman Emperor. Her face was long and thin like her mother's, but she had most of his nose in the middle of it. He worried that it looked better on him than on his daughter.

"That sounds all right to me," Irene said. She looked at George. He nodded. She looked at Theodore. He pulled a sour face. He was a couple of years older than Sophia, and at the age where he pulled a sour face at anything his parents suggested. Irene chose to make the best of that she could: "I know you're not fond of leeks. Will you put up with them tonight because everyone else in the family is?"

"I suppose so," he mumbled; sometimes soft answers from George and Irene were harder for him to take than furious shouts would have been. George, though, was not long on furious shouts. He'd had a bellyful of them from his own father, and didn't see that they'd done much good in making him behave.

Irene carried the hares and partridges upstairs; like a lot of artisan families, George's lived over their shop. Before too long, a delicious smell floated down into the work area. No customers had come in since George showed up with the game, and it was getting dark outside, so he felt no hesitation about shutting the front door and letting down the bar. He didn't expect anyone would need new boots or to have a sandal repaired so badly as to come to the shop with a torchbearer—and, in the unlikely event somebody did do that, he could always open the door again. He and the children went upstairs after his wife.

It was lighter up there than down below: safer to put windows in the second story of a building, because they were harder to break into there. Even so, Irene had lighted a couple of lamps. The smell of burning olive oil was part of the characteristic odor of Thessalonica, along with woodsmoke, garbage, and manure. George paid no attention to the smell when he stayed in town, but it forcefully brought itself to his attention when he came back after some time away, as with his day of hunting.

Irene ladled the stew into earthenware bowls; Sophia carried them and horn spoons to the table. Irene brought in bread and honey to go with the stew. Before the family began to eat, they bowed their heads. George said grace, thanking Christ that they had enough to fill their bellies. When he was done, he glanced toward the heavens. Though all he saw were the beams of the roof, he knew God watched over him.

The blessing reminded him of what had gone on in the woods earlier that day. "I saw a satyr this afternoon," he remarked after he'd taken his first bite, and then, in much the same tone of voice, "Good stew."

Theodore gaped at him; Sophia made the sign of the cross. They and their mother all exclaimed—they knew George too well to let that calm, casual tone lull them. Irene, not surprisingly, was the first one to put words to her thoughts: "I hope it was from far away, and that the creature didn't bother you."

"It didn't bother me." George took another bite. Deliberately, he chewed. Deliberately, he swallowed. "I gave it some of my wine—not too much. I didn't want it drunk."

"You should have driven it away, Father." Now Theodore crossed himself, to show what he meant. "Those nasty demons can't stand against the sign of the true faith."

"I know that." George hid his smile. In going against what his father had done, Theodore had—no doubt altogether without intending to—become perfectly conventional. George ate some more stew, then went on, "As things worked out, I'm glad I didn't." He told of what the satyr had said about the Slavic wolf-demon and what that demon had done to the priest.

His wife, his son, and his daughter, all made the sign of the cross then, to turn aside the evil omen. For good measure, Theodore also pulled at the neck opening to his tunic and spat down it, an apotropaic gesture older than Christianity, and one a priest might have frowned to see.

"What are we going to do?" Sophia asked. "If these barbarians and their horrible demons come against Thessalonica, how shall we be saved?"

"We have strong walls, we have soldiers, we have priests, we have faith in God," George answered. "If all those aren't enough, what will be?"

Sophia nodded, reassured. Irene's eyes met George's. Neither of them said anything. He knew what his wife was thinking: that all the things he'd named might not be enough. And it was true. Not long before Sophia was born, Sirmium, a city perhaps as great as Thessalonica, had fallen to the Slavs and Avars. Life in the Roman Empire was hard these days, and no one could say it might not get harder.

After supper, Irene and Sophia washed the dishes in a basin of water. By the time they were done, full darkness had fallen. Against its almost palpable presence, the flames from the lamps and the flickering light they cast seemed tiny and weak, the next thing to lost. George thought of the Slavs and Avars moving down toward the Aegean, and of Thessalonica, a Christian light in a sea of pagan darkness.

He went to the window and looked out. Most of Thessalonica was dark now, with a glow of candles and of holiness coming from the churches, more lights up on the walls, and here and there one moving through the streets as prominent people undertook to travel through the night. Footpads traveled through the night, too, but did not advertise their presence.

"Close the shutters, George," his wife said, yawning. "Let's go to bed." Few people—mostly the rich, who could afford the lamps and candles they needed to turn night into day—stayed up long past sunset. Nor was darkness the only reason for that. When you rose with the sun and worked hard all day, you were ready to go to bed by the time night came.

The room to the left of the hall as you walked up it had been shared by Sophia and Theodore. These days, since they'd come to puberty, it had a wooden partition down the middle that turned it into two cubicles. George kept telling himself—and anyone who would listen—he would enlarge the doorway one day soon. He'd been saying it for so long, he didn't believe it himself anymore.

He used a lamp from the kitchen to light one that rested on a stool by the bed in his own bedchamber, then, in orderly fashion, carried the first one back to where it belonged, blew it out, and used what glow came through the doorway from the second to guide him up the hall. By the time he returned, Irene was already in bed. He used the earthenware chamber pot, took off his shoes, undid his belt and took it off, and got in himself, still wearing the long tunic he'd had on all day. The straw of the mattress rustling under him, he leaned up on one elbow and blew out the lamp on the stool. The bedroom plunged into darkness.

Despite that darkness, Irene did not want to go to sleep at once. "A satyr," she said in a low voice, one that, with luck, the children would not overhear. "I know of them, of course—everyone knows of them—but I never heard of anybody meeting one before, not even in the stories my old grandmother told me when I was little."

"Neither did I," George said, "not around a city that's been Christian as long as Thessalonica. But up in the north it's all helter-skelter; things are bubbling like porridge in a pot over a hot fire. The Roman soldiers and the Avars and Slavs keep going back and forth and round and round, but every year, in spite of what the soldiers do, there are more pagan Slavs settling on land that ought to be Roman."

"I know," Irene answered. "From what I hear in the marketplace, the Roman generals spend more time quarreling among themselves than they do fighting the enemy."

"I've heard the same thing," George said. "It worries me." Irene caught her breath at that. Her husband was a man who worried a good deal, but hardly ever admitted it out loud. He went on, "And when the Slavs settle on land that ought to be Roman, their gods and demons settle on land that ought to be Christian."

"That wolf—what it did to the priest . . ." On top of a wool blanket she had woven herself, she shuddered.

"Satyrs, now, and the other creatures from the old days," George said musingly, "people believe in them, yes, but not the way they used to, so no wonder the true faith of Christ is stronger than they are. But the Slavs, they believe in their powers the same way we believe in the power of the Lord. That makes the wolf—and whatever other things they have like him—dangerous to us Christians."

"Do you think the Slavs will come down as far as Thessalonica?" Irene asked.

"Farther west, bands of them have pushed deeper into Greece than we are," he replied: Irene was not the sort of woman to be fobbed off with vague reassurances, especially when those were likely to be false. "So yes, they could come to Thessalonica. Taking the city is another question. God surely guards us here."

"Yes, surely," Irene agreed, but less confidently than he would have expected from her. She was worried, too, then.

She lay on her left side, facing him; he lay on his right. He set a hand on her hip, partly to reassure her, partly as a sort of silent question. He'd learned early in their marriage not to take her when she didn't feel like being taken; the anger and arguments following that lasted for days, and were far more trouble than brief pleasure was worth. She, on the other hand, had learned not to deny him unless she was emphatically uninterested. For the most part, the compromise—about which they'd never said a word, not out loud—worked well.

If she'd flopped down onto her belly, he would have rolled over, too, and gone to sleep. Instead, she moved toward him, sliding across the linen of the mattress cover. He held her for a while, then peeled her out of her tunic and took off his own. Her body was warm, familiar, friendly in his arms. They seldom surprised each other in bed these days, but they made each other happy. As far as George was concerned, that counted for more.

Afterwards, he and Irene both used the chamber pot again, then redonned their tunics. The night was warm enough to sleep without those, but neither of them felt like startling their children in the morning. George fell asleep almost at once.

Breakfast was leftover stew, along with more bread. Irene sighed, then said, "I wonder how many women have prayed for a way to keep food fresh longer than a day or two."

"God has bigger things than that to worry about," George said.

"Evidently," his wife answered, leaving him with the feeling that he'd been punctured, even if he couldn't quite tell how.

He didn't have time to worry about it long; with the rest of the family, he went downstairs and got to work. Whenever they didn't have anything else to do, they worked on heavy-soled sandals in assorted sizes. Some farmers outside of town would make their own, but those were usually crude rawhide affairs, and didn't last. George had spent years building up a reputation for solid craftsmanship. *When you buy from George, you get your money's worth*, people said.

Once, a couple of years before, Theodore had remarked, "You know, Father, if we made the leather thinner, it would wear out faster, and people would have to come back sooner to buy more."

He'd obviously thought he was being clever. Because of that, George had been gentle when he said, "The trouble is, son, if the leather wore out faster, people would have to come back sooner, yes, but they wouldn't come back to *us*. They'd pick another shoemaker, one who gave them sandals that didn't fall to pieces in a hurry."

And, sure enough, the first customer of the morning was a farmer named Felix. "Good to see you're still here," he said to George in backwoods Latin. "I'm not fixing a hole this size, I don't think."

He held up a sandal. The sole was mostly hole. What wasn't hole was bits of leather, some tanned, some not, that had been sewn on over the course of years. George wouldn't have wanted to walk around in a sandal like that even without the latest hole, but held his peace. What Felix did with—or to—shoes was his business. George did take the ruined one to remind himself how big a foot Felix had. "We made a pair about that size a few days ago, I think," he said, and looked on the shelves set against the back wall. "Sure enough." He held out the sandals. "Try these on—see how they feel."

Felix did. His gnarled hands had a little trouble with the small bronze buckles, but he managed. He walked back and forth inside the shop. A smile came over his weathered face. "That's right nice," he said. "I'd forgotten walking doesn't have to feel like you've got a sack of bumpy beans under each foot."

"Glad you like them," George said; starting off the day with a sale always struck him as a good omen.

Felix, all at once, looked less happy than he had a moment before. "Guess I shouldn't have said that. Now you're going to charge me more on account of it." He cast an apprehensive eye toward George. "What are you going to charge me?"

"That's a good pair of sandals—you did say so yourself," George answered. "I was thinking . . . six miliaresia."

"Half a solidus?" Felix exclaimed. He made as if to throw the shoes at George. "I figured you'd say something more like two."

After an argument they both enjoyed, they split the difference. Felix also promised to bring a sack of raisins to the shop the next time he was in Thessalonica. Maybe he would and maybe he wouldn't. The four silver coins he did pay were enough for George to turn a profit on the deal.

"How are things treating you these days?" the shoemaker

asked, to make sure no bad feelings lingered after the haggle—and because life would have been boring if he let people out of his shop without finding out what they knew.

"Not bad, not bad," Felix answered. "Always a lot of fairies and such about, there away from town. It's quiet here, God be praised: everybody inside the walls believes in Him, pretty much. Not like that out in the country, you know. Old ways hang on."

"That's so," George agreed. "I saw a satyr myself yesterday, as a matter of fact."

"Oh, yes, I've seem them, too," Felix said. "I chase my daughters into the house when they're about, just on account of you never know—you know? But these I saw a few days ago, they weren't like anything I seen before. Pretty women, they looked like, with long yellow hair and with wings on their backs. Not angel wings, with feathers and all—more like beetle wings, all clear and shimmery. I made the cross at them, like a good Christian ought to, but they stood there and smiled at me. It was like they never seen it before."

"Maybe they hadn't," George said, and told him about the wolf. "New people on the move, new gods and demons moving with them."

Felix clicked his tongue between his teeth. "Hard times, sure enough," he said. "Well, God will protect us, I expect. I hope He will, anyhow." He headed out of the shop, then turned back. "The sandals feel good, George. I thank you for that." With a wave, he was gone.

George turned back to his son. "There, do you see, Theodore? Do a proper job and your customers come back to you."

"Yes, I see, Father." Theodore grinned mischievously. "Make four miliaresia every five or six years from a farmer and you can use it to buy gold plates to eat off of."

The shoemaker didn't know whether to smack the youth or start laughing. He let out a strangled snort, which satisfied neither of those impulses. If God did protect

Thessalonica, he thought, it would be either because He ignored the younger generation or because He was even more merciful than the Holy Scriptures said. As George pondered those two choices, he realized one didn't necessarily exclude the other.

He was delicately tapping an awl to produce a tooled pattern on a boot for a prominent jurist when Dactylius stuck his head into the shop. "Archery practice this afternoon!" the little Greek jeweler exclaimed. He carried a bow and had a quiver on his back. "Have you forgotten? I'll bet you have!"

"You're right, I did forget," George admitted. "I start doing this fine work" —he pointed to the boot— "and I don't think about anything else."

"Go on, dear," Irene told him. "Germanus won't be expecting those boots for at least another week. You'll have plenty of time to finish them."

"You're right." He didn't know why he bothered saying that; Irene was generally right. To Dactylius, he said, "I'll go get my bow and arrows—be right back." He hurried upstairs, grabbed the bow off the pegs where he'd hung it, and picked up his own quiver. He slung it over his shoulder as he returned to the ground floor.

Dactylius was hopping from foot to foot, as if he needed to visit the latrine. He seemed all the more excitable when paired with stolid George. "Come on!" he said. "Rufus will yell at us if we're late."

One of George's eyebrows quirked upward. "He'll yell at us if we're not late, too. You go to church to pray You go to militia practice to get yelled at."

Taking no notice of that, Dactylius grabbed him by the sleeve of his tunic and dragged him out into the street. Behind him, he heard Irene laugh softly. He was never late enough to matter, and most of the time his punctuality had nothing to do with Dactylius. For that matter, he kept the jeweler out of trouble more often than the other way round.

The practice field was just that: a field in the southeastern part of the city, not far from the hippodrome and fairly close to the sea. In the time of George's great-grandfather, a grandee had had a mansion there, but no one had ever rebuilt the place after it burned down.

A scrawny brown dog sprawled in the grass and watched the militiamen at their exercises. The commander of the regular garrison, up in the citadel on the high ground at the northeastern corner of Thessalonica, would either have laughed or suffered a fit of apoplexy to see it. The amateur soldiers were indifferent archers, poor spearmen, swordsmen longer on ferocious spirit than skill.

George knew he'd never use his bow as well as a professional soldier, even if he did bring back game when he went out hunting. Dactylius shot straighter than he did, though his own bow had a stronger pull. After he missed a shot from a range where he should have hit, he yanked a new arrow out of his quiver and made as if to break it over his knee.

Another of his fellow militiamen, a gangly, curly-haired man named John, not only had the gall to hit the canvas target but then said, "You might as well shoot that arrow, George. After it's gone wild, someone who knows what he's doing may find it. If you break it, it's gone for good."

"I'll have you know I bagged two rabbits and two birds yesterday," George said with dignity.

"Aye, and if the bunnies carried bows, they'd have bagged you first," John retorted. You didn't want to get into an argument with him; he made his living, such as it was, by going from tavern to tavern telling jokes. People said he'd come from Constantinople, that he'd been run out of town when some of his jokes there got too pointed to suit the men in power.

In the militia, though, your mouth would take you only so far. Rufus, the squadron commander, was a gray-haired veteran who'd fought the Ostrogoths in Italy under Narses the eunuch. He had one blue eye, one brown eye, and one nasty disposition. "Let's see you hit it again, John, before you make like you're the Second Coming."

"You couldn't have your second coming till a month after the first one," John muttered. But he made sure Rufus didn't hear him. George blamed him not at all for that. Rufus had to be nearing his threescore and ten, but George wouldn't have wanted to fight him with any weapons or none.

John nocked his next arrow, drew the bow back to his ear, let fly—and missed, almost as badly as George had done. Rufus laughed raucously. John muttered again. This time, not even George could make out what he said. The shoemaker decided that was probably just as well.

Somebody shot an arrow at the dog. The shaft thumped into the ground six or eight feet away from the beast. The dog never moved. "He's in the safest place he could be," Rufus said, and laughed again.

"I would hate him, if only he weren't right," Dactylius said. "We have to get better." His face was probably more intent than when he was setting a ruby into a golden necklace. He aimed, shot—and missed.

"You lugs are all hopeless." Rufus rolled his eyes. "Come on—all together now." A ragged volley followed. "By Jesus, the Virgin, and all of the saints, what will you do if the Slavs and Avars ever do come down on Thessalonica?"

"Probably something like this," John said, shivering as if he were about to freeze to death. "Or maybe this." He gave an alarmingly realistic impression of a man suddenly seized by diarrhea. "Or this." Now he mimed jumping onto a horse and galloping away as fast as he could go.

George was a sober, serious fellow most of the time. He found himself laughing helplessly at John's antics. He would have felt worse about it, but everyone else was laughing, too. Rufus had a soul as flinty as any this side of a tax collector's, but he guffawed with the militiamen he commanded. "You're a funny fellow, all right," he said to John. "I'd like you better, though, if your work with the bow weren't so funny."

John's next arrow not only hit the target, it pierced the center of the bull's-eye. "How about *that*?" he said triumphantly.

"That's even funnier than when you were doing the fellow shitting himself," Rufus said, leaving the comic, for once, altogether at a loss for words.

On their way back to their places in the workaday world, several of the militiamen, George among them, stopped in a tavern for a mug of wine. "Maybe even for two mugs of wine," George said, liking to spell things out as precisely as he could beforehand.

"Maybe." Dactylius sounded nervous. He might have been a trooper in the militia, but his wife Claudia, whose gray eyes and fair skin spoke of Gothic blood, was larger and brawnier and of a sharper temper than he.

The taverner, a long-faced, swarthy man named Paul, seemed gladder to see the militiamen than was his wont. He filled their mugs up to the top and didn't scrutinize the coppers they passed across the bar as if certain every other one was a counterfeit. "Are you feeling well, host of ours?" asked a plump fellow named Sabbatius.

"As well as a forest when the birds fly south for the winter," Paul answered in a gloomy croak. "Aye, the birds are flying, sure enough."

"Are you making riddles?" Sabbatius asked, swigging at his wine. He was liable to stay for more than a mug or two—or three or four.

"I don't think he is," George said. He studied Paul. "I think he's heard something. You *have* heard something, haven't you?"

"Good thing you make shoes instead of asking the questions when the torturer's doing his job," the taverner said. "Aye, I've heard something, and if it's so, you militiamen are going to be all that's in the way between us and trouble for a while."

"What do you mean?" Four or five of the amateur soldiers asked the question at the same time.

Paul shrugged. "My line of work, you do hear things. Some of the things you hear, you wish you hadn't, if you know what I mean. This is one of them. If I did hear right, most of the regular garrison is heading out of town."

"Christ have mercy!" Sabbatius said, beating George and several others to the punch. "Why do they want to go and do a fool thing like that?"

"Don't know that they want to," Paul answered. "When you're a soldier, though, you don't do what you want to. You do what they tell you to. Way I hear it is, Priscus the general is in trouble against the Avars and the Slavs somewhere off in the back of beyond"—he pointed vaguely toward the northeast—"and he needs soldiers, so off they're going to go."

"That's not so good," George said. He looked around the tavern, then back to Paul. "Would *you* want Thessalonica defended by the likes of us?"

"If I say no to that, you people will throw things at me," Paul replied, a smile stretching his face in unfamiliar directions, "but if I say yes I'll be lying. What am I supposed to do about that?"

"I *will* have two mugs of wine after all," Dactylius said, as if that were a matter more important than the regular garrison's leaving Thessalonica.

While the taverner filled his mug with a dipper, George pondered the question he'd asked. In due course, he told Paul, "Maybe you ought to join the militia, too. Then you'd have no one but yourself to blame for whatever might go wrong."

"Aye, maybe I ought to at that," Paul said. "I don't have forty years on me yet, and if I'm no Hercules, I'm no tun of suet, either, like some people I could name." He looked pointedly toward Sabbatius.

The chubby militiaman glared right back. "Step out into the street and we'll talk some more about that," he offered.

Paul reached under the counter and pulled out a stout club studded with nails. He set it on the bar. "If I step out into the street, I do my talking with this," he said. Sabbatius' sword was a better weapon, but he didn't push it, peering down into his mug of wine instead. Paul grunted and put the club away.

"You do join the militia, join our company," George said. "And bring your friend there." He tapped the bar to show what he meant. "Rufus sees that club, he won't just let you join, he'll try to steal it from you."

"Maybe I will," the taverner said again. Most of the time, that meant, *Not on your life, but I'm polite about it*. This time, George thought it meant he probably would.

Dactylius gulped down that second mug of wine and hurried out of the tavern. George's opinion was that he shouldn't have poured it down so fast; he was walking at a slant. If he was working on anything delicate, it wouldn't turn out so well as it might have. Claudia would notice, too—as far as George could tell, Claudia noticed everything, whether it was there or not—and make Dactylius regret it.

Although Sabbatius liked to drink, he was next to sidle out the door. He'd been staring down where Paul had stowed the nasty club. He was bold enough shooting at targets in the field, and at practice with swords, too. George got the idea, though, that he'd found the notion of having nails pounded into his own personal, precious flesh distinctly unappealing.

George left the tavern a few minutes after Sabbatius. He hurried back toward his shop—this was news more important than having seen a satyr. No one could know for certain what the latter portended, but anybody this side of an idiot was able to see the garrison's leaving Thessalonica meant trouble.

When Sophia saw him coming up the street, she ran out of the shop, exclaiming, "Father, guess what! You'll never guess what!"

"I don't know," George said agreeably. "What? Once you've told me, I have something to tell you, too."

"I was in the market square buying some parsnips for

Mother," Sophia said, her eyes snapping with excitement, "And people were saying the regular army is going to march out of town, to go help with the wars God knows where. Isn't that important? Isn't that worth hearing?"

"Well, yes, it is," he admitted.

He was never a man who got very excited about anything. His stolidity this time, though, irked his daughter. "You must be angry at me for telling you my news and not waiting to hear yours," she said. "What *was* your news, anyway?"

"It doesn't matter." He set a hand on her shoulder. "You've already heard it. What's your mother going to do with the parsnips?"

"Bake them with some snails she's gathered over the last few days," Sophia answered. "She finally has enough to cook."

"That sounds good," George said. "Let's go back to the shop. Don't you have some work to do? I know I've got plenty, and I spent longer at practice than I thought I would." He didn't mention going into Paul's tavern. What point, now? The rumor had to be all over Thessalonica by this time. He consoled himself by remembering rumors weren't always true.

The garrison marched out of the city three days later. They wore their mailshirts and helmets, which struck George, who stood watching as they headed out of Cassander's Gate, east down the Via Egnatia and away from Thessalonica, as a bad sign, a sign they expected to have to fight at any time. Many of them had painted either the cross or the labarum—☧—on their shields to help ward off whatever gods or demons the Slavs and Avars might call up. The labarum replaced the old pagan eagle atop their standards, too.

Bishop Eusebius stood just outside the gate, blessing the soldiers as they filed past him. "May you go with God, and may God go with you," he said. His silk vestments, more splendid than the cloak of the general commanding the garrison, gleamed in the sunshine. "In the name of the Father, the Son, and the Holy Spirit, go forth and defend the Roman Empire against its enemies, defend our Christian folk against all traps and tricks of the devil."

Eusebius put on a brave show. His long, lean face was lit by a pious certainty George sometimes wished he could match. The shoemaker's broad shoulders went up and down in a shrug. He was as he was, as Eusebius was as *he* was.

After Eusebius was done, the city prefect, a rotund fellow named Victor, came forward to make a speech of his own. He and the bishop eyed each other warily, neither altogether certain of his own power or trusting the other very far. Victor cleared his throat a couple of times, then began, "Glorious citizens of the equally glorious city of Thessalonica, we remain strong, we remain steadfast, we remain courageous, we—"

We remain bored, George thought. Victor not only liked to talk, he liked to hear himself talk. Eventually, he might come to the point. Meanwhile, George could stop listening for a while. He admired a pretty girl not far away. The wind was blowing her tunic tight against her body, so that she might almost have been naked.

Looking with lust in your heart at a woman not your wife was a sin. George knew as much. He also knew that, had Irene been standing there beside him and caught his eye straying toward that girl, she might have stuck an elbow in his ribs, but she would have been laughing while she did it. He sometimes thought she had more forgiveness for human frailty than the church did.

He started listening again, on the off chance the prefect was getting around to anything important—assuming, as might or might not have been justified, that he ever did get around to anything important. At the moment, he was saying, "—our magnificent metropolis, guarded by God, certain of protection from our patron saint, warded by our walls—" Not being in the mood for alliteration, George daydreamed a little while longer.

Victor began to shift from foot to foot. That either meant

he was coming to the point or that he needed to break off and run for the jakes. Hoping it was the former, George began paying attention once more. His optimism was rewarded, for the prefect declared, "And so, citizens of Thessalonica, my delegation and I shall travel to the imperial city, there to petition his imperial majesty, the splendid Roman Emperor Maurice, to send from elsewhere in the Empire, from lands less threatened by barbaric inroads, a new contingent of soldiers to take the place of those who have gone to fight. In the meanwhile, of course, I am certain our militia will continue to offer complete security for Thessalonica."

Had he been truly certain of that, what need would he have had to go to Constantinople to ask Maurice for replacement troopers? There were times when George thought he should have become a priest; his mind was made for logic-chopping. As usual at such times, he shook his head. He enjoyed the trade he'd learned from his father. A logical shoemaker might be an uncommon beast, but by no means an unnatural one.

Such musings did not keep him from joining in the applause Victor got. Being a member of the militia himself, he recognized its shortcomings. Professional soldiers were bound to know their craft better than amateurs like himself. The sandals he turned out, after all, were better than the ones rustics made for themselves. Had that not been true, he wouldn't have been able to feed his wife and children. The way Theodore ate these days, George needed to be good at his trade.

Bishop Eusebius' face was a study in mixed emotions. He took Victor's getting applause almost as a personal affront; his model was his predecessor Ambrose, who had made the Emperor Theodosius do penance for a massacre his men had carried out in the hippodrome of Thessalonica. On the other hand, with Victor and other secular notables departing for Constantinople, Eusebius would be the most important man in Thessalonica for a while. That he liked fine.

Victor said, "I am certain the holy bishop here will pray for the success of my mission and for my safe return."

"What?" The prefect had succeeded in startling Eusebius. Like George, the bishop must have figured out that much of what Victor said wasn't worth listening to. Eusebius did recover quickly. "Yes, of course. I shall pray for your safe journey, your success, and your eventual safe return." Did he place a little extra stress on that *eventual*? George wasn't sure.

The ceremony broke up after that. Some people went up onto the gray stone walls of Thessalonica to keep an eye on the departing city garrison for as long as they could. George would have reckoned that an insult to the militia if he hadn't noticed that a fair number of those wistful spectators were militiamen. He wondered if he ought to go up himself. The militia would be keeping watch for the city now.

In the end, he decided not to bother. He expected he'd have plenty of chances to do actual patrolling; why bother with rehearsals, in that case? On the way back to his shop, he passed under the triumphal arch of the Emperor Galerius, celebrating his victory over the Persians. Galerius was three hundred years dead, more or less. The Persians were still very much around; Maurice had finally won a long war against them five years before.

George looked at the arch. Galerius, arrogant in stone, stared back at him. "It does make you wonder what the point of all that fighting was," George murmured. Galerius didn't answer.

"Hello, Father," Theodore said when George came through the front door. "How does it feel to be a leading defender of the city?"

"Strange," the shoemaker answered. "How does it feel to you that I'm a leading defender of the city?"

His son grinned at him. "Is there any way I can get out of town, like the prefect is doing?"

"Children have no respect for their elders these days," George said. "If I'd told my father something like that—"

He paused. He had told his father things like that, and a good many times, too. Most of the time, the old man had thrown back his head and laughed like a loon.

"You started to say something?" asked Theodore, who was, if you resisted the temptation to strangle him, a fairly good specimen.

"Maybe I did," George said. "But what's the use? You wouldn't listen, anyway." In a different tone of voice, that would have been wounding. But George sounded somewhere between resigned and amused. Theodore grinned again and went back to the boot he'd been mending.

The shoemaker went back to work, too. Those fancy tooled boots wouldn't get done by themselves, and he'd never heard of a spirit or fairy that would make shoes for you while you lay in bed.

He went back to the boots, tapping the awl one careful stroke at a time with his light hammer. He had to bend close to the last to see what he was doing. A day spent at uninterrupted fine work like that left him with a pounding headache. One of these years before too long, if God let him live, his sight would lengthen, and then the fine work would be beyond his power. Then Theodore would have to take over the lead in the shop, and George would do whatever his sight let him do, and would probably take a hand in training up his grandsons in the trade.

When the sun went down and shadows filled the shop, the family ended their work and cleaned up. "I wish we had a slave," Sophia said. "That would make life a lot easier."

"Your mother and I have talked about buying one, now and again," George said, setting the tools he'd used back onto the pegs he'd set in the wall to hold them. Each tool had its own set of pegs, on which it hung neatly.

"Have you really?" Sophia sounded surprised. "You've never done it when I was around."

"Could we afford to buy a slave?" Theodore asked.

"Probably," George said. Irene nodded. Now both their

children looked surprised. George went on, "I don't expect we'll get one any time soon, though." His wife nodded.

"Why not, if we can afford one?" Sophia said. "It would save us a lot of work, and besides—" She paused, uncertain how to go on. At last, she said, "If you've got a slave, if you don't have to do all your own work, that means you're better off than a lot of the people around you."

Before George could answer, Irene spoke with great firmness: "I can't think of a worse reason to buy a slave than social climbing."

"That's right," George said, knowing he couldn't have put it so well himself. Sophia and Theodore let out simultaneous, identical disbelieving snorts. They were at an age where social climbing mattered intensely. George remembered that. He'd got over it. He expected they would, too.

"Besides," Irene said, "the work wouldn't disappear as if a priest had exorcised it. The slave might do the housework so we didn't have to, but we'd have to make more shoes and fix more shoes and sell more shoes to buy the food and clothes and medicines and whatnot we'd need to give the slave."

"That's right," George said again. "It's not what you pay to buy a slave that counts. It's the upkeep. We could afford to buy one, but I don't know how long we could afford to have him here."

"We'd find a way," Theodore said with the innocent confidence of youth.

"That's not the only problem, you know," George said. "Most of the slaves in the market these days are Gepids or Slavs. They don't speak Latin, they don't speak Greek, and God only knows if they understand anything about work. If they run away, you're out everything you paid for them, with no chance of getting a copper back from the dealer."

"Some people must manage in spite of all those troubles," Sophia said, "or nobody would have slaves."

"*Some* people," George said pointedly, "must raise up

children who don't talk back to them. Come to think of it, though, I've never heard of any. When you can afford a slave, Theodore, or when your husband can, Sophia, then we'll see what you do. Meanwhile—"

"Meanwhile," Irene broke in, "we still have a lot of work to do, and not much light left to do it in, mostly because a couple of people I could name have been grumbling instead of doing what they're supposed to." She picked up a sandal and made as if to clout Theodore in the ear with it. He got to work, but he didn't stop grumbling. That satisfied George, who remembered doing a deal of grumbling in his own younger days.

Rufus lined up his charges and gave them their orders: "Walk your stretch of the wall. Try not to fall off and break your fool neck. The challenge is 'St. Demetrius.' The answer is 'St. Nicholas.' If somebody can't give you the right answer, he's got no business up on the wall at night."

"What do we do then?" Dactylius asked nervously.

"It depends," the militia officer answered. "If you can tell it's just some cursed fool from inside the city, just send him down. If it's anybody sneaking up onto the wall from outside, try and kill the bastard and yell for help like the devil's about to drag your soul to hell. Anything else? No? All right, first shift, up onto the wall. Second shift will relieve you about the start of the fifth hour of the night."

George had first-shift duty tonight, along with Dactylius. The two of them climbed to the battlements near the Litaean Gate. George peered west. In the deepening evening twilight, the Via Egnatia was a gray stone ribbon heading west toward the sea, some days' journey away. Beyond the sea lay Italy. Past that, George's knowledge of geography faded fast.

The moon, full or near enough, rose in the southeast, in Capricorn, with the bright silver lamp of Jupiter not far away. Even after night fell, there was enough light to see where to put your feet, and to see shapes moving out beyond the wall. There was, in fact, enough light to see shapes moving out beyond the wall whether they were really there or not.

"I wish we could carry torches," Dactylius said.

"That would be fine," George said. "If there are any Slavs out there sneaking up on us, they'd know where to aim when they started shooting."

"Urk," Dactylius said: a sound that made no word in either Latin or Greek, but one full of meaning nonetheless. "I hadn't thought so far. If to see I am more easily seen, I'll do without the torch, and gladly."

"Good fellow." George liked Dactylius, though he wondered what had prompted the jeweler to join the militia: a less warlike man would have been hard to imagine.

Mosquitoes buzzed as the two militiamen patrolled their stretch of wall. One of the bugs bit George behind his left knee. He said something pungent he'd learned from Rufus. Dactylius laughed. Then a mosquito bit him, and he said something even more sulfurous. He laughed again, this time self-consciously. "You wouldn't let Claudia know I talk like that among my fellow warriors, would you?"

"Perish the thought," George said. Maybe Dactylius was a militiaman because Rufus left him feeling less henpecked than Claudia did.

Something moved, out beyond the ditch. George saw it. So did Dactylius. "What is it?" he hissed.

"It's a man," George said. That was better than naming it a demon or a pagan god, but not much. His hand closed over the hilt of his sword. The leather grip comforted him, even if it wasn't shoe leather. Beside him, Dactylius started to say something but stopped, perhaps because his tongue was cleaving to the roof of his mouth. George didn't say anything. He knew better than to try. If he opened his mouth with his heart pounding the way it was, all of Thessalonica would hear the noise.

He went to the edge of the wall and peered down into

the night. Sure enough, that was a man. What was he doing down there, away from the monastery to the west of the city? *Spying out the land*, was the first answer that leaped into the shoemaker's agile mind.

Then the man came out from the shadows of some bushes into moonlight. That moonlight gleamed off his tonsure. He looked up toward the wall with complete uninterest and began to sing, loudly and off-key, in Greek.

"Christ have mercy!" George exclaimed, his voice an explosive whisper. "It's a drunk monk, that's all."

"You're—you're right." Dactylius spoke in tones of wonder, as if he'd seen a revelation straight out of the Apocalypse of St. John.

The monk wandered away. He'd developed a list from the wine he'd taken on, as a ship would list after taking on water. Anger washed through George, sweeping away fear. After a moment, the anger flowed away, too, replaced by a more characteristic sour satisfaction. "I don't even have to think up things I'd like to do to the bastard for giving me such a start," he said to Dactylius.

"Why not?" the jeweler asked. "I was thinking of things like that."

George's smile was broad, almost beatific. "Because before long that fellow's going to have to go back to his monastery, and the abbot there will take care of everything we could dream up, and more besides."

"Oh, my," Dactylius said, almost as if he'd had another vision, but this one of the pleasant sort.

They paced back and forth along the wall for most of another hour. Nothing happened. That suited George fine. He would have been delighted to go home after his turn was up, slide into bed next to Irene, and, if he woke her up, say, *Nothing happened*. She would be happy and relieved. He was already happy and relieved, the monk having turned out to be a monk.

He wondered when he would be relieved in a different sense of the word. The moon was a good way up in the sky. Hours were hard enough to gauge during the day, let alone by night, but he thought the men who would replace him and Dactylius should be climbing to the top of the wall soon.

He promised himself he wouldn't tell them about the monk.

A moment later, he too forgot about the poor sot. From out of the blackness of the woods to the north and west of Thessalonica came a long, cold, fierce, hungry howl. All the adjectives formed in George's mind as the howl echoed and reechoed in his ears. None of them described it. He'd heard wolves before; when winter came down hard, they often drew near the city to see what—or whom—they could take. He did not believe for an instant that this sound had anything to do with any wolves he'd heard during hard winters, though.

Beside him, Dactylius jumped and crossed himself. George did not blame the excitable little jeweler in the least. "That's *not* a wolf," Dactylius said, as if someone had declared it was. He seemed to realize as much; after a brief pause, he went on, "But what else could it be?"

"It was a wolf—of sorts." George spoke with an odd certainty, as if his mouth had adjusted to the horrid hunger of that sound faster than his wits had. After a moment, his wits caught up. "It must have been one of those wolf-demons the satyr was telling me about when I went hunting a few days ago."

"Christ have mercy," Dactylius exclaimed. Such an oath would have been plenty to drive away any of the old pagan Greek spirits who heard it. For a moment, George hoped it had had the same effect on the Slavic demon. But then the wolf howled again, and was joined a moment later by another. The two howling together were more than twice as bad as one howling alone. They made George feel as if he, up on the walls of Thessalonica, were on an island of faith and piety in the middle of a dark sea . . . and that the sea was rising, threatening to wash over him and his little island as if they did not exist and were of no account.

"Devils!" Dactylius whispered.

George did not argue with him. George knew he could not argue with him. Those were devils out there. Instead, he said, "Devils don't prevail against God. That's what the Scriptures say."

He did a better job of reassuring his friend than he did for himself. He believed he'd told the truth, but it was a long-term kind of truth. How many Christians had been martyred for the faith before it prevailed in the Roman Empire? If God chose for His own reasons to give Thessalonica over to the foe who knew Him not, He would do that. George could only hope that was not what He had in mind.

No, that wasn't the only thing he could do. He could also do everything in his power to keep the barbarians out of the city. God might offer the way, but men had to provide the means.

"St. Demetrius!"

At first, George thought that was only in his own mind, seeking intercession with the divine. Then he realized the call had come from someone else. "St. Nicholas!" he answered.

"Thought you were asleep up here," Sabbatius said, advancing to take his turn on sentry-go. "Did you hear the wolf a few minutes ago?"

George looked at the tubby newcomer. "I thought it was your stomach growling," he said. But he could not stay jocular long. "Yes, we heard it."

He and Dactylius descended from the wall and lighted torches at one burning down there by the base so they could find their way home. They carried their weapons home with them, too, which was enough to repel any thieves who might have skulked through the streets of Thessalonica in the darkness.

Irene had thoughtfully left a lamp burning downstairs. George carried it up to the bedroom. He tried to slide into bed as quietly as he could, but woke her. "Those horrible wolves," she said drowsily. "I didn't dream them, did I?"

"No," he answered, truthful before he wondered whether a lie might have served better. Irene nodded and went back to sleep. Some time later, George wished his own rest would have come so easily.

II

Sophia came running back from the market square with turnips in her hands and excitement on her face. "Come quick, everybody," she called as she hurried into the shop. "There's going to be a procession out to the monastery of St. Demetrius—you know, the one with the healing spring."

George looked up from the fancy boots he had almost finished ornamenting. "What kind of procession?" he asked.

"Remember Menas the nobleman?" Sophia said. "The one who hasn't been able to use his legs since his horse threw him a few years ago?"

"Yes, I remember Menas," George said. Beside him, Irene nodded, too. He went on, "He's lucky he's rich, to have bearers put him in a litter and take him wherever he wants to go. We've all seen him in church." Irene nodded again. This time, so did both their children. "A poor man," he finished, "a poor man would probably have to stay in his bed the rest of his days, and those wouldn't be long, either."

"Will you let me tell you?" Sophia burst out. She pretended to throw a turnip at him. Now he nodded.

She said, "St. Demetrius sent him a dream, he said, that if he goes out to the monastery and bathes in the spring, he'll be able to walk again."

Irene crossed herself. "May it be so," she said.

"Aye, may it be so," George agreed. His spirit was not quite so broadly generous as his wife's, though, so he could not help wondering why God and the saint had chosen to give that dream to Menas rather than to some poor and wretched paralytic whose state, as he'd suggested to his daughter, was liable to be far worse than that of the nobleman.

His shoulders went up and down. When God needed a shoemaker to advise Him on how to run the world, no doubt He would inquire. In the meantime, He would do as He pleased, not as pleased George.

Theodore said, "If St. Demetrius promised a miracle, that would be something worth seeing, wouldn't it, Father?"

"You see a miracle whenever you take bread and wine and communion," George said. "What I see is a young scamp who wants some time off from work." He put down his awl. "I wouldn't mind a little time off myself. Let's go."

Theodore whooped. Sophia set the turnips on the counter. "What shall we do if a customer comes in while we're away?" Irene asked, resisting even after her husband had given up.

"What shall we do? We'll miss him, that's what," George said, which, while literally true, earned him a glare from Irene. He went on, "A lot of the people who might come in, you know, will be parading along with Menas, too."

"I suppose so." Irene weighed it like a judge considering evidence, and in the end gave a nod George would have described as judicious. "Yes, I suppose so." The decision made, she brightened. "That will be exciting, won't it, if the saint does work a miracle for us?"

"Yes, it will," George said. That was also true. If it left him imperfectly satisfied with the way the world was arranged, he had no one to blame but himself. Maybe God had some special reason in mind for restoring to Menas the use of his legs.

And maybe Menas would bathe in the spring without having the use of his legs restored. Till the event, you couldn't tell. Satan might have sent the dream, deceiving the nobleman to weaken not only his faith but also that of everyone who watched him bathe. Or he might have had the dream all on his own, imagining he saw St. Demetrius because he so badly wanted to walk again. Once more, no way to know till the moment.

"Come on," Sophia said. "They're not going to wait for the likes of us before they start. If we don't hurry now, we'll have to hurry to catch up or we won't be able to see a thing."

She and Theodore waited for no more discussion from their obviously stodgy parents; they headed out the door. George and Irene looked at each other, started to laugh, and followed. George closed the door after them.

They were far from the only people hurrying toward the market square. Seeing that, the shoemaker caught his wife's eyes and gave her his best I-told-you-so look. She did her best job of pretending she hadn't seen it, which left the match a standoff.

"Oh, good!" Sophia exclaimed when they got to the square. "He hasn't left yet." Sure enough, there in the middle of the crowd sat Menas' litter, the poles above the seat where he reclined supporting a brightly dyed canopy that kept the sun off his noble head. Also there, gorgeous in his vestments, stood Bishop Eusebius. If this was a true miracle, he intended to wring from it every grain of advantage he could.

Not everyone in the market square had come to join the procession. Some people remained intent on doing the business of an ordinary market day. And others, detecting out-of-the-ordinary opportunities to turn a profit, appeared in the square when they ordinarily would not have. There stood Paul the taverner, for instance, with a jar of wine and a dipper, selling drinks for a couple of folleis apiece. He was doing a brisk business.

George waved to him, calling, "I thought you were talking about joining the militia. Where have you been?"

"I'll get there, never fear," Paul said. "I'm a busy man; you can't expect me to do everything at once."

"Have it your way," George answered. Maybe the taverner would come, maybe he wouldn't. George hoped he would. He liked Paul, and anyone who could run a tavern and keep it from being a place where men went at each other with knives a couple of times a day—which Paul's emphatically was not—had the makings of a pretty fair underofficer in him. Besides, if Paul joined his company, he might offer his fellow militiamen discounts on his stock in trade. George liked that idea, quite a lot.

"Look!" Sophia said. "They're starting. We got here just in time." The sniff following that comment spoke volumes on her opinion of parents who had almost made her late for such a spectacle.

The canopy shielding the limp-limbed Menas from the sun rose several feet as his bearers lifted the litter in which he lay. Eusebius preceded it on the way out toward Cassander's Gate, by which the soldiers had left a few days before. The bishop sang the Trisagion—the Thrice-holy—hymn: "Holy one, holy mighty one, holy immortal one, have mercy on us!"

Many voices swelled the hymn as the procession passed under the arch of Galerius and out through the gate. George sang as loudly as anyone, and not much less musically than most. A God Who would not have mercy on poor but sincere music sent up to glorify His name would have been a hard and unmerciful God indeed.

For a wonder, no one in the crowd added the Monophysite clause— "Who was crucified for us"—to the Trisagion. That probably would have led to cries of heresy and touched off a brawl if not a lynching, and would hardly have been an auspicious way to advance toward a hoped-for miracle.

Singing still, the bishop and Menas in his litter led the procession toward the monastery of St. Demetrius. The monastery stood near the top of Cedrenus Hill, north of the Via Egnatia. It looked as much like a small fortress as a place of contemplation and worship, having been built in the days when the Goths rather than the Slavs were sniffing around Thessalonica. Those strong stone walls might come in handy again.

The track up to the monastery was steep and winding and full of rocks. Someone complained blasphemously about breaking a strap to his sandal. George dared hope the fellow would come in before long to have the damage repaired.

Then such notions left him as the procession drew near the spring, which bubbled forth from a cleft in the rock of the hillside. The setting, in the middle of a wooded glade, with the monastery's walls visible through the trees off to one side, did not seem appropriate for any but prayerful thoughts.

Something was carved into the stone not far from the origin of the spring. George, curious as usual, pushed his way through the crowd so he could read the inscription, which was written in square, old-fashioned Greek letters: GLORY TO THE SHRINE AND TO ASCLEPIUS, WHO CURED MY ILLNESS HERE: I, GAIUS THYNES, WRITE THIS IN THE SECOND CONSULSHIP OF THE EMPEROR TRAJAN.

He whistled softly. This had been a healing place for a long time. He didn't know exactly how long Trajan had been dead, but he knew it had been hundreds of years. Back then, Asclepius had ruled the spring. Sometime in the centuries since, St. Demetrius had taken it from him. But the saint had kept it as a place of healing.

Menas' bearers undid the side curtains that kept the curious from staring into the rich paralytic's litter. Two of them bent, reached inside, and brought out their employer, who kept one arm around each of their necks. Menas had a tough, fleshy face, arms as big and strong as a stonemason's, and a broad, powerful chest. His legs, though, were pale and shriveled and useless.

Bishop Eusebius anointed his forehead with purified oil, sketching a cross there that gleamed in the sun. The bishop raised his hands in prayer, declaiming, "Myrrh-exuding great martyr Demetrius, heal your servant Menas in the name of God—Father, Son, and Holy Spirit. Amen."

"Amen," George said, along with everybody else. Here in the glade by the hillside spring, he no longer doubted Menas had had a true dream. Why St. Demetrius had chosen to aid the noble rather than some other cripple remained beyond the shoemaker's understanding, but the saint seemed to have done just that. The very air felt pregnant with possibility.

"Put me in, boys," Menas said to the bearers, his gruff voice matching his appearance. But then he spoke in tones of wonder: "It's almost like being baptized again, isn't it?"

"In no way," Eusebius answered. "Baptism seals your soul, where the spring, even if God is kind, will heal only your body."

Menas bowed his head, outwardly accepting the bishop's correction. George, though, could still see his eyes. Eusebius might speak slightingly of the body, but Eusebius was not imprisoned in his. "Put me in," Menas said again, even more urgently than before.

Grunting a little under his weight, the bearers obeyed, placing him in the little pool the spring formed before its water flowed on down the hill. Eusebius called once more on St. Demetrius.

Like everyone else, George sensed the moment when the healing began. Maybe the bishop's prayer had brought it on. George, though, was more inclined to feel it happened of its own accord, or rather that St. Demetrius would have interceded whether Eusebius had been there to pray or not. Power thrummed in the air, in the ground, and most of all, no doubt, in the water in which Menas lay and which poured over him out of the cleft in the rock. George breathed deeply, as if hoping he could suck some of that power into himself and bring it down out of this place and into his day-to-day life in Thessalonica.

Menas splashed about in the pool, as if he were bathing. That reminded George he ought to visit the city baths himself one day soon. They weren't so busy as they had been before Thessalonica became a Christian town (or so the bath attendants said, whether to drum up business or from a genuine tradition handed down with their strigils), but they were open.

Bishop Eusebius started to send up yet another prayer to St. Demetrius. He had hardly begun when Menas gasped. It took a good deal to silence a bishop in the middle of a prayer, but that gasp did the job. It was as if all the power immanent in that place had sprung forth in a single awe-smitten inhalation of breath.

Menas stood up in the pool.

For a moment, George simply accepted that. Menas' strength and agility seemed so natural, he took them for granted. Then memory caught up with vision. Half a man had gone into the pool, but a whole man came out, water dripping in sparkling streams from the hem of his tunic. His legs, which had been thin and wasted, were now as thick and solid as his arms.

"Thank you, St. Demetrius," he said. "Bless you, St. Demetrius." He turned to the men who had borne him in the litter for so many years. "Take that cursed thing back to my house and burn it. I'm never going to get into it again." Nobles often traveled through the streets in litters, not least to show those who weren't nobles how important they were. George, though, could understand why Menas was willing to forgo that particular kind of aggrandizement.

"Let us thank God for the miracle He has given us this day!" Eusebius said. George gladly thanked God for letting him witness a miracle. Miracles were by their very nature rare; had they happened every day, they would hardly have been miraculous.

"How will you celebrate this miracle?" someone called to Menas.

The burly noble mulled that over, but not for long. "I am going to celebrate it with my wife," he declared, a reply that made George realize Menas' legs had not been the only parts of him that did not work. A good many other people realized that at about the same time as the shoemaker. Their ribald whoops echoed through the glade that had been full of the sounds of prayer only moments before.

Eusebius looked furious. He raised his eyes to the heavens, perhaps hoping divine wrath would follow hard on the heels of divine mercy. If so, he was disappointed. The day remained bright and warm and clear, and no lightning bolt came smashing down on the people in the grove.

"He *is* going in unto his wife," someone behind George said, "and the Scriptures do tell us it is better to marry than to burn."

"Menas has been crippled a long time," George observed, "so I wouldn't be surprised if he's burning now."

With determined stride, the noble headed away from the spring. The procession back to Thessalonica was a lot less orderly and less united in purpose than the one that had led to the sacred spring. Some people still hymned God's praise. Bishop Eusebius remained incandescently angry. The men who had carried Menas about for so many years looked worried, and George understood why: with the noble walking again, would he still have work for them?

But most people, like the shoemaker, were chiefly concerned about getting back to the city so they could return to work. "Come on," he said, gathering up his family. "Miracles are all very well, but you can't eat them."

"No?" Sophia said. "What about the loaves and fishes?"

"And manna from heaven?" Theodore put in.

"All I know about them is that they didn't happen in Thessalonica," George returned. "And this wasn't our miracle: it was Menas'. The only way it can do us any good is for him to want to buy shoes from our shop."

Irene sighed. "That would take another miracle, I fear."

Songs rang out in the city when word of the miracle came. Paul did a brisk business selling wine to the people returning from the monastery of St. Demetrius. Several other taverners came out to try to do the same. George hoped Paul, who had been thoughtful enough to get there ahead of everyone else, reaped the reward for his cleverness.

After the cool freshness of the glade around the sacred spring, after the power that had manifested itself there at the spring, going back into the cramped, dark shoemaker's shop, stinking of leather, made George sigh. Then he shook his head. "If I wanted to work outdoors all the time, I would have to be a farmer or a woodsman." He enjoyed the woods and the fields—but not that much. "Talking with sheep or partridges is not my idea of spending time in good company."

"And what is your idea of good company?" Theodore asked with a glint of mischief in his eye. "Half-drunk militiamen?"

"Better than sons who don't show their fathers proper respect," George shot back, which won him a giggle from Irene and, better yet, sudden silence from Theodore. That was rare enough to come close to being a miracle in and of itself.

But George did not bask in the warm glow of victory for long. Picking up his tools was anything but delightful. All at once, no matter how skillfully he punched a pattern into leather, he had trouble believing any of it mattered. What was the point? Why did he bother?

And then, when he was feeling at his lowest, the rich man who had ordered the boots came into the shop. "Those are splendid," Germanus exclaimed. "Much better than I thought they'd be." Not only did he put them on and wear them out of the shop, he paid George a couple of miliaresia more than the price on which they had agreed.

George stared after him, the weight of the money sweet

in his palm. "Do you know," he said slowly, looking down at the coins, "in its own little way, that may be a miracle as wondrous as the one God worked for Menas through St. Demetrius."

Neither his wife nor his children argued with him.

On the practice field near the hippodrome, John put down his spear and pointed up the street. "May I be sent to eternal damnation if that isn't Paul!" he exclaimed in delight.

George's opinion was that the profane tavern performer risked eternal damnation whenever he opened his mouth. That, however, did not seem a helpful comment, the more so as John was all too likely to agree with it. The shoemaker contented himself by saying, "It does look like him, doesn't it?"

Dactylius, whose trade had left him a trifle shortsighted, peered in the general direction from which the taverner was coming. "Yes, that is Paul, isn't it?" he said, a good deal later than he should have.

Rufus set hands on hips and awaited the new arrival. "So you think you can be a soldier, do you?" he growled.

"I don't see why not," the taverner answered. "If you can do the job, it can't be too hard."

The veteran's smile was fierce and predatory. "God will punish you for that—and if He doesn't, I will." His sword slid out of its scabbard with a sound like a snake's hiss. "Let's see what you can do."

In the practice that followed, Rufus could have killed Paul a dozen times over. Everyone saw as much. But Paul refused to let it worry him, and, after Rufus finally resheathed his sword, the taverner did well not only with the bow but also with the spear.

Rufus rubbed his chin, considering. At last, he said, "As long as you keep them away from you, you may live. If they get close, run for your life like you've got Satan on your tail. How does that sound?"

"See what kind of wine *you* get served the next time

you stick your nose into my tavern," Paul said, which made Rufus let out a carefully rationed grunt of laughter.

John greeted the new volunteer with a sour expression. "You were supposed to be funnier than that," he said.

Paul's face glistened with sweat. He looked down his nose at the other militiaman. "People were saying the same thing about you the last time you came and did your routine in my place."

"Shall we get back to drill?" Dactylius asked, eager as usual to spread oil on troubled waters. "We all need to get better. Has anyone heard anything about what the city garrison is doing?"

"Not a word," George said, and everyone around him nodded. He didn't let it worry him; he hadn't expected news so soon. He wondered whether any word would get back to Thessalonica before the soldiers came home to tell the tale themselves. With so much disorder south of the Danube, maybe not.

Rufus came striding over. He was an old man, yes, but a tough old man, a frightening old man. When he transfixed Dactylius with a glare, it was as if he'd shoved a spear into him. "Here's something for you to think about," he rumbled. "Suppose you're a scout in the woods. You make a noise or some fool thing, and about twenty different Slavs all start running right toward where you're at. What do you do then?"

"Run!" Dactylius exclaimed, turning pale at the prospect.

George snorted, then tried to pretend he hadn't. The little jeweler had given an utterly honest answer. If it wasn't the one Rufus was looking for, though, Dactylius was going to be in trouble. George wasn't the only one laughing, either, and some of the others didn't try to hide it.

Rufus turned that fearsome gaze on them. " 'Run' is the right answer," he said. "You're outnumbered like that, what else can you do? But what should you do while you're running?"

"Pray to God for a miracle like the one He gave Menas," Dactylius said.

"Pray to God you don't shit yourself while you're running," John said.

"One case of long odds, one case of a big mouth," Rufus remarked. He turned to George, as he often did when he wanted a question answered in a particular way. "What should you do while you're running?"

"If you can, you should probably lead the Slavs back toward the main body of your force, so you won't be so outnumbered when they catch up to you."

"That's the right idea," Rufus said approvingly. "Don't just run. Think while you're doing it. Your wits are as good a weapon as your sword." He glowered at John. "That's true for most people, anyhow." The tavern funny man blew him a kiss, as if he'd paid him a compliment. The look Rufus sent up toward God was as grim as the ones he gave the militiamen.

Dactylius said, "But what if you don't want the enemy to know where your main mass of troops is? What do you do then?"

For once, Rufus' sour features uncurdled. "That's a good question," he said, in tones implying a good question was the last thing he'd expected. He turned to George again. "What are some of the things you might do?"

George thought before he spoke. The answer here was less obvious than the other for which Rufus had asked him. At last, he said, "One thing you might do is try to make the enemy think you have a lot of soldiers close by, even if you don't."

"That's right." Rufus' big, gray head went up and down, up and down. "A friend of mine saved himself from the Goths—or was it the Franks?—back in Italy, doing that very thing. You got to think fast when you're fighting, on account of you don't usually get the chance to think slow. Now let's get back to work, so you don't have to think about fighting at all. The more you think in hand-to-hand, the worse off you're going to be."

John looked around at his fellow militiamen. His gaze finally fell on Sabbatius. "We're in good shape there, by the Mother of God. Some of us have trouble thinking even when we're not in hand-to-hand."

Sabbatius' pudgy face reddened. "Are you practicing your jokes on me? You're not as funny as you think you are, I'll tell you that." He would have sounded more impressively angry, though, had he seemed more certain John was really insulting him. In truth, Sabbatius wasn't so bright as he might have been.

Despite that, George said, "Enough." He was looking at John as he went on, "The idea is, we're all supposed to be on the same side. If you make people hate you, they won't help you when we really have to fight."

John's eyes widened. In spite of everything, he didn't look to have realized that the militia might have to fight. He lobbed insults as automatically as he breathed. To underscore the point, George threw back his head and did his best to imitate the fearsome howl of a Slavic wolf-demon.

Before John could say anything, insulting or otherwise, Rufus nodded again. "George has it right," he declared. "I remember in Italy, when one part of the army didn't get along with the rest. You couldn't trust them at your back, so you were more afraid of them than of the Goths. Works the same way here. If you get in trouble, you have to know your chums are going to come and pull you out of it. If you can't be sure of that, you might as well give up and go home before you ever start."

George nodded. That made sense. Rufus commonly made sense, though he had such a rough tongue that you sometimes wished he'd keep quiet more often. If you could stand to listen to him, though, it usually repaid the effort.

Sabbatius did his best to look sly. It put George in mind of a public woman trying to look chaste, but that he kept to himself. Turning to Paul, Sabbatius said, "You see? You'd better keep us in wine if you expect us to take care of you."

"No, that's not what Rufus meant," Dactylius said

earnestly. "We don't help each other from hope of reward. We help each other because that's what we need to do when we go fight."

"Most of you lugs understand what I'm talking about," Rufus said. "The ones who don't . . ." His shoulders moved up and down in a shrug. "All we can hope is that God will have mercy on them when they see Him, on account of we already know they're going to see Him pretty fornicating quick."

That comment left the militiamen—perhaps even including Sabbatius—thoughtful when they returned to their exercises.

Mosquitoes buzzed in the night. Crickets chirped. Somewhere not far outside the walls of Thessalonica, an owl hooted. Since it was nighttime, George knew the pagan Greeks would have taken that for a good sign, a sign Athena was nearby. Even he, good and believing Christian though he was, got nervous on the rare times when he heard an owl calling by daylight.

He looked out from the wall, west toward the woods and toward the monastery of St. Matrona, which was a little fortress in its own right. It was far enough from the city that it disappeared from view, or nearly so, at night or during the misty days so common by the sea.

Beside George, Sabbatius whistled while he walked. The shoemaker glanced over at his companion in some annoyance, though Sabbatius was only another dim shape in the darkness. "Can't you put a stopper in that?" George said. "If there are barbarians lurking in the bushes, they'll know just where we are."

"So what?" Sabbatius answered cheerfully. "You can't shoot a bow for anything during the night, and I like to whistle."

"I'd like it more if you did it less often, or if you did it better," George told him, that seeming likelier to have good results than something like, *If you don't quit making noises like a starling with its tail caught in a door, I'm going to sew your lips shut.*

He might as well have said exactly what he meant, for Sabbatius grumbled, "You're as bad as John," and subsided into hurt silence. Since it was silence, George had no trouble putting up with the hurt that informed it. When he didn't apologize, that only hurt Sabbatius more.

Somewhere out in the woods, a wolf howled. Sabbatius gasped and tried to yank out his sword and nock an arrow at the same time, thereby succeeding none too well at either task.

"I think that's only a wolf, not one of the Slavs' demons," George said. "Hearing it doesn't make your blood turn to water."

"No, eh?" Sabbatius was breathing hard; the howl had given him a good fright. "Well, I think it was one."

"All right," George said. "I might be wrong." He didn't feel like arguing about it. For one thing, he had no way to prove he was right. For another, arguing with Sabbatius wasn't usually interesting enough to be entertaining. He yawned. The two of them had the middle watch this time. Eventually, he would be able to go home and go back to bed. At the moment, *eventually* felt a long way away.

Sabbatius, in a touchy mood, decided to be offended because George wouldn't passionately insist he was correct. "You must not think you know much," he said loftily.

Next time, by the Virgin, I'll bring needle and thread and I will *sew his lips shut*. One thing he did know, though, was not to quarrel with a fool. "We are supposed to be on the same side," he reminded Sabbatius.

"Well, yes," his comrade said, with the air of a man making a great concession, "but—" He stopped suddenly with a wordless exclamation of dismay, flailing his hands around his head. "Gah! A bat! It almost flew into my face."

"They eat bugs, I think." George scratched a mosquito bite. "I'm in favor of anything that eats bugs."

"This one looked like it wanted to eat me," Sabbatius returned. "Didn't you see its glittering eyes?"

"I didn't see it at all." That was true, but it had the effect of offending Sabbatius all over again, as if George had called him a liar. George had done nothing of the sort, but trying to convince Sabbatius of that would have been more trouble than it was worth. He sighed and kept quiet.

And then, suddenly, the bat was fluttering in front of him. He'd never paid bats much attention; they skimmed through the night, when he mostly stayed indoors. He was sure, though, he'd never seen one like this. Sabbatius might not have been bright, but he knew what he'd seen: the bat's eyes did glitter, red as blood.

Its teeth glittered, too, as if it wanted to sink them into something larger and more flavorful than a moth or a mosquito. Of itself, George's hand shaped the sign of the cross. The bat's eyes no longer glittered; just for a moment, they glowed, as if torches had been kindled behind them. Then the creature flew away: or, for all George knew, it simply disappeared. At any rate, it no longer flapped its wings in front of his face.

He turned to Sabbatius. "You were right. That was a large bat."

"What? You mean you did see it, too?" Now Sabbatius sounded amazed.

"I don't know whether it was the same one you saw, but I saw a bat, yes." When George changed his mind or found he'd made a mistake, he said so, straight out. He never had quite figured out why that caused so much surprise and even consternation among his fellow human beings, but it did, more often than not.

"It was a nasty sort of thing, wasn't it?" Sabbatius said.

Soberly, he said, "I've had visitors I liked better—even my mother-in-law, come to think of it." That was a slander upon Irene's mother; before Helena had died of the plague in the epidemic a couple of years earlier, she had been as pleasant a woman as anyone could want to know.

"You can be a funny fellow, George—you know that?"

Sabbatius said. "And you're not mean when you're funny, the way John is."

"Oh, I don't know," the shoemaker replied. "My mother-in-law, God rest her soul, would have thought you were wrong." He let a judicious pause stretch. "But Irene would be angry if I called her a bat."

"Heh, heh—if you called her a bat. Heh, heh." Sabbatius' shoulders shook with laughter. "That's good. I wish I'd thought of that, so I could have said it for myself."

Very likely, Sabbatius *would* be saying it, at any chance he got. People who hadn't heard it before might be impressed. For those who had heard it, it would soon be one more cliche in Sabbatius' arsenal. George sometimes wondered how—or if—his companion thought when he didn't have a maxim handy.

The shoemaker strode along the wall, looking out into the darkness beyond the city with fresh intensity. Looking availed him little. For all he knew, a vast army of large bats with glittering red eyes and glittering white teeth flapped and flew out there, just beyond where his eyes could reach.

All at once, he turned and strode to the opposite side of the walkway atop the wall, the side that let him see down into Thessalonica. In the middle of the night, though, the city was nearly as dark as the rough and overgrown country beyond it.

"What are you doing?" Sabbatius asked. "It's almost like you think the bats are spying on us, or something."

George hadn't thought that. No. George hadn't fully realized he thought that. But once Sabbatius said it, he knew it was true. He wished the satyr he'd met had mentioned these bats along with the wolves. Then he would have had a better idea of whether he was shying at shadows. With the notion firmly planted in his mind, he was going to worry till he found out about them one way or the other.

He shook his head. No again. If he found out about the bats one way, he would stop worrying. If he found out about them the other, he'd worry more than ever.

He kept on staring into Thessalonica, though he knew it was likely to be futile. With so few lights burning, he wasn't likely to spot a bat if one was there to be spotted, and even less likely to recognize it for what it was.

No sooner had that thought crossed his mind than something flew in front of a torch burning outside a little church in the heart of the city. It was gone almost before he'd seen it. And even if it had been there, it might well have been a nightjar, swooping after insects drawn to the light of the torch.

So he told himself, again and again. He wished he would have had an easier time making himself believe it.

When Rufus and Dactylius—as odd a pair in their way as George and Sabbatius were in theirs—came up to take the before-sunrise shift on the wall, George told them of what he and his partner had seen. "I don't know what it means," he said, "but you ought to know about it."

"If the sign of the cross will make the creatures run—uh, fly—away, we should be all right," Dactylius said.

Rufus drew his sword from its scabbard. "This has the shape of the cross, too," he said, holding up the weapon. "If we can't drive off the cursed things, we can always kill them."

He lived in a simple world: not the same sort of simple world as did Sabbatius, for he clearly saw more facets to it than did the rather stupid militiaman, but simple in the sense that he firmly believed every problem possessed an uncomplicated, direct, and usually obvious solution. George wished he could believe something as satisfying as that.

"Anything else?" Rufus asked. George and Sabbatius shook their heads. The veteran went on, "Well, I expect a hero like Dactylius and me'll be able to keep any giant bats from flying off with the city till the sun comes up. Why don't you boys go on home and get some sleep?"

That was uncomplicated, direct, and obvious. So far as George could see, it overlooked no hidden difficulties.

Some problems *were* simple. George descended from the wall and headed back to the dwelling above his shop. He kept looking for bats all the way there, though. That he saw none relieved him only a little.

George peered back toward Thessalonica, though hills hid it from view. He liked living in the city, but he also liked escaping from it from time to time. With luck, he'd bring back some game for Irene to throw in the pot or some mushrooms to make a stew more interesting. Without luck . . . He shook his head. Here he was in the fresh air, away from city stinks. If that wasn't luck, what was?

He looked around. Somewhere not far from here, he had met the satyr that had started him worrying about the Slavs and Avars and their gods and demons. He hoped he would meet the creature again, or another of its kind. Bishop Eusebius—any priest—would have set a penance on him for entertaining that kind of hope.

His broad shoulders went up and down in a shrug. For one thing, he hoped he might learn more from the satyr than he had at their previous meeting. And, for another, he was curious. He tried not to admit that even to himself, but he had never been much good at such mental games.

So long as he stayed on the road—the track, really—he was unlikely to meet up with the satyr or any other supernatural creature. Almost all the men who used the road these days were Christians. They carried the power of their faith with them, making areas they frequented uncomfortable for lesser powers. Not only that, rabbits were easier to find off the beaten track.

And so George plunged into the woods. He had a bow and an arrow in his hands, a full quiver on his back, and a knife at his belt. If brigands wanted him, they would have a busy time of it before they finally pulled him down.

He moved as smoothly and quietly as he could. He was no great scout, to slip among the trees with neither animals nor men having the slightest notion he was anywhere nearby. He knew that—and if he hadn't known it, Rufus would have got the idea across to him in no uncertain terms. But he seldom came home empty-handed when he went out hunting, so he supposed plenty were worse at the game than he, too.

Something behind a bush moved. George nocked the arrow he carried, then settled into immobility. Out from behind the bush came . . . a mouse. George let out a silent sigh. If he hit the little animal with an arrow, there wouldn't be enough left to take home. *I should have brought along a cat*, he thought, smiling at the conceit.

In a leather sack on his belt he had some cheese, some bread, a little flask of olive oil in which to dip the bread, and a fine, fat onion. He also had a wineskin on his belt. He knew he could drink water instead, but that didn't mean he wanted to. Besides, the sweet scent of wine might help lure a satyr his way, as it had before.

When shadows and his belly both said it was more or less noon, he sat down on a log to eat the food Irene had packed for him. The mouse was the nearest thing to game he'd seen all day. If he didn't come across something—or even that patch of mushrooms he'd thought about before—by evening, his wife would have some pungent things to say to him when he got back to town. He shrugged. That had happened before. It was sure as need be to happen again.

He had bread in one hand and the little flask of oil in the other when a hedgehog, perhaps disturbed by his sitting on the log, came out and scurried over to a nearby drift of leaves, in which it took refuge. He knew people who ate hedgehogs when they caught them. He didn't get up and go after this one. He wasn't any of those people.

He tore off a piece of the loaf Irene had baked, put oil on it, and had just taken a bite when a couple of men came out of the woods. They froze when they saw him. He froze when he saw them, too—all but his eyes, which flicked this way and that till he'd made exact note of where he'd set down his bow.

One of the newcomers had a bow of his own. The other carried several javelins. Those might have been good for hunting deer—or for hunting men. Both of them wore long wool tunics with fierce beasts embroidered in bright colors at the chest and shoulders. George had never seen tunics like those before. After a moment, he realized the strangers were Slavs.

But for the tunics, they didn't look outstandingly peculiar. True, they wore beards, but some Roman rustics wore beards, too. They were stocky and fair-skinned, with light brown hair shiny with grease of some sort. One of them had light eyes, the other dark. They wore, he noted, excellent boots.

They seemed as nonplused to encounter George as he was on meeting them. He didn't want to fight unless he had to. Holding up the bread, he called in Latin, "Come and share. I have enough." He didn't, not to satisfy three men, but a little hunger was supposed to be good for the soul.

The Slavs didn't come forward. They didn't go back, either. He called to them again, this time in Greek. They spoke back and forth to each other in a coughing, guttural language George had never heard before.

At last, when he was wondering whether he ought to grab for the bow, they did approach him. Both of them held right hands up, palms out. Either they meant peace or they were trying to lull him into thinking so.

One of them took out bread of his own, a lumpy-looking, dark brown loaf nowhere near so fine as the one Irene had given George. The Slav tore off a chunk and handed it to the shoemaker. In return, George offered him some of his own loaf. The Slav took a bite and looked pleased.

George held out the little flask of olive oil. The Slav took it, sniffed, made a face, and passed the flask to his comrade. That fellow also looked disgusted. The two of them spoke emphatically in their own language. George didn't understand a word of it, but odds were it meant something like, *How can you stand to eat that stuff?*

As far as he was concerned, bread by itself was boring. That went double for what the Slav had given him: it was dense and chewy and, he guessed, made from a mix of barley and wheat. It would, no doubt, keep a man alive for a long time, although after a while he might not want to go on living on such rations.

Then the Slav with the dark hair took out a flask of his own. It proved to hold not olive oil but honey. With honey, the bread definitely became more palatable. George shared out his cheese. The Slavs approved of that. They gave him some sun-dried pears and plums in return.

He untied the rawhide cord around the neck of the wineskin and handed the skin to the blue-eyed Slav. The fellow swigged, his larynx working. He passed the skin to his darker friend, who also drank. Courteously, though, he made sure he did not empty the skin before returning it to George.

After everyone had finished eating, the Slavs tried talking with him some more. The effort was vigorous but useless. They spoke their own guttural language and fragments of another that sounded even stranger—maybe it was the Avars' tongue. Whatever it was, it made no sense to George. He gave them Latin and Greek, the only two languages he knew. As he'd already concluded, they didn't understand those.

By signs, he showed them what he'd been doing out in the woods. They laughed at his impression of a hopping rabbit. He laughed, too, as he bounded about, but he was careful not to let them get between him and his bow. When he was done bounding, he did his best with gestures and questioning looks to ask why they were here.

They looked at each other and talked for a couple of minutes in their own incomprehensible language before trying to reply. When they did, their gestures were anything but clear. Maybe that was because they weren't very good at sign language. On the other hand, maybe it was because they didn't want him to understand why they had suddenly appeared only a few miles outside of Thessalonica.

Maybe they were hunting for animals; from the way they leapt and crept and shaded their eyes with their hands, that was possible. And maybe they were hunting for Thessalonica itself; that was as plausible an interpretation. They didn't ask George where it was. Had they done so, he might have told them; it wasn't as if a city that size was hard to find.

Face to face with two veritable Slavs, he decided to learn what he could from them, even if they had not a word in common. Pointing to them to get their attention, he threw back his head and imitated as best he could the howls he had heard from the woods, the howls he believed to have come from the throats of the Slavic wolf-demons the satyr had described.

He hadn't known he owned such a gift for mimicry. The wailing cry that burst from his throat was almost as frightening as those he had heard on the walls of Thessalonica. He did not judge that merely by his own reaction to the noise he made. The woods around him grew suddenly still, as they might have at a real wolf's—or a real wolf-demon's—howl.

And the two Slavs, after starting when he first began that cry, nodded and grinned to show they recognized it and to show they understood he meant a spirit of their folk rather than a mere fleshly beast of prey. They spoke several incomprehensible sentences. Once more, though he followed not a single word, he assigned meaning to the whole: something like, *Yes, those are ours. Pretty impressive, aren't they?*

He wished he really could have talked with the barbarians, so he might have learned more and brought it back to Thessalonica. That he was thinking of getting back to his home city again was a sign he didn't believe the Slavs intended to try murdering him. But he still stayed wary enough to remember exactly where his bow was.

Then one of the Slavs clumsily made the sign of the cross. George didn't think for a moment that meant the fellow was a Christian. And, indeed, the barbarian followed the gesture by pointing and saying something that was plainly a question. *That's the god you follow, isn't it?*

"Yes, I'm a Christian," George said, first in Latin and then in Greek, the two sentences sounding very much alike. He crossed himself, slowly and reverently, showing the Slav how it should be done. Having done so, he looked up into the heavens but not at the sun, not wanting to give the barbarians the mistaken notion that it was his god.

They asked him something else. He couldn't figure out what it was. The one with brown eyes pointed roughly in the direction of Thessalonica and made the sign of the cross once more. He crossed himself over and over again, then raised an interrogative eyebrow at George.

"Oh, I see what you mean," the shoemaker said. "Yes, everyone in Thessalonica is a Christian." He nodded vigorously. About then, he realized he wasn't being fair to the Jews in the city, but people were hardly ever fair to the Jews, so he felt no great urgency about redressing the balance now.

The blue-eyed Slav crossed himself, then strutted around looking fierce and dangerous, then looked another question at George. What the question was supposed to be puzzled him. He scratched his head.

A moment later, he had the answer. "Yes, God is a strong god. God is the strongest god. God is the only true god." The words meant nothing to the two Slavs. George crossed himself, then flexed his biceps, then nodded back at the barbarians.

He wished the Lord would give him a miracle like the one He had granted to Menas. No miracle came, though. Or perhaps one did: the Slavs understood him, not the least of concerns when he and the barbarians had no words in common. George glanced heavenward again. *Art Thou so subtle, Lord?* he asked silently, and got no answer.

He did get what was, if not miraculous, at the least a

display of God's lovingkindness: having shared with him food and drink and such conversation as could be carried on with hands and bodies and faces, the two Slavs picked up their weapons and, instead of trying to use those weapons against him, waved, nodded, and went back into the woods.

"Hail and farewell," George called after them in Latin. When they had disappeared among the oaks and beeches, he allowed himself the luxury of a long sigh of relief. Meeting them had been far more dangerous than encountering the satyr. As beasts, long hunted, grew leery of men, so the satyr rightly feared the superior power of the Christian God. But the wild Slavs were unfamiliar with His might, and so it held no terror for them.

George shook his head. "No time for philosophy now," he said out loud. "Whatever else it's good for, it doesn't fill your belly." He got to his feet, set an arrow in his bowstring, and went on looking for rabbits. He made sure he walked in a direction different from the one the Slavs had chosen, lest they think he was following them and decided they'd made a mistake by not picking a fight with him in the clearing.

Maybe God, having worked a small, subtle miracle (if He *had* worked a small, subtle miracle and it hadn't been skill at pantomime or blind luck) for George, was keeping a closer eye on him than He had before. Or maybe George was keeping a closer eye on the terrain around him than he had before. Or maybe the shoemaker had simply wandered into a country more richly stocked with rabbits than that through which he'd been going during the morning.

Whatever the reason, in the space of a couple of hours he'd killed five, and would have had a couple more if he'd been a better archer. He recovered one of the shafts with which he'd missed; the other hit a rock and splintered, and he couldn't find the iron point no matter how hard he looked.

He wondered if he ought to hunt more while his luck was so good, but decided against it: he was not the sort of man much given to pushing anything to extremes. Moderation was not the only thing that made him decide to head back to Thessalonica. Also in his mind—in quite a prominent place there—was that, having encountered two Slavs in these woods, he might come on more, and one happy outcome was no guarantee of a second.

Even the gate guards were militiamen these days, though not from his company. He showed them the rabbits. They congratulated him. He said not a word about the two easy kills he'd missed.

He didn't say anything to Irene about the kills he'd missed, either. As best he could, he downplayed his confrontation with the two Slavs. He knew perfectly well his best was not good enough, and that he would hear about it later from her. For the moment, in front of the children, she matched his restraint.

Theodore was excited by the meeting. "You should have fought them, Father." He made cut-and-thrust motions with an awl, as if it were a sword.

"Rufus would laugh at you," George said. "I'd laugh at you myself, if I weren't worn out. When one man goes out looking for two to take on, it's most often because he's drunk his wits away."

His son let out a loud sniff. It was, George thought, no wonder they recruited soldiers from among lads of about his son's age: they were strong, aggressive, and, most of all, stupid. If their superiors ordered them to rush out and get themselves killed, they'd do it, and thank the officers for the privilege.

Sophia said, "Somebody besides us should know the Slavs have come so close to the city."

"Yes, I think you're right," George answered with a sigh. He touched the rabbits he'd set down on the counter. "I wanted to bring these home first of all, so your mother could start dealing with them. But as soon as I'd taken care of that, I figured the best thing I could do was pay a visit to Bishop Eusebius."

✧ ✧ ✧

Getting to see the prelate of Thessalonica would not have been easy for an ordinary shoemaker at any time. Getting in to see him when he was not only prelate but also *de facto* prefect of the city would have been doubly difficult. But when George went to the basilica of St. Demetrius, he knew the magic words that got him past the lesser priests and scribes. Those lesser worthies hustled him past the silver-domed ciborium topping the saint's tomb, past the basilica's brilliant wall and ceiling mosaics, and straight into the little office adjoining the church wherein the bishop labored when not performing the divine liturgy.

In that office, Eusebius looked more like a bureaucrat than a prelate. The desk behind which he sat was piled high with papyri; ink smudged the fingers of his right hand. He was scribbling a note when George came in, and set down his reed pen with every sign of relief.

"What's this I hear?" he asked in a Greek so educated and archaic, George had trouble following it. "Is it accurately reported to me that you met two of the revolting barbarians in the woods earlier today?"

"Yes, Your Excellency, I did." George stuck with his Latin, the tongue in which he felt most at home. Eusebius understood him and motioned for him to go on. The bishop probably thought him on the uncultured side. That didn't bother him. By Eusebius' standards, he *was* on the uncultured side. He described the meeting with the Slavs and his attempt to explain Christianity, or at least its potency, to them.

"Well done," the bishop said, making the sign of the cross. "*En touto nika.*" As if making a great concession, he turned that Greek into Latin: "*In hoc signo vinces.*" Then he returned to his own preferred language. "Very well. You shared your food with the barbarians. What, beyond their mere presence, prompted you to report all this to me? You understand, their presence is of some concern in and of itself with the garrison gone, which is why I had you admitted to my presence, but—"

"I've come to bring this to your notice for two reasons, Your Excellency," George said. "One is that the Slavs, as best they could without using words, made it plain to me that they were looking not just for supper but for Thessalonica."

Bishop Eusebius' attention had wandered. Now it snapped back to the shoemaker. "That is not good," he said. "With the war that has gone on between us Romans on the one hand and the Slavs and Avars on the other, I do not want to hear reports that the barbarians are seeking our God-guarded city." He held up a beringed, elegantly manicured hand. "Do not mistake me. By that I do not mean I am ungrateful for your having brought this word to me, only that I wish you had no need to do so."

"I understand," George assured him. He studied the bishop with an odd mixture of distaste and admiration. The word that came to mind for Eusebius was *slick*, slick as fine olive oil or an icy pavement. Slickness could be wonderfully useful or unexpectedly dangerous, depending on circumstances. George gave a mental shrug, thinking, *As if I have the power to pass judgment on those placed over me*. Aloud, he went on, "The other reason I thought I ought to bring them to your notice is because they admitted the wolf-demons that have been howling outside the walls belong to them."

"Did they?" Eusebius said softly. Yes, George had his attention now. "What did they say of them? Tell me everything you remember." George got the distinct impression that, if Eusebius was dissatisfied with his report, he would go after more detail with lash and rack and heated pincers.

"They didn't *say* anything, Your Excellency, since we couldn't talk with each other," the shoemaker replied. He detailed the exchange, then added, "I've heard, Your Excellency, that these demons can attack a priest even after he's made the sign of the cross. Is that so?"

Eusebius' eyes went hooded, unfathomable. George knew what that meant: the bishop was figuring out whether to lie to him and, if so, what sort of lie to tell. But, at last,

Eusebius answered, "Yes it is, as a matter of fact, though I'll thank you for not spreading it broadcast through the city. I also remind you that evil is no less evil for being powerful, only more deadly."

"I understand that," George said—did Eusebius take him for a lackwit? Well, maybe Eusebius did.

"You did not hear of the vicious power of these demons from the Slavs you encountered today?" Eusebius asked. He answered his own question: "No, of course you did not, for by your own statement you and they had no words in common." His gaze sharpened. "Where, then, did you hear this about them?"

George abruptly wished he'd kept his mouth shut. He didn't know whether lying to the bishop or telling him the truth was the worse choice. Eusebius had told him the truth, or at least he thought the bishop had. He decided to return the favor: "A satyr told me, the last time I was out hunting in the woods."

Eusebius hadn't been looking for that. His eyebrows climbed up toward his hairline, and he let out a hiss that made George wonder if he were part viper on his mother's side. Then he crossed himself, as if the shoemaker were himself a relic of a creed outworn. When George failed either to vanish or to turn into some loathsome demon, the bishop regained control of himself. "That is a—bold admission to make," he said, picking his words with obvious care.

"Why?" George asked stolidly. "Without the satyr, you wouldn't have had this news, and I think it's important, don't you?"

"On that we do not disagree," Eusebius said. "On a good many other matters, I suspect such a statement would be as false as any from Ananias' lips."

"Maybe," George said, stolid still. "But I didn't come here to tell you about anything else."

Underneath that impassive shell, he was troubled. Once a bishop started worrying about—and worrying at—your theology, he generally didn't let go till he'd made you sorry you ever crossed his path. And Eusebius, being more aggressively pious than a lot of his fellows, had a worse name for that than most.

The inspiration—if not divine, certainly convenient—struck George. "Because you're prefect now, Your Excellency, or pretty much prefect, anyway, I was sure you wouldn't want any danger to come to Thessalonica."

"Of course not," Eusebius said at once. "Protecting the city is the most important thing I can do, the garrison being gone and the secular leaders away petitioning the Emperor Maurice." Sure enough, George had managed to distract him, to make him think of Thessalonica rather than satyrs.

"How can we fight demons that defeat even holy priests?" the shoemaker asked, wanting to keep Eusebius' mind away from him and on the bigger picture. *That's only proper*, George thought, remembering the mosaics that made the basilica of St. Demetrius so splendid. *If you look at one tessera, you don't see anything in particular. But if you look at what all the tiles do when they're working together . . .*

He'd also chosen the right question to ask Eusebius. The bishop said, "We can—we shall—we must—do two things. First, we must reconsecrate ourselves and bring our lives into closer accord with God's will, so that other powers will be less able to get a grip on us. And, second, we must make certain the walls of Thessalonica remain strong and the militia alert. For have you not seen how such sorceries seek to weaken not just the spiritual but also the material defenses set against them and those who make them?"

"Yes, I have seen that, Your Excellency," George answered, surprised now in his turn: he hadn't figured Eusebius would reckon material defenses as important as he obviously did.

The bishop said, "What else have you learned of the powers the Slavs, in their ignorance, prefer to the holy truth of God?"

He did not ask where George had learned whatever else he'd learned. The shoemaker took that as a tacit promise not to raise the issue of satyrs anymore. He didn't mention his source again, either, replying, "I hear they have other powers nearly as strong as the wolves. I cannot really speak about that because of what I've seen with my own eyes, though when I was on sentry-go one night, I did see a bat, or maybe two bats, that weren't like any natural bats I've spied before."

"Are you certain of this?" Eusebius asked.

"No, Your Excellency," George said at once. "Plenty of people must know more about bats than I do, but I can't think of anyone who knows less. Who pays attention to bats?"

"Who, indeed?" the bishop said. "Well, God willing, perhaps we shall yet be able to keep Thessalonica from being interred in a blood-filled, barbarous sarcophagus. If this be so, you, George, shall have played no small part in the preservation of the city, thanks to this information you have brought me. I am grateful, and no doubt God is grateful as well." He started fiddling with his pen, a sure sign he'd given George all the time he'd intended.

George rose and, after bowing to Eusebius, made his way out of the prelate's office. As he strode up its central aisle, he paid more attention to the basilica of St. Demetrius than he was in the habit of doing. Just being inside the church dedicated to the martial saint made him feel stronger and braver than he did anywhere else in the city: more like a real soldier than a militiaman.

After walking past the ciborium and then out of the basilica, he turned back toward it and sketched a salute of the same sort as he might have given to Rufus. If St. Demetrius could extend his influence over all of Thessalonica, if he could make everyone feel stronger than without his intercession . . . that might help, if the two Slavs George had encountered outside the city were, as he feared, the harbingers of more.

But, as George walked north and mostly west back toward his shop, his home, his family, and away from the shrine, the feeling faded, until he was only himself again, and oddly diminished on account of that. He forced his shoulders to straighten and his stride to lengthen. Even without the saint's beneficent influence close by, he remained himself.

"Blood-filled, barbarous sarcophagus," he muttered under his breath, which made a woman walking in the other direction give him a strange look and move a little farther away from him. He didn't blame her; he would have moved away from anyone mumbling about a blood-filled sarcophagus, too.

It's Eusebius' fault, he thought. The bishop pulled out funereal images at any excuse or none. George glanced toward the walls of Thessalonica. Surely, they would not be the walls of a stone coffin to enclose the corpse of the city.

He shook his head. "He's got me doing it," he said, which made someone else give him a sidelong glance.

Irene rounded on him when he walked in the door. "I thought you weren't coming back," she said indignantly. "I thought Eusebius wouldn't let you come back. You told him about the satyr, didn't you?" She didn't wait for him to answer. "I knew you were going to tell him about the satyr. Why did you go and tell him about the satyr?"

"It was either that or tell him lies," George answered. "Would you rather I told a holy man lies?"

"Of course I would," Irene answered with the same certainty and lack of hesitation George used when imparting what was, with luck, wisdom to Theodore or, more rarely, Sophia. *How could you be so foolish as to think otherwise?* her tone demanded.

George usually accepted such rebukes from her, because he knew he usually deserved them when he got them. Today, though, he balked. "I went to tell the bishop about the Slavs and about their demons," he said. "It was only natural for him to ask how I knew what I knew. When he did ask me that, I didn't see what choice I had but to tell him the truth, so he could know how seriously to take the news I was giving him."

Irene muttered something under her breath. George thought it was "Men!" but felt disinclined to inquire more closely. As with theology, some of the more subtle points of marriage were better taken on faith than examined under the piercing lamp of reason. In any case, Irene had a good deal to say that wasn't under her breath: "If he had taken you seriously, George, he might have felt he had to do something like ask questions about how you came to be talking with a satyr, not chasing it off with the sign of the cross." The look in her eye said she still wondered the same thing; she was more pious than he. She went on, "Would you really have liked, say, a couple of years' penance for doing that?"

"No, I wouldn't have liked that," he admitted. "But I didn't think he would do anything to me, because the news was more important than how I got it." Before she could interrupt, he held up a hand. "And I was right. Remember that—I was right." He felt no small sense of pride; in an argument with Irene, he seldom got to say that.

As things turned out, it did him no good even when he did get to say it. "It was a foolish chance to take," Irene retorted. "What you gained by doing it wasn't worth the risk."

"I thought it was," George said, but that took the argument out of the realm of fact and back into opinion. He tried a slightly different tack: "It's done now, and it worked out all right." Irene thought that over, then grudgingly nodded. That meant the argument was over, too, which suited George fine.

III

More people began encountering Slavs in the woods. A couple of men who went out hunting didn't come back. George was on a search party that went out after one of them. He found no trace of the missing hunter. He found no trace that the man had fallen foul of the Slavs, but nothing to prove the fellow hadn't, either. Whatever had happened to him, he never showed his face in Thessalonica again. George, along with most other people, suspected the worst.

The roads from the north grew crowded with farmers fleeing the ever-growing presence of the Slavs—and, presumably, their Avar overlords, though the Slavs were the folk on everyone's lips. Some of the peasants took refuge in the city. Others kept going, hoping to find lands the barbarians would not penetrate.

With the peasants came priests and monks, driven from churches and monasteries by the inroads of the barbarians. The monks, many of them, took refuge in the monasteries surrounding Thessalonica; the priests came into the city itself, to help serve its churches while theirs lay under the control of the Slavs and Avars. Suddenly the divine services had far more officiants than were needed, so that the holy men had to take turns performing them. When the refugee priests were not celebrating the liturgy, they gathered in the market square and told their harrowing tales to whoever would listen and perhaps toss a follis or two into the begging bowls they put out in front of them.

George wondered whether the copper coins they collected would go to the ravaged churches from which they had fled, to the churches of Thessalonica in which they sheltered, or into their own pouches. He did not know whether others had that same doubt. People who were clever enough to have the question occur to them were also clever enough not to voice it.

The priests drew considerable crowds. George listened along with everyone else, but kept his money to himself as long as the priests talked about the merely human destruction they had experienced or seen. The world was a harsh place, and war unceasing: unfortunate, certainly, but also unsurprising.

But then one of the refugees, a man who, by his theatrical gestures and carefully balanced sentences, had had more than the usual share of rhetorical training, said, "Nor is the energy from this vicious and brutal plunder and rapine derived from this world alone. For the Slavs and Avars bring with them a new host of barbarous powers against whom the true God and His Son Jesus Christ shall have to contend and whom They shall have to overcome by virtue of their superior prowess."

Someone—not George—called out, "Doesn't the Lord cast out all demons?" After a moment, the shoemaker recognized John's voice. Not content with scoring points off people in the taverns he frequented and off his fellow militiamen, now he was trying to get a priest angry at him. If John lived to be old, George would be astonished.

The priest, however, took the question seriously, answering, "In the end, the triumph of the Lord is inevitable: so it has been written; so it shall be. But the path to that end is not known, and much misery surely lies along it until it be traveled to the fullest."

George waited to hear what John would make of that. The tavern comic made nothing whatever of it, falling silent instead. As silently, George wished his friend would show such good sense more often.

"For now, the spirits attending the Slavs and Avars, being puffed up with arrogance on account of the victories those folk have won over us Christians, vaunt themselves and exult in their strength, and are difficult even for pious folk to withstand successfully," the priest said, which was not only true but explained to his audience why he and his fellows had had to retreat from the Slavic powers instead of easily beating them, as the old pagan Greek spirits were beaten these days. "We must do not what we want to do, but what God wants us to do."

His audience murmured in approval. But then, unfortunately, John started up again, asking the priest, "What does that mean, what God wants us to do? Should we be more fierce, so we can beat the barbarians and make their powers weaken, or should we be more pious, so God will take better care of us?"

The priest gaped at him. If he'd just answered *both*, he would have done well and probably made John shut up, an act of virtue in itself. But John had asked whether it meant one or the other, and the priest (whose wits were, excusably, perhaps not at their swiftest then) took it that way and that way only. Any reply he gave, then, was but half a truth and, worse, contradicted the other half.

After tossing the priest a couple of coppers, George elbowed his way through the crowd and caught John by the arm. The tavern comic whirled. He started to grab for the knife on his belt before he saw who had hold of him. Just in case he didn't feel like stopping—his temper could turn nasty—George squeezed a little harder. He had large, strong hands. "Come along with me," he said in a pleasant tone of voice.

"Suppose I don't feel like it?" John said. He wasn't

going for his knife, but he wasn't coming along, either.

George started walking. He did not let go of John. Since he was bigger and stronger than his fellow militiaman and sometimes friend, John got moving, too. He yelped. Then he cursed. If he did try to take out that knife, George figured he'd kick him where it would do the most good. If that didn't distract John, he didn't know what would.

"Turn me loose," John said.

It was not an angry shout, and did not seem like a threat. George considered. "Will you come along if I do?" he asked. John did not say yes. But John did not say no, either. George chose to take that as assent, and let go of his arm. John did keep walking. Once they reached one of the little side streets that opened onto the market square, George stopped, turned to him, and said, "Do you want to know a secret? Getting a priest going in circles is cheap sport."

"I liked it well enough," John answered. "Priests always pretend they know everything. That makes them more fun to bait—same with drunks in taverns."

"Baiting a drunk is one thing," George said. "Nobody but him made him drunk. But it's not that priest's fault he's here. All he did was keep from getting murdered by barbarians or eaten by wolf-demons. You can't blame him for not knowing which end of the awl to hold right now."

"Who says I can't?" John demanded. "And if he's not to blame for the way he acts, who is?" If John couldn't play logic-chopping games with the priest, he'd play them with George.

The shoemaker, however, didn't feel like playing. "Why don't you ask the khagan of the Avars? I'll bet he'd give you a better answer than that priest could."

John glared at him. George looked back steadily. That look didn't abash Theodore anymore, but John hadn't been exposed to it so often. He shuffled his feet like a boy caught stealing grapes. "Sometimes you're too serious for your own good," he grumbled.

"Yes, that's probably true," George said, which only

made John eye him with even more annoyance than he had before. George could make no sense of that. When he realized he could make no sense of it, he started laughing. He didn't explain what he found funny. John got angrier still.

The next time George went out hunting, he saw neither satyrs nor Slavs. That suited him fine. He also saw one rabbit, and missed it, which pleased him and his wife not at all. "Look on the bright side," he told her. "I don't have to go tell anything to Bishop Eusebius."

"Thank God for that," Irene said. "You got by with saying too much to him once. Doing it twice would be tempting fate." This was the first time she'd admitted George had got by with telling the bishop about the satyr. He decided to accept that, and gladly, and not worry too much about the rest of what she'd said. Concentrating on the good and not letting the rest get under his skin was one of the reasons his marriage went along as well as it did.

Dactylius came in just then. Sure as sure, he was carrying bow and arrows and had a sword on his belt. Sure as sure, he said, "You've forgotten again."

"I don't know what difference it makes," George answered sourly. "I can't hit anything today anyhow." But he got his own weapons and headed down to the practice field with the jeweler.

They went past St. Demetrius' basilica along the way. The broad doors were open. The hexagonal silver roof of the ciborium not far inside the entrance glittered, catching a little of the slanting late-October sun.

The reflections drew George's eyes to the church. His glance was wary, as if he expected Bishop Eusebius to burst out and rush toward him with either more questions or, just possibly, with red-hot pincers. Nothing of the sort happened; the only person who did come out of the church was a gray-haired woman wearing black, who had probably gone in to pray for the soul of some recently deceased relative.

George did hit the mark a few times. No one harassed him for not shooting better, because Paul the taverner seemed unable to frighten the targets, let alone hit them. "Next time, you don't want to drink up all the wine in the place before you take your shots," Rufus told him.

"I did no such thing," Paul said indignantly. "It's only that other people have had more practice than I have."

"Well, in that case, go gather up your arrows—if you can find them all; God only knows where some of them have got to—and shoot off another quiverful. This time, at least try to shoot 'em toward the targets." Rufus pointed at the bales of hay.

"You don't want to give him too hard a time, or he'll cut you off at his tavern," John said, stirring up trouble.

He got it. Rufus expressed in great detail what he would do if Paul presumed to take so rash a course. *Cutting it off* was one of the milder things he came up with. His bloodthirsty bellowing formed the background to Paul's search for his missing arrows. The taverner took a long time to find them, despite or maybe because of Rufus' running commentary.

"No wonder Jesus had nasty things to say about publicans," John remarked. That got him back in Rufus' good graces, but made Paul send him such a dirty look, George wondered if he'd ever be welcome to perform at the taverner's place of business again. Sometimes paying attention to something more than the moment's joke was a good idea.

By the time Paul did stick the last arrow into his quiver—and by the time Rufus counted them all (counted them twice, in fact, when he lost track on his fingers the first time)—daylight was fast draining out of the sky. "I think you did it on purpose," the militia commander said. "Now all you lugs get off with less work than you might."

"Maybe we could get enough torches to keep on practicing even after sunset," Dactylius said.

"Maybe we could light *you* up instead," Sabbatius

muttered. "For once, we get off easy, and you want to spoil it?"

Rufus, fortunately, did not hear that. "It'd be too expensive," he told Dactylius. "Bishop Eusebius, if it's for the church, he'll pay whatever it takes. But if it's for anything else, you got to cut the coppers out of him with a knife. You'd think so, anyhow, way he bellyaches." He stretched and grunted and pointed northwest, back toward the part of the city where most of the militiamen lived. "To hell with it. Tonight, we go home."

Not even Dactylius argued with him after that. George, for instance, knew Irene would be glad to see him home. Carrying his gear with him, he trudged off the practice field.

"Who's for some wine?" Paul asked when they neared his tavern. After a moment, he added, "Everyone can come on in." Rufus kept walking. Paul sighed. He was more worried about profit than about the insults he'd taken from the veteran. Sabbatius did go in. Knowing him, he would be there well into the night and wake up with a thick head in the morning.

"What about you, George?" Dactylius asked.

The shoemaker shrugged. "Not tonight, I don't think," he answered. "I have some work that could use finishing." He shook his head. "I always seem to have some work that could use finishing. Ah, well—if you intend to keep eating, better to be too busy than the other way round."

"That's true." Dactylius nodded several times, rapidly. "A man who isn't doing anything can't sell anything, and a man who can't sell anything isn't going to eat."

As they drew near the basilica of St. Demetrius, George sniffed. The air in Thessalonica always smelled smoky, what with so many fires going to cook food and heat homes. Still . . . The militiaman came round a corner. George pointed. Sure enough, a black cloud was pouring out of the open doors of the church.

For a moment, everyone simply stared in dismay. As in any city, fire was the great fear in Thessalonica. Once every generation or two, a great blaze would level whole districts. Again, the shoemaker thought of all the fires burning all the time: lamps, cookfires, hearths, smiths' fires, potters' ovens. . . . No wonder the flames got loose every so often.

"It's the saint's ciborium burning!" Dactylius said.

Priests were dashing out of the basilica, past the six-columned dome erected over St. Demetrius' tomb. Layfolk from nearby buildings came running. Those who had buckets of water splashed them onto the blaze. George could see at a glance that that was like trying to hold back the ocean with a spoon—the fire was far past putting out. If God was kind, it would not spread to the rest of the church, or to any other building in Thessalonica.

"Not much wind," Rufus said. "Sparks won't go flying all over the place." He'd been thinking along with George, then. "Something, anyhow," he grunted.

Dactylius, who spent his days working with precious metal, eyed the silver dome of the ciborium. It wasn't solid silver, but silver laid over wood—wood now burning. "That's going to melt," he said. "It will run just like water, and splash down onto the floor above the tomb."

"It'll be where anyone can grab it, you mean," Rufus said, and Dactylius nodded. Rufus transformed himself from a tired old man walking home with his companions back into a militia officer. "We'll have to form a perimeter around it, then, and keep people who don't have any business inside the church from getting too close till the priests can gather up the metal."

He drew his sword and advanced on the ciborium. George, Dactylius, and the rest of the militiamen in the group followed him. Dactylius had known what he was talking about: already melted silver was dripping down from the dome of the ciborium; smoke rose from the marble on which it landed. How much silver had been in the dome? It had to be hundreds of pounds.

"God bless you!" the priests called as the militiamen

took up their stations around the monument to St. Demetrius.

"I want to tell you, He'd better," Rufus said grimly.

George would gladly have echoed the officer. The church was filling rapidly, and not all the people were those the shoemaker was delighted to see. The smoke and the outcry the fire had created combined to bring out gawkers of every sort, from the merely curious to those who appeared at disasters to see what profit they could make from them.

When this latter sort saw the silver melting and dripping down to where they might get their hands on the lumps and globules, their expression reminded George of the look dogs wore in front of a butcher's shop. He'd never seen so many hungry, avid, hopeful faces all together.

"Why don't you go home?" he suggested to some of them. "Nothing here belongs to any of you."

"Not yet," a skinny man said. His friends laughed.

Priests and militiamen together lacked the numbers to keep the swelling crowd from doing as it would. The priests were not even armed—no, some of them had makeshift bludgeons, not that those would amount to much. George did not want to draw his sword, for fear of turning crowd into mob. Many of the Thessalonicans staring at the silver had weapons no worse than his.

"When it gets a little darker, they'll likely rush us," Rufus said. "That way, nobody will be able to tell for certain who does what."

"I think you're right," George said, "and it gets dark a lot faster this time of year than it did a couple of months ago, say." *When I get home, Irene will yell at me for being seven different kinds of fool for letting myself get caught in what's likely to be a riot*. That was his first thought. Only after it had gone through his mind did he think to wonder how and if he would get home once the riot got rolling.

Through smoke still thick enough to make him cough and force tears down cheeks no doubt sooty, the stretch of sky he could see got darker and darker. Color seemed to leach from the bricks of the basilica of St. Demetrius and the other nearby buildings.

In the gathering gloom, someone hissed, "Come on. Let's get it. They can't hardly spy us now." The serpent's voice must have sounded like that when it was tempting Eve in the Garden of Eden.

Only a few feet away from George, Rufus suddenly jerked, as if he'd been hit by an arrow. For a moment, the shoemaker thought that was what had happened. Then he felt the power in the air, strong enough to make the hair stand straight up on his head. He looked around wildly, wondering if lightning was about to strike.

But it was not lightning, or not mere lightning. Rufus' eyes were wide and staring. Whatever he saw had nothing to do with the burning ciborium or the thieves gathering around it. His mouth started to move. At first, no words came from it, as if the power about to speak through him had trouble matching its needs to those of his flesh and blood.

Then it did speak, in a voice that would have made George's hair stand on end if it hadn't been doing that already: "Men, citizens—barbarians around the wall!" After a moment, Rufus, or Whoever was using him as a channel, cried out again: "They've appeared unexpectedly, but all of you, all of us, we'll hasten with arms for our homeland!"

Rufus repeated himself twice more, using, so far as George could tell, the identical words each time. By the time he fell silent, staggered, and almost fell as he came back to himself, the basilica was nearly empty. Almost everyone who had heard him had rushed to obey.

He turned toward George, who was having all he could do to keep from rushing to the walls at that very instant himself. "The saint . . ." Rufus began, and then tried again: "The martyr . . ." He shook his head. "Something happened," he muttered, "but what?" He might have been the only person in the basilica of St. Demetrius who did not know what he'd said.

George started to explain, but a cry of wonder from behind him made him stop before he'd got out more than a couple of words. A priest was pointing at the wreckage of the ciborium. Wreckage it remained, but it was no longer burning. "We did not put out this fire," he exclaimed, his eyes almost as round as Rufus' had been. "God put out this fire."

"Christ and God helped us, with the intercession of the glorious martyr," Rufus said, again in a voice not quite his own. "The fire is quenched, and nothing here destroyed by it." Where before he had given orders to the crowd, now he commanded the priests: "Shut the doors to the church and gather up the silver in peace and quiet. And remember that this place remains in good order because of what the martyred saint established."

The veteran shivered like a man coming out of a warm house into an icy wind. Gently, cautiously, George touched him on the arm. "Come on," the shoemaker said. "The Slavs are attacking the walls."

"They are?" Rufus exclaimed. "What are we wasting time here in the church for, then?" Now he was himself again, and no one else. "Let's get moving. We'll teach the whoresons a lesson they'll remember one cursed long time."

He trotted out of the church at a ground-eating lope. George followed, along with the handful of other militiamen who had resisted the call that came through Rufus and stayed by the man himself. Behind them, the doors to the basilica slammed shut, with their bars thudding down to hold them so. Inside, the priests would be collecting the spilled silver . . . in peace and quiet.

People were running through the streets of Thessalonica, brandishing the spears and bows and swords and knives and occasional axes they had snatched up from their homes. "This is marvelous," Rufus said. "I wouldn't have thought even the barbarians at the gates would get everybody moving this way. I wonder what did it."

"It was you," George said, but Rufus, now, paid little

attention to him when he tried to tell what had happened. Power had not only filled him, but filled him to overflowing, so that he had neither memory nor even great interest in what he had set in motion. So, at any rate, it appeared to George, who was viewing it from the outside. He wondered what being filled with the power of the saint felt like. He doubted he would ever know.

Many of the townsfolk, not being part of the militia, had no assigned place on the walls. They went up anyway, and shouted curses and abuse at whoever was on the far side. George supposed that would do Thessalonica no harm; if any of those curses stuck to the Slavs, it might even do some good.

His own place on the wall was on the western stretch where he and his comrades in the militia had taken their turns as watchmen, near the Litaean Gate. That meant traversing most of the city, as St. Demetrius' church stood over in the northeastern part of town.

"Here we are," Rufus said when they reached their proper section of the wall. The old veteran sounded winded. George did not blame him, and contented himself with a nod by way of reply. When you made shoes, you sat or stood in the same place all day, which did not do wonders for your endurance. George's heart thudded like a drum.

Climbing the stairs up to the wall made it beat even harder and faster; he wondered if anyone had fallen over dead rushing to the defense of Thessalonica. They gained the walkway and looked out into the gathering dusk. His heart pounded harder still, now not from exertion but from astonishment and alarm.

Beside him, Rufus murmured, "Sweet Mother of God, it's a whole swarm of them."

The word was better than any George had found to apply to the Slavs. Thousands of men milled around outside the city, all of them carrying weapons of one kind or another. Some looked to be mounting attacks against the monastery of St. Matrona, leaning ladders against its walls and trying to climb up them. The monks overturned some of those ladders as George watched, and threw stones down onto the heads of the Slavs down below.

"Do you know," he said, discovering he had breath enough to speak again, "I think they think they're attacking the city wall."

"They couldn't be that stupid," Rufus said, but then, after he'd watched them for a couple of minutes, he shook his head in wonder. "I take it back. Maybe they *could* be that stupid."

"It's getting dark," George said. "There's a little mist in the air. They must have taken the long way round to get at Thessalonica from the west, because everything we've heard about the fighting is that it's been off to the east and north. So here they've come, they've never been anywhere near the city before, and what do they do? They see strong walls, so they think they're doing the right thing by storming them."

"You make sense," Rufus said, a compliment that delighted the shoemaker. His superior went on, "Now how long will they take to figure out that a city's bigger than a monastery?"

The Slavs did not take long. Some of them kept on assailing the monastery. More, though, drawn by the more distant walls and the people on them, came on and discovered Thessalonica. No sooner had they discovered it than they began to try to take it. They flung javelins and shot arrows at the militiamen and simple citizens on the wall.

An arrow slammed into the stonework not far from George's head. He heard the shaft snap, much as he did when he broke one of his own arrows hunting rabbits. But the Slav who'd shot this arrow had not been out for game. He'd had killing George in mind, or if not George then Rufus or someone else nearby. *He wanted to kill me*. Once lodged in George's mind, the thought would not leave. *He did his best to kill me*. This was not practice, shooting at a target. This was not drill. The Slav had meant it. This was war.

More arrows flew. One zipped past George's head, hissing like a snake. The first realization he was a target had shocked him. The second . . . He pulled an arrow of his own from the quiver, nocked it, and shot it at one of the barbarians down below. He didn't know whether he scored a hit or not—the Slav was running around among several others, and they were hard to tell apart: growing harder by the moment, too, as the light failed.

He also had other troubles. "We should have practiced shooting from the top of the wall," he said to Rufus. "It's a different business from shooting on the level."

"Aye, you're right—it is," the veteran answered. "Have to talk to the city prefect about that, or maybe to the bishop."

"You should talk to the bishop," George said. "If he won't listen to the man the saint spoke through, whom will he hear?"

"Nobody, maybe," Rufus said. Having dealt with Eusebius not long before, George thought that had a chance of being true. Eusebius, he suspected, listened to himself first and everyone else afterwards. But with Thessalonica being in his hands more than anyone else's this side of St. Demetrius, he might well pay attention to anything that would help him defend the city.

Sabbatius and Paul came up onto the wall then. Paul was somber and self-contained; Sabbatius reeked of wine. The contrast did not particularly surprise George. A taverner who got too fond of the goods he sold would not stay a taverner long: his business would fail, and he'd end up drinking at someone else's.

Sabbatius stared down at the Slavs. "Mother of God!" he muttered. "How many of 'em are out there? Must be ten or twenty myriads, easy."

"Even if you're seeing double, there aren't that many—not anywhere close," Rufus said. He scratched his chin. "I don't know if there're ten myriads of people *inside*

Thessalonica, let alone twenty. Three, four thousand Slavs out there, five at the most."

"There have to be more than that," Sabbatius said. Rufus gave a single scornful shake of his head. If George had to choose between a guess by a drunken militiaman and another by a soldier who'd been gauging the size of armies most of his life, he knew which one he preferred.

"Anyway," Rufus said, "the point isn't how many of 'em there are, the point is how to make there be fewer of 'em. Why don't you stop jawing and start using that cursed bow—or don't you remember you have it along?"

Sabbatius did start shooting at the Slavs. George could not tell what effect his arrows had; a lot of missiles were flying out from the wall. Somebody said, "If the jawbone of an ass was good enough for Solomon to fight with, why not for Sabbatius, too?"

"Hullo, John," George said without turning around. He loosed another arrow himself, then went on, "I thought I'd see you up here."

"It's the place to be right now," John said in affected, upper-class Greek.

George snorted. "Pity the Slavs don't speak any civilized language—you could slay them with laughter."

"Me?" John said. "Considering the way you shoot, making them laugh themselves to death would be your best chance." He let fly, then grunted in satisfaction. "There, you see? I got one. I'm funnier than you are, and I'm a better man with the bow, too."

"To say nothing of more modest," George murmured.

"That's ri—" John began, and then stopped, sending a chilly glance toward the shoemaker. George felt a moment's pride; not everyone could trade words with John and come off the winner. He knew he couldn't do it himself very often.

But then his small satisfaction was swept away, for out of the woods rode four or five men who sat their horses as if they were the centaurs that might still linger in the remotest valleys of the most rugged upcountry. But centaurs wore no armor, neither the man half nor the beast, and these men and their horses were both clad in scalemail that would ward them against anything but a direct and lucky hit.

They rode up to and through the Slavs, who parted before them as the citizens of Thessalonica might have parted before the Roman Emperor, had he come to worship at the church of St. Demetrius. They halted within bowshot of the walls. Under their iron helmets, their faces, as well as George could make them out in the fading light, were flat, strong, impassive.

"Avars," Rufus muttered under his breath. As soon as he spoke the name, George knew he had to be right. No wonder the Slavs treated them like lords: they *were* the Slavs' lords.

Calm as if they had come to visit rather than to attack, the Avars studied Thessalonica's works for a minute or two, then turned their horses away from the walls and rode back into the gathering darkness. Once more, the Slavs stood aside to let them pass. Shadows reached out for them, and they were gone.

Neither side started up the fighting again for some little while after that. "Those men had a power in them, and not a small one," George said quietly. "I wish Bishop Eusebius would have been here on the wall with us, to show them we have a power that can stand against theirs."

Rufus surprised him by shaking his head. "The less the enemy knows about you, the better off you're going to be," the veteran said. "That's true every which way, not just with plain weapons."

After a little thought, George nodded. "You're probably right," he said. Then he pointed to the Slavs, who were beginning to resume the racket they had abated when the Avars appeared among them. "We've found out about *them*, that's for certain."

But Rufus shook his head again. "Not yet. Not hardly. Not so it matters." He too looked out toward the barbarians. They were starting to light fires out there on the cleared ground between the city and the woods. "Me, I've got the feeling we're going to have plenty of time to find out more."

The strangest thing about the early days of the siege of Thessalonica was how close to normal everything felt. The only difference in his life George noticed was that going out to hunt had become impossible—which was, he realized, just as well, for it would have been decidedly unwise. He did not think the Slavs would share bread and honey with Romans they chanced upon in the woods, not anymore.

Not even his times up on the wall changed much. He still served his usual four-hour shifts, sometimes during the night. There was always the chance the Slavs would mount an assault against Thessalonica's formidable curtain of stone, but, after St. Demetrius had warned the townsfolk of their presence and kept them from coming up over the wall by surprise, they contented themselves with shooting occasional arrows at the garrison.

Indeed, as time went by, many of them left the immediate neighborhood of Thessalonica, so that the city hardly seemed under siege at all. Sometimes, looking out from the walkway atop the wall, George could not set eye on a single enemy warrior.

"They're out there," Rufus said one afternoon when he remarked on that. "Oh, they're out there, never fear. If they weren't out there, we'd have traffic on the Via Egnatia getting into the city from east or west. Seen any?"

"No," George said. "I wish I had." He lowered his voice, as if passing on a secret, and, in fact, he wanted no one but Rufus to hear his next words: "If we don't get some traffic, we'll be hungry by and by."

"That's so," Rufus answered, also discreetly. "Constantinople, now, Constantinople gets grain from Egypt. An enemy can besiege Constantinople till everything turns blue, and it won't do him any good at all. We aren't so lucky. We've had a few ships in from southern Greece, but not many, and not much in 'em."

"Maybe we should sally, try to drive them away," George said. "Then traffic could start moving again."

"Probably nothing to move right now, anyhow," Rufus said gloomily. "If the Slavs are here, they're in the farm country and backwoods villages, stealing their wheat and barley and wine. No, best thing to do is wait 'em out. Maybe God will send them a plague. That happens in a lot of sieges."

"Happens in towns, too." George remembered the outbreak of bubonic plague in Thessalonica not so long before. Hundreds, maybe thousands, had died.

After a while, Dactylius and John came up onto the wall. George hurried back to his shop; he was convinced his being away from it so regularly would make it founder. Irene was convinced he was out of his mind; Theodore, on the other hand, was convinced a soldier's life was far more exciting than that of a shoemaker. One day, George intended to sit him down with Rufus, to see if anything resembling sense would penetrate his head.

George had just finished nailing a new heel onto a boot (not a boot he'd made, he was pleased to note) when Claudia came into the shop carrying a pair of sandals. "Hello," George said, setting aside the newly repaired boot. "What can I do for you today?"

"Have you seen my husband?" Claudia's voice throbbed with melodrama. She was one of those people who found day-to-day life too dull to be readily tolerable, and spiced it up with imaginary worries when no real ones were handy. And when real ones were handy— "I live in dread of the day when the messenger will tell me my beloved Dactylius has died a hero's death for his city."

She clasped both hands to her bosom. It was a fine, well-rounded bosom; the gesture might have belonged in a pantomime show but for the inconvenient sandals. Sophia excused herself and hurried upstairs. Theodore coughed and coughed. Irene kept her face utterly expressionless. She worried about George, and made no secret of it, but made no production of it, either.

And George did not tell Claudia that the likeliest way for Dactylius' untimely demise to occur at the moment was death by boredom. Instead, showing restraint he felt sure St. Demetrius would have praised, he said, "I think he'll be all right. The wall is very strong."

"So they say," Claudia answered, as if *they* were notorious liars. "For myself, I wish Dactylius would just stay in the shop with me."

Given a choice between closing himself up in a shop with Claudia all day and going out to fight the fierce barbarians, George would have taken on the Slavs even without a sword to hold them at bay. That was something else he couldn't tell her; he was wider through the shoulders, but she overtopped him by two or three digits.

"What's wrong with the sandals?" George asked, hoping to turn her away from morbid worries about her husband and toward something simple.

"I broke a strap on this one—see?" She showed him the problem.

"Yes, I can take care of that," he told her, and then, to make conversation, added, "How did it happen?"

He realized that was a mistake the moment the words were out of his mouth. Claudia drew herself up to her full, formidable height. Her gray eyes flashed. It wasn't quite so impressive a manifestation as when St. Demetrius had spoken through Rufus, but it wasn't supernatural, either: it was only her temper coming out.

"That stupid slut next door kept throwing her garbage in front of *my* place, and so I hit her with the shoe," she explained. "I don't think you sewed the strap on very well."

George examined it again. It hadn't broken at a sewn seam. She'd hit so hard, she'd torn the leather. From under his eyebrows, he glanced up at her. No, getting on her bad side was not a good idea. She might well have been more dangerous to the Slavs than a good many militiamen on the wall, her husband included.

"I'll take care of it," he said again. With almost anyone else, he would have pointed out in no uncertain terms that the problem was not of his making. But Claudia was his good friend's wife . . . and, even if she hadn't been, he suspected he'd have kept his mouth shut.

Instead of sewing the broken strap back together, he took it off the sandal and replaced it with a new one. That took a little longer, but meant the sandal wouldn't rub Claudia's ankle when she wore it again.

She tried it on after he gave it back to her. After a judicious pause, she nodded. "Yes, that will do. I hope it holds together, though."

"It should," George answered. "Of course, the next time you hit your neighbor, you might want to think about using something like a brick instead."

Claudia considered the joke with such chilling seriousness that George once more wished he had the words back; he'd wanted to make her smile, not to make her murder the woman next door. But at last she said, "No, a brick would have hurt her more than I intended then. I would have to be truly angry to use a brick." She took a couple more steps in the repaired sandal and nodded. "It does feel good, George. I'll tell Dactylius I've been here. You know you can drop by the shop." She wrapped her mantle around her and swept away.

"What will you get me at Dactylius', Father?" Sophia asked, as eagerly as if she were a little girl rather than a young woman. The shoemaker and jeweler did not charge each other money for their services, but traded them back and forth.

"I don't know," George answered. "Some bit of polished brass—a ring, maybe, or a thin bracelet. Fixing a sandal strap isn't enough for me to bring home gold inset with rubies and pearls, you know." Nothing he was likely to do was enough for him to bring home gold inset with precious gems. He'd long since resigned himself to that.

"That woman." Irene shook her head. "She reminds me of a jar with the stopper in too tight left in the fire too long. One day it will burst and hurt half a dozen people with flying potsherds. And yet Dactylius dotes on her."

"Of course he does," George said. "Do you think he'd dare not to?"

Theodore chuckled, Sophia giggled, and Irene wagged a severe finger at her husband. "You are a wicked man. All the time you've been spending in the company of the militia is making you sound like John."

"I got the better of him the other day, up on the wall," George boasted, and recounted the exchange he'd won.

"That's funny, Papa," Theodore said, clapping his hands together. "Now will you tell us all the ones where he bested you?"

"If you want to hear those, you can go ask John," the shoemaker replied with dignity. Then he gave his son a cuff on the side of the head, not hard enough to hurt, not soft enough to be ignored, to remind the youth to preserve at least some vestige of respect for his parents.

"It's all right, George," Irene said.

"I know it is," he answered. "I want to make sure it stays that way."

As long as only Slavs were besieging Thessalonica, George didn't worry much about the ultimate safety of the city: they hadn't impressed him as being particularly dangerous fighters. That was as well; he and his fellow militiamen weren't particularly dangerous fighters, either.

"The ones who bother me are those Avars," he said to Dactylius as they waited for relief so they could return to their shops and homes after a morning stint on the wall. "We haven't seen much of them since that handful the first night of the siege, but if they weren't real soldiers, there're no such animals."

"They were fierce-looking, all right," Dactylius said, "but I don't think you worry enough about the Slavs. There are so many of them. Look at the way their powers are coming in and doing things the ones that have been here forever wouldn't even try in the face of Christian men."

"That's so," George admitted unhappily. "I wish it weren't, but it is. I hope that satyr I saw up there in the hills is all right. He's not a Christian power, true enough, but he'd been here a long time, like you say."

Dactylius made small disapproving noises. "As a good Christian man myself, I say we should have nothing to do with the old powers." His voice was prim. "The sooner we forget all about them, the sooner they'll vanish from the earth."

In principle, George agreed with him. In practice, he found the supernatural powers still lingering in the land that had once been theirs interesting in the same way he found old inscriptions and old coins interesting—relics of what had once been of great import to people.

He said, "I wish the Slavic powers would vanish from the earth if I forgot about them. Trouble is, they're too much in the minds of the Slavs for that to happen."

"What we need to do is convert the Slavs and Avars to Christianity," Dactylius said. "Then their powers will vanish away, as they deserve to do."

"That would be wonderful." George pointed out to a couple of Slavs sitting on the yellowing grass out beyond archery range. They were passing a wineskin back and forth. After a while, one of them rolled over and went to sleep. "They don't look ready to convert right now, worse luck."

"That's so," Dactylius said. "Maybe in the time of my children—if God blesses Claudia and me with children who live."

George thought about making love to Claudia. She was a well-built woman, and far from homely. All the same, had she been his wife, divine intervention would almost surely have been necessary for them to start a family. On the other hand, she might simply seize little Dactylius and have her way with him when the mood took her. George turned a snort into a cough; he didn't want his friend to know what kind of thoughts were running through his mind.

The Slavs did not try to break into Thessalonica during the rest of their watch. When the sun had swung through a third of its arc across the heavens, Paul and John ascended to the wall to take their places. John peered out at the Slavs, most of whom seemed utterly uninterested in the siege. "Another day of martial combat!" he cried. "And now to rush at the foe with a fearsome—" After a look of intense concentration, he broke wind.

"There you go," George said. "If the breeze were blowing in the right direction, you'd save the city single-handed."

"That wasn't my hand, you blockhead," John said. After a little more chaffing, he and the taverner began patrolling their stretch of wall while Dactylius and George went down into the city.

As usual, a crowd of women had gathered around the cistern in the neighborhood. Thessalonica's water came from nearby streams and rivers through underground pipes the Slavs and Avars had not yet discovered or tried to destroy. It still filled all the cisterns and flowed unhindered from fountains not only on street corners but also in several churches.

Among the chattering women stood Irene. Spotting George, she lowered the water jug she carried from her shoulder and waved at him. He waved back, looking around to see if she had Sophia with her. Sometimes it was hard to tell them apart from a distance—and sometimes not from a distance, too. But no; Sophia wasn't there this time.

Just then, the roof of the cistern flew off. Concrete chunks, some of them as big as a man, spun through the air. One of them smashed a house. More, by luck or providence, came down on empty ground. But some landed with horrible wet squashing noises.

The women near the cistern screamed and scattered. "Irene!" George cried, and ran toward them. He had almost reached his wife when the power that had hurled the roof off the cistern stood up inside and looked around.

It was roughly man-shaped, but five or six times as

tall as a man. It looked old, old. Its hair, what there was of it, was moss-green, and its long, straggling beard was also made of moss. Its skin hardly seemed skin at all, but rather wet bark.

Maybe George's shout, deep among shrill, had drawn its attention to him. Whatever the reason, it turned his way. Its eyes were red, like burning coals. When he looked into them, he felt his will dripping away like olive oil out of a cracked jar.

It reached out a hand—no, more a misshapen paw—toward him. As a drowning man will reach for anything his fingers touch, so the shoemaker made the sign of the cross. A satyr would have fled in terror. This horrifying apparition kept right on groping for him.

But the holy sign had not been altogether without effect. He had his wits back, and his will. He snatched an arrow from his quiver, set it in his bow, and took aim at the gigantic . . . Slavic water-demon or -demigod, he supposed the thing was.

Irene, whose presence of mind he often admired, had not dropped the water jar she'd filled at the cistern. A smaller version of the green-bearded thing popped out of it and grabbed George's arm, spoiling his aim. The touch of the power was clammy and piercingly cold.

Dactylius smote the smaller water-demon with his sword. What might have been mist or might have been ichor sprayed out from the wound. Irene did drop the jar then. Water splashed up and out from it. The small apparition of the demigod went from a single one to a multitude of tiny ones spread out in the bigger puddles among the cobblestones.

George started stamping the tiny ones, as if they were so many cockroaches. They crunched under his sandals like cockroaches. The great demigod in the cistern roared and bellowed as he crushed its smaller simulacra—or perhaps they were all part of the same entity, so that the big one felt the pain he inflicted on the others as if on itself.

More water-demons began springing out of the jars of other women who hadn't dropped them. George and Dactylius shouted for the women to do just that. Crockery crashed on cobbles. And George and Dactylius and Irene fled away from the cistern as fast as they could run.

"Do you suppose," Dactylius panted, "these horrible things—are in every—cistern in the city?"

"I hope not," George answered, just as short of wind. "I hadn't—thought of that. I wish—you hadn't—either."

Their flight carried them past the church of St. Elias, the church nearest their homes and shops. It was close enough to the cistern for a couple of priests to have come out to try to learn what the commotion was about. Irene stopped and gasped out an explanation. The priests exclaimed in dismay. "Heathen powers loose in our God-guarded city?" one of them, Father Luke, said. "We'll exorcise them forthwith."

"Have a care," George told them, still trying to catch his breath. "These things are *strong*, Your Reverence. You didn't see the roof go flying."

"A roof is a material thing, a thing of this world," the priest replied. "In matters of the spirit, the power of God shall overcome all others. Did not He, through the intercession of St. Demetrius our patron, vouchsafe a warning that our city was about to be attacked?"

"Yes, He did, no doubt about it. I was there, and I saw it with my own eyes and heard it with my own ears," George said. "But the Slavs are such raw pagans, their powers are strong in the world of the spirit, too." As he had so many times by now, he warned them of the wolf-demon that had slain a priest.

One of the men who had come out of St. Elias' church turned pale and made as if to go back inside. Father Luke remained unperturbed. "This means only that our own faith shall have to be stronger. Come, Father Gregory. If we fear the pagan spirits, we give them power over us."

Father Gregory looked anything but delighted at the prospect of facing a water-demon of the might of this one. But facing a water-demon was liable to be as nothing when set against facing Father Luke—to say nothing of facing Bishop Eusebius. Muttering something that might have been a prayer or a curse, Gregory followed his colleague up the street toward the cistern.

"Go back to the shop," George told Irene. "Let the children know you're all right."

"What are you going to do?" his wife demanded.

He pointed to the priests. "You never can tell what sort of help they might need, or who might be able to give it to them." He still didn't know what an arrow might do to the demigod or whatever it was. On the off chance he might have to find out, he started after Father Luke and Father Gregory.

Dactylius followed him. So did Irene. He wondered for a moment why she chose such inconvenient times not to listen to him. He had no time to argue, and the only way to force her to go back would be to drag her, which would mean he couldn't help Father Luke. Resolving to take it up with her later (a wasted resolution if ever there was one, as he knew even at the time), he hurried to catch up with the priests.

Then Father Luke, confusing things further, spun around on his heel and ran back into the church. He emerged a moment later, leaving George mystified. "Let's go!" he said, and go they did.

The open square by the cistern was almost bare of people: of living people, at any rate. A couple of women were down and not moving under shards of what had been the roof. Others writhed and wailed. The liquid puddled around them was red and sticky and of no interest to demons concerning themselves only with water.

"By She Who bore God!" Father Gregory gasped when he got his first glimpse of the water-demon looming out of the cistern. A few smaller copies—or parts—of the demigod still stood in puddles left by shattered water jars. They were hideous, too, but hardly worth noticing with the great one about.

Those red eyes swung toward the newcomers. The demigod made a strange, wet, bubbling noise, something that sounded as if it might be a question about what people were doing coming toward the cistern rather than running away from it. *A good question*, George thought. He wondered what he was doing, too. But he kept doing it. Each foot kept going in front of the other.

Father Gregory shouted, "In the holy name of God, go back to whatever accursed place spawned you!" He made the sign of the cross.

He must not have been listening when George warned of what the Slavic powers could do. Or, possibly, he hadn't believed George, who was, after all, only a shoemaker.

A power from the days of the pagan Greeks would have been routed. A power from the days of the pagan Greeks, though, could never have made its way into Thessalonica in the first place, not when the city was warded by God through St. Demetrius.

Far from being routed, the water-demon roared angrily and reached out for Father Gregory. As it was several times longer than a man, it had a correspondingly longer reach. George shot an arrow into its arm. A slight mist sprinkled down onto him. Other than that, the shaft had no effect.

Dactylius aimed for the thing's torso. In what might have been the shot of his life, he sank an arrow that should have pierced the demigod's heart. It seemed, however, not to have a heart: at any rate, his arrow did no more good than George's had.

"Run!" George shouted. He didn't know whether he meant it more for Father Gregory, on whom the water-demon's hand was closing, or for Irene. No, that wasn't true: he did know. He wanted his wife away from the power. The first denial must have sprung from embarrassment at putting her safety above that of the holy man.

It didn't matter. Neither his wife nor the priest listened to him. The huge hand closed on Father Gregory. He screamed like a lost soul. Considering his circumstances, that seemed fitting enough. He called on God and the Virgin and on Christ, using the holy names as if they were curses. They did no good against the Slavic demigod. George, in the midst of his own terror, was saddened but not surprised. Revenge and reverence were not the same.

Father Luke ran toward the cistern. The water-demon reached out its other hand toward him. George and Dactylius both sent arrows into that arm. The shoemaker never knew for certain whether that did any good. What he did know was that, when the demigod snatched at the priest, it missed.

Instead of grabbing again at once, it chose to pay attention to Father Gregory, whom it had already seized. It raised him high, then threw him down onto the cobbles of the square. Blood splashed out from his body when it struck, as if he too were a shattered jar. He screamed no more.

That brief hesitation, though, had let Father Luke reach the side of the big concrete basin with the wrecked roof. He pulled a small jar out from inside his robe, yanked off the stopper, made the sign of the cross over the jar, and tossed it up into the cistern. The demigod reached down to treat him as it had his colleague. Father Luke waited, unafraid. A moment before those great hands grabbed him, George heard a small splash: the jar had gone into the water.

The demon disappeared.

Silence slammed down in the square, silence punctuated by distant screams. George realized he'd been hearing those with the back of his mind for some time, which was a good argument in favor of the notion that the water demigod had appeared in every cistern in Thessalonica. As he stood there still half-stunned by his escape, those screams changed in tone from terror to amazement, which was a good argument in favor of the notion that, whatever Father Luke had done, whatever force he had called upon, had rid every cistern in Thessalonica of the demigod in the same instant.

On legs still wobbly with fright, George walked up to him, taking a few steps around the smashed horror that had been Father Gregory. "Bless you, Your Reverence," he said, most sincerely.

"Bless you for your courage," the priest answered, sounding as shaken as the shoemaker felt. "Without courage and faith, I fear, we shall be lost in the dark days that lie ahead."

George nodded. He looked back toward what was left of Father Gregory. The other priest had proved not to have quite enough of either, there when the ultimate test came. George suspected Father Luke would have found a way to prevail even without . . . whatever he'd thrown into the cistern. George's bump of curiosity, always easy to excite, began itching furiously now. "What was in that jar, Your Reverence?" he asked.

"Water from the baptismal font," Father Luke answered. "Fighting fire with fire is as ancient a proverb as I know. Here I thought it better to—"

"—Fight water with water," George interrupted, an enormous smile stretching itself across his face. The priest showed himself a man of enormous charity as well as piety: he did not get angry with George for stepping on his line.

Dactylius and Irene came up then. George put an arm around his wife. She shivered against him for a moment, but then said, "I'll have to buy a new jug to replace the one I broke here."

More than jugs had been broken in the square. Along with Father Gregory, several women lay there. Some might be helped. One was groaning and shrieking and clutching her leg, which streamed blood out onto the cobbles. A big chunk of concrete from the roof the demigod had destroyed lay by her.

George used his sword to cut a strip from the bottom of her tunic to bandage the leg. She screamed abuse at him all the while, as if the tunic were more important than anything else. He took no notice of that; the lower part of the leg was out of true with the rest. "A bandage isn't all she needs," he said, pointing. "That leg is broken."

"I'll fetch a physician," Dactylius said. "This could have been Claudia, as easily as not." George might not have bet on the water-demon against Claudia, but he knew the little man was right. Dactylius hurried away.

Father Luke came up to the woman and prayed over her. His entreaties might have eased her pain a little, but no more than that. Routing the Slavic demigod was a matter of power against power. Something as mundane as a broken leg wasn't, barring a miracle. Barring—

"Pity we can't take her to the healing spring outside the city," George said. "But the Slavs have to be prowling there nowadays."

"It is the will of God," Father Luke said. "We are in His hands."

He believed that with every fiber of his being. Not least because of his strong faith, he'd been able to vanquish the water-demon. But had he not had the wit to bring with him water from the baptismal font, all his faith would have done him no good. George, shorter on faith, tried to be sharp of wit. He had trouble understanding how God's purpose included things like a broken leg inflicted, so far as any man could tell, at random.

Father Luke would have called him presumptuous for wanting God's purpose to make sense to a mere man. He supposed the priest would have had a point, too. Some of his own purposes didn't make sense to Theodore and Sophia, who were in essence his equals, not inferiors, as he was an inferior to God. Even so . . .

He waited by the woman till Dactylius brought back the doctor, who took one look at the leg, nodded, and began the business of setting it. "I told him it was broken," Dactylius said, "so he brought the boards for splints."

"Good," George said. He turned to Irene. "Do I remember rightly? Wasn't I on my way home from a stretch on the wall?" He glanced at the sun to gauge the time. "Not very long ago, either." He shook himself, like a dog coming out of a pond. "Only seems a year's gone by since then, I guess."

"Bless you," Father Luke said again as he and his wife left the square. Weary and worn as he was, he walked straighter. When a priest like Father Luke blessed you, you felt blessed.

He wondered what the priests of the Slavs and the Avars were doing, now that their effort to make it impossible to draw water inside Thessalonica had failed. Wailing and gnashing their teeth, with any luck at all. But they probably wouldn't go on wailing and gnashing their teeth for long. They'd probably bring more of their gods and demons to bear against the God-guarded city.

He shrugged. The Thessalonicans couldn't do anything about that till it happened, if and when it did. Not only did they have God guarding them, they also had the militia. George had got almost to his own street before he wondered whether that counted for or against them.

Irene put her hand in his. "You were very brave," she said.

"I was what?" George said. Father Luke had praised his courage, too. He had trouble following that. "If I hadn't done what I did, I figured something worse would happen. If that's courage, then I'm—"

"Someone who talks too much," Irene said firmly. He was about to make an indignant denial; she could truthfully have accused him of a good many things, but not that. After he opened his mouth, though, he shut it without saying anything. If his wife thought he was brave and he went around denying it, didn't that count for talking too much?

When he and Irene walked into the shop, their children looked up from the shoes they'd been repairing. "Where's the water jar, Mother?" Sophia asked.

Irene and George looked at each other and started to laugh. Sophia spluttered in annoyance; how dared her parents share what was obviously a joke when she had no idea why it was funny?

Theodore said, "What's been going on out there, anyway? People have been running back and forth and shouting things that don't make any sense. And a while ago it sounded like a building fell down, or something like that. Are the Slavs throwing rocks—?" He paused, stood up, and set hands on hips. "I *said*, are the Slavs throwing rocks at us?"

His parents were laughing harder than ever, which irritated him and Sophia both. After a while, George stopped laughing. When he did, he felt as if he ought to start shaking instead. Laughing was better.

Little by little, he and Irene explained to their children what had in fact happened. By the time they were through, Theodore had turned very red and looked about ready to burst. "All that was going on not three stadia from here, and we didn't know anything about it?" he exclaimed in what, to his credit, tried very hard not to be a shout but didn't quite succeed. "If I'd been there, I'd have—" He made cut-and-thrust motions that merely betrayed how little he knew about handling a sword.

"Thank God you weren't there," George said, which only inflamed his son further. "The best adventures are the ones that happen to somebody else, believe you me. This isn't a story, son. The priest and the women who are dead, they're *dead*, and they won't come back to life till Judgment Day. The woman with the broken leg, she may be crippled for as long as she lives. And any one of them could have been me or your mother as easy as not." He saw he wasn't reaching Theodore, who was at the age to believe nothing bad could ever happen to him. George turned to Irene for support, only to discover she wasn't there to support him: she'd gone upstairs while he was talking, and he hadn't noticed. He might as well have been Victor, the city prefect, who liked to hear himself talk.

Irene came down a moment later, carrying a cup of wine in each hand. She gave one to George, who gulped it down faster than was his usual habit. Instead of scolding him, she drained her cup, too. George took it from her and went upstairs himself. When he returned with both cups filled, she took one from him and drank it as fast as she had the first. As she had not been behind him on that first cup, he was not behind her on the second.

Her eyes were a trifle glassy as she looked toward Sophia and said, "You can fix supper tonight." She spoke with unusual emphasis.

"All right, Mother." Sophia had enough sense to know when not to argue. She went on, "That will be easy, anyhow, because we don't have much besides bread and beans and oil and some prunes."

"You can live a long time on bread and beans and oil," George said. "People only a little poorer than we are live on them their whole lives through." He spoke more loudly than was his usual wont, too; so much wine drunk so fast made the world seem a very certain place.

"That's true," Theodore said, "but the world would be a boring place without some meat every now and then." He smacked his lips.

George was fond of meat, too. He sighed. "Can't go out hunting. Can't hardly keep cows or sheep inside the walls. Pigs, some pigs, and chickens. They eat anything. Ducks, maybe. And fish. The Slavs can't keep us from fishing in the sea." He sighed again. "Anything like that will cost plenty, even now. Pretty soon, oil will cost, too. After a while, beans and bread will cost."

"Bishop Eusebius won't let that happen. He won't let the merchants make beggars of us all," Irene said confidently. She had more faith in the bishop than George did. He didn't want to do complicated thinking right now, but after a moment decided she might well be right. Eusebius was too good a Christian and too good a politician both to let a handful of men aggrandize themselves at the expense of the rest.

Theodore's thoughts, meanwhile, had gone off on another tack. "Everything you said about how strong the Slavs' powers are must be true, Father," he said, a sentence to warm the cockles of the heart of any father of an adolescent male. "For that water-demon to show up in the middle of this city—"

"It's a worry," George agreed. He tried to imagine a satyr strolling into the marketplace of Thessalonica. He couldn't. Such a thing might have happened when Galerius was Emperor, but three hundred years had gone by since then, and those powers overpowered by a greater power.

"This is the first time they've tried anything so horrid," Irene said. "What will they do next?"

The question hung in the air. George looked out the door. All he could see was the shop across the narrow street. He couldn't see the wall, let alone what lay beyond it, not with his fleshly eyes. His mind's eye reached further. Somewhere out there, the chieftains of the Avars would be deciding what to do next. If they and the Slavs they led succeeded with it, whatever it was, the city would fall. That was very simple. For once, George wished things might be more complex.

IV

Axes rang in the woods around Thessalonica. George watched an oak tremble, sway, fall. A crew of Slavs began lopping off branches and cutting the trunk into lengths they found useful. Not far away, a mounted Avar watched his subjects.

"He's working hard, isn't he?" John said, pointing out from the wall to the horseman, who, but for occasionally pointing, wasn't doing anything much.

"Not so you'd notice," George answered, "but the Slavs are working harder because he's there."

"The noble comes round to see how his building is going up, you'd best believe the carpenters work harder," John said. "Me, I'm funnier when I know the fellow behind the bar at the tavern is listening to me. If he doesn't like what he's hearing, I have to try to find someplace else to work the next night."

"Carpenters build buildings," George said. "What do Slavs build? They can't be making a village out there, can they?"

"I know what they're making," John said: "they're making trouble."

"They've already done that." George looked along the wall instead of out from it. No sooner had he done so than he stood more erect and gripped his bow more firmly. Out of the side of his mouth, he said, "Here comes Rufus. Think of him as the fellow behind the bar."

John obviously did think of Rufus that way, for, like George, he did his best to project an air of martial ferocity. Like George's, his best left something to be desired. Rufus surveyed them with his brown eye, with his blue eye, and with both eyes together. He looked dissatisfied all three ways. "God must be watching over Thessalonica," he said, "if it hasn't fallen with the likes of you two holding off the Slavs and Avars."

George didn't argue with the veteran; on the whole, he agreed with him. And John surprised Rufus by putting an arm around him and kissing him on the bristly cheek. "Thank you, great captain," he said in a voice gooey with counterfeit emotion. "You've made us what we are today."

Rufus wiped his cheek with the back of one hand. "The good news about that is that it's true," he said. "And the bad news about it . . . is that it's true."

Another tree went over with a crash. The Slavs started trimming it as they had the oak they'd felled a few minutes before. "What *are* they doing out there?" George asked Rufus.

The veteran clapped to his forehead the hand he'd just used to wipe his cheek. "God help all of us if you're as I made you," he said. "Anyone with enough sense to rub his fingers on his tunic after he blows his nose can see that they're cutting the timber they need for siege engines."

"Siege engines?" George and John spoke together. John went on, "They're barbarians. They don't have any cities. What are they doing with siege engines?"

"They don't have cities, no," Rufus said. "That's not the point. The point is, *we* have cities. If they want to take them away from us, they have to get inside. The way to get inside a walled town is with siege engines. They know that; they may be barbarians, but they aren't stupid."

By the way he said it, his opinion was that the two militiamen *were* stupid. George's ears got hot. Rightly or wrongly, he prided himself on his wits. Having Rufus scorn them was bitter as wormwood to him. He said, "All right, they know what they need to do to break into our cities. But how do they know? Siege engines can't be easy to make."

"Anything is easy—if you know how to do it," Rufus said. "And they do." His face darkened with anger. "The Avars were besieging some town up near the Danube, way I heard the story. I forget the name of the place; this was, oh, I don't know, ten years ago, something like that. They caught a soldier outside the walls, fellow called . . . called . . . Bousas, that was it."

"They learned to make siege engines from us Romans?" George said, appalled. "Did this Bousas tell them how?"

Rufus nodded. "That's what he did, all right. They were going to kill him. He told them to take him back to this town, whatever its name was, and the people there would pay ransom to get him back."

John's chuckle was cold and cynical. "Didn't happen, eh?"

"Sure didn't," Rufus agreed. "One of the nobles there was either screwing Bousas' wife or else wanted to screw her, I misremember which, and he persuaded the people not to give the Avars even a follis for Bousas."

"And Bousas paid them back?" George said.

"That's what he did, all right," Rufus repeated, with another nod. "Said he'd give 'em the town if they let him live, and then went on to teach 'em how to make stone-throwers." He scowled. "That's how they've taken so many towns since, and that's how they know about engines."

George was a man who liked to get to the bottom of things. "What happened to Bousas, and to his wife, and to the noble who kept the people from ransoming him?"

"If Bousas isn't dead, he's still with the Avars," Rufus answered. "I don't know what happened to the woman or the other fellow. Whatever it was, my bet is that it wasn't pretty. I've seen what happens to towns in a sack." His lined face went very harsh for a moment. George wondered what pictures he was watching inside his head, and hoped Thessalonica wouldn't find out.

John said, "If the Slavs do break in, nice to know it's on account of our sins and not theirs, isn't it?"

"Maybe we should sally and break those engines, or else burn them, before the barbarians can bring them up against the walls," George said.

Rufus studied the ground outside the wall. After what must have been a couple of minutes, he regretfully shook his head. "I wish we could, but I don't think we can. Too stinking many Slavs out there—Slavs here, there and everywhere. They can afford to waste whole great stacks of men holding us off, and we can't afford the ones we'd have to spend. Anybody says the militia ought to try it, I'm going to say no as loud as I have to, to make people listen. If we had some regulars, now—"

Regulars would have armor to match the scalemail the Avars and their horses wore, and most of them would be mounted, too. If the militiamen fought the Slavs out in the open, they would lack the advantage in weapons and position and be outnumbered to boot. George decided Rufus was right.

Then the veteran looked thoughtful. "Wouldn't want to send militiamen out against the Slavs in broad daylight, I sure wouldn't, not unless things were different from the way they are now. Sliding a postern gate open at night, though, and going out and seeing what we could do then . . ." His eyes didn't match, but they both saw clearly.

So George thought, at any rate. John hopped straight up in the air, a motion startling enough to make a couple of Slavs look up from their carpentry and point his way. "At *night*?" he said with anger that sounded genuine. "You're going to try to take my audience away? I like that!"

"Don't worry about it, pup." Rufus set a hard, much-scarred hand on his shoulder. "Nobody'd be listening to you anyway." He tramped on down the walkway atop the wall, leaving John, for once speechless, behind him.

✧ ✧ ✧

More and more Slavs came down from the northeast. More and more Avars came with them, to make sure they stuck to their work. With alarming speed, a variety of siege engines took shape under the Avars' direction. George, who knew plenty about shoes but had never been besieged before, needed help telling one sort from another. Rufus gave it.

"You see the ones on the broad bases?" he said. "The ones that taper up till they're thinner on top? Those are the stone-throwers. They'll try and knock the wall down so the barbarians can swarm through the breach."

"That's what all those things are for, isn't it?" George said.

"Well, of course it is, but there are different ways of going about it," the veteran answered, tossing his head in annoyance at the shoemaker's naïveté. "Those hide-covered sheds shaped like triangles, they're going to hang battering rams from those. You see that log with the pointed iron beak? That's going to be a ram. They'll bring that little present up to the gate or try and fill in some of the ditch in front of the wall so they can come right up close and pound away."

"And the shields all piled over there?" George looked out to the very edge of the forest. Even from that distance, the shields were obviously not of the ordinary sort. They were bigger than those either militiamen or regulars carried, and extravagantly faced with iron.

"Tortoises," Rufus said. "The Slavs'll stand under 'em and try to dig out the stones at the bottom of the wall so the ones above 'em fall down. Of course, life gets interesting under a tortoise. I've been under one a time or three, and it's something I could do without."

Interesting was not the word George would have used. The Thessalonicans already had piles of stones waiting along the walkway. They also had stacked firewood and collected a goodly number of iron pots in which to boil water. All of the stones and the boiling water would come down on the Slavs. Maybe the shields would hold off the rocks. Could they hold out scalding water?

"What we need," John said, "is St. Demetrius coming down and working another miracle. I mean, a miracle besides talking through a homely old sinner like our captain here."

"For a follis, two at the outside," Rufus growled, "I'd go and tell Bishop Eusebius to lower your worthless carcass down in front of the wall and use it to pad the stonework against the boulders the barbarians are going to fling at us. Any boulder that bounced off your hard head would be gravel the next instant, that's certain sure."

"You've got your nerve, running down miracles," George said to John. "What do you think God will do to you for that?"

John flashed his impudent grin. "God is a god of mercy, right? That means He'll forgive me, I hope."

"Now there's a doctrine that would get Bishop Eusebius hopping mad," George said. John *did* have his nerve; George, as often with his friend, didn't know whether to be admiring or horrified.

"Who's running down miracles?" a deep voice behind them demanded. George turned. There stood Menas, solid and blocky and altogether cured of his paralysis. The noble had a helmet on his head and a stout hammer in his hand. He looked like a man with whom no one sensible would want to trifle. "Where would I be today without God's kindness?"

John started to answer him. Afraid of what the answer would be, George stepped on his fellow militiaman's foot. John hissed like a viper. George didn't care about that. To Menas, he said, "I'm sure you must fit into God's plan for saving Thessalonica."

"What?" Menas snapped. That thought plainly hadn't occurred to him; all he'd worried about was God's plan for saving Menas. He had a fine glower, one that no doubt struck terror into the souls of everybody who owed him money. "You're the shoemaker, aren't you?"

"That's me," George answered evenly.

"I'll remember you," Menas rumbled. He strutted

off, chest out, thick legs striding along as if they hadn't been useless sticks for years. Maybe that strut was what made a couple of Slavs shoot arrows his way. The shafts missed, but Menas moved a lot faster and with a lot less self-conscious magniloquence after they zipped past his head.

John whistled. "You don't want to get important people angry at you, George." He spoke with unwonted sincerity. "I know about that. Why do you think I'm not living in Constantinople anymore?"

"I don't know," George answered. "They're supposed to have good taste back there; that probably has something to do with it."

Rufus gave him an admiring look. "The Slavs shoot poisoned arrows every now and then. I wonder what they did for poison before your tongue came along."

"You people don't need me," John said. "I think I'll go off into the garden and eat worms."

"Thessalonica's not *that* hungry yet," Rufus told him, "and besides, your stretch on the wall here isn't up yet, either. We're stuck with you a while longer."

But out beyond the walls, the sounds of logging and carpentry went on and on.

People filed into the church of St. Demetrius to pray for the salvation of the city and to listen to what Bishop Eusebius had to say both about divine aid and about what mere men needed to do to save Thessalonica.

"We'll meet you across the square from the church after the service is over," Irene said. George nodded. His wife and Sophia took the stairs up to the women's gallery. He and Theodore walked on down the central aisle of the basilica, to get as close to the altar as they could. Not only did that give them a more concentrated feeling of the saint's warlike power, it also let them have a better chance of actually hearing Eusebius.

George looked up toward the filigreed screen intended to keep men at prayer from being distracted by looking at and thinking about women. In a way, it did exactly what it was supposed to do. In another way, it failed, for he kept trying to spot Irene and Sophia through the screen's ornately patterned holes.

Chanting priests swinging thuribles advanced toward the altar from either side. Clouds of incense drifted up from the censers: fragrant frankincense and bitter myrrh. Like any church, St. Demetrius' was steeped in those fragrances even without their reinforcement. When George smelled them, his thoughts automatically went to holy things.

And here came Bishop Eusebius, gorgeous in silks encrusted with pearls and precious stones. He made his way to the altar and celebrated the divine liturgy with a zeal that matched the meaning of his name in Greek: "pious." As he usually did, he conducted the services in Greek. George did not mind that, even if Latin was his preferred tongue. Maybe the powers that had lived in this land before Christianity might also hear petitions in Greek.

Had he spoken that thought to Eusebius, the bishop would no doubt have berated him. But then, being a bishop, Eusebius was no doubt on intimate terms with God. George was just a shoemaker, and not inclined to be picky about which powers helped Thessalonica against those of the Slavs and Avars.

When the service was completed, Eusebius addressed the congregation: "Brothers and sisters under God, we must remember always that we are in His hands. And we must remember always that our fate is in our hands as well as His. If we do not prove ourselves worthy of His aid, we shall not receive it. Instead, we shall be chastised for the multitude of our sins. The instruments of His chastisement lurk beyond our walls.

"I have heard it said the pagans number a double handful of myriads, a hundred thousand men. I do not know if this be true, but it would not surprise me. Our own numbers are not so large, but numbers alone I do not fear, for is it not written, and written truly, 'How should one chase a thousand, And two put ten thousand to flight, Except their Rock had given them over, and the Lord had delivered them up. For their rock is not as our Rock'?"

The rhetoric was strong and heartening, and lifted George's spirits. But then he wondered, as he had once or twice before, what the men who talked with the powers and gods of the Slavs and Avars were saying to their followers. They had no Holy Scriptures, of course, but he would have been surprised if they told their fellow barbarians anything much different from Eusebius' words. All men believed their gods the mightiest, till the test came.

Then George had a truly appalling thought, one that had not crossed his mind till now: *what if the men who talked with the powers and gods of the Slavs and Avars were right, and Bishop Eusebius mistaken?*

He shivered like a man out at night in a cold rain. The Avars and the Slavs who did so much of their fighting for them had beaten the Romans at least as often as they had tasted defeat. What did that say about the relative strength of the powers involved?

He did not care for what he thought it might say. Brooding thus, he missed some of what Eusebius was saying; his attention returned to the bishop in midsentence: "—is because God demands much of us Romans. If we sin, He punishes us, as we deserve. If we want Him to stay His hand and not bring His flail down upon our backs, we must live our lives in holiness, showing Him we deserve to be saved."

A hum of approval ran through the basilica. How many people would give up gambling and blaspheming and fornicating because of the bishop's words, though? Bishops had been inveighing against sin since the beginning of Christianity, yet sin remained loose in the world and loose in Thessalonica.

Eusebius said, "We are men. We are sinners. We are

imperfect. God does not expect all of us can be saints; He knows our hearts too well. But He does expect each of us to do all he can. If all of us, together, do enough, our foes shall not prevail against us."

George always felt clever when he thought along with someone, especially with someone who was clever himself, as Eusebius undoubtedly was. As alarm had a little while earlier, pride made him miss a few of the bishop's words: "—pray that we shall be brave enough to withstand the barbarians' onslaught, which cannot now long be delayed. And we shall also pray that the measures we take against the foe, both on the walls and in the spiritual realm, shall be crowned with success."

"Amen!" The response came loud and strong. George joined in along with everyone else. Nobody in Thessalonica was crazy enough not to want to be delivered from the Slavs and Avars. Even the Jews were probably praying for that deliverance. The Slavs and the Avars wouldn't hate them for being Jews, but would hate them for being Romans. The Jews got a poor bargain, any which way.

Eusebius stooped and picked up something that lay behind the altar. He held up a large iron grappling hook. "With defenses such as this, we shall turn aside the engines of the barbarians. Let us pray virtue into them."

"Amen!" the worshipers cried out again.

"The Lord God shall see that we do all we can in our own behalf, and, being merciful toward us and filled with lovingkindness, shall grant us a measure of His strength as well." Eusebius waved the grappling hook about. If he'd gone fishing with it, he might have snagged a whale. But whales were not its intended prey; it was made for catching rams and their sheds.

Just for a moment, George thought the grappling hook glowed with a light that did not spring from the candles and lamps in the basilica of St. Demetrius. Before he could be sure he hadn't imagined it, Bishop Eusebius set down the hook with a clank of iron and held up another. Again, he and the Thessalonicans prayed. Again, George thought he saw a glow surround the hook with light apparently not from any natural source. Again, he admitted to himself that he couldn't be sure.

Another clank of iron heralded Eusebius' setting down the second hook and picking up a third. All in all, the congregation must have sought to pray virtue into at least a dozen grappling hooks. George wondered how the bishop kept track of which ones had been prayed over and which hadn't. Did one of them, by some mischance, have a double dose of divine power prayed into it while another went without? Or could Eusebius sense the difference between a grappling hook the Lord had been invited to fortify and one He had not?

"When the enemy attacks, we shall all stand fast," Eusebius declared. "The liturgy is accomplished. Go in peace, but knowing you shall be tested in the fire of war."

"We'll smash them, won't we, Father?" Theodore said eagerly as they walked out of the church. "God will help us."

"I hope so." George's eyes went to the ruins of the ciborium, and to the smoke stains still blackening the columns and ceiling nearby. God had helped then, dousing the flames and speaking through Rufus to get the people up onto the walls when the Slavs first appeared in large numbers.

But, even as he walked across the square to the meeting place on which he'd agreed with Irene, he heard drums thundering outside Thessalonica: not drums calling men to battle—alarms would have come from the wall had that happened—but more likely summoning the gods and demons of the Slavs and Avars to fortify the onslaught that was to come. Men against men, walls against siege engines, God against gods . . .

"There's Mother." Theodore pointed. George waved to Irene. Theodore, having spotted her, cast his eyes on some of the other women—younger, unmarried women—coming out of the basilica. Some people might have disapproved of such concupiscent thoughts on the heels of the divine liturgy. In theory, George disapproved of them, too. In practice, he remembered having done the same thing when he was a youth. And, for that matter, he still looked at pretty girls when he got the chance, even if he had no intention of doing anything but looking. He remembered the one he'd seen when the garrison marched away.

That, unfortunately, made him remember the garrison *had* marched away, something he would sooner have forgotten. The militiamen had kept Thessalonica safe so far, but the Slavs and Avars hadn't yet seriously assaulted the walls. Soon—maybe as soon as tomorrow—they would. Having a couple of thousand professionals in place alongside people like him would have made him rest easier of nights.

"Well, let's go home," Irene said when she'd made her way through the crowd to George's side. Then she spoke to Sophia, in a low tone George didn't think he was meant to hear: "Don't stare at them that way, dear. You're supposed to be—reserved."

"*Mo*ther!" Sophia's reply hit the indignant high note every young woman seems to find by instinct. Her ears turned pink.

George knew young women eyed young men, too. He smiled to himself; by the way Irene addressed her daughter, that was supposed to be a secret of sorts. He shrugged. One of these days, if he found the right chance, maybe he'd tease his wife about it.

"I always feel better coming out of church after the liturgy," Irene said. "It reminds me of how much in God's hands I am."

"Yes, Bishop Eusebius said the same thing," George answered, and let it go at that. His own faith, while real, was harder to kindle.

But after a few more paces, Irene said, "While Bishop Eusebius was praying over those hooks, though, I couldn't help but wonder what the Slavs and Avars were doing at the same time."

"Yes," George said again, this time in an altogether different tone of voice. He set a hand on his wife's shoulder. "I'm glad our parents thought we were a good match for each other. They were right in more ways than they knew. I was thinking the same thing myself."

"Were you?" Irene walked on a little farther. "Well, you wouldn't believe me if I told you I was surprised, not after all those years you wouldn't. And since I'm not surprised, anyhow—"

They both laughed, easy and happy with each other. Theodore and Sophia looked at them not quite as if they'd suddenly sprouted second heads, but certainly as if they were peculiar. Maybe they were. George thought about Dactylius and Claudia. He would have been astonished if they knew this camaraderie. But then, a lot of things about that marriage astonished him.

"Do you know," Irene observed, "I think Dactylius and Claudia would have been happier together if one of her babies had lived."

"You're right—he's said as much." George let it go at that. Had his wife been watching Theodore and Sophia watching them, too? If she had, her thoughts had gone from there in exactly the same direction as had his. Coincidence? George didn't believe it. It had happened too many times. Whatever it was, he liked it.

George and Sabbatius had the dawn-to-midmorning shift the next day. As was his habit, George reached the stretch of wall near the Litaean Gate a quarter-hour or so early. That gave him the chance to shoot the breeze with Rufus and Paul, who'd been up there to watch the Slavs and Avars through the late hours of the night, and to see for himself what the besiegers might be up to.

He also saw something new: one of the grappling hooks Bishop Eusebius and the congregation had blessed in the basilica of St. Demetrius. Attached to a good length of chain, it lay on the walkway above the gate. Rufus said, "They'll try and break in where it's easiest, same as we would. They won't try knocking down stones if knocking down timbers will do the job for them."

"That makes sense," George agreed. He peered out toward the encampments of the Slavs and Avars. A light mist kept him from telling what they were doing. He turned his head back toward the east. Here came the sun, rising red through the ground fog. Before long, it would burn the fog away. George wondered whether he really wanted to see the full range of the barbarians' armaments after all.

Paul yawned. "I'm for bed," he said. Footsteps sounded on the stairs leading up to the wall. "And here comes Sabbatius. Since I'm not leaving us shorthanded—" The taverner started for the stairway.

"Wait," Rufus said. He spoke rough army-Latin, which Paul, who used Greek by choice, didn't follow at once. Rufus ran after him and grabbed him. "Wait, curse you!" he said, shouting now. He still spoke Latin. "Don't you hear? They're moving out there."

They were, too, in a way they hadn't done since the earliest days of the siege. Shouts and clankings and the sounds of heavy things being dragged along the ground came out of the thinning mist. All at once, George understood why Rufus seemed to have forgotten his Greek: Latin was the language he'd used when he was a soldier, and he thought he was about to be a soldier again.

The mist thinned a little more, and the people and things moving through it came closer to the city. As they did so, cries of alarm and horn calls rang out up and down the wall. This would not be another quiet day. *Too bad*, George thought; he'd grown fond of quiet days.

"Do you think they're going to attack?" Sabbatius asked, staring out at the battering ram moving slowly toward the gate, and at the swarms of Slavic archers who ran along beside and in front of it. No sooner were the words out of his mouth than an arrow hummed past his head and shattered off the stone behind him.

Rufus clapped a hand to his forehead. "No, fool, I think

they've come to get drunk with us and dance the *kordax*." He kicked his legs high in a couple of steps from the obscene dance. Then, apparently deciding sarcasm was wasted on Sabbatius, he pointed to the grappling hook. "Let's throw that over the side and show the sons of a thousand fathers they aren't going to have everything their own way."

"What if they try to run up ladders, too?" George asked.

"You sound like Dactylius," Rufus said. "With the horns screaming like that, we'll have more men on the walls soon enough. First things first."

Since that was good advice—advice he'd given a good many times himself—George took it. He trotted with his fellow militiamen to the grappling hook. As soon as he grabbed the chain, he knew the prayers in the church of St. Demetrius had been effective. He felt strong and brave and able to overcome anything, as a man touched by the power of the military saint should have felt.

Rufus himself handled the hook. He said, "We'll show it to 'em, let 'em know we have it ready and waiting." He looked tough and confident, too. "If they come on anyhow, I'll hook the shed like I was fishing for bream, and then we all pull hard as we can, and shout for help, too. God willing, we lift the shed up and twist it so the ugly lugs under it get what they deserve. Everybody ready?"

When no one said no, he tossed the grappling hook over onto the outer surface of the wall. The iron rang off the gray stone.

George stood right behind the militia officer, ready to do whatever he ordered. The shoemaker stared out toward the shed advancing on the Litaean Gate. Against the massive construction of timber and hides, against the iron-headed log inside, the grappling hook seemed small and unreliable.

But, although the Slavic archers kept swarms of arrows in the air, the shed halted outside archery range from the wall. A couple of Slavs came out of it and pointed toward the gate. No, George realized joyously, they weren't pointing to the gate, but to the hook hanging over it. If it worried them, it stopped worrying George.

An Avar rode up to the shed on his armored horse and shouted to the Slavs, gesticulating angrily. George didn't need to know any of the barbarians' languages to understand what he was saying: something like, *Why don't you pick that thing up and get it moving again?*

The Slavs' answering gestures were every bit as emphatic as those of their overlord. The Avar looked toward the gate himself. He made a sign with his left hand. When nothing happened, he jerked his horse's head around hard and rode off at a gallop.

"We've beaten them!" Sabbatius exclaimed.

"Not yet," George said.

Paul agreed: "That fellow on the horse is heading back for friends. The business I'm in, I've seen that kind of thing more times than I can count. One chap loses a fight, he goes off, he comes back with some friends, and they have another go at it."

"Aye, that's how it'll be here, I think," Rufus said. "They haven't gone to all this trouble to quit before they use their toys."

They weren't going to use them right away, though. Rumor raced round the circuit of the wall, confirming what George had hoped: all the rams the Slavs and Avars had built were now halted. "What are they waiting for?" Paul asked, as if his comrades could see into the mind of the khagan of the Avars.

"I think we're going to find out," George said, pointing to the Avar who now walked up toward the ram stalled in front of the Litaean Gate. Instead of wearing scalemail like all the other Avars George had seen, this one was fantastically decked out in furs and feathers and fringes.

"He's an ugly customer, isn't he?" Sabbatius said with a scornful curl of the lip. "If that's what the Avars wear when they aren't in armor, no wonder they're in armor so much."

"He's one of the people who treat with their gods,"

George said, wondering what kind of gods or powers the Avars had. Unpleasant ones, probably. The shoemaker went on, "You can see it in how he carries himself. You can feel it, too, the way you can with the bishop."

"I still say he's ugly," Sabbatius said. Since George was a long way from finding the Avar attractive, he let that go. Sabbatius had a gift for fixing on the least important aspect of almost any matter and clinging to it as if it were at the core of the question.

The Avar studied the grappling hook. George watched him rub his chin in consideration, as a physician might have done while evaluating a patient with a fever whose nature he did not immediately recognize. Whatever the fellow saw did not satisfy him. He walked past the shed holding the ram and up toward the wall.

"Shoot the son of a whore!" Rufus shouted as soon as he came within arrow range. The command, while eminently sensible, was also to some degree wasted, for the archers on the wall—more of them now than had been there a little while before—were already sending arrows at the Avar.

None bit. George could not see any of them swerving aside or disappearing or bursting into flames. They all simply missed. The odds of that happening by itself struck him as somewhere between astonishingly poor and astonishing. Sure enough, the Avar had powers of his own.

"Christ with me!" John shouted, drawing an arrow back to the ear. When he thought he needed divine help, he called for it. George wondered what God thought about that.

Maybe God decided He wasn't going to answer John's prayer, considering some of the other things John said and did. Maybe the Avar's own gods protected him. And maybe his arrow would have missed with or without invocations of God and gods—John's archery, like that of most of the militiamen, was not all it might have been.

Whatever the truth there, the Avar remained uninjured on ground that had enough shafts sticking out of it to resemble a porcupine's prickly back. He drew his sword and waved it at the gate. Through the chain attached to the grappling hook, George sensed the power in that sword at war with the one the prayers of Bishop Eusebius and the people of Thessalonica had imbued into the hook.

"He's strong," Paul whispered, feeling that same clash of forces, and then, "What's he doing now?"

The Avar in the outlandish costume raised the sword high and then stabbed it deep into the dirt. The wall shivered, as if from a small earthquake. The Avar capered—angrily, if George was any judge. He must have expected more.

One of the other Avars called a question to their priest or wizard or whatever he was. He shook his head. Yes, he *was* angry; his whole body seemed to radiate fury. He capered some more, in slack-jointed style that would have won him applause as a mime. He pulled the sword free and stabbed it into the ground again. The wall shook once more, but not very much. The wizard shouted in his unintelligible language. He waved his arms. The fringes and furs and feathers sewn to his fantastic tunic fluttered and flapped. Nothing else happened.

He turned to the Avar in scalemail and shouted again. The warrior made as if to argue with him, whereupon the fellow's shouts turned into screams. George didn't know what he was saying, but wouldn't have wanted it said to him.

Reluctantly, the Avar captain accepted the rebuke and the instructions that had led to it. He shouted something himself. The Slavic archers in range of his voice trotted away from the walls of Thessalonica and back toward their encampments. All around the city, the same shouted orders went out to the Avars' subject allies. George could not see all around the city. As far as he could see, though, the Slavs were giving up the fight for now.

"That's done it!" Sabbatius cried gleefully. "We've shown them they've got no business messing with good Roman men!"

His words were almost lost in the cheers that rose from

the wall as the defenders of Thessalonica watched the Slavs withdraw. Despite those cheers, Rufus shook his head. "They don't think the attack will work now—that's plain enough," he said. "But they haven't done all this work so they could go off and leave it. They'll be back."

"But—" Paul, for once, sounded as confused as Sabbatius. "That crazy fellow out there, whatever he was, he saw that the power we prayed into the grappling hook was stronger than anything he could do against it."

"No." Like Rufus, George had caught the distinction his other comrades were missing. "He saw that what he tried now didn't work. That doesn't mean he can't try something else. Doesn't mean he *won't* try something else, either. I wish it did."

Sabbatius scowled like a child learning he would have to go to school not only on the first day he'd just survived but also for months to come. "Why, the dirty, cheating son of a poxed ewe!" he exclaimed.

George looked at Rufus. Rufus looked down at the ground. Looking down at the ground didn't help. The veteran and the shoemaker both started to laugh, and then started bleating out at the Slavs and Avars. Sabbatius and Paul joined them. The bleating spread along the wall. More than a few feet away from the people who'd started it, the militiamen had no idea why they were making noises like sheep, but any derision aimed at their foes seemed worth sending.

The Slavs stared up at the Romans on the wall. Some of them made peculiar gestures. George stopped bleating and started laughing again. "They think we're cursing them!" he exclaimed.

"Good," Rufus said, and bleated louder than ever. So did George, wishing the bleats really would do something to the Slavs and Avars.

Even more suddenly than it had begun, the bleating died down. George looked around to find out why, and saw Bishop Eusebius coming down the walkway in his shining vestments. He waited for the bishop, a somber sort, to make some cutting remark about the racket the militiamen had been creating. But Eusebius surprised him. In a great voice, he cried, "Sing out, you lambs of God!"

George didn't sing out, not at first. He cheered instead, along with most of his companions. But then he did bleat, and hoped that, with Eusebius' blessing, the sound would gain potency in the spiritual realm. The words of the psalmist ran through his mind: *Make a joyful noise unto the Lord, all ye lands*. Bleating probably wasn't the sort of joyful noise the psalmist had had in mind, but George didn't fret about that.

Eusebius came up to Rufus and said, "I see it is the same here as it is all along the circuit of the wall: they have not dared attack us, feeling the power of the Lord our God." He pointed to the chain from which the grappling hook hung down over the Litaean gate.

Rufus cleared his throat. "Don't like to contradict you, Your Excellency, but it looks to me more like they haven't attacked *yet*. This Avar . . . I don't know . . . priest, I guess, he tried to overthrow the power in the hook. He didn't do it, but I wouldn't swear he can't do it. You know what I'm saying?"

"I do," Eusebius answered. "I wish I did not, but I do. We shall be tested in all ways. I pray only that we shall not prove like Belshazzar the king of Babylon, who was weighed in the balances, and found wanting. May our city not be given to the Slavs and Avars, as his kingdom was given to the Medes and Persians."

"The Persians," George muttered. Off in the distant east, the Persians still contended with the Roman Empire. When God gave a gift, He gave a long-lasting one—though who heard anything of the Medes these days?

As the Avar wizard's preposterous costume had drawn Roman eyes to it, so Eusebius' bright silks stood out among the drab wool and linen tunics the defenders of Thessalonica wore. The Slavs, who had been standing around dejectedly after their overlord's spells failed to beat down the power in the grappling hooks, now took fresh spirit and began shooting arrows at the bishop.

None of them touched him; his holiness shielded him from them, as the Avar's power had kept Roman shafts from piercing him. However holy Eusebius was, though, George and his comrades could not match him. They ducked down behind the outer wall of the walkway. "Be careful with those arrows," Rufus said to Sabbatius when one rebounded back near them. "Remember, the Slavs sometimes poison the points."

"I wasn't going to touch it," Sabbatius said, and gave himself the lie by jerking his hand away. Again he reminded George of a schoolboy, though schoolboys commonly drank their wine well enough watered to keep from getting drunk.

Bishop Eusebius said, "By my presence, I am bringing you brave men into danger. I shall withdraw." He went over to the stairway and back down into Thessalonica. The storm of arrows died away.

Indeed, but for the short advance of the battering rams, it was as if the efforts of the Slavs and Avars had never been. Paul laughed nervously. "Does it usually get so quiet so fast?" he asked.

"A lot of things about this siege strike me as peculiar," Rufus answered. "When I was fighting the Goths, now, and then the Lombards, it was Christian against Christian. Oh, they were heretics, but that's a small thing. Their saints had the same powers as ours, near enough. With the Slavs and Avars, it's like they aren't sure what their powers can do to us, or about what God and the saints can do against them. They're feeling us out as they go."

"I don't want any Avar feeling me," Sabbatius said emphatically. Everyone else tried explaining that it was a figure of speech. Regretfully, George saw again that he didn't need to be drunk to be stupid.

As the sun crossed the sky, Romans went down from the wall and resumed their normal occupations. George's shift on duty was long past, but he didn't feel like descending while Rufus stuck to his post. And the sudden slackening of the assault in which the Avars had apparently put so much effort and so much faith—in several senses of the word—struck him as being as odd and suspicious as it did the veteran. If something was about to happen, he wanted it to happen while he was here to see it and to try to do something about it, not to hear about it after it was done.

Now the light shone in his face, not at his back. He wondered if the Slavs and Avars would renew the attack because of that. He didn't think so; the sun still blazed high in the southwest, casting only fairly short shadows. It wouldn't interfere with the Roman archers' aim.

"Hello!" Rufus said suddenly. "Here comes that cursed wizard or priest again. What sort of deviltries does he have in mind now?" He made the sign of the cross, to rout whatever demons or powers might be lurking to aid the Avar.

If the gesture bothered the fellow, he did not show it. He was not alone this time: a couple of fair-haired, shaggy-bearded Slavs accompanied him. Reading the attitudes of the three of them as best he could across a furlong or so, George guessed the Avar was doubtful and the Slavs to either side of him more confident.

"What are they doing?" the shoemaker asked, leaning out over the wall to get the best view he could. The Slavs were still shooting arrows, but only every now and then; he ignored them.

Although the Slavs' overlord, the Avar wasn't doing anything to speak of. He stood there while his minions labored; if they succeeded, he would reap the benefit. One corner of George's mouth twisted in a rueful smile. Barbarian in funny clothes though he was, the Avar had a lot in common—more than he knew, no doubt—with a good many Roman nobles.

The Slavs' magic, like their costumes, was less showy than what the Avars practiced. They simply went to work, as if . . . *As if they're making shoes*, George thought, pleased with the comparison.

"What are they doing?" This time, Paul said it, not George. Had George heard it back in the taverner's place of business, it would have meant something like, *Are they making so much trouble, I'll have to throw them out?*

Snap! George didn't hear that. He felt it through the soles of his shoes. "What the—?" he said, and peered all around. Nothing seemed out of the ordinary. His comrades must have felt the same strange sensation, for they were looking around, too.

Seeing nothing amiss on top of the wall, he looked out over it. The Slavic wizards seemed delighted with themselves. One of them was holding what looked like a two-foot length of darkness. George tried to convince himself he was seeing a snake or a length of lead pipe or something of the sort, but he couldn't. It looked like a length of darkness.

Where had it come from? Somewhere close to him, he judged, or he wouldn't have felt that curious snap. He looked down. Had the Slavs sorcerously severed the chain that held the grappling hook? He thought he should have noticed the clank as the hook fell to the ground, to say nothing of the lessened weight he and the others were holding.

But no—there was the hook, with chain intact. Most men, having seen that, would have looked no further. But George's nature and his trade both impelled him to examine things carefully. The chain was intact, but about two feet of its shadow were missing. The sun shone on that piece of the wall of Thessalonica as if no stout iron links impeded its passage.

"See what they've done!" he exclaimed, and pointed out the stolen shadow to his fellow militiamen.

"I see *what*," Rufus said, scratching his head. "I don't see *why*."

"I don't, either," George said. "But they wouldn't have

done it for no reason." He was as certain of that as he was of sunrise tomorrow morning.

One of the Slavic wizards kept hold of the piece of shadow they had seized. The other heated a sword in a fire. Before long, the blade glowed red. The Slav had no trouble keeping a hand on the hilt, though. *More magic*, George thought. His suspicions, already wild, grew wilder.

The Slav with the sword drew the blade from the blaze. The other one, the one with the shadow, held it out in front of him, a hand at either end. The Slav with the sword brought it up, then, slashing down with one swift stroke, sliced the shadow in two.

Once cut, it vanished. George looked to see whether it reappeared on the wall at the same time. It didn't. That gap remained. He pursed his lips. *Something* had changed. After a moment, he realized what it was. He still had a hand on a length of the grappling-hook chain. All he felt beneath his fingers now was sun-warmed iron. The protective power St. Demetrius had given the grappling hook when so beseeched in the basilica dedicated to him was gone, cut off as abruptly as the shadow had been.

Before George could do anything more than note that, Sabbatius said, "Something's wrong here," and then, "The hook! It's just—a hook."

That was inelegant, but it had more accuracy than Sabbatius usually managed. Nor were the Romans the only ones to note the change. The Slavic wizards leaped in the air in delight at what they'd accomplished. The Avar who had used their service patted them on the shoulder, as if they were a couple of horses that had hauled his cart faster than he'd expected.

He shouted back toward a couple of mounted Avars, his voice as harsh as a raven's caw. The men in scalemail shouted, too. George could not understand what they said, but their tone spoke for them. *Now we can get on with it* was what they meant.

Moments later, their signal drums started booming.

That meant, *Now we can get on with it*, too. Up on the walls of Thessalonica, horns called the militiamen to alertness. Did their brassy music sound faintly alarmed? George hoped that was his imagination, but he didn't think so. He said, "I'd bet the Slavs took our protective magic off all the grappling hooks on the whole circuit."

"I never thought of that," Sabbatius exclaimed. The only thing past the end of his nose he was in the habit of thinking of was his next cup of wine.

Rufus nodded soberly. "I'm afraid you're right," he said to George, and then coughed a couple of times. "Well, we'll just have to beat them" —he pointed down over the wall— "on our own hook."

George stared at him. "You've been spending too much time listening to John," he said, as if passing sentence after a crime.

"Maybe I have," the veteran said. "That doesn't mean I'm wrong, though. Look!" He pointed out beyond the wall. "The Slavs have decided it's time to go back to work."

"The Slavs have decided the Avars will slaughter them if they don't get back to work," George said. It amounted to the same thing.

"Arrows! Get back!" Shouts rang out up and down the wall, warning any of the defenders who weren't so alert as they might have been. Cries of pain rose, too, as some of the arrows found their mark.

The militiamen shot back. Here and there, a Slav crumpled. But more warriors took the place of those who fell. The besiegers seemed to have an unlimited store of missiles. They made the defenders keep their heads down most of the time.

Rufus did not enjoy the luxury of being able to take cover. "Here comes the cursed ram," he announced, and shouted for more men on the chain. "Come on, friends, this is how we earn our pay."

"What pay?" someone said. "Nobody's paying us a half-follis, and we're all losing money because we can't work at our proper trades."

"You're getting paid," Rufus answered. "You do a good job here, and the bastards down there won't cut your throat like a sheep's, rape your wife, bugger your little boy, and burn down your house with your old toothless father in it. You don't think that's pay enough?" The fellow who had complained kept very quiet after that.

Here came the shed sheltering the battering ram. It was heavy, and could not move very fast. George would have been glad had it moved even slower. Every foot the Slavs inside made it lurch forward brought it so much closer to the gate above whose housing he stood. If the Slavs and Avars got into Thessalonica, that complainer and his family wouldn't be the only ones who suffered.

Rufus jerked the chain back and forth. The grappling hook clanked against the stonework over the gate. "When they get close enough, I'm going to try and snag 'em," he said. "Then everybody on the chain pulls like a madman, we throw rocks down on the Slavs' heads, and our bowmen fill them full of arrows." He grinned, showing off the few worn teeth left in his mouth. "Sounds easy, doesn't it?"

"Everything sounds easy," George said. "It's only when you try doing it that it gets harder."

"You're learning," Rufus said.

George risked another glance out over the wall. As the shed with the ram advanced, it left behind the corpse of a Slav who'd taken a shaft in the neck. Most Roman arrows, though, either glanced off the hides of the roof or were turned by the big shields the barbarians at the front of the shed carried.

"Won't be long now," Rufus muttered. "Come on there, logfish, let me get my hook in you."

Nearer and nearer to the gate crawled the shed. George could hear the panting of the men who hauled it forward. Peeking out between the Slavs with the big shields was the iron-faced head of the log that would try to break down the Litaean Gate.

"All right," Rufus said. "Let me have some more chain, boys, enough to do what I need to do."

The big rough iron links, some of them blushing red from a light coat of rust, paid out through George's hands. Rufus leaned over the edge of the wall as if he were all alone. The Slavs sent a blizzard of arrows at him. None of them stuck. It was either incredible luck or the lingering protection of St. Demetrius. The veteran maneuvered with the hook, trying to snag the front end of the roof pole.

The Slavs were maneuvering, too. The ram thudded against the gate, which groaned like a wounded man. *Thud!* Another groan of timbers and bars and hinges.

"Now!" Rufus shouted before the ram could strike again.

George pulled with everything he had in him. The chain swiftly moved up a couple of links' worth, then stuck as it lost its slack and took on the full weight of the shed. Down below, the Slavs shouted in anger and alarm. George pulled again, along with everyone else on the chain. They gained a quarter of a link. He set his sandals against the rough stone of the walkway and kept on pulling.

The Slavs tried to free the hook from the shed; George could feel the chain twist a little in his hands. But it was taut now, and gave the barbarians nothing to work with. A quarter of a link, half a link, a link at a time, he and his grunting, cursing comrades gained.

Other militiamen flung stones at the Slavs under the shed, then dropped bigger stones. The defenders of Thessalonica also popped up to shoot arrows at those Slavs, quickly ducking back to escape the shafts Slavic archers aimed at them.

"Pull!" Rufus bellowed. "Pull and bear to the left. That way, you'll—"

He didn't need to say anything more. With a rending crash, the shed tipped over on its side. Some of the Slavs inside screamed as the log with which they had intended to smash through the Litaean Gate smashed them instead. Those who could picked themselves up and fled for the woods, some of them helping wounded comrades along.

"Shouldn't we get out there and burn that shed?"

George asked Rufus. "That way, they can't sneak back at night to try to drag the thing away, repair it, and use it against us again."

Before, Rufus had been set against any sally. Now he pursed his lips and looked thoughtful. "Out through the postern gate," he muttered, half to himself. "Wouldn't take long, wouldn't be much risk." He smacked fist into palm in sudden decision. "We'll try it." He told off a dozen men, George and Paul among them. "Take torches and take oil. You want to make sure that when you set the fire, it sticks and spreads. You'll only have the one chance."

The militiamen got what they needed and hurried down the stairs. Rufus came with them and outshouted the militiaman in charge of the postern gate, who seemed in no mood to risk opening it for anything. "If you don't bet, you can't win," George told him.

"That's right. That's exactly right," Rufus said. "We can hurt the sons of whores, but not if we stand around here flapping our jaws instead of going out there and doing something about it."

He set a hand on the hilt of his sword, as if to challenge the postern gate commander. That worthy, though hardly half his age, wilted rather than responding. George and his comrades drew their swords. The gate opened. They dashed toward the tumbled shed.

The Slavs shouted, some in excitement, more in alarm. They had not expected the Romans to rush out at them. Some fled, others stared. Only a few had the presence of mind to start shooting at the newcomers.

George slashed at a Slav standing between him and the shed. The Slav turned the blow with a large, clumsy shield. He cut at George. They traded swordstrokes. The shoemaker got him on the forearm. He dropped his sword, running for the woods and shouting in his guttural language. George did not pursue him past the shed, though he might easily have caught him. *First things first*, he reminded himself.

He smashed a jar of olive oil against the timbers. Paul

thrust a torch into the oil. Flames and thick black smoke rose, not only there but elsewhere along the length of the shed. "We've done what we came to do," George called to his comrades. "Now we go back."

Back they went, running bent low to the ground to offer the Slavic archers the smallest target. Just before they reached the postern gate, though, one of them cried out in pain and crumpled, an arrow through his calf. The Slavs had helped their wounded—how could Romans do less? George heaved the fellow up and helped him limp into the city.

The postern gate slamming shut was one of the sweetest sounds he'd ever heard. Militiamen slammed bars into place to keep the gate secured. Some of the bars were gray and weathered, having stood up to sun and rain for years. Some, though, were of fresh, new-cut timber, and rested on shiny, rust-free iron brackets. George was heartily glad they'd made the postern gate stronger.

He and his comrades, all but the wounded man, hurried back up to the top of the Litaean Gate. "I want to watch that shed burn," Paul said, stressing the last word. "You were right, George; now they'll have to build another one if they want to attack us here."

"Yes," George said, but less happily than he would have thought possible before they'd burned the shed and the ram. Lots of Slavs swarmed out there; running up another shed wouldn't take them that long. And besides— He looked south, then north, along the wall. "I don't *think* they've broken into the city anywhere else, but—"

"They haven't," Rufus said. "If they had, you'd hear the screaming in Constantinople. It couldn't have happened without our knowing about it."

"I suppose you're right," George said. "That's good. They—" The wind shifted and picked up a little, coming now from out of the west. That meant it blew the smoke from the shed straight into the faces of the defenders atop the Litaean Gate. George broke off and started to cough. His eyes stung. Tears ran down his face.

If he looked anything like the rest of the men up there, the soot was turning his face black, too. And not only his face, either . . . John came up to Rufus and said, "If you wanted your hair dark again, why didn't you just dye it instead of going through all this?"

"Ahh, to the crows with you," Rufus said, and then he had a coughing fit, too. He spat. His saliva was black. He stared at it in disgust. "By the saints, maybe burning the shed wasn't such a good idea after all. If the Slavs put ladders against the wall now, they'll be up here with us before we know they've even started climbing."

Like a lot of what the veteran said, that had truth mingled with the jest. Through streaming eyes, George tried to peer through surging smoke to see what the Slavs were doing. He couldn't see much. He hoped that meant they weren't doing much. If it didn't, he'd get more practice using his sword.

Cheers rang out, off to the north. He didn't know what that meant, but he had hopes. When the cheers weren't followed by cries of alarm, he decided the hopes were justified. "I think we just threw them back up there, too," he said, and then coughed some more.

Eventually, the shed burned itself out. By the time it did, George felt like a smoked sausage in a butcher's shop. The westering sun shone red as blood through the last few puffs of smoke from the fire. Wearily, Rufus said, "I don't think they're going to come back for any more tonight. And if they do, it's going to be somebody else's worry, not mine." With that, he went down into Thessalonica.

George stayed on the wall till he saw enough men were coming up to replace those going down. Once he was sure of that, he went home, too. A lot of grimy, smoke-darkened men walked through the streets of the city. Some men, George had heard, had skins naturally that color. He'd never seen any, but it might have been true.

Irene gasped when he walked in through the front door of the shop. "What's the matter?" he asked in genuine puzzlement.

She pointed to him. "You're black, and you've got blood all over you."

He looked down at himself. Sure enough, blood had sprayed onto his tunic. His right hand—his sword hand—was bloody, too, along with being filthy. "Don't worry," he said. "It's not mine."

His wife dipped a rag in a pitcher of water and handed it to him. "I don't know whether that tunic will ever come clean," she said, "but you can wash yourself." Obediently, he scrubbed the blood and soot from his skin. The rag turned a color halfway between rust and gray. "You missed a couple of places," Irene told him, pointing to his cheek and to his left shin.

When he scrubbed at those, he discovered they hurt. He also discovered he hadn't been altogether right: he had cuts in both places, cuts that started bleeding again when he got them wet. "Wonder how I picked those up," he said, bemused.

Irene looked more horrified than ever. Theodore, on the other hand, seemed struck with awe. "You mean you got wounded, Father, and you didn't even know it?" he exclaimed.

"I guess I did," George answered. Irene started to cry. George put his arm around her. "They're not really *wounds*, darling." He'd seen wounds; he knew that was true. "They're just *scratches*, like." What you called something could be as important as what it really was. What you called something, for that matter, could determine what it really was. Names were powerful.

Irene said, "The Slavs were trying to kill you." He recognized the astonished indignation in her voice; he'd felt the same thing when he first realized the difference between exercises and war.

"Well, they didn't," he said, and squeezed her tighter. "And I helped burn one of their battering rams and the shed it came in."

That made Theodore look not just proud but jealous. It did little to reassure Irene, though. "You mean you went outside the wall?" she said, and shivered when he nodded. "When you didn't come home after your regular shift on the wall was done, I knew something was wrong. No, I knew it before then, when men started running through the streets shouting about an attack. Waiting and praying and praying and waiting come very hard, let me tell you."

"We threw them back," George said. "They couldn't sneak into the city—St. Demetrius stopped that. And they couldn't batter their way into it—we stopped that ourselves." His chest puffed out with what he hoped was pardonable pride.

Sophia came into the shop through the back door in time to hear him. In tones of reproof, she said, "The blessings of the saint on the grappling hooks couldn't have hurt, Father."

"Couldn't have hurt," George admitted, "but they didn't help, either." Sophia and Irene and Theodore all stared at him; he had to remind himself that they hadn't been up on the wall. He explained: "The Slavs and Avars found a magic to cut through the power in that blessing."

His family exclaimed in dismay. "How can we beat them if they defeat our power?" Sophia said.

"We managed, just now," George said. His daughter looked puzzled. He went on, "Powers or no powers, we're still men, and so are they. It was a straight-up fight on the wall today, and we won it."

"And outside the wall, too," Theodore said. "I wish I could have been out there instead of you."

"Instead of, no," George said. "Alongside me—that may happen, son. You haven't got much practice with weapons, but you don't need much practice to fight from the wall."

Theodore looked about ready to explode with joy and excitement. Irene looked about ready to puncture George with an awl. She hadn't been delighted to hear her husband had gone down and fought outside the wall. To hear her son sounding so eager to imitate his exploits left her shaking her head about the male half of the human race.

Sophia sniffed, not scornfully but in a practical sort

of way. "I think supper is about ready," she said, and went upstairs to check. Her voice floated down to the shop: "Come eat, everyone."

Supper was a porridge of peas and beans and onions, with bread and salted olives alongside. "Good," George said. "Good as anything we could have had before the Slavs and Avars came." It would have been a plain supper then and was rather a fine one now, but that didn't mean he was wrong—not quite. It tasted all right and filled his belly. In the end, what else mattered?

Daylight's twelve hours were short as autumn drew on toward winter, while those of night stretched like clay in a potter's hands. George hoped the Slavs and Avars wouldn't use the long night hours for deviltry. He intended to use every last moment of them for sleeping.

With a yawn, he said, "I'm turning in. Fighting a war is harder work than making shoes." A lot of warfare, he'd discovered up on the wall, consisted of doing nothing. The moments when he wasn't doing nothing, though, he knew he'd have those moments printed on his memory till a priest chanted the burial service above his corpse.

No one argued with him, but what he'd said didn't mean making shoes was easy. His wife and daughter washed the supper dishes in the last fading glow of twilight. When full darkness fell, everyone went to bed.

Lying there beside George, Irene asked, "Have we beaten them back for good, then?"

For the first time in all the years since they'd wed, he got the feeling she wanted him to lie to her. Try as he would, he couldn't do it. "I don't know," he answered, "but I don't think so. They'll try something else, or maybe the same thing over again, to see if it works better the second time."

"Oh," she said in a small voice. "All right." It wasn't, not by the way she said it. But he didn't hear her. He'd already fallen asleep.

V

Some nights, George did not want to go straight to bed. After the noble Germanus gave him a good price for a second pair of embossed boots like the ones he'd bought before the siege of Thessalonica started, the shoemaker, coins jingling in the pouch he wore on his belt, went over to Paul's tavern to spend some of his profit as enjoyably as he could.

He was glad to duck inside. "Close the door!" someone yelled, even as he was doing so. It was chilly outside, but fire kept the tavern cozy.

He looked around for people he knew. Sabbatius sat at a table by the wall, not far from the fire. He didn't see George. He was already slumped against the wall, half asleep. In the couple of years they'd been in the same militia company, George had never found out what he did for a living. Drink, mostly, as far as the shoemaker could see.

Paul was frying in olive oil some squid a customer had brought in. Fishing boats still sailed out onto the Gulf of Thessalonica to help keep the city fed. They didn't go far from shore, though, not when autumn storms could blow up almost without warning. The hot, meaty aroma of the sizzling squid sent spit squirting into George's mouth.

He made his way toward the taverner, who used wooden tongs to take one of the squid out of their bath of bubbling oil and pass it to the fellow who'd given them to him to cook. "Hot!" the man yelped, sticking burned fingers in his mouth. Paul gave him the other fried squid. He burned his fingers on that one, too, but then began to eat.

"Red wine," George said. Paul filled his mug. He lifted it in salute. "A pestilence on the Slavs!"

Everyone who heard that toast drank to it. George poured down the wine, tossed another follis on the counter, and held out his mug for a refill. This time, he sipped instead of guzzling. He was a moderate man, sometimes even in his moderation.

Somebody waved. George pointed to himself. "No, I don't want you," John said. "I'm trying to talk that dipper on Paul's wall over there to sit by me."

Shaking his head, George plunked himself down on a stool by John. "Are you going up there tonight?" he asked, pointing to the little raised podium where entertainers performed.

"Easiest way I know to earn my wine," John said.

"It wouldn't be for me," George said. "I'd sooner have the Slavs shooting arrows at me than stand up there and tell jokes in front of a big crowd of people."

"Yes, well, when they don't laugh, they're meaner than the Slavs, too," John said, a faraway expression on his lean face—he was, George thought, probably remembering times when they hadn't laughed. After a moment, one of John's eyebrows rose almost to his hairline. "They're generally drunker than the Slavs, too," he added.

"You can joke about making jokes," George said. "What *do* you do when they don't laugh?"

"Die," John said succinctly. "It happens. If it happens too often, you have to go out and work for a living. I've done that, too. Telling jokes is more fun—and besides, I'm no good at anything else."

"Oh, I don't know," George said. "You could work in a stable, because—"

He didn't get away with it, not this time. "—Because I already know everything about horseshit," John finished for him. "Ha. Ha. Stage fright isn't the only reason you don't go up there, pal."

"I'm not going to argue with you," George said. "I tell jokes the way you make shoes. I admit it." He looked sidelong at John. "Of course, when I make shoes, I don't run the risk of having to get out of town in a hurry because I've made somebody with more money than me angry."

"What? You mean you didn't tool GERMANUS LIKES PRETTY BOYS into those fancy boots you made for him?" John said. "I'm disappointed in you. Maybe you did it in tiny letters, or in fancy ones that look like part of the design till you see them just right?"

George coughed, which wasn't a good idea, because he'd taken a swig of wine a moment before. "I don't know that Germanus does like pretty boys," he said once he wasn't trying to choke to death.

"Neither do I," John said cheerfully. "That wouldn't stop me from telling jokes about him, though." He took a sip of his own wine, making a point of doing it neatly. A moment later, though, he looked glum, which added close to ten years to his apparent age. "Of course, that's why I don't live in Constantinople anymore, which I suppose proves your point."

A barmaid came around with a bowl of salted olives. Before the Slavs came, a big handful had cost only a quarter of a follis. They were up to three quarters of a follis now, but that was still cheap. George bought some and ate them one by one, spitting the pits onto the rammed-earth floor. By the time he'd finished them and licked his fingers clean, he was thirsty again. He called for another cup of wine. The wine was where Paul really made his money.

John ordered more wine, too. When the girl brought it to him, he slipped an arm around her waist and said,

"After I get done tonight, why don't we go someplace quiet and—"

She twisted away, shaking her head. "I've heard about you. If you don't like me in bed, you'll call me names so nasty, they'll make me cry, and then you'll tell jokes about me tomorrow night. And if you do like me, you'll sweet-talk me till I don't know up from down—and then you'll tell jokes about me tomorrow night. No thank you, either way." She went off, her nose in the air.

George had heard John tell a lot of jokes about a lot of different women, which made him think the barmaid was likely to be right. John peered down into the cup of wine the girl had given him. Harsh, black shadows from the hearthfire and the torches on the wall kept George from reading his expression.

After a while, Paul thumped his fist down on the bar in front of him, once, twice, three times. The racket in the tavern faded, though it did not vanish. Paul said, "Now, folks, here's someone who can keep us laughing, even with the Slavs all around. Come on, tell John what you think of him."

"Not *that*!" John exclaimed as he bounced to his feet and, seeming like a builder's crane, all built of sticks, with joints in curious, unexpected places, made his way up to the little platform that might at another time have housed a lyre-player or a fellow with a trained dog. Most of the people in the tavern clapped for him. A few *did* tell him what they thought—likely those who'd been his butts in the recent past.

He ignored them, with the air of a man who'd heard worse. "Being a funny man is hard work, you know that?" he said, swigging from the cup of wine he'd brought with him. "I was trying to talk a girl into bed with me, and she turned me down, just on account of I'm a funny man."

"Who says you're a funny man?" a heckler called.

John turned to Paul, who was dipping up a mug of wine behind the bar. "You've got to stop feeding your mice so much. They keep squeaking for more while I'm doing my show." He waited to see if the heckler would take another jab at him; he disposed of such nuisances with effortless ease. When the fellow kept quiet, John shrugged and resumed: "Like I was saying, she told me that if I didn't like her, I'd insult her and then tell jokes about her, but if I did like her, I'd say all sorts of nice things to her—and then I'd tell jokes about her." He waited for his laugh, then went on, "So you see, friends, this isn't easy work."

George looked around the tavern till he spotted the barmaid who'd turned down John's advances. She stood with both hands pressed to her cheeks. She hadn't said yes—and, by the same token, John hadn't waited till the next day to tell a joke about her, even if it was the same joke she'd told about him. George envied the comic his ability to take something from everyday life and incorporate it into his routine as if he'd been using it for years.

Thinking about the way John told jokes kept him from paying attention to the jokes John was telling. He started listening in the middle of one: "—so the Persian king had this new woman brought in before him, and he looked her over, and she was pretty enough, so he said, 'Well, little one, tell me, are you a virgin or what?' And she looked back at him, and she said, 'May it please you, your majesty, I am what.' "

About three quarters of the people in the tavern got the joke and laughed. "What?" several people said at the same time, some of them smugly, showing they understood, others sounding bewildered enough to prove they didn't.

"Day after tomorrow," John said, "I promise you, an angel of the Lord will come in here and write it out in letters of fire, but it probably won't do you any good, because if you can't figure that one out, it's a sure bet you can't read, either."

"*Oh*, John," George said softly. This was how his friend got into trouble: when he started insulting his own audience, they stopped thinking he was funny. George instinctively understood how and why that was so. Clever though he was, John had never figured it out.

But tonight, John steered clear of that danger, at least for the moment. "Talk about your miracles, now," he said with a wry grin. "Isn't it wonderful how God gave Menas back his legs just in time for him to run away from the Slavs?"

That got a laugh, too, but a nervous laugh. Some people were probably nervous about John's questioning the will of God, others about what Menas would do to John if the joke got back to him. George, who prided himself on being a thorough man, was nervous about both at once.

"It's all right," John said soothingly. "I saw another miracle, too: when St. Demetrius told Rufus to let the rest of us know the Slavs were attacking, old Rufus didn't swear once. If that's no miracle, what is?"

George looked around again, and saw he wasn't the only one doing so. He didn't spy Rufus in the audience, which meant nothing would happen to John right away. Sooner or later, though, the veteran would hear about the joke. That was the way life worked. Rufus had been around a long time. He might laugh it off. If he didn't, being a shoemaker would have nothing to do with why George wouldn't have have cared to stand in John's sandals.

If John knew he'd skirted trouble again, he didn't let on, but then, he never did. He went on with another story: "Did you hear about the fellow who got an audience with the Roman Emperor by claiming he was God? The Emperor told him, 'You'd better think about this, because last year a man came before me saying he was a prophet, and I ordered his head cut off.' And the fellow looked at him and said, 'Your Majesty, you did the right thing, because I did not send that man.' "

More people groaned than laughed over that one, but John didn't mind. If anything, he looked happy: the silly story let him slip away from the dangerous ground on which he'd been treading. Listening to him tell more tales, George fully realized for the first time that he wasn't just spinning one story after another; they all fit together in a pattern as elaborate as any a mosaicist could make with colored tiles. And part—much—of the art here lay in concealing from the audience that a pattern existed. *One more reason*, George thought, *I couldn't match what John is doing*.

"Do you know," John said, "our friend Sabbatius there" —he pointed to Sabbatius, who seemed to have slept through his entire performance— "has never seen a drunken man in his life?"

"Oh, come on now!" Several people said that, or words to that effect, at the same time. Nobody who came regularly to Paul's tavern—or to any of a good many others in Thessalonica—could fail to know Sabbatius was a tosspot of epic proportion.

But John only grinned his lopsided grin. "It's true," he insisted. "He drinks himself to sleep before anybody else, and he doesn't wake up till long after everybody else is sober again. Deny it if you can." No one could; he got an appreciative hand instead. Raising his voice to a shout, he called, "Isn't that right, Sabbatius?"

The plump militiaman thrashed and almost fell off his stool. "Wuzzat?" he said thickly, before sliding back into deeper slumber.

"Isn't he wonderful?" John said, more quietly now. He looked out at the people packing the tavern. "And aren't you all wonderful? And don't you wish you could be sure *your* name would never, ever show up in one of my stories? Best way I can think of is to make me too rich and happy ever to think of you in an unkind way." He nudged with his foot a plain earthenware bowl up there on the platform with him.

Quite a few people made their way over to him and tossed coins into the bowl. George watched their faces as they went back to their seats or to the bar. Some looked pleased: they'd rewarded a man who'd entertained them. More, though, wore a tight, intricate expression, almost as if they'd made up their minds to have a tooth pulled to end continuous pain. They were the ones who feared John would mock them next.

"How does it feel to be a blackmailer?" George asked when money stopped rattling into the bowl and John carried it back to the table.

"Don't know yet," the comic answered. "Let me count the take first." He dumped the bowl out onto the tabletop. Shuffling coins into stacks, his fingers were as quick and deft as a money changer's. He let out a little happy grunt at spotting silver among the bronze. "Ah, isn't that nice? Somebody gave me a miliaresion. And here's another. Good, good—one would be lonely by itself." In a couple of minutes, the reckoning was done. "Tonight," John declared, "being a blackmailer feels pretty good."

"Don't go away, folks," Paul called. "In half an hour or so, the special duo of Lucius and Maria, who've sung in Sicily and Illyria, will give you old love songs and some new ones all their own. I'm sure you'll want to stay and hear them—they'll send you home in a happy mood."

"Now I know when to leave," John said, scooping his take into a leather pouch. "I've heard Lucius and Maria, by God. They're funnier than I am. The only difference is, they don't mean to be."

George hadn't heard them. He said, "If they're that bad, how have they been able to perform in all those places?"

"Are you kidding?" John rolled his eyes. "They stink up a town once, they get run out, and they bloody well have to go somewhere else—in a hurry. And so, before they come on, I'll bloody well go somewhere else, too. Good night."

But before he could escape, the barmaid whose intended insult he'd turned to his own purposes came up to the table. "That wasn't very nice, what you did there," she said, hands on hips.

John said, "The best stories come from what really happens. Anybody silly enough to tell me not to use one would probably marry a eunuch."

She glared at him. "Is that all that matters? That I gave you a story you could use to make people laugh?"

"Of course not," he answered, which, with John, was as likely as not to mean *yes*. He leered. "I told you beforehand, I had something else in mind."

Confronted with a line like that, George would have poured, or maybe broken, a jar of wine over John's head. Like anyone else, he judged other people by his own standard, and so was astonished when the barmaid said, "That's right, you did," in a purr that announced she suddenly had something else in mind, too. She and John left the tavern together.

Muttering to himself, George got another cup of wine from Paul (the barmaid having disappeared) and settled down to see whether Lucius and Maria were as bad as John had claimed. They weren't. They were worse.

After a stint on the wall early the next morning, George went back to his shop to get some work done. He wasn't working so much as he would have liked these days, not with the siege. People were still buying shoes; he'd sold several pairs to refugees who hadn't bothered putting on any before fleeing the Slavs and Avars.

Having sewn the last strap onto a sandal, he looked into the box where he kept little bronze buckles. It was empty. When he made an exasperated noise, Theodore said, "I'm sorry, Father—I used the last ones in there a little while ago. Haven't we got any more?"

"No, those were the last," George answered. "I'll have to walk down to Benjamin and buy some new ones." He grumbled something inaudible even to himself: more time when he wouldn't be able to get anything useful done.

Theodore must have figured out what that grumble meant. "You could send me, Father," he said.

"I could. . . ." George considered. Not without a certain amount of regret, he shook his head. "No, I'd better not. He'd skin you alive on the price. He'll skin me, too, but not so bad."

"I'm not afraid of him," Theodore said. "Just because he's a Jew—"

"I'm not afraid of him because he's a Jew," George answered. "I've got the better of plenty of them. I'm afraid of him because he's Benjamin."

Like most of Thessalonica's Jews, Benjamin lived and had his shop in the southwestern part of the city. The whole street echoed with the taps and clangs of hammers on metal: Jews dominated the bronze- and coppersmithing trades.

Benjamin looked up from his work when George walked into the shop. The bronzeworker was a few years older than George, lean and wiry and dark. "Ah, good morning, good morning," he said in Greek. "I thought you would be one of the bishop's men, and that order is not yet ready."

George scratched his head. "If you don't mind my asking, what would Bishop Eusebius want from you?"

"Arrowheads, of course," the Jew answered, holding up a file with which he'd been sharpening one. "I'm supposed to deliver another five hundred day after tomorrow, but if they wanted them today, I couldn't do it."

"Arrowheads. I should have thought of that," George said.

"Iron points are harder, of course, but when you're in trouble you use everything you have," Benjamin said, and George nodded. The bronzeworker gave him a tired smile of sorts. "You, though, I do not think you have come for arrowheads."

"Well—no," George said, and smiled back. "I've finally gone through that last batch of buckles you sold me, and I wanted to buy some more."

"I have a few," Benjamin said, "but not many. You're lucky you came in today, George. After I finished this order I'm working on now, I would have melted them down for the next one."

"I *am* lucky, then," George said. He'd been dealing with

Benjamin for a long time; the man did good work. Finding someone else who had buckles or could make them would have been an annoyance at least, and, with bronze going into arrowheads, might have been impossible. "Let's see what you've got."

Benjamin showed him the couple of dozen buckles he'd made. They were, without a doubt, up to his usual standard of quality. The Jew coughed apologetically. "I am going to have to ask more for them. Otherwise, melting them down would pay me better."

"How much more?" George asked warily. He didn't think Benjamin was lying to him. He wished the bronzeworker were lying; that would have made the dicker easier.

"For most people, I would double the price," the Jew said. "For you, half again as much. We've been doing business a long time, and you've always been fair with me." He looked thoughtful. "And besides, don't I remember that you did something brave when the city had trouble with the cisterns a while ago?"

"I did what needed doing. You don't think about things till afterwards." Praise made George nervous. He turned the subject, at least to some degree: "How did this part of the city come through the attack from the Slavs' water god or whatever he was?"

"The Lord be praised, we had no trouble here," Benjamin said. "The demon did not show itself at the cistern that serves us."

Us Jews, he meant. George stared. "Not at all?" he asked.

"Not at all," Benjamin said.

Again, George didn't think he was lying. He leaned his chin on his hand and thought about what that might mean. Maybe the Slavic demigod had experience dealing with the powers of Christianity and had never run up against anything Jewish before. Maybe the Jews, a minority everywhere in the Roman Empire and an unhappy minority to boot, prayed harder than most of Thessalonica's Christians and so averted trouble. One other possibility occurred to him, not one that made him happy but one he thought he could not ignore, either: maybe the Jews held on to a bigger piece of truth than did his own coreligionists.

"Why do you suppose that was?" he asked Benjamin, curious to hear what the Jew would say.

"Why? I don't care about why," Benjamin said with complete and utter sincerity. "All I care about is that it did not happen, for which I praise the Lord."

George had trouble understanding anyone who didn't care about why, but he hadn't come down here to understand Benjamin; he'd come down to buy bronze buckles from him. Half again the usual price wasn't outrageous, not with the way everything had shot up in Thessalonica. But a day without haggling was like a day without sunshine. "Maybe a third again as much—" George began tentatively.

Benjamin shook his head. "Half again keeps you even with the arrowheads. Anything less and I'm better paid to melt down the buckles."

"Don't do that. I'll pay you. I'll pass it along to my customers, so they can grumble at me, the same way I'm grumbling at you." George laid money on the counter in front of the bronzeworker. "If we run out of other copper, we can melt down folleis."

"No profit in it—not yet," Benjamin answered. George had meant it for a joke, but the Jew had plainly made the calculation.

The shoemaker took the buckles and started out of the shop. He almost ran into a youth coming in. The youngster showed clearly what Benjamin had looked like at about twelve. His dark stare wasn't aimed at George for having almost collided with him, but at everyone not a Jew for everything that had happened to all the Jews for the past two thousand years.

Benjamin said, "It's all right, Joseph. George is a very good . . . customer."

"All right, Father," the youth said, and bobbed his head

to George. "I'm sorry, sir. I didn't mean to bump you." He sounded as if he meant it. His eyes, though—George did not fancy facing those eyes.

"No harm done, Joseph," George said, speaking to him as if he were a man. Joseph nodded, polite but distant. Suddenly, George wished with all his heart that Benjamin had called him *a good man*, not *a good customer*. No help for it. The Jews didn't have it easy, and they saw no point in making it easy for anyone else. He didn't suppose he could blame them. Buckles jingling in his belt pouch, he left the bronzeworker's shop.

"The Lord keep you safe," Benjamin called after him. He waved to show he'd heard, but feared he'd gone too far for the Jew to see the gesture.

He'd intended bringing the buckles straight back to his shop and getting to work, but found himself waylaid when he walked past Dactylius' place. The little jeweler dashed out the door toward him as fast as if he'd had a swarm of Slavs on his tail. "Come on in, George," he said, grabbing his friend's arm. "Your wife and daughter deserve some pretties—Claudia told me you fixed her sandal."

"I'd almost forgotten," George said. "Listen, Dactylius, I really ought to—"

Dactylius wasn't listening to him—or letting go of his arm, either. "Come, come, come," he said. It was either come or pry him loose with a stick. George came.

As soon as he walked inside the jeweler's shop, he sneezed. That happened about every other time he went into the shop, which smelled of hot metal and of the abrasive powders Dactylius used to shine it and to polish his precious stones.

"Here, let me give you these while I still can," Dactylius said, presenting him with thin bracelets of bright bronze.

From the back room, Claudia asked in indignant tones, "What goes on? What are you giving away now, Dactylius? The whole shop, most likely." But when she came out to see what was going on and found the shoemaker there, her manner changed. "Oh, it's you, George. That's all right, then."

George hefted the bracelets. More ordinary ornaments he had never seen. "Why wouldn't you be able to give me these later?" he asked.

"Why? Because they wouldn't be here later, that's why," Dactylius said, as if that were self-explanatory. Seeing it wasn't, he motioned George over to his worktable. "There. Now do you understand?"

"Oh. You've gone into the arrowhead business, too," George said. "Well, yes, all right, that does make sense. Benjamin the bronzeworker is doing the same thing, for the same reason."

Dactylius nodded. "Yes, I can see how he would be."

Claudia, though, let out an indignant screech from the doorway to the back room. "They have *my* husband, my brilliant artist of a husband, doing the same thing as a no-account Jew? Darling, you have to tell the bishop you're quitting, and right this minute. The insult!"

"I want to think about that before I do it," Dactylius said.

What George wanted to say to Claudia was, *Are you out of your mind?* What he did say was, "An arrowhead doesn't care who makes it."

"That's not true," Claudia said, advancing on him so she could argue nose-to-nose with anyone presumptuous enough to disagree with her. "How is the holy Bishop Eusebius supposed to bless an arrowhead made by some nasty Jew instead of a good Christian man?"

It was a good question—a better question, in fact, than George had looked for from Claudia. After discarding two possible answers, he came up with one he hoped might satisfy her: "Since the bishop gave Benjamin the work, he doesn't seem worried about it."

Claudia sniffed. "That's his foolishness." A moment before, he'd been the holy bishop Eusebius; now he was a fool. Had she been born a man, Claudia might have had a fine career in the law courts. She went on, "I still say it's a shame and a disgrace for Dactylius and a Jew to both be doing the same thing."

"We're all inside the city together, dear," Dactylius said hesitantly.

"Maybe if we gave the Jews to the Slavs and Avars . . ." Claudia began.

"I don't think that would be a good idea," George said with what he thought of as commendable restraint.

"It probably wouldn't satisfy them," Claudia agreed mournfully. That wasn't what George had meant, or, for that matter, anything close to what he'd meant. He supposed he should have been happy he'd got her to reconsider, whatever the reason. After thanking Dactylius again for the bracelets, he beat a hasty retreat.

Sophia smiled when he gave her the bangle, but said, "Couldn't you have found something nicer?"

"Not the way things are now," George answered, and explained what both Benjamin and Dactylius were busy doing. He added, "Claudia isn't very happy that her husband has had to come down in the world so."

"Claudia isn't very happy," Irene said with an air of finality. "I'm just glad you managed to get the buckles."

"Some buckles," George said. "Fewer than I would have liked." He shrugged. "You do the best you can with what you have. When I've used all these, I'll make boots for a while. If we haven't got rid of the Slavs and Avars by then . . . well, we're liable to be down to eating leather by then instead of turning it into shoes."

Sophia made a face. "You're making that up!" She looked at him. Real worry replaced playacted disgust. "No. You're not."

"You do the best you can with what you have," George repeated. "If you don't have much, you do the best you can with what little you do."

"I hope it won't come to that," Irene said.

"So do I," George said. "But that doesn't mean it won't. We all hoped the plague wouldn't come to Thessalonica again—but it did." He looked around the shop. "Well, if it comes down to eating boiled leather, we'll have a better supply than almost anyone else."

"That's true," Irene said with a smile.

Sophia giggled. "I'd like to see Dactylius eat his stock in trade."

"He couldn't do it," George agreed solemnly. "But do you know what? I wouldn't be a bit surprised if Claudia could."

Dactylius pointed out from the wall. "What are they doing out there?" he said. "They ought to be trying to get inside the city every moment of the day and night." He sounded indignant, as if the Slavs and Avars were falling down on the job.

"You work all the time yourself," George said, and Dactylius nodded vigorously. "I work all the time myself—or I did, before this siege turned everything topsy-turvy." Even if he was almost out of buckles again, with no great prospect of getting more, he still wished he were back in the shop. "But the Slavs and Avars don't seem to do things the same way we do. They make a push and put everything they have into it. If it doesn't work, they loll around for a while till they're ready to try something else."

Lolling around they certainly were, for the time being, anyhow. They sat around campfires (days were chilly now, nights frankly cold), passing wineskins back and forth. Some of them shot dice. Some sang songs whose music echoed in George's head even if the words were unintelligible.

"If Rufus saw them like this, he'd scream for a sally right now," Dactylius said. The thin little jeweler seemed to puff himself out into the shape and choleric aspect of the veteran. George clapped his hands; it was a fine bit of mimicry.

But applause or not, he shook his head. "He's seen them this way, and he's all for sitting quiet. They may be idle, but they haven't forgotten what they're supposed to be doing. See how they have sentries round all the engines, ready to protect them if we do stick our noses outside the gates? I wouldn't be surprised if they were trying to lure us out."

"Maybe so," Dactylius said, not sounding as if he believed it. He hesitated, then went on, quite as if he wasn't changing the subject, "I am still making arrowheads, you know."

"No, I didn't know," George said, "but I thought you would, because you have too much sense to do anything else." Then it was his turn to hesitate. "I hope your wife's not too upset over what you're doing."

"I managed to persuade her it was necessary." The jeweler's smile was wry. "Every now and then, I do win an argument."

"Good for you," George said, wondering whether to believe it, wondering whether his friend fully believed it. "Nobody should win all the time, unless it's us Romans over the barbarians, and that's not the same thing." Claudia, now, Claudia was as fierce as any Avar ever hatched, but Dactylius undoubtedly knew more on that score than he did.

A troop of Avars came by, armored men on surprisingly big armored horses. Just by the way they rode, they gave the impression of owning everything they surveyed, and owning it beyond hope of challenge. George hadn't seen many of the nomads since the siege began. Compared to the numbers of their Slavic subjects, he didn't think there were many Avars. But every time he did see a few, he understood why the Slavs obeyed them.

"I wouldn't want to go up against those fellows in the open field," he said, "not even if I were betting a copper follis to win a gold solidus."

"Not even a half-follis," Dactylius agreed. "But we're not in the open field, and so—" He plucked an arrow from his quiver, set it to his bow, drew it back with a sweet, swift motion, and let fly.

George started to chide him, because he thought the Avars were far out of range, especially for a small man like Dactylius, who couldn't pull a strong bow. But the arrow kept going and going and going. . . . "Good shot!" George exclaimed. "Oh, good shot!"

Dactylius cried out in exultation when the shaft he'd launched struck one of the Avars in the side. He cried out again a moment later, this time in anguish, when it rebounded from the fellow's scalemail shirt. The Avar looked down at the arrow, then up at the wall. He shook his fist and kept on riding.

"I had him," Dactylius moaned. "By St. Demetrius, I had him—and he got away." He sent another arrow at the troop of nomads. This one fell twenty cubits short, as George had expected the other to do. It was as if Thessalonica's patron saint had helped that first arrow along—only to see it fail in the end. If that was an omen, it was one for which George did not care.

He set a hand on Dactylius' shoulder. "You couldn't have done any better," he said. "You did better than I thought you could. If you shoot like that against the Slavs when they come to shoot at us, a lot of them won't go back to their encampments."

"I know," the jeweler said. "I hope I can. But for a few seconds there, killing that Avar seemed like the most important thing in the world. I thought I'd done it, and then—" He shook his head. "It's not fair."

"No," George agreed. "It's not." But for their part, the Avars would no doubt say it wasn't fair that God and St. Demetrius had watched over Thessalonica and kept them from sacking the city. Fairness, like beauty, was in the eye of the beholder. When no two people could agree on what it meant, did it matter? George had trouble seeing how.

The Avar Dactylius had shot but not wounded made his horse pull up and looked over toward Thessalonica again, as if deciding he wouldn't brook the insult after all. He shouted something. George wouldn't have understood it had he heard it clearly, which he didn't.

"Hello," the shoemaker muttered under his breath. He might not have understood the shout, but he understood what sprang from it: out of one of the Avars' tents near the woods came the priest or wizard who had tried to ruin the holy power in the grappling hooks on the walls of Thessalonica but had succeeded only in causing a minor earthquake.

"What's he carrying with him?" Dactylius asked.

"Looks like a mirror," George answered. "He's in an even uglier getup than he was the last time we saw him, isn't he?" Instead of looking like some weird animal, half furry, half feathered, the Avar now resembled nothing so much as a tree all shaggy with moss. He even wore a great, untidy wreath of leaves on his head.

He came trotting up to the horseman who had called for him. They talked together for some little while. The mounted Avar kept pointing back toward the wall, and toward that portion of it where George and Dactylius stood. Dactylius let out what could only be described as a giggle. "I don't think he's happy I almost let the air out of him," the jeweler said.

"I'd say you're right," George answered. "The next interesting question is, what can he do about it?" To turn any harm aside, George made the sign of the cross. The Avar wizard *had* shaken Thessalonica's wall, even if he hadn't toppled it. George didn't want that kind of power aimed at him alone—or, come to that, at him and Dactylius together.

The mounted Avar, having said his piece, rode on to rejoin his comrades. The priest stood staring at the wall. Even across a couple of furlongs, he seemed to be staring straight into George's face. George stared back, unable to take his eyes away. He felt the weight of the Avar's persona pressing on him, and pressed back as strongly as he could.

That seemed to take the Avar by surprise. Abruptly, he turned away and went back into the tent from which the horseman had summoned him. Dactylius tapped George on the forearm. "Did you feel that?" The jeweler spoke in a whisper, though the wizard was far away.

"Yes, I did," George said. "I didn't know you did, too." Some of his pride in resistance faded. If the Avar had set that mental grip on more than one Roman at once, he was stronger than any single foe of his.

"What do you suppose he's doing in there?" Dactylius pointed to the tent into which the Avar had returned.

"I don't know," George answered, "but I think we'll find out."

He hardly thought himself worthy of being compared to Elijah or Jeremiah as a prophet, but that prediction was soon borne out. The Avar emerged from the tent carrying not only the mirror but what looked like a wooden pail of water. He set the mirror on the ground; as he did so, the sun angled off it for a moment, the flash proving to George what it was. He began to dance around it. Every so often, water splashed out of the pail onto the ground and onto the mirror.

Clouds crowded the sky, which moments before had been sunny though pale. What had been as good a day as any Thessalonica might expect in November quickly changed to one warning of storm. "Magic!" George exclaimed; nothing natural could make the weather turn so fast.

Cold rain began pelting down onto the wall almost as soon as the word passed his lips. Dactylius pointed. "Look!" he exclaimed. "It's not falling on the Slavs out there."

He was right. The rain seemed confined to Thessalonica alone. Past twenty or thirty cubits beyond the wall, the weather remained as it had been. George started to say something, but thunder crashed, deafeningly loud, right above his head. He staggered and almost dropped to one knee.

Another crash came, even louder than the first. George stared up into the sky. He'd never heard thunder like that. Were those just cloud shapes, or did they look like Avars thumping great drums? When the thunder rang out again, he was convinced of what he saw. Those shifting shapes, all thirteen of them, were real.

After yet another peal of thunder, rumblings continued for some time, like aftershocks from an earthquake. The rumblers were cloud shapes, too: little men or gnomes with enormous feet, all made of mist.

"Avar rain and thunder spirits!" George shouted, pointing up into the heavens. He hoped Dactylius would perceive them, too.

Before he could find out whether his friend did, an utterly mundane arrow hissed past his face. He reached for his bow to shoot back at the Slavs, then cursed the Avar wizard as foully as he knew how. No rain fell on the Slavs; their bowstrings were dry. Those of the men on the walls of Thessalonica, though, were soaked and useless.

The thunder spirits thundered. The smaller, less fearsome rumblers rumbled. The Slavs out beyond the walls kept on shooting. George and the other defenders were powerless to reply.

"Where's Bishop Eusebius?" Dactylius shouted. "He could put a stop to this."

Wherever Bishop Eusebius was, he was nowhere close by. Peering through the curtain of rain all around Thessalonica as if through a glass, darkly, George saw more Avars come out to confer with their priest. "I don't know why they're wasting time talking," he said. "They'll never have a better chance to attack the walls than now."

"Look!" Dactylius pointed not to the cloud creatures in the sky, not to the Slavs and Avars beyond the rain, but to the head of the stairway leading up to the wall. "It's Father Luke!"

That made George feel as good as seeing the bishop might have done. Father Luke was of lower rank, but George and Dactylius had already seen what his holiness could do. George said, "You beat the one water demon, Father. Can you beat these new ones as well?" He pointed at the thunderers and rumblers up in the sky.

"I don't know," the priest replied, putting a hand up over his eyes so he could see the Avar powers without raindrops continually blowing in his face.

"You don't know?" Dactylius sounded horrified. "Are we just going to stand here and drown, the way people did in the great Flood?" He looked about ready to drown. The drumming rain made his hair run down over his face like so many wet snakes and plastered his tunic to him so tightly, George could count his ribs.

In a way, Father Luke's answer horrified George, too. In another way, it pleased him. A more arrogant priest would have claimed abilities he lacked and tried to do more than he could, as Father Gregory—the late Father Gregory—had done by the cistern. If nothing else, Father Luke had humility, a virtue in any Christian man and all the more vital in a priest.

"God provided in the Flood, telling Noah to build his Ark," Father Luke said. "I have faith God will provide for us now, if not through me, then surely through someone else."

Again, George did not quite know what to make of the response. Admiring the depth of Father Luke's faith, he had trouble sharing it. He knew he had not the temperament of a man like Job, to go on unceasingly praising God regardless of the misfortunes befalling him.

Instead of criticizing the priest, though, he tried to nudge him into action: "You routed one water demigod with water of your own from the baptismal font. Can you do the same with these—?" Before he could say *things*, the thirteen thunder spirits let loose with another crash, one so enormous he thought it would split his head open.

Father Luke's shrug was not encouraging. "They are there" —he pointed up into the sky— "while I remain down here. I see no way for the sanctified water to come in contact with them, as it did with the Slavic demon in the cistern."

"All right, you can't do that," George said, following the logic without liking it. "What *can* you do? You have to be able to do something."

"And you'd better do it soon, too," Dactylius added. He sounded both insistent and frightened, neither of which George wanted. The shoemaker aimed to make Father Luke figure out what he could do and then to have him do it, not to alarm and rattle him.

Father Luke, fortunately, seemed neither alarmed nor rattled. "I can pray," he answered.

It was, after all, what a priest was good for. Even so, George would have preferred a response somewhat more aggressive. He was beginning to feel as much like a drowned rat as Dactylius looked. "Well, if that's what you can do, you'd better get to it," he said roughly. "The Slavs out there aren't going to be content with shooting at us up here on the wall, not for long they won't. Pretty soon they'll try knocking it down again."

"You're right, of course." Father Luke looked up to the heavens again. Now he paid no attention to the thunder spirits or the smaller rumblers, nor to the rain beating into his face. "I take my text from the Book of Genesis: 'And God said, Let there be light: and there was light.' "

Knowing the priest's piety, and knowing also how he had beaten the Slavic water demigod, George expected the Avars' sky powers to be routed and the sun to break through. That did not happen. The rain kept falling. More thunder boomed, as if those powers were laughing at Father Luke's effort to disperse them.

Dactylius let out a cry of dismay that showed how much confidence he had placed in Father Luke. George glanced over toward the priest. Father Luke's long face was set in thoughtful lines. Seeing George's eyes upon him, he nodded slightly. "It is as you have said all along," he remarked. "The powers of the Slavs are strong, and now I see that the powers of the Avars are stronger still. Since the Avars rule the Slavs, I suppose I should have expected as much."

"What can you do about it?" George demanded. Another shattering roar from the heavens emphasized the thunder spirits' strength more than the priest's words could have. Somewhere not far down the wall, a militiaman screamed when an arrow pierced him. Caught in the tightly defined circle of rain, the defenders could offer no reply.

"What can I do?" Suddenly, despite building catastrophe, Father Luke smiled. For a moment, George thought he saw in that smile the sun he'd hoped the priest would be able to restore. Father Luke said, "I could not make those powers quit this place against their will: they were too strong for that. Suppose instead, though, I give them everything they want?"

Through drumming rain, through rumblings and thunderings above, Dactylius hissed to George: "He's gone mad."

"I don't think so," George answered, though he had not the slightest idea what the priest intended.

As Father Luke had before, he stared up into the sobbing sky. As he had before, he chose words from the Book of Genesis, but words of different import, perhaps inspired by Dactylius: " 'On the same day were all the fountains of the great deep broken up, and the windows of heaven were opened. . . . And the waters prevailed, and increased greatly on the earth . . . And the waters prevailed exceedingly upon the earth; and all the high mountains that were under the whole heaven were covered.' "

"What's he *doing*?" Dactylius said fretfully. "Is he trying to drown us all?"

"No, I don't think so," George said. "The rain's no worse than it was." Before saying anything more, he paused and looked out from the wall. Something had changed. He was sure of that, but had trouble identifying what it was. And then, all at once, he laughed with glad surprise and bowed to Father Luke. "You did it, Your Reverence!"

"Did what?" Dactylius squawked. And then, a beat behind the other two, he understood. He too bowed before the priest.

"God gets the credit, not I," Father Luke said. It was too wet for George to be sure his eyes twinkled, but he thought so. It was too wet all around Thessalonica, not just in the narrow circle to which the rain and lightning and thunder and rumbling had been confined. Now, like any proper storm, this one spread over the whole land.

"Give them what they want," George said musingly.

"They must have been angry, penned up in such a narrow space." Father Luke's voice was amiable. Rainwater splashed off the tonsured crown of his head. "Now they can do as they like, where they like."

"And if the Slavs and Avars don't care for it—what a pity." George laughed out loud. Even standing here soaking wet in the chilly rain, being alive felt monstrous good. He vastly admired cleverness, and what could be more clever than turning the Avars' powers against the priest who had loosed them in the first place?

That, Father Luke had done. The storm of arrows that had joined the rainstorm to assail the militiamen on the walls of Thessalonica now died away: archery with wet bowstrings was as impossible for the Slavs as for the Romans. If the barbarians had planned anything more than sweeping the walls bare of defenders who could not shoot back, the sudden extension of the rain made them think again.

George peered out toward the Avar wizard who had summoned the thirteen thunder spirits and their lesser rumbler cousins to torment Thessalonica. He could see even less now than before, what with the rain extending all the way from him to the wizard. Was that angrily dancing figure the Avar, or just a Slav irked at having his sport spoiled? The shoemaker could not be certain.

Lightning crashed out of the heavens, striking near the dancer, whoever he was. The thunder that followed almost at once made George clap his hands to his ears. He felt as if he were standing inside God's biggest bass drum. "Lord, have mercy!" he gasped.

"He has had mercy on us," Father Luke said. "Without His help, our city would have fallen. But that wasn't what you meant, was it?"

"Not exactly," George said, his head still ringing.

"I hope the Lord had no mercy at all on that cursed Avar," Dactylius exclaimed. "I hope that lightning bolt burned him to ashes, and I hope the ashes wash into the sea and are gone forever. That's what I hope." He stuck out his chin, daring the other two to disagree with him.

"*I* hope the Avars leave off attacking us and accept our faith," Father Luke said. George snorted—that was a pretty sentiment, but how likely was it? Father Luke's eyes twinkled again. After a moment, he went on, "That failing, Dactylius' hope sounds good enough for me."

"Do you think the lightning did cook the Avar priest?" George asked.

"What I hope and what I think are, I fear, two different things," the priest replied. "Those are the powers with which he is intimately familiar; I think he will be able to bring them back under his control."

George sighed. That made more sense than he wished it did. And Father Luke proved a good prophet, as George himself had, not long before. The rain soon eased off; the thunder stopped. A brisk breeze sprang up and blew away the storm clouds. "Here comes the sun," George said happily. The sunshine was watery, but it was sunshine.

And there in the sunshine stood the Avar priest. Now that George got a good look at him, he saw his bizarre costume was soaked and, with any luck at all, ruined. The wizard stared toward the wall and shook a fist at—no, not at George; it had to be at Father Luke. And the priest nodded back toward the Avar, recognizing the other's skill and potence.

"You ought to blast him with an anathema," Dactylius said.

"I do not think he fears my anathemas," Father Luke said. "I do not think he fears any Christian power. Only greater acquaintance with us will teach him the true strength of the Lord."

That was as temperate an answer as George could have looked for from any priest. But the Avars and the Romans had struggled against each other now for most of a decade. The war remained unwon on either side, which, he presumed, also meant neither God nor the gods and spirits of the Slavs and Avars had prevailed.

He might have been able to say something to that effect to Father Luke, as he could not have to Bishop Eusebius. But when he opened his mouth to speak, his teeth chattered so loudly, he could not. He and the rest of the militiamen on the wall had stood in the driving rain longer than the Avar wizard had done, and were more drenched than he. The breeze was chilly, too.

Father Luke took off his cloak, which was thick even if soaked, and wrapped it around George's shoulders. "That's all right, Your Reverence," the shoemaker said, trying to shrug it off. "Here, you keep it."

"I may not be the Son of God, to give up my life for mankind, but I should be a poor sort of priest indeed if I did not give up my cloak for a friend," Father Luke said.

Just then, Dactylius sneezed. That gave George the excuse he needed to shed the cloak: he passed it to Dactylius. The jeweler tried to protest, too, but kept on sneezing. That let George and Father Luke ignore him, and left them both warm in spirit if less so in body.

John and Sabbatius came up onto the wall to replace George and Dactylius. So far as George knew, nobody had told Sabbatius that John was in the habit of making jokes about him. One of these days, Sabbatius would find out, and there would be trouble. Not wishing either to borrow or to cause the latter, George kept his mouth shut and headed for home.

When the shoemaker got to his shop, Irene said, "Wasn't that a dreadful storm a couple of hours ago? I see you're still all wet, poor thing, and the roof has a new leak in it, too. I put a bowl down under it to catch the drips."

"It was quite a storm," George agreed. If it had seemed nothing more than that to his wife, he was as well pleased.

"Storm like that, I'm glad the Slavs didn't attack," Theodore said. "They could have caused all sorts of trouble, and you might not have noticed them in the rain till too late."

"That's true, too," George said, and sneezed as vigorously as Dactylius had up on the wall.

"Come upstairs. Get out of that wet tunic." Irene took charge of him with brisk efficiency. "Drink some warm wine with honey in it. That will make you feel better."

"If I don't feel better, I won't notice after I drink enough of it," George said.

Ignoring that, Irene maneuvered him much as Rufus might have done up on the wall. And, sure enough, in dry clothes and with hot wine in him, he did think the world a kindlier place than he had when he was all wet and shivery. He stretched the upper for a boot he was working on over the last and smoothed the leather with a round file.

"That's good work, Father," Theodore said, looking over his shoulder.

He paid more attention to it himself than he had been doing. "It is, isn't it?" he said, surprised at how surprised he sounded. Looking down at his hands, he added, "They know what they're up to, anyhow. Now if I could only leave them behind to work while the rest of me goes upstairs to supper or off to the tavern, that would be pretty fine."

Theodore snorted. "While you're at it, why not wish for a bronze man, like the one the Poet says Hephaestus made to help him with his work?"

"Why not indeed?" George said mildly—too mildly to suit his son, who might have been hoping for an argument, as he often did these days. He went back to work himself.

George let his hands guide the file over the leather once more, since they'd proved they could tend to that by themselves. When Theodore had learned to read Greek, the teacher taught him Homer, from whose poems boys had been learning to read for more than a thousand years. Even now, in these Christian times, the *Iliad* and the *Odyssey* gave the old gods a shadowy life they would not have had without them.

Was that good or bad? Homer wrote so well that, while you were reading him, you couldn't help believing in his gods and heroes—George remembered as much from his own days in school. No wonder some bishops would sooner have had students taught from the Holy Scriptures alone, thereby interring the memory of the pagan gods for good.

"But the words are so fine," George murmured. While he'd mused, his hands had smoothed out the whole toe of the boot. He opened and closed them, almost as if to make sure they were still willing to respond to his will. Maybe he'd come closer to imitating Hephaestus than either he or his son had thought.

That night, Irene said, "Something more happened today than you let on in front of the children—or in front of me, either, come to that. What was it?"

He didn't bother asking how she knew. They'd slept side by side more than half their lives; he often wondered if she knew him better than he knew himself. "It wasn't an ordinary storm," he said, and went on to explain how the thirteen thunder spirits and however many little rumblers there had been had let the Slavs shoot at the Romans for a while without fear of reprisal, and how they'd nearly let the Slavs do worse than that, too.

Irene shivered, then took him in her arms, as much, he judged, to reassure herself he still lay beside her as because the night was chilly. "That is a terrible thing," she said in the quiet dark: "That the power of the Lord could not rout these sky-things the Avars worship."

"It is a terrible thing," George answered, remembering how frightened he'd been when Father Luke's first prayer failed to drive the thunder spirits and rumblers away from Thessalonica. "It's what I've been saying: the powers feed off the belief the Slavs and Avars give them."

"God doesn't feed off our power. He gives us power, the way He did with Rufus in the church of St. Demetrius. The pagan powers from the old days that still lurk here fear Him. Why don't these others?"

"Because they're stronger," George said patiently. "I think Father Luke did very well. When he saw he couldn't force the Avar powers out of the sky, he went with them instead of against them. He used their own nature to get them to drench the barbarians along with us, and that ruined whatever plan the Avars had."

"It worked, but was it right?" Irene asked. "Satan will give you what you want, too, if you ask it of him. Asking is the sin."

"I don't think Father Luke sinned. I think he did what he had to do. And I think he was clever to come up with it so quickly after the first prayer failed."

Irene shivered again, and held him tighter. "I hope you're right."

"So do I," George said. He didn't want to think about what being wrong might mean. That his wife was holding him, and he her, gave him something else to think about. Since he was a man, what that something was soon became evident. Irene laughed a quiet laugh, deep down in her throat, and reached between them.

They made love with their tunics hiked up rather than naked; the night *was* cold. They were generally happy with each other in bed, one reason they got on well with each other outside the bedroom. Tonight, though, Irene responded to his caresses with more fervor than she'd shown in . . . he couldn't remember how long. Her excitement drove his, too.

Only afterwards, his tunic down past his knees again to warm as much of him as it could, did he wonder whether Irene also had a good many things she was trying not to think about.

He yawned and snuggled closer to her. She was already nearly asleep. All the jokes said that was something men did, but it happened with her more often than with him. Not that he wasn't sleepy himself, no indeed. Soon after her breathing grew deep and regular, his did, too. The last thought he remembered having was a vague hope that she would find herself worried more often.

✧ ✧ ✧

"You! Shoemaker!"

The gruff growl made George look up from his work. There in the doorway stood Menas, looking large and well fed and unpleasant. One look at his proud, meaty face said he remembered and still resented George's remark up on the wall: he was the sort of man who would remember for a long time anything diminishing his self-importance.

No help for it. "What can I do for you today, sir?" George asked.

"I hear you've been telling lies about me," Menas said heavily.

"No, sir," George said, surprised now. "So far as I know, sir, I haven't said anything about you at all."

"Lying again," Menas said. "Well, you'll pay for that, too. You're going to tell me the stinking joke going through the taverns, the one that says God gave me my legs back so I could run away from the Slavs, that isn't yours?"

"No, that's not mine," the shoemaker said. But he had heard it—where? At Paul's tavern, coming out of John's mouth, that was where. He'd worried it would land John in trouble with Menas. He'd never imagined it would land *him* in trouble with the noble instead.

"Not only a liar, but a bad liar." Menas thrust out his big, square chin. "If it's not your joke, wretch, whose is it?" His thick-fingered hands opened and closed, opened and closed, as if around the neck of anyone rash enough to tell jokes on him.

"I'm sorry, sir, but I don't know that." George lied without hesitation. If he threw John to this wolf—no, this bear, a better description for Menas—how was he supposed to live with himself afterwards?

"Of course you don't—it's yours. Who else would have wanted to tarnish God's miracle by calling me a coward?"

"I've never wanted to tarnish any of God's miracles," George replied with absolute conviction.

Menas would hear none of it. He shook his fist at the

shoemaker. "Not a true word comes out of your mouth. Tell me you didn't say to my face that God's curing me didn't mean anything in particular, and that He cared more about the city than about any of the people in it."

"That's not what I said, sir," George told him, aware as he spoke that he had no hope of being believed. The noble had closed his mind, locked the door, and thrown away the key.

"You mocked me then and you've made vicious jokes about me ever since," Menas declared, heedless not only of George's denials but also of having mentioned only one joke bare moments before.

George stood up. If he could not convince Menas he had done him no harm, maybe he could convince him he might do harm if provoked. "Sir, I tell you again I did not do those things, but I also tell you you're starting to make me sorry I didn't."

"You're not sorry," Menas said. "You don't know what sorry is. But I tell you this, shoemaker—you're going to find out." He turned on his heel and stamped up the street, waves of indignation rising from his back as heat rose from a blacksmith's forge.

Theodore and Sophia both stared at George. "He's an important fellow, Father," Sophia said worriedly. "I wish he weren't angry at you."

"I wish he weren't, too," George answered steadily.

"That's not your joke," Irene said. "I know who tells jokes like that." To his relief, she did not upbraid him for protecting John.

"Do *you* know who told that joke?" Theodore asked. George nodded. His son burst out, "Then why didn't you tell Menas?"

"Because a man who betrays his friends has no friends left after a while—and doesn't deserve any, either," George said. "And because, if Menas weren't angry at me for this, he'd be angry at me for something else. He's decided he's going to be angry at me, and he's the kind of man who doesn't change his mind about things like that."

"It's one thing if a farmer or a butcher is angry at you," Sophia said. "All they can do is insult you in the street, or something like that. But if Menas is angry at you, he could . . ." She paused, trying to think of the worst thing she could. After a moment, she went on, "He could set lawyers on you."

"Heaven forbid!" Irene exclaimed. George would have said the same thing if his wife hadn't beaten him to it. He didn't have a lot of money; the next rich shoemaker of whom he heard would be the first. Not only would he find it hard to fend off the attacks of lawyers trained in Berytus or Constantinople (and find it all the harder because judges would surely be prejudiced in favor of the lawyers' wealthy, prominent client), he would also be tied up in court for so long, he wouldn't be able to tend to what business he had. Serving on the militia gave him that kind of trouble, but half the men—better than half the men—in Thessalonica had it now. If Menas decided to persecute him by prosecuting him, that wouldn't be so.

"We'll just have to see what happens, that's all," he said. "Maybe—" He stopped.

"Maybe some Slav will shoot him in the face with an arrow," Theodore said. "Shooting him in the heart wouldn't do—I'm sure it's too hard for an arrow to hurt."

"Theodore . . ." George's voice carried a warning for a couple of reasons. Theodore hadn't bothered keeping his voice down. If word of what he'd said got to Menas, the noble would have another reason for hating George. And the shoemaker did not feel comfortable about wishing anyone dead. He'd had the thought his son had spoken aloud, but he'd stopped before he said it. Words, he told himself, were what gave thought power.

Theodore said, "Sometimes I think you're too kind-hearted for your own good."

George walked over and swatted him in the backside. He leaped into the air with a yelp. "There," George said. "Think again." Theodore did his best to look indignant, but couldn't help laughing—especially when his sister and mother were laughing already.

But Irene quickly turned serious again. "What are we going to do?" she asked.

"I know what I'm going to do," George said: "I'm going to finish this sandal I was working on. As for the rest, I won't worry about it till it happens—if it happens." He hoped he convinced Irene with that *if*. He wished he could convince himself.

VI

Standing up on top of the wall, George shivered. The day was bright, but cold enough to make him wish for trousers. "We ought to be warmer here than down below," John said. "We're closer to the sun, aren't we?"

"Close enough to bake your wits, anyhow," Rufus said. John grinned at him, unperturbed. George wished John would stop making jokes. He didn't think he'd get either of his wishes, but made them anyhow.

He hadn't told John of the trouble from his joke about Menas—what point? It wouldn't have abashed the tavern comic, and might have given him ideas for new vile jokes . . . although John, being John, never seemed to have any trouble coming up with those ideas.

Rufus pointed out toward the Slavs. "They look like trying anything?"

"Not today," John said. "Quiet as the basilica halfway through one of Eusebius' sermons, except the Slavs are too far away for you to hear them snoring."

"*Oh*, John," George murmured, as he sometimes did when John went too far in middle of his routine. John took no notice; John seldom took notice of anything. George spoke to Rufus: "I'm not sure he's right. They were stirring about when we first came up onto the wall, though they haven't done much the past couple of hours."

"Maybe they were stirring so quick because they've got dysentery going through their camp." John mimed a man dashing for the latrine. He didn't need to say anything to be funny; sometimes, as now, he was funnier when he let his body do the talking for him.

Rufus laughed; you couldn't watch John trying to hurry and at the same time trying to clench every part of himself without laughing. But the veteran said, "Dysentery's no joke. I've been in camps where it came calling. Sometimes more soldiers die of a flux of the bowels than from swords and spears and arrows and what have you."

George waited for John to crack wise about soldiering's being a shitty job, but his friend disdained the easy laugh. If he was casting about for one more worthy of his talents, he never got the chance to use it. Instead, he spoke in a voice so flat and unemphatic, it commanded immediate attention and belief: "You were right, George. The Slavs are up to something."

"They sure are," Rufus said, both brown eye and blue going wide. His voice rose to a formidable shout: "Sound the alarm! The Slavs are attacking the city!"

The first horns on the wall might have rung out before he shouted, but they might not have, too. Afterwards, George never was sure. He was sure a whole ungodly lot of Slavs were rushing at the wall. Some of them carried picks, others sledgehammers, and still others the big shields he'd noted at the edges of their encampments.

He was slow adding up what all that meant, not least because another host of Slavs, these keeping their distance from Thessalonica, filled the air with arrows. George ducked behind the battlement to snatch an arrow out of his own quiver, stood up quickly to shoot it, and then ducked down once more.

Rufus wasted no more time in taking cover, but Rufus had seen everything once and most things half a dozen times. He knew what the Slavs intended, and announced what he knew to everyone else: "They're going to try making tortoises and undermining the wall!"

"Have we got enough things to drop on them?" George asked.

"We're going to find out, aren't we?" Rufus said, not the most reassuring answer the shoemaker could imagine. The veteran's bowstring twanged as he shot at a Slav. His curses said he'd missed. While setting another arrow to the string, he went on, "They're not doing a very good job of it. They should set up the tortoises before they move on the walls—they'd take fewer casualties that way." His critique of the Slavs' performance was milder than some he'd given the militiamen on the practice field.

George shot at a Slav carrying one of the oversized iron-faced shields. The fellow clutched at his leg and fell. The shield bounced away. Before he could recover it, three more arrows pierced him. None of them finished him off, though. He managed to get the shield back and slowly crawl away from the fighting. In the abstract, George pitied him; if he lived, he would be a long, painful time healing. At the same time, though, he wished his first arrow had killed the Slav instead of merely wounding him.

He lacked the leisure to contemplate the inconsistency of those two notions. He lacked leisure for anything. His life reduced itself to groping for arrows, nocking them, finding a target, drawing the bow, and letting fly. That Slav was an exception; with most of the shafts he loosed, he had no idea whether he'd hit or missed.

A good many Slavs sprawled in death or writhed in torment on the ground in front of the walls of Thessalonica. Quite a lot of shieldmen reached the walls, though, and raised their shields up over their heads to protect themselves and their comrades with picks and crowbars from whatever the Thessalonicans rained down on them.

"That's not how Bousas would have taught them to do it," Rufus said reprovingly. "They should know better, if they learned from a proper Roman."

"I don't think this is one of those times when the pedagogue will come across their backsides with a stick if they're sloppy," John said. "Sieges aren't marked on neatness."

"They're wasting men," Rufus insisted.

"They don't care," John replied, accurately enough. "You think the Avars are going to break down and bawl because some stupid Slav gets an arrow in the ribs he might have turned if he was careful?" His mobile features suggested an aggressively indifferent barbarian.

Rufus seemed inclined to carry the argument further. George, for once, found himself on John's side. The Avars had already shown they didn't care what happened to their Slavic subjects, so long as they got into Thessalonica. And then the Slavs started pounding away at the city walls, a distraction that made both John and Rufus forget what they'd been talking about.

George felt the pounding through the soles of his feet. He seemed to hear it the same way, as if it had traversed his entire body before reaching his ears. The noise or feeling was alarming. If the Slavs could get enough stones out from the bottom of the wall, the masonry above the place where those stones had been would fall down, too. And, since George was standing on top of that masonry . . .

He grabbed a large stone from a pile on the walkway, picked it up, and, grunting with effort, carried it to the edge of the wall and dropped it on the attackers below. A loud and satisfying crash said it had landed on one of the upheld shields of a tortoise down there. He hurried back to the pile for another stone. He was just about to fling it down onto the Slavs, too, when an arrow hit it and tumbled, spinning, up over his head.

"Thank you, Lord," he said sincerely, and let the stone fall. Had he not been holding it, or had he already dropped it, the arrow would have pierced him. That was another of those chances of war that did not repay close contemplation.

"Here, pick something they'll feel," Rufus said. His

stringy, corded muscles bunched as he stooped and seized a rock George reckoned Hercules would have had trouble lifting. Up it came, though. Maybe fighting frenzy impelled the old man. Or maybe, George thought with no small awe, St. Demetrius was once more lending a subtle hand in the fighting. How else could Rufus carry that weight?

George was not the only militiaman to stare as the veteran brought the stone to the edge of the wall and cast it down. Not only did he hear a crash when it hit, but also hoarse screams.

"There's a tortoise with a broken shell!" John shouted.

Not far down the wall, a couple of Romans lifted a cauldron from a hastily lighted fire, wrapping rags around their hands so the hot iron handles would not burn them. They tipped the boiling water in the cauldron over the edge of the wall. George capered in glee at the shrieks that rose immediately afterwards.

The Romans did not get off scot-free there. One of them dropped his half of the cauldron, howling in pain and clutching at the shoulder from which an arrow had suddenly sprouted. "Get down into the city and have that seen to," his comrade said. The militiaman made his way toward the stairs, hand still clapped over the wound and bright blood running out between his fingers.

Rufus pawed through the pile of stones, casting aside with such fervor those he didn't care for, everyone nearby had to step lively to keep toes from getting smashed. When he finally found the one he wanted, George stared in astonishment. He had no idea why, or for that matter how, people had carried it up to the top of the wall in the first place. It looked too big and heavy for any two men to lift, let alone one.

Rufus took hold of it. His lips moved silently. Prayer? Curse? George couldn't tell. The veteran strained—whatever power was in him, he was pushing it as far as it would go, maybe farther. No. Up came the stone, not so smoothly as the one before but up nonetheless. Staggering a little, Rufus got it to the edge of the wall, set it down so he could pant for a moment like a winded dog, and then, with what looked to be all the strength he had in him, shoved it off.

George heard a crash, but no screams. The feel of the pounding under his feet changed subtly. "I don't think anyone in that tortoise is left alive," he said in tones of wonder. "You just wrecked it."

"Good," Rufus told him. If this was a miracle, it didn't leave him confused and dazed, as he had been when St. Demetrius spoke through him. Instead, he sounded ready to pick up another stone and heave it down onto the Slavs. That was exactly what he did, though the one he chose this time was small enough not to leave George wondering whether he'd had divine help handling it.

After casting another stone at the Slavs (and not worrying in the least whether he was without sin), George traded arrows with some of the archers down on the ground. When he was shooting—or flinching from shafts flying far too close to his face—he thought about the impossibly large stone Rufus had lifted. Impossibly? He shrugged. Maybe not. Men in battle could do strange things. He'd already seen that for himself, limited as his experience was. If he believed half the tales he'd heard—

There stood Rufus, solid and bandy-legged, about the least likely man (or so anyone with sense would think) through whom God would choose to work a miracle—but God had already worked one through him, no matter what any man with sense would think. So maybe He had worked two.

"You, George! You fallen asleep there?" the subject of the shoemaker's musings demanded in his rough soldier's Latin. "You've got no business doing that. John hasn't been telling his jokes up here, after all."

"Stick out your tongue," John told him. Rufus did, a gesture more contemptuous than obedient. A physician would have been proud of John's wise, thoughtful nod. The words that followed, though, were less than Hippocratic: "I remember George said he was missing one of his files. Now I see where it's turned up."

"You go on like that, see where you turn up in a little while," Rufus retorted. "Somebody else doesn't do it for me, I'll put you there."

John picked up a heavy stone and made as if to throw it at the veteran. "Here—catch," he said, but then hurled it down on the Slavs.

"Brothers, the lot of us," George said. He shot at a Slav—and missed. After some halfhearted blasphemy, he went on, "How are we doing? The wall doesn't feel so much as if termites are nibbling at it." Were his feet feeling what he wished them to feel, or had the Slavs' efforts to undermine the wall really slowed down?

Rufus said, "I think you're right. Lord knows I hope you're right. But I tell you this—right now I'm not going to stick my head out and look down to the bottom of the wall to find out if you're right."

"That's sensible," George said. "I'm not, either."

"It *is* sensible," John said, apparently to no one in particular. "How did he ever manage to come up with it?"

"When this fighting is done—" Rufus began in a voice thick with menace. But he broke off, shaking his head. "Ahh, what's the use? I should have known better than to try making a soldier out of you. But near as I can guess, we may drive the Slavs off this time, but there's never going to be a time when all the fighting's done."

"I pray you're wrong," George said, "but I think you're right."

"It's as sure as burying your money back of your house," Rufus said. He looked around. A couple of militiamen were lugging a great jar of water up the stairs to pour it into the cauldron to heat. More men were carrying stones in upside-down shields.

"Are we going to have enough things to throw down to make them give over before they bring down a stretch of wall?" John asked—the question on everyone's mind.

"If God is kind, we will," George answered. So far as

he could tell—with the possible exception of Rufus' lifting those two enormous stones—the fight here was of men against men, not of God against the powers of the Slavs and Avars. He'd meant what he said as a general wish, then, not as a prayer for divine intervention.

Rufus picked up another stone, braved looking out over the wall in that storm of arrows to see where it would do the most good, and threw it down. The crash that came back was particularly loud and satisfying. "That one went where it was supposed to," John said.

"You'd best believe it did," Rufus said, flexing his elderly biceps and twisting into a pose that put George in mind of the statue of an athlete from pagan times: or rather, of something the pagan sculptors had never made, the statue of a former athlete as a grandfather.

It put John in mind of something else. "You go prancing around like that anywhere near the baths, they'll drag you off to gaol for unnatural vice," he said.

"The most unnatural vice I've ever tried is putting up with you," Rufus said. That prompted John to pull out an arrow and shoot it at the Slavs. Rufus smiled, probably because he'd hoped to accomplish something on that order.

George threw another rock down on the Slavs himself. The pile of stones on the walkway was much smaller than it had been. Men were still bringing more up to the top of the wall, but not nearly so fast as they were being used. That pile and the others like it had been accumulated over days; they couldn't be maintained when they were used up in hours. If the defenders ran out before the Slavs had had all they could stand . . .

"If we can't drive them off like this, will we have to sortie?" he asked Rufus.

"Maybe so," the veteran said unhappily. "I don't want to do it, you understand, but I don't want the wall crumbling under me, either."

Methodically, almost mechanically, the defenders kept dropping stones and boiling water onto the Slavs. They knew they were hurting the foe; the screams and shrieks from the ground said as much. But war, as George had discovered, was not merely a business of hurting the enemy. It meant hurting him more than he could endure. Were the Romans doing that? The Slavs had already shown they could endure a good deal.

Grunting, George lifted and flung another stone. The pile was small indeed now, hardly higher than his knees. Once it was gone, what then? Rushing out and fighting the Slavs seemed a better choice than helplessly staying up here and waiting for the wall to fall down, but neither alternative struck the shoemaker as highly desirable.

"Shall we sortie?" he asked, as he'd done before.

"If we have to, we have to." Rufus' face twisted. "Damn me to hell if I like the idea, but damn me to hell if I like the idea of letting the cursed Slavs do whatever they please, either."

"That's what I was thinking," George said. "When the other choice is worse, a bad choice can turn good."

The militia captain made no reply for a moment. His lips moved as he worked that through. "You're right," he said at last. He cocked his head to one side. "You managed to put enough twist on that to make a priest happy." Not sure whether he was being complimented or mocked, George maintained a discreet silence.

And then John, who left no doubt when he was insulting someone—as he often was—let out a howl of pure joy. "They're running away!" he shouted a moment later.

George and Rufus shouted, too. George slapped the veteran on the back. Rufus not only endured the familiarity, he grinned wide enough to show off the worn and snaggled teeth still in his mouth. The world soon interfered with that little stretch of unexpected delight, as the world has a way of doing. Rufus, remembering he was a captain, shouted, "Let's give the bastards a going-away present. Grab your bows, lads!"

Along with the rest of the men on the walls, George shot at the Slavs till they fled out of range. As the warriors from the tortoises withdrew, the archers who had supported them also moved away from the wall. That let the Romans peer down at the ground without the risk of taking an arrow in the face.

"We dented them," George said, which would do for an understatement till a bigger one appeared. It was, in some instances, only literal truth; many of the big, reinforced shields the Slavs had brought up against the walls of Thessalonica were broken, while others had their iron facings badly battered.

A good many dented men lay under the wall, too, men whose shields had proved unable to protect them from the stones and arrows the Romans had showered down on them. A couple of them were almost as badly smashed as poor Father Gregory had been after the Slavic water-demigod hurled him to the cobblestones by the cistern. This too was war. George wished Theodore had come up on the wall beside him, to see the reality of what he thought so great and glorious.

Not all the Slavs who lay below the wall were dead. Groans and shrieks still rose from those whose crushed limbs or burns kept them from retreating with their comrades, and from a couple who dragged themselves along with their hands because they were dead from the waist down.

"Let's finish them," Rufus said. Some militiamen had already begun shooting at the helpless Slavs, and precisely aiming stones at those right under the wall. That was a hard, unpleasant business. One by one, the screams and their makers died till none was left.

Into the grim silence following that last death, Rufus said, "I think most of us can come down off the wall now. They aren't going to be able to nerve themselves for another attack any time real soon."

"What do we do if you're wrong?" John asked.

Rufus shrugged. "If you're still up on the wall, you fight 'em. If you're down in the city, you come running back and you fight 'em. If they're already down into the city before you get back here, it's the end, but you fight 'em anyway, and you keep fighting 'em till they kill you. Any other questions?"

"What good would other questions do me?" John returned. "You've only got one answer."

Only when he turned to head down the stairs into Thessalonica did the comic's shoulders sag and his stride lose its jaunty spring. "Mother of God, I'm so tired," he said over his shoulder to George, who was a couple of steps above him. "If those bastards keep coming after us like this, sooner or later they're going to break in."

"If they *can* keep coming at us, I think you're right," George answered. "But we've given them a fine set of lumps every time they've tried. How many men did they lose today? It had to be hundreds. Rufus is right—they'll take a while getting over that."

"Maybe you're right," John said. "Maybe Master One Blue and One Brown is right, too. But maybe not. You think the Avars care how many Slavs the ravens peck the eyes out of? It's like spending other people's money. If Paul tells me I can drink all I want at his place and he's paying for it, why should I stay sober?"

"People aren't miliaresia," George said. "After a while, the Slavs will start saying no when the Avars send 'em out against the wall to be slaughtered."

"And a fat lot of good that will do them." John jumped off the last step. "If they don't come out here against the walls, the Avars will do the job on them for us, sure as God made the world in seven days."

George thought that over. He decided the tavern comic was probably right. "I don't think I'd care to be a Slav right now," he observed.

"Leave the 'right now' out of it, if you please," John said. "I can't think of any time I'd want to be a Slav." He turned off at the side street that led to the furnished room where he lived.

On reflection, George couldn't think of any time when he would have wanted to be a Slav, either. He waved to

John, who, filled with himself as he often was, didn't see or didn't notice—in any case, John didn't wave back. Sighing, George headed on home himself.

Several people on the street had blankets over their tunics like sad excuses for cloaks. George didn't blame them. Now that he wasn't up on the wall fighting for his life, he realized how raw the day was and wished he had a cloak himself. As was the way with such things, wishing did him little good. Along with wishing, he hurried. That not only made him a little warmer than he would have been otherwise, it also got him home sooner.

George was growing resigned to gasps of relief and excited exclamations whenever he walked through the door into his shop. They helped him understand why armies, whenever they could, fought far from home. It wasn't so much to keep their own lands from being ravaged, as he'd always thought. More likely, it was so the soldiers could get away from their families and not have them fretting every minute of the day and night.

"Are you all right, Father?" Sophia said now, hurrying toward him. "You've got blood on your tunic."

"Do I?" George looked down at himself. "Why, so I do." He pulled the hem of the tunic up a little so he could inspect his legs. "It isn't mine. I've said that before and been wrong, so I wanted to make certain this time and not look foolish."

"What was it now?" Irene asked in a voice so flat and dull from holding in worry that it might as well have been a scream. "We hear people running and people shouting, but we never really know what's going on till you come home. We're always afraid till then, too."

"I'm all right." George held up both hands so his wife could see as much. Then he stood on one leg like a stork, and then on the other. That made Sophia and Theodore laugh, and even Irene's smile was a little warmer than dutiful. He went on, "What was it now? The Slavs tried knocking down the foundations of the wall. It didn't work.

We killed a lot of them and made the rest run away."

Put that way, it sounded easy, the result seeming foreordained. The few sentences said nothing of the way the wall had shuddered under George's feet when the Slavs attacked it with picks and pry bars, nothing of the fear that it would do more than shudder, and would come tumbling down like the walls of Jericho in the Bible story. George felt not the least bit guilty at keeping such knowledge from his family. He wished he had no part of it himself.

Theodore said, "I'll bet you butchered them."

"We hurt them," George agreed tonelessly. "I was thinking at the time that you should have been there." Theodore looked proud till he went on, "Seeing what a man looks like after a rock this big" —he gestured with his hands— "lands on his head would keep you from going on and on about what you don't begin to understand."

Sophia made a small, disgusted sound. Irene looked down at the leather strap she was sewing to a sandal and didn't say anything. Theodore did think about what his father said; George gave him credit for that. But it didn't sink in. George could see as much.

Maybe he should have talked about the men who'd had rocks fall on them but didn't die right away, the men with crushed limbs or broken backs. Maybe he should have talked about the men who'd screamed and screamed after a cauldronful of boiling water came down on them. Maybe he should have— He shook his head. None of it would do any good, not till Theodore saw it for himself and, more important still, understood in his belly that it could have been he as easily as any luckless barbarian.

"I'm not afraid," Theodore said, which so decisively proved he'd paid George no attention that the shoemaker, instead of uselessly arguing with him, walked over to his bench to get to some of the work the siege had kept him from doing.

He'd just picked up his awl and noted how smoothly the wooden handle fit against his palm and fingers when

Irene said, "Will you come out back with me, please, dear? I want to know whether you think the fennel is ready for picking."

George muttered under his breath. Irene knew far more about the herbs she grew back there than he did. He couldn't remember the last time she'd asked his opinion about them. The last time he'd offered it unasked, she'd made a point of ignoring him. And he had more work to do in less time than he'd ever known before. He started to say as much. Before he did, though, he looked over at his wife. Without a word, he set the awl down on the bench and walked out with her to have a look at the fennel.

"Seems fine to me," he said, pointing at the wispy, light green plants that stood almost as tall as he did.

Irene gave him the stare she reserved for times when she caught him being deliberately obtuse. "Of course it's fine," she said with an edge to her voice. "But I can't very well talk about Sophia right there in front of her, can I?"

"Why not?" George asked. "You talk about me when I'm right there all the time."

Irene's left foot began tapping the muddy ground of the herb garden, a sure danger sign. "How much do you know about Constantine, the son of Leo the potter?" she asked.

"Say, as much as I know about any of the young men who live on this street," George answered. "He doesn't wear baggy tunics with puffy sleeves and cut his hair short the way the young toughs do, so I suppose he's not so bad as some. Why do you want to . . . ?"

His voice trailed off. Looking back, he realized it should have trailed off a couple of sentences sooner. Irene's foot was tapping harder, which showed exactly how stupid he'd been. "Yes, that's right," she said, as if he'd asked the right question. "Sophia has noticed him. She's done rather more than notice him. This morning, she told me she thought he was the sweetest thing God had made since the fruit in the Garden of Eden."

"Oh." George suppressed a strong urge to retch. "Oh, dear." He'd never particularly noticed young Constantine. What he had noticed was a fellow huskier than most whose beard, which he did not shave very well, had some red patches in it that were startling when seen with the dark hair on top of his head. "Is she serious, or is it just . . . foolishness?" That wasn't the word he wanted, but he couldn't find a better one.

"She thinks she's serious, so she might as well be," Irene answered, a thought convoluted enough to have made Bishop Eusebius proud.

"Am I going to have to talk to Leo?" George asked, and then, as much to himself as to his wife, "Do I want to talk to Leo?" As he had asked it, he answered his own question: "Constantine's not the worst match I can think of."

"No, he's not," Irene agreed. "But he's not the best, either. We have to think about this, and we have to see whether Sophia changes her mind again day after tomorrow, too. I remember there were boys who—" Now she was the one who broke off.

George waggled a finger at her. "Ha! I'm usually the one who makes mistakes like that." With his wife still flustered, he went on, "Some of the boys who might have caught her eye, well, I think I'd be praying the Slavs and Avars would sack the city before the wedding."

"God forbid." Irene's voice was serious, but her eyes danced. "As you said, it could be worse. I was wondering if Theodore had his eye on anyone in particular, but he hasn't shown any signs of that. It won't be long, I expect."

"No, but for now he hasn't." George said nothing more. At Theodore's age, he'd had his eye on every pretty girl who walked past the open door, but he'd left it to his parents to find him one with whom to make a life. His gaze flicked back to Irene. Would he have chosen her on his own? He didn't know, but his mother and father had done well by him.

"I can guess what you're thinking," Irene said, and

laughed a little. That laugh meant she wasn't guessing: she knew he'd eyed all the girls when he was younger. She continued, "With Sophia, it's not anything we have to worry about right away, I don't think. But if she's still serious come summer—"

"All right," George said. Summer seemed farther away than Jerusalem, farther away than Gaul, farther away than the island that was supposed to lie beyond Gaul, the island whose name, for the moment, he'd entirely forgotten. He clicked his tongue between his teeth. That would bother him till he remembered, no matter how useless knowing the name of an immensely distant island now surely infested with barbarians was.

He grunted. Thessalonica was infested with barbarians. To think of them, he didn't need to worry about . . . "Britain!" he said happily.

"What *are* you talking about?" Irene asked.

Before he had to come up with an answer, Sophia called, "How much can the two of you say about fennel, anyway?"

"They're not talking about fennel," Theodore said in a voice George didn't think he was supposed to overhear. "They're talking about one of us—unless they're talking about both of us."

"I know *that*," Sophia replied indignantly, as if her brother had mistaken her for a halfwit. "But I don't want to come right out and say it, do I?"

George suffered a coughing fit at the same time as Irene made wheezing noises, the way some people did when flowers bloomed in springtime. Had their children been a little farther away—*on the island of Britain, for instance*, George thought—both of them would have howled laughter.

As they went back inside, Irene found a way to make them both serious again. She asked, "Now that the Slavs and Avars have found they can't knock the wall down with crowbars and such, what do you think they'll try next?"

"I don't know if they've found they can't knock the wall down this way," George answered. "I just think the Slavs took as much punishment as they could stand right then, which may not be the same thing." He considered. "They seem to be taking turns, soldiers one try, powers the next. We still don't know all the different powers they have, but my bet is, we'll find out."

"Find out what?" Theodore asked when they came into the workroom.

"Find out who's been trying to listen to every word we say," his father answered with a growl that concealed memories of trying to find out what his own parents had been up to when he was Theodore's age and younger.

"Is the fennel all right?" Sophia asked, mildly enough to keep George from thinking she was practicing one of John's routines.

"The fennel is fine," George said. "The two of you, on the other hand, are nosy. Irene, which of them do you suppose is nosier than the other?"

"Both," Irene said, which confused George but confused Theodore and Sophia even more, thereby accomplishing its purpose.

Claudia came in with the sandal George had repaired not long before. Now it had two broken straps, not just one. Despite that detail, Claudia said, "You didn't fix this very well, George."

"I am sorry," George replied, examining the damage. "If you use a shoe to hit people, you know, it won't wear so well as it would if you only walked in it."

"That's not very good." Claudia's voice was indignant. Not only did irony roll off her like dye from a well-greased area of leather on a boot, she also remained as convinced nothing was ever her fault as if she were an aristocrat rather than an artisan's wife. "Shoes should be strong enough to stand up to whatever you do to them."

"I'll try to get this back to you in a couple of days," George said resignedly. He knew he wasn't going to make her see the world or her place in it any differently. What Dactylius saw in her—except someone bigger and stronger and fiercer than he—was beyond the shoemaker.

Claudia's pale eyes flashed fire. "A couple of days?" she said.

Not being married to her, George could take a firmer line than her husband. "Yes, a couple of days, I'm afraid," he answered. "I have a lot of work here that I'm trying to do, and I don't have a lot of time to do it. You can blame that on the Slavs and Avars, if you like, along with everything else."

"I do. Oh, I do," Claudia said. "They've done nothing but make my life miserable ever since they got here. As far as I'm concerned, they ought to go away and never come back."

"As far as I'm concerned, they ought to go away and never come back, too," George said, though he concerned himself with the Slavs and Avars more for what they were liable to do to Thessalonica as a whole than for how they were inconveniencing him in particular.

Claudia let out a melodramatic sigh she probably meant to be martyred instead. "All right, George. A couple of days, since you're the one who says so." She swept out, dissatisfied but doing her best to bear up under the disappointment: an actor in a mime troupe couldn't have conveyed the emotion more clearly.

Once she was gone and George was sure she wouldn't make any sudden reappearances, he said, "I admire Claudia—I really do." That drew from the rest of his family the disbelieving exclamations he'd expected. He held up a hand. "No, wait. Hear me out. How many other people in this whole city can you think of who make me *glad* to go up on the wall and fight the Slavs and Avars?"

No one answered him, by which he concluded he'd won his point.

George and Theodore jostled for places near the altar in St. Demetrius' basilica. Up in the women's gallery, Irene and Sophia were probably doing the same thing. They sometimes came home from church with stories of pushing and shoving. Once or twice, they'd come home with bruises on their arms.

Theodore twisted past a plump man. Turning back to his father, he said, "I'll bet Dactylius' wife watches the divine liturgy from wherever she pleases."

"Claudia? I'll bet you're right, son," George answered. Then he stopped and really listened to what Theodore had said. That meant he all but had to kick the plump man out of the way to keep up with his son, but he didn't care. He didn't even snarl back when the plump man used several expressions not often heard in church. Theodore had thought along with him as effortlessly and accurately as Irene sometimes did. The boy—no, the young man now—had had a lifetime of practice doing just that, of course, but his lifetime hadn't been very long, not to George's way of thinking. The shoemaker suddenly felt more like a grandfather than a father.

Deacons and acolytes and altar boys scurried up and down the aisle, keeping it clear so Bishop Eusebius could advance to the altar. A rising hum of conversation said he was on his way. George craned his neck, but taller people around him kept him from seeing the bishop. Rumor declared Eusebius would say something important this morning, which was why George and his family had come to St. Demetrius'. Rumor, frustratingly, was mute about what the bishop would say.

Celebrating the divine liturgy in a church as splendid as any outside Constantinople was of itself enough to leave George convinced the longer walk than usual had been worth making. But when Bishop Eusebius finally got around to his sermon, more jostling and pushing and shoving started up, with everyone trying to get closer to hear him better.

"My children," he began, "the vicious barbarians outside our gates still seek to inter Thessalonica in a sarcophagus of their design." George smiled to himself; Eusebius remained fond of trotting out tombs and coffins. "Thanks to the power of God and of our own holy saint, we have thus far prevented them from achieving their wicked ends."

The bishop went on, "But our hold on safety is not secure. Far from it! The Slavs and Avars, being ignorant of the power of the one true God, have at their beck and call a host of vile powers, whom they have summoned again and again to try to overwhelm us. They have come too close to success."

A murmur of agreement ran through the basilica, much of it, George thought, from militiamen. He added his small part to the murmur, whispering to Theodore, "They certainly have." His son nodded but waved for him to be quiet so they could hear what Eusebius was saying.

George had, to his annoyance, missed a few words. "—so they think we can use our own power, the power of truth and righteousness, only for defense," the bishop declared. "But, my fellow Christians, I tell you they are mistaken. God not only heals His flock, He curses the wolves who seek to pray upon it. Let us beseech Him to curse the Slavs and Avars, who so plainly need to become acquainted with His wrath."

Back in Paul's tavern, George had casually wished a pestilence on the Slavs. He was sure half the people in Thessalonica, likely more, had expressed similar wishes. That was not the sort of thing Bishop Eusebius was talking about. A shiver ran through George. When a bishop formally asked God to bring a curse down on an evildoer's head, the Lord was likely to deliver.

Eusebius said, "God has granted such prayers before," echoing George's thought. The bishop went on, "When Pharaoh of Egypt would not let the children of Israel depart his lands in peace, God visited upon him the Ten Plagues. Did Pharaoh of Egypt oppress the children of Israel more harshly than the khagan of the Avars oppresses the people of Thessalonica? I think not, my children."

Was Eusebius right? George wondered. The Slavs and Avars had ravaged the countryside and killed and wounded a number of militiamen on the walls, but they hadn't enslaved the Thessalonicans or forced them to make bricks without straw. And they'd been here for weeks; they hadn't held the Thessalonicans in bondage for generations. But if the Avars ever broke into Thessalonica, what they would do was liable to be worse than anything Pharaoh had visited upon the Israelites. George gave Eusebius the benefit of the rhetorical doubt.

The bishop went on, "When the wicked Assyrians, who knew God not, besieged Jerusalem, the Lord sent a plague into their camp, so that they had to give over the siege. What He did for Jerusalem, He shall surely be willing to do as well for this famous city of Thessalonica, which, as He has shown, He enfolds under His protecting arm."

Thessalonica did indeed have a name for being a God-guarded city. And it was more than a name, or Rufus would not have been inspired to warn of the Slavs' onset. That thought passed through George's mind in a moment. The one that followed and stayed longer was curiosity about how Benjamin the Jew would have felt, listening to Eusebius going on about miracles worked on behalf of his people, not on behalf of Christians.

If that inconsistency bothered Eusebius, he gave no sign of it, continuing, "What God has done in days gone by, He can surely do again, for, as we have seen with our own eyes, my children, the age of miracles is not yet past. And so let us with full hearts and reverent spirits offer up a prayer to God our Lord that He have mercy upon us now as He did upon the Israelites in days gone by and smite the Slavs and Avars with plagues and pestilences such that they are compelled to withdraw from the environs of this God-protected city, and such that they suffer from the aforesaid sickness as they deserve for the suffering they have inflicted upon us. Let us pray that they are requited as justice demands."

That was a prayer to conjure with, literally and figuratively. George shivered again. He could think of no one who could hope to come through safe based only on justice, with no mercy thrown onto the scales to temper the verdict. How much more would that be true of the

Slavs and Avars than of people at least acquainted with the Christian faith?

Someone stepped on his foot. He looked around. There stood Menas, who, by the smug expression on his fleshy face, hadn't done it by accident. George sent up a prayer of his own, for some undiluted divine justice to come to the nobleman who had taken a dislike to him.

Bishop Eusebius looked up through the beams of the roof to the heavens beyond. "We pray, O Lord our God, that Thou savest Thy city of Thessalonica and Thy Christian people in it" —not a word about the Jews in it, George noted, despite Eusebius' citations of the Lord's aid to the Israelites in days gone by— "by smiting the Slavs and Avars with loathsome plagues and diseases, showing forth Thy power in that way and making the barbarians whom Thou hast accursed withdraw in terror and disorder. Amen."

"Amen," the worshipers in the basilica said solemnly, Menas and George for once agreeing. George hadn't been willing to pray for Menas' getting an arrow in the face when Theodore suggested it. He wondered if he really ought to be praying for dysentery or the bubonic plague to visit the Slavs and Avars in their camps. How was one different from the other?

The only answer he could come up with was that, when he prayed for something dreadful to happen to Menas, he would be praying for his own personal advantage. When he prayed for the Slavs and Avars to take ill, he was praying for the well-being of all the Christians (and even the unmentioned Jews) in Thessalonica. He hoped that was enough of a difference.

A moment later, he remembered that Menas was himself not only a Christian, but one whom God had directly aided through a miracle. A prayer for some misfortune to land on him was much less likely to be acceptable than one for the discomfiture of the pagans beyond the wall.

That made George feel better, but only for a little while. Out beyond the wall, the gods of the Slavic wizards and

Avar priests would find their prayers the more acceptable. How did that leave George on the moral high ground?

He wasn't sure it did. The powers and gods the Slavs and Avars reverenced were both true for them and powerful, as he had seen. His chief hope was that God would prove more powerful. That took things out of the realm of morals altogether, and into the realm of brute force.

Brute force mattered. Anyone who had ever walloped a child for doing wrong knew as much. But . . . George cast a speculative eye Menas' way. Maybe he should have asked God to let the nasty noble stop an arrow with his face. God only knew what Menas had asked Him to do to George.

The Slavs, George reminded himself. *The Avars*. Once they abandoned the siege, life would return to normal. Then he could worry about Menas and his ilk. Till then, the survival of the city had to rank ahead of his own.

Another reason to pray for the plague to visit the barbarians, he thought, and did so.

"The divine liturgy is over. Go in peace," Eusebius said. As George and Theodore filed out of the church, the shoemaker reflected that that farewell offered a strange contrast to the catastrophe the bishop and the congregation had called down on the heads of the warriors besieging Thessalonica.

As soon as they were outside, Menas said, "Do you know what I was praying for, shoemaker?"

"Something unpleasant for me, I don't doubt," George answered, and the noble smiled unpleasantly to show he was right. Shrugging, George said, "If I were you, sir, I'd spend more time praying camels fit through the eye of needles. If they don't, you'll have trouble fitting through the doors to the kingdom of heaven. Now, if you'll excuse me, I have to meet my wife and daughter."

He felt Menas' eyes boring into his back as he walked away. Theodore set a hand on his arm. "That's telling him, Father! That's telling the big-bellied toad he can't mess around with you."

"Oh, I can tell him that," George answered. "I can tell him any number of things. Whether they're true or not . . ." He shook his head. "That's different."

In a strange way, George enjoyed mounting to the stretch of wall near the Litaean Gate that had become almost as familiar to him as his workshop. Up here, at least, he knew who his enemies were and from which direction they were likely to strike.

Rufus and John stood on the wall now. "God bless you, George," John said. "You're as reliable as my bladder after three mugs of wine."

"Thank you so very much." The shoemaker made as if to examine John's neck, then whistled as if astonished. "I see Rufus still hasn't tried strangling you. I wonder why not."

"I'm an old man." Rufus got into the spirit of raillery in a hurry. "This sprout here, he's too quick for me to catch him."

"I love you both." John planted a big, wet kiss on George's cheek, which led both of them to make disgusted noises. "You're as bristly as a boar's back," John exclaimed. "But, like I said, you're here, which means I don't have to be. See you soon, I expect." He strode toward the head of the stairs, whistling one of Lucius and Maria's better tunes—not that that was saying much.

"Who's up with you, George?" Rufus asked.

"Sabbatius," the shoemaker answered.

Rufus made a face. "I'm liable to be up here a while, then. By St. Demetrius, I'm liable to be up here his whole time on the wall, if he's gone and got outside a whole great lot of wine the way he sometimes does."

"I can only think of once when he didn't come up at all," George said, "and if you didn't put the fear of God into him then, he'll never have it."

"If he were in the regular army, I wouldn't have just screamed at him," the veteran answered. "He'd have got himself a beating, or else someone would have taken a sword to his thick neck. You can't do that kind of thing. I should have given him worse than he got as things are. With us under siege here, the militia *are* the regular army. I must be getting soft."

George found that unlikely. He reckoned it unwise to say how unlikely he found it. In lieu of saying any such thing, he pointed out from the wall and asked, "Any sign of the Slavs' coming down with the plague?"

Rufus shook his head. "Not so I've noticed, anyhow. That kind of curse, if God grants it, usually comes later than you wish it would." Motion at the top of the stairs made his eyes flick in that direction. "Speaking of curses coming later than you wish they would—"

Actually, Sabbatius wasn't late, or wasn't very late, anyhow; George had been early. "Hail!" Sabbatius said. He smelled like wine past its best days, but he usually smelled like that.

"A good day to you," George told him. There were people with whom he would sooner have spent his time up on the wall—the faces of almost all the members of his militia company flashed before his eyes—but telling Sabbatius what he thought of him wouldn't solve anything. It wouldn't even mean they could avoid stints together. It would just make them snarl at each other. George saw no point to that.

Rufus didn't leave right away. George sometimes wondered if the militia captain had set up housekeeping on top of the wall. Aside from that, Rufus also had a habit of staying around longer than usual when Sabbatius was coming up for his turn, no doubt to make sure Sabbatius could get through that turn without falling asleep or starting to see things that weren't there.

Except for squinting against sunlight that didn't need to be squinted against, Sabbatius seemed in good enough shape this morning. He walked out to the edge of the wall to see what the Slavs and Avars were up to, which was more than he often did. When he started to laugh, George wondered if he was seeing snakes and aurochs instead.

But he pointed to show the shoemaker and Rufus what he was seeing. "Look!" he exclaimed. "They've got the galloping trots."

Sure enough, a couple of Slavs were squatting just beyond archery range from the wall. A couple of more were running for the trees. One of them, realizing he wasn't going to make it, also suddenly assumed an undignified posture. More and more of the besiegers seemed afflicted.

"Isn't that nice?" Rufus said happily. "One of their cooks must have tossed something bad into the stewpot last night, and now they're paying for it. I've been in armies where things like that happened."

"Look at them," Sabbatius said again, in high glee. "The whole bunch of 'em'll be sick by this afternoon, looks like."

George stared out at the Slavs. "Do they just have bad stomachs," he asked, "or is that the plague Bishop Eusebius asked for?"

"What?" Rufus snorted and started to laugh. "You think God's answering Eusebius' prayer through the Slavs' arseholes? Because . . ." He couldn't go on, but doubled over, grabbing his knees as he guffawed.

"Do miracles have to be fancy?" George said. "You know dysentery. Have you ever seen a whole army come down with the runs as fast as this?"

"A whole army down with the runs? Plenty of times," Rufus answered. "It would happen to the Goths and the Franks all the time. They were too stupid to keep from pissing and shitting in rivers upstream from their camp, and I'll bet the Slavs and Avars are, too. But as fast as this?" He rubbed his chin. "Mm, maybe not. They were fine an hour ago, sure as sure they were."

"They aren't fine now," Sabbatius said. "Look at 'em go!" George wondered if he'd intended the double meaning, or, for that matter, even noticed it. Sabbatius went on, "Shame it's so far into fall, most of the flies are gone. Otherwise, they'd be biting 'em on their bare bums, just like they deserve." His pronouns were tangled, but his meaning seemed clear.

"If we attack now, could they fight back?" George asked Rufus.

"Probably," the veteran answered. "You don't die from the runs, most of the time—you just wish you did. If somebody's really trying to kill you, you'll yank up your trousers fast enough, and that's the truth. I remember back in Italy, there was this Lombard, and he—"

What the incontinent Lombard did or did not do, George never found out. Sabbatius pointed out over the wall again, saying, "Look. Here's that ugly Avar bugger with the funny clothes again, and he's got some Slavs with him who're cursed near as ugly and funny-looking as he is."

Sure enough, the Avar wizard or priest or whatever he was and the Slavic sorcerers who had defeated Bishop Eusebius' charm on the grappling hooks had their heads together now. The way they were seriously discussing things, now and then pointing toward the stricken Slavs, left George sure of what they were talking about. Their manner almost made him laugh; in different vestments, they might have been Eusebius and some priests hashing over a fine theological point.

Rufus said, "You don't see any of the likes of them running for the slit trenches, mind you."

George kicked himself for not having noticed that. What it meant wasn't hard to figure out. "They have some way of turning aside the curse, then."

"I'd say you're likely right," Rufus answered, nodding. "Wish you weren't, but I think you are. Next question we get to have answered is whether they can protect the odds and sods in their army, not just themselves."

"How can they do that?" Sabbatius said indignantly. "This isn't Eusebius cursing them—it's *God* cursing them. You can't keep God from doing what He's going to do to you."

"You can if you've got gods of your own—or maybe

you can, anyhow," George said. "Some of those gods are pretty strong, too, not like the pagan ones we're used to. Those gods, they've been fighting God for hundreds of years, and they're worn out and beaten. The gods of the Slavs and Avars are running up against God for the first time now. They have all their strength and power still, and that means they can put up a good fight, same as the Avars and Slavs do against Roman armies."

He might as well have been talking to one of the paving stones of the walkway. "You can't keep God from doing what He's going to do to you," Sabbatius repeated, as if George hadn't spoken at all.

Out beyond the wall, one of the Slavic wizards might have accused another of heresy. The reaction was about the same as if one Christian priest had accused another of heresy, anyhow: the offended party first struck a dramatic pose, almost as if he were turned into a statue illustrating denial, and then, that failing, punched his accuser in the nose. The two of them rolled around on the ground, hitting and kicking each other till their companions pulled them apart.

After that, their deliberations went more smoothly. The Avar walloped one Slav, but the lesser wizard accepted the rebuke in the same way a junior priest might have accepted chastisement from Bishop Eusebius. The Avar priest stared in toward Thessalonica. From where he stood, he would have been peering more or less in the direction of the basilica of St. Demetrius, though the walls hid it from his gaze.

A small chill ran through George. "He knows where their sickness is coming from," the shoemaker said. "It *is* a curse."

Rufus grunted. "Well, he would, wouldn't he? If it's not a natural sickness, they've got to figure we gave 'em a present. Question is, what can they do about it?"

The Slavic wizards were shouting, not at one another for a change, but at one of their sick comrades. The fellow came over to them with dragging stride. The complaint with which Eusebius' curse had afflicted him had not slain, but, as Rufus had said, he looked unhappy about being alive.

As if they were physicians, the Slavs examined him from head to foot, staring intently at him and running their hands over his body. One of them had him bend over so he could look at the bodily part that was the most immediate source of his difficulty. "Thorough," George remarked. Sabbatius held his nose and cackled like a hen.

One of the Slavs—not the thorough one—made the sick warrior straighten up. Then he slapped him, first on the right cheek, then on the left, then on the right, and then on the left again. He and his colleagues made passes over the sick Slav's head and in front of his belly. Then they had the fellow open his mouth.

"Did you see that?" Rufus said.

George wasn't sure what he'd seen, but answered anyhow: "The little gray cloud that came out of his mouth? It didn't look like the steam you breathe out on a cold day, did it?" He scratched his chin. "I wonder what it was. I wonder what it meant."

"I know!" Sabbatius exclaimed. "I know!" He bounced up and down in his excitement, like a usually slow schoolboy who saw something his smarter classmates had missed. "They're getting rid of the evil eye. My granny used to use a ritual like that. She's from Illyria, where the Slavs have been trouble for years. Maybe they got it there; I don't know."

"The evil eye!" Rufus said. "This isn't the evil eye. It's a curse of God. I was in the basilica when Bishop Eusebius asked us to pray for it. You can't get rid of the curse of God the way you get rid of the evil eye."

"You can't, huh?" Sabbatius pointed. "Tell that to him." And, sure enough, the Slav on whom the wizards had tested their technique seemed much livelier than he had been the moment before. He hugged his belly. George hoped that was torment, but it turned out to be delight.

"It isn't right," Rufus insisted, as if his eyes were lying.

"Maybe it is," George said slowly. "What's the evil eye but a kind of curse? If you can lift one kind of curse with that ritual, why can't you lift another one if you're strong enough? And we've already seen how the Slavs and Avars worry more about their gods than they do about ours. We have priests protecting our people against their curses. Their wizards are protecting them against us."

That was just what the Slavic wizards were doing. As soon as they'd cured their first patient, they began shouting again. Two Slavs came over to them this time. The Avar priest danced in front of them. The Slavic wizards performed the same rite as before, although they slapped the face of only one. Both men, however, rocked back on their heels as if slapped. A small cloud of smoke came from the mouth of each. And both warriors walked away far happier than they had approached.

"Sabbatius," Rufus said with sudden decision, "go run to the church of St. Demetrius and bring the bishop here."

"Me?" Sabbatius' eyes widened. "He won't listen to me."

"Tell him what the Slavs and Avars are doing out there," Rufus answered. "He'll listen, I promise you." His voice roughened. "Now get moving, curse you. I'll hold your place here—don't worry about that."

Sabbatius left. By his expression, he would sooner have stayed and stood around than moved quickly. You argued with Rufus at your peril, though. George said, "I hope he doesn't stop into a wineshop as soon as he's out of sight."

"If he does, I'll kill him." Rufus spoke as matter-of-factly as if he were talking about slicing bread. That made him both more believable and more frightening than if he'd ranted and raved.

Out beyond the wall, the Slavic wizards summoned four of their fellow tribesmen. The Avar priest briefly danced in front of them, capering, George thought, like a fool. Then the Slavs singled out one warrior to be slapped. All four of them might as well have been, though, by the way they staggered. All four of them opened their mouths. Four little clouds of vapor escaped. Four Slavic soldiers suddenly seemed free of their diarrhea.

One of them ran and got his bow and started shooting arrows at the Romans atop the walls of Thessalonica. The Romans shot back. When half a dozen arrows fell close by him, the Slav lost the nerve or anger that had sustained him. He turned and ran away. The Romans kept shooting. One shaft caught him in the left nether cheek. He let out a howl George could hear from the wall.

"Let's see your cursed wizards fix *that* pain in the arse!" Rufus shouted out to him. George laughed out loud.

But the Avar priest and Slavic wizards paid no attention to the wounded warrior. This time, eight hangdog Slavs stumbled up before them. Again, the Avar performed as if he were a dancing bear. One Slavic sorcerer slapped one Slavic soldier. All eight Slavs might have been slapped. They all opened their mouths. They all expelled vapor—and, apparently, their illness with it. They all walked away as healthy men would walk.

"What would be next?" George counted on his fingers. "Two eights make—sixteen."

And sure enough, the Slavs and the Avar cured sixteen soldiers next. Rufus' lips moved: he was probably performing the same mental arithmetic as George. "It'd be—thirty-two—this time, wouldn't it?" he said, and the shoemaker nodded, having just reached the same answer. Rufus went on, "If they keep doubling up like that every time, they'll curse their whole stinking army in a jiffy."

George turned his head. "Here come Sabbatius and Bishop Eusebius," he said.

"Good," Rufus said. "Now I don't have to kill Sabbatius." Again, he sounded as if he would have done it without a second thought.

Robes swirling around him, Bishop Eusebius came out onto the walkway. Sabbatius followed. The bishop did not look out from the wall. Instead, rounding on Rufus, he said, "This man you sent tells me the barbarians have the power to defeat the curse of the Lord. Can such a thing be true?" He did not sound as if he believed it.

Rufus was a man who said what he thought. In his rough Latin, he answered, "No, of course not, Your Excellency. I lied just to get you up here and to get you angry at me. I like having important people angry at me."

Eusebius' eyes flashed. George, who already had an important person angry at him, feared the militia captain's pungent sarcasm had achieved its announced purpose. Before Eusebius vented the anger he plainly felt, George said, "See for yourself, Your Excellency."

Turned from the personal toward the real, Eusebius watched as the Slavic wizards cured thirty-two warriors of the disease with which the bishop's curse had tormented them. When the small, dark clouds of vapor had sprung from the mouths of the sick Slavs, and when the warriors walked away no longer sick, Eusebius made the sign of the cross, as if to say no spiritual power but his own had any business being effective.

"Can you stop them, Your Excellency?" George asked. "Can you bring the curse back to its full strength?"

"I can try. I will try." Eusebius drew himself up to his full height—which would have been more impressive had he been taller. He began to pray: "Lord God, I beseech Thee: do not abandon the folk of Thessalonica to the Slavs and Avars. Punish the barbarians, smite them as they deserve for taking no thought of Thee or of Thy truths, and—"

He went on in that vein. He seemed prepared to go on in that vein for some time. He had, however, attracted the notice of the Slavs and Avars. George thought they would try to disrupt his petition to the Lord with a storm of arrows, such as they had sent his way the last time he'd come up onto the city wall and into their presence.

Instead, the Slavs went on curing their fellow tribesmen while the Avar priest or wizard began what was plainly a petition to his own powers. And, as plainly, those powers were heeding him, as God had heeded Bishop Eusebius. "I am hindered," the bishop said indignantly. "I can sense I am hindered. In the name of Christ, Who cast forth demons, I command this hindrance to cease!"

The Avar priest staggered. He glared toward the wall. Evidently he was no more used to having his power thwarted than was Eusebius. As the bishop had done, he redoubled his efforts, dancing harder than he had before and shouting to his gods so loudly that George had no trouble hearing him across more than a bowshot of ground. Were noise the only criterion for piety, he would have defeated Eusebius.

He did not. The bishop's quiet prayer discomfited him, and also discomfited the Slavic wizards with whom he'd been working. Rather than curing their warriors thirty-two at a time, they had to drop down to batches of eight, sometimes four. But they did keep curing them.

Eusebius groaned. "Who would have expected the pagans to be so strong?" he said, and shook his fist out toward the Avar who was keeping him from keeping the Slavic wizards from curing the Slavic warriors. "Almighty God, invincible God, a plague is but a small thing next to what Thou canst do. I pray Thee, smite them now with thunder and lightning!"

George hoped for a levinbolt from the clear blue sky to crisp the Slavs and Avar. He hoped for one, but did not expect it. Nor was his hope granted. The Avar priest, after all, was the one who controlled the thirteen thunder spirits and the rumblers. Going straight against the Avars' powers, from all he'd seen, did not work.

"Your Excellency," he said, "sometimes it's better to work with what the powers out there can do than to ignore them." He explained how Father Luke had turned the sorcerous storm against the Avar who had created it.

"I have heard this sordid tale already," Eusebius replied in a voice chillier than the weather. "Father Luke is serving a penance for undue familiarity with these demonic powers."

"He saved us all," Rufus exclaimed. "Doesn't that count for more than how he did it?"

" 'For what is a man profited, if he shall gain the whole world, and lose his own soul?' " Eusebius answered, smug as any theologian with a quotation from Scripture handy.

"He didn't do it for gain," George said stubbornly. "He did it to save the city and save the people."

It was useless. He knew it was useless. A layman arguing theology with a theologian was like a militiaman taking on a fully armored regular soldier: a gifted amateur might prevail, but that wasn't the way to bet. Eusebius, fortunately, kept his temper. Indeed, the look he gave George was pitying. That made the shoemaker angry, which was also useless: as well have a gnat angry at a horse.

Out beyond the wall, hampered but not stopped, the Slavic wizards went on curing their countrymen. Bishop Eusebius tried again to break their power to do so, tried again and failed again. That did anger him, as if someone had changed the rules to a game without telling him first. He stomped off in high dudgeon.

"We're not going to win all of them, looks like," Rufus said.

"No," George agreed. "And now it's their turn."

VII

When George went into the church of St. Elias, he found Father Luke alone there, praying in front of the altar. The priest turned and greeted him with a smile. "Welcome, George," he said. "God is always glad to see you here."

"I didn't come here for myself," George answered. "I came here for you, Your Reverence. You've done more than anyone else to keep the Slavs and Avars out of Thessalonica, and what have you got for it? Penance, I hear. It's not right."

Father Luke's smile did not shrink, nor did it seem grudging. "So my superior has ordered: so shall it be. Disobedience is not a sin I want on my conscience. I have too many others."

Men who talked about their many sins commonly had very few: that was George's experience, at any rate. "Nonsense," he said roughly. "You're the holiest man I know."

The priest made a deprecating gesture. "You do not know me so well as you think you do, my friend. And I tell you again, what Bishop Eusebius did, what he commanded me to do, he had every right to do and to command. I speak truly: did I not believe it, I have means of recourse."

George frowned. Within Thessalonica, Eusebius was ecclesiastically supreme along with being *de facto* city prefect. If Father Luke didn't care for anything he did, the priest had no one to whom to appeal—no one in the city, at any rate. The shoemaker's eyes widened. "You would—?"

"Of course I would," Father Luke said. "If I believed the holy Bishop Eusebius had trampled on my rights as a priest, I would not hesitate for an instant before writing to Cyriacus in Constantinople. The patriarch has the authority to bring back under rein any cleric who outrages propriety."

He obviously meant what he said. From that, George concluded he also meant he didn't believe Eusebius' infliction of penance on him was wrong. Maybe that was part of holiness, too. If it was, it was a part George didn't fully understand. "If it hadn't been for what you did," he said, "you wouldn't be arguing with the bishop; you'd be arguing with that Avar out there, the one who brought the storm down on the city."

"That is possible," Father Luke admitted. "And yet—" He quoted the same verse from the Book of Matthew that Bishop Eusebius had used.

"What does it profit you to die," George returned, "when you have a weapon in your hand that might let you live?" He would have given up against Bishop Eusebius. The priest, though, took argument as a sport, not a personal affront.

"If using that weapon to save your body damns your soul to all eternity, dying might well be the better course to take," Father Luke said.

"If I saved myself by worshiping Satan and working abominations, then you might be right," George said. "But that's not what you did. That's not anything like what you did."

"The difference is of degree, not of kind," Father Luke

said. "I follow the Son, and thought I stayed within the limits of what is permissible for Christian men. Bishop Eusebius thought otherwise. I willingly accept his judgment."

"But—" George gave up. Had Father Luke felt resentment, the shoemaker might have fanned it with resentment of his own. Against acceptance he had no power, and he knew it. "Your Reverence, so long as you're content—"

"I am," the priest assured him. He smiled again. "I do thank you for your concern. You are not the first to have expressed it; I told the others what I am telling you now." From smile, he went to outright laughter. "Some of them were harder to dissuade than you. One suggested something I could not in good conscience even hear, though I do not think he meant it seriously."

George had a sudden vivid vision of Rufus proposing that Eusebius be flung off the top of the wall into a dungheap. He didn't ask who; he didn't ask what. But he would have bet his guess was near the truth.

"Can I do anything else for you today, George?" Father Luke asked.

"No," the shoemaker said. He checked himself. "No. Wait. Yes. Maybe you can. What do you know about Constantine, the son of Leo the potter? What do you think of him?"

"Constantine?" Father Luke's eyes sparkled. "Are you thinking of a match?"

"I'm trying to find out if I should be thinking of a match," George said.

"Ah." The priest nodded. "You are a prudent man—except when you go butting into the affairs of the clergy." George's ears heated. Thoughtfully, Father Luke went on, "He's a big, strapping lad, isn't he? Truth to tell, past that I can't think of anything remarkable about him, for good or ill. He seems a decent enough young man, whatever that may be worth to you."

That's not good enough for Sophia, was George's first

thought. On the other hand, he knew himself well enough to understand he wouldn't have reckoned the city prefect's son good enough for his daughter, not if the lad were also handsome and saintly in the bargain. He let out a rueful chuckle. "Thanks, Your Reverence. I'll do some looking and some more asking of my own, then. No hurry with this, God be praised, or I don't think so, anyhow."

"All right, George," the priest said. "I'm sure you'll do very well, whatever choice you and Irene make for Sophia."

Irene would be looking and asking on her own, too. Irene, very likely, had already started doing just that. What she thought of Constantine, and of Leo, and of Leo's wife (whose name, at the moment, escaped George), would carry enormous weight. If George approved and she didn't, the marriage would not even be broached. If she approved and George didn't . . . he didn't know what would happen then, in spite of being in theory unquestioned head of the household. He was glad they thought alike most of the time.

Nodding to Father Luke, he left the church and headed back toward his shop. And there, heading the other way, his arms full of straw, came Constantine the son of Leo. He was indeed a strapping lad, with shoulders wider than George's, which was saying something. His walk was something less than graceful, but George's would have been, too, had he borne a like burden.

Constantine nodded at George, politely enough. He was nothing special to look at (so the shoemaker thought, anyhow; his daughter evidently had a different opinion), and pimples splashed his cheeks and chin. George nodded to him in return. He looked back over his shoulder at Constantine. To his surprise, the potter's son was looking back at him, too. Each of them tried to pretend he'd done no such thing.

Why was Constantine looking over his shoulder? The likeliest explanation occurring to George was that he'd noticed Sophia and wanted some notion of what her father was like. That was unsettling. So was the idea that what some youthful lout thought of him might be important.

When George returned to the shop, he and Irene went out to inspect the fennel again. He caught the glance that went from Sophia to Theodore, but did his best to seem as if he hadn't. Once he and Irene were out among the herbs, he told her of what little Father Luke had had to say about Constantine.

"Yes, that sounds about like what I've heard," she answered with a brisk nod.

"Does it?" George said. "And where have you heard all this?"

"Why, from Zoe the weaver's wife, and from Julia—you know, the widow who sells fish because her husband sold fish—and even from Claudia, though she hasn't the slightest idea why I was interested, and from—" Plainly, Irene was ready to go on for some time.

George, however, was not ready to let her. He interrupted with a cough. "If you've heard all this, dear," he said, bearing down a little on the endearment, "why haven't I heard any of it? From you, I mean."

"Oh, you would have," she said blithely. "In due time, you would have. Once I knew enough to make up my mind."

"Once you knew enough to make up *my* mind," George returned. Irene stuck out her tongue at him. He did not take that for a ringing denial. "Well, I gather he's not so good, but he's certainly not so bad, either. What does that leave us? To make up our own minds, I suppose."

"We would have anyway," his wife said. "The best thing we can do now is wait. She can't even think of marrying till after the siege is over, and she doesn't have to think of it even then. She's a long way from being an old maid—fifteen is nothing to worry about. She may decide there are other fish in the sea before we need to do anything about Constantine."

"So she may," George said. "So there are. Some of them have shells and claws. Some of them have lots of arms all covered with suckers."

"My dear, any boy Constantine's age seems to have lots of arms covered with suckers." Irene cocked her head to one side. "Or isn't that what you meant?"

"By now, believe me, it's hard to tell," George said. They both laughed, and went back into the workshop laughing still. Sophia and Theodore eyed them suspiciously, sure they were up to something. Since they were, they tried all the harder to pretend they weren't.

"Do you know," George said to Dactylius as they paced along the wall, bows in hand, quivers on their backs, "I used to come up here when the weather was fine, just for a promenade: take a little walk, you know, and get out of the city stink for a while if the wind was blowing in the right direction. I'm not going to do that anymore. I've seen altogether too much of this awl."

"If you weren't a shoemaker, that would make even less sense than it really does," Dactylius answered. "As things are, it leaves my ears ringing."

George took two or three steps before realizing his friend had topped him, a measure of how badly he'd been topped. He sent Dactylius a reproachful look. "John and I are the ones who make jokes like that."

"Contagious as the—" Dactylius had probably been about to say *plague*, but remembered George had lost family from it. "—the grippe," he finished.

"Can't trust anybody anymore," George said, mock-serious. Dactylius smiled in something like triumph.

The little jeweler pointed out toward the tent where the Avar priest or wizard made his home, and to the smaller ones nearby that belonged to the Slavic wizards. "I wish they hadn't chosen to camp near the Litaean Gate," he said. "If they were somewhere else, we wouldn't be able to watch them getting ready to work all their magic."

"Oh, I don't know," George said. "For better or worse, I want to know what's going on as soon as I can. It wouldn't stop happening if we didn't find out about it till it came down on us like a building falling over."

"I suppose not," Dactylius said, "but if I didn't see them at their sorceries, I wouldn't worry about them so much."

"Of course you would," George said, having known his friend for many years. "You'd just be shying at shadows, not at anything real."

Dactylius sighed. He wasn't ignorant of his own faults; like most mortals, he had trouble doing anything about them. "You're probably right," he said.

"Besides" —George sent Dactylius a sidelong look— "sometimes you cause the trouble you complain about afterwards. If you hadn't bounced an arrow off that Avar's corselet, that priest of theirs wouldn't have tried to drown the city with a thunderstorm."

"In the end, though, it showed the power of God," Dactylius said, and George supposed that was true. But it had also shown the strength of the powers upon which the Avar had called. Dactylius continued in musing tones: "I wonder what they'll try next."

"No way to tell." George didn't want the jeweler working himself up into a swivet over the incalculable. But then, being who *he* was, the shoemaker tried to figure out what he'd just said could not be figured out. "The storm had spirits of the air in it, and maybe spirits of water, too. That water-demigod was certainly one of those. And when the Avar tried to take the bishop's blessing off the grappling hooks, the earth shook, even if it didn't shake very hard."

"Earth and air," Dactylius said, musing still. "Water and— It'll be something to do with fire, I'd bet."

"I think you're right," George answered. "I hope you're wrong." He knew he was the one who would start worrying, start shying at shadows, now. Fire was a constant dread in every city, Thessalonica no less than others. Once it started spreading, you could do so little to put it out.

"What can we do?" Dactylius whispered, echoing his thoughts.

"I don't know." George pointed toward the Avar priest's tent. "Keeping an eye on what he's up to strikes me as a good idea."

"Well, of course it does," Dactylius exclaimed, and then had the good grace to turn red. "You have me this time, don't you, George? A little while ago, I said I wished that tent was somewhere else."

"That's true." George bowed to Dactylius, as he might have done before the city prefect. His friend looked puzzled. He explained: "You also just admitted you were wrong. That doesn't happen every day, or every month, either."

"Oh." Dactylius looked abashed. He started to say something more, chewed on it, and shut his mouth tight instead. George thought he could guess what his friend hadn't said: that, living with Claudia, he'd had practice confessing he was wrong, whether he was or not. George would not have chosen to live with Claudia. But then, Dactylius hadn't exactly chosen to live with her, either. His parents had done it for him—or rather, to him.

One of the Slavic wizards came out of his tent and looked toward Thessalonica. His shoulders moved up and down: not a shrug, George thought, more likely a sigh. Seen by himself, the Slav, like the couple of his compatriots whom George had encountered in the woods, didn't seem threatening. When you put him together with all his compatriots, though . . .

Dactylius said, "He looks like he's sick of the whole business."

"He does, doesn't he?" George said. "Well, I'm sick of the whole business, too, but I'm sticking with it. I suppose he will, too, worse luck for us." He described his conceit of a moment before for his friend, then added, "You take me by myself and I'm not what you'd call dangerous, either. But think of me as one part of the Roman Empire and I look different."

Dactylius studied him carefully. "No, you don't."

"You're not making this easy," George said, clucking. "Now if you think of the whole massed weight of the Empire—" As he spoke, he waited for Dactylius, who seemed in a whimsical mood this morning, to crack a joke about the weight of the Empire's making the wall fall down. But, since he didn't complete his sentence, Dactylius never got the chance. Instead, George pointed out toward the wizard. "Hello. He's got company."

The other Slavic wizards were coming out of their tents, too, and studying Thessalonica with the same intent look the first one had given the city. And here came the Avar priest or wizard in his costume of furs and leather and fringes. As always, George shivered when he saw him. The Avar carried a lot of spiritual force. Had he been born a Christian and a Roman rather than a barbarous pagan, he might well have become a bishop.

Pointing again, this time toward the Avar, George said, "Can you imagine him in Eusebius' vestments?"

Dactylius gaped, then made a noise half giggle, half squeak. "Easily," he said.

And Eusebius, born a barbarian, might have been out there in furs and leather and fringes, trying to rouse his powers to break into Thessalonica and overcome the God Who held them at bay. He wondered what he himself would have been, had his life begun among the Slavs or Avars rather than the Romans. Probably not a shoemaker; from what he'd seen, the enemy had no one who made shoes for everyone else, each man being his own shoemaker and cobbler. George shrugged. He could have found something else to do.

"What are they doing?" Dactylius asked, a question of more immediate import.

"I don't know," George said. "If I had to guess, though, I'd say it's nothing we're going to like very much."

The Slavs and the Avars had huddled together like small boys before a mime show they'd thought up. That George recognized: they wanted everything right. When they broke apart, the Avar priest shouted something that was, as usual, unintelligible from the wall. Also as usual, it got prompt results. Several Slavs with the harassed look of slaves began building a great fire from so much wood and brush that George, who'd often been chilly because Thessalonica lacked fuel, grew warm with angry jealousy.

One of the slaves thrust a torch into the brush. The fire caught swiftly. Flames leaped higher than a man. The Slavic wizards drew close to the blaze, whether for warmth or for the sake of ritual George could not tell. Staring out at the fire, Dactylius sighed longingly.

Another Slav led a billy goat up close to the fire, tethering the beast to a stake driven into the ground. The Avar priest walked all around the goat, raising his hands and chanting in a scale that had little to do with any sort of music George had heard before.

When the Avar got round behind the goat, he drew a knife from his belt; firelight flashed off the edge of the blade. With one swift motion, he reached down and castrated the goat. Blood spurted. The animal gave a bleat of startled agony. A moment later, the Slavic wizards took up the strange chant the Avar had been using.

He, after holding the goat's testicles aloft as if in triumph, flung them into the heart of the fire. It flared up for a moment in a blaze more nearly white than honest red-gold. The Avar priest and his Slavic acolytes—for so they seemed to George to be—began a new and different chant, one the shoemaker thought might be a name: "Odkan Galakan Eke! Odkan Galakan Eke!" They called the name or phrase over and over again, till it echoed in George's mind.

Dactylius crossed himself. "The goat!" he said. "Look at the goat."

Watching the Avar and the Slavs, George had almost forgotten the poor unfortunate animal, whose role in the ceremony he had assumed to be over. Now he found he was mistaken. "Holy Virgin Mother of God," he whispered, and also made the sign of the cross.

It had no effect. The woman now riding on the goat (she might have been Odkan Galakan Eke; George thought of her thus, rightly or wrongly he did not know), though plainly supernatural, was as plainly not the Virgin Mother of God. Half again the size of a man, she and her clothing seemed made all from fire.

Her tunic might at first glance have been woven of crimson silk, but was in fact flames. Her face was the color of melted butter, but glowed like the fire that would have melted it. Her eyes . . . George looked away from her eyes. Something more than mere fire blazed there, the mother substance from which all fire sprang. Men were not meant to see such directly.

"What are they going to do?" Dactylius said, staring at the beautiful and terrible being who rode the goat without consuming it.

"I don't know," George answered with a small shudder. Talking about the Slavs' and Avars' using fire against Thessalonica was one thing. Having them actually go and do it was something else, something daunting. "I wish Father Luke were up here with us."

"I was thinking of Bishop Eusebius, but you're right," Dactylius said.

When the fire goddess appeared atop the castrated goat, the Slavic wizards drew back from her in what looked to George like awe and wonder. That made the shoemaker think they'd never seen her before, and that, even though they'd helped evoke her, she was likelier to be an Avar power than one of their own. The way the Avar priest shouted at them, as if drawing them back to a task they'd forgotten but still needed to finish, strengthened that impression.

They began a new chant, this one low and rumbling, altogether different from that which had summoned Odkan Galakan Eke. On her bleeding mount, the fire goddess stirred restlessly. Dactylius whispered, "I don't think she likes what they're doing."

"I don't think so, either." George whispered, too, not wanting to draw the notice of that beautiful, flaming, unearthly creature in any way. He added, "Question is, will we like it any better?"

Chanting still, the Slavic wizards picked up swords and

spears and thrust them into the fire that had summoned Odkan Galakan Eke. Despite the fierce blaze, the wooden spearshafts did not catch. The fire goddess writhed again. "She *doesn't* like that," Dactylius insisted.

Had George been a fire goddess, he wouldn't have liked it, either. The Slavic wizards seemed to be trying to wound the bonfire, not to sustain it. One of them took a spear out of the flames, another a sword. Each pointed his weapon at Thessalonica. All the wizards, and the Avar who led them, cried out together.

The outcry looked to have mollified Odkan Galakan Eke. She stretched out a long, shining arm toward Thessalonica, as if she too were holding a weapon in it. But the fire goddess did not hold a weapon; she *was* a weapon. For a moment, her voice joined with those of the Avar and the Slavs. All the hair on the back of George's neck rose in alarm. The Avar had power, wielded power: George had been forced to acknowledge as much. But Odkan Galakan Eke *was* power, power raw and terrifying.

And then, suddenly, she was gone. The bonfire, suddenly, was but a bonfire. The billy goat, which had been awed into silence while the fire goddess rode him, began to bawl once more, though his bawling would never restore what the Avar had taken from him.

Dactylius and George looked at each other. "Did they fail?" Dactylius asked. "Did they offend her so she fled?"

"Not to look at them, they didn't," George answered, pointing out at the Avar and the Slavs, who did indeed look pleased at what they had wrought. Why they were pleased, George did not understand. As far as he could see, they hadn't changed anything, as they had done with the water-demigod and, more subtly, with the magic aimed against the blessed grappling hooks.

From further north along the wall, one of the Romans called to another: "Say, Bonosus, let me light a torch at your fire, will you? Ours went out some way. Don't know how, but . . ." The voice trailed away. George would have bet the speaker was shrugging a hapless shrug.

After a brief silence, another militiaman, presumably Bonosus, answered, "I would if I could, Julius, but ours is out, too. Funny, ain't it?"

"They were careless," George said with more than a hint of smugness. "It's a good thing we've kept our fire—" He glanced toward the fire at which he and Dactylius had been in the habit of warming their hands. He did not say *going*, as he'd intended, for the fire wasn't going anymore.

"How did that happen?" Dactylius asked, realizing the same thing at the same time.

"Don't know," George answered. "It hasn't rained, and you wouldn't think a gust of wind could . . ."

His voice trailed off again. Dactylius' eyes got big and round. "You don't think—?" he began.

He and George both seemed to be speaking in half-sentences. The shoemaker said, "What I think is, the Avars and the Slavs and their fire goddess didn't fail at all. I think they did just what they intended to do, and I think" —he took a deep breath— "I think every fire in Thessalonica may be out right now."

"That's—that's terrible, if you're right," Dactylius exclaimed. "How will people get any work done? Smiths, potters, jewelers too . . ." He stopped, looking even more appalled than he had before. "How will people cook their food? Christ and the saints, how will people stay warm?"

"I don't know the answers to any of those questions," George said. "I don't know if any of those questions have answers." *They may all have the same answer: people won't*, he thought.

The growing commotion down in the city suggested he and Dactylius had been right. People came running out onto the streets: looking in rather than out, George watched them pointing and gesticulating. He couldn't hear what they were saying; only a confused Babel of Greek and Latin came to his ears.

Dactylius tried to make the best of the Avars' successful magic: "They can't have put out the fires in the churches.

Those are holy, and—" He cut himself off again, looking foolish.

"Turning into a Persian fire-worshiper, are you?" George asked, spelling out the reason for his friend's confusion. He wondered if any Persians were in the city. Merchants from the distant eastern land did come here every so often when their kingdom was at peace with the Roman Empire, as it had been these past five years. But he did not recall any of them being around now. *Too bad*, he thought. He would have liked to take advantage of their faith, false though he reckoned it.

And then he spied, along with the townsfolk of Thessalonica, some tonsured priests. They looked as bewildered and bereft as anyone else. Dactylius saw that, too, and groaned. "Look at them! They must be without fire, too."

"I don't know about *must* be, but it's the way to bet," George agreed.

"How will we bake our bread?" Dactylius demanded.

George didn't know the answer to that, either. And then, all at once, he did, or he thought he did. "Remember when the water-demigod showed up in all the cisterns in Thessalonica at the same time?" he said.

"I'm not likely to forget it," Dactylius replied with feeling.

"No, I suppose not," George said. "But the point is, the water-demigod didn't really show up in *all* the cisterns. There was one it kept clear of."

"I didn't know that," Dactylius said. "Which one was it?"

"The one in the Jews' quarter," George answered. "As soon as our shift up here ends, that's where I'm going to go to see if I can't get fire that's proof against the Slavs' magic. I don't know whether I can, mind you, but I think it's worth a try."

"If you do, you'll be like—" Dactylius' face furrowed with concentration. "What was the name of the fellow who stole fire from the pagan gods?"

"Prometheus," George said. A priest might not have approved of how quickly he brought out the name, but knowing the old stories and believing them were two different things. So he told himself, at any rate.

John and Sabbatius came up a little later to replace their fellow militiamen. When George explained what he intended to do, John shook his head. "Paul won't be happy with you," he said.

"Why is that?" George asked in honest puzzlement.

"Think for yourself—don't make me do the work. With the way he cooks, having all the fires in town go out is the best thing that could happen to his place," the tavern comic said.

"I'll tell Paul you said so," George replied, which made Sabbatius laugh nastily. John laughed, too; unlike his comrade, he could tell George was kidding.

Dactylius trailing along behind him, George descended from the wall. Before heading to the Jews' district, the shoemaker stopped in St. Elias' church. If any Christian man was likely to have a fire going, he thought Father Luke the one. But the church proved as dark and chilly as the rest of Thessalonica. Shaking his head at the strength of the barbarians' magic, George went on down toward the Jewish quarter.

"What do we do if the Jews have no fire, either?" Dactylius asked.

"Pray that Father Luke or Bishop Eusebius can figure out how to get some," the shoemaker said. "The priest is pious enough for God to hear him, and the bishop is tricky enough for anything at all." If Eusebius wanted fire badly enough, he was liable to call on Prometheus and then convince his congregants the Titan had been a Christian saint.

At first, the Jewish quarter seemed no different from the rest of Thessalonica. As many people were on the streets, and they seemed as excited as their Christian fellows. But that was simply how the Jews lived their everyday lives. Listening to them, George realized they were exclaiming and gesticulating over the ordinary things of life, not over the morning's prodigy. He took that for a hopeful sign.

"Just where are you going?" Dactylius asked. "If you walk into the shop of some Jew you've never seen, he's more likely to set his dog on you than to give you fire."

"If he has any fire to give, that is," George said. "But I'm not going to walk into the shop of some Jew I've never seen. I'm going to walk into the shop of a Jew I've been doing business with for years."

Sudden understanding lit Dactylius' face. "That bronzesmith friend of yours, do you mean? The one who was also making arrowheads?"

"Benjamin's not my friend, not exactly," George answered; the regret he felt at that surprised him. He went on, "I don't think he has any friends who aren't Jews. But he won't turn me away if he can help. I don't think he'll turn me away, anyhow. We're about to find out." He led Dactylius into Benjamin's shop.

The Jew looked up from the arrowhead he was sharpening; by his posture, he might not have moved since George last saw him. "I rejoice to see you, George," he said in polite Greek. "And who is your friend?" When George had introduced Dactylius, Benjamin nodded to the little jeweler. "Yes, I know of you. Your work has a good name. From the couple of pieces of it I have seen, it deserves such a name."

"For this I thank you." Dactylius sounded more constrained than he usually did. He was probably hoping—and likely to be hoping in vain—Claudia's loud opinions about Jews had never reached the bronzeworker's ears.

If they had, Benjamin made no mention of them. He said, "How can my poor shop help the two of you?"

George looked around. He saw no lamps burning. He saw no lamps that looked as if they'd recently gone out, either. "Have you fire?" he asked.

Benjamin's eyebrows rose. "Have I *fire*?" he said, as if ensuring he'd heard correctly. "Not on my person."

He ran his hands up and down his wool tunic in what was as near an approach to a joke as George had ever heard from him. When his visitors neither laughed nor even smiled, he grew serious himself. "You ask as if this is a matter of no small importance. I shall see for myself." Without another word, he ducked into the back room.

When he returned a moment later, he was carrying a lamp whose smoky wick showed he had just lighted it. "Thank God!" Dactylius exclaimed, and then, turning to George, "You were right all along."

"It is a lamp," Benjamin said, setting it down on his worktable. "Having a lamp is good, yes, but so good?"

"Right now, yes," George told him, and explained the magic the Slavs and Avars had worked against fire in Thessalonica.

Benjamin listened till he was through, then said, "If you need this fire, take it. I give it to you. God protects our fires. Hundreds of years ago, He made a flask of pure oil, enough for only one day, burn for eight until more could be brought. This was after we Jews had driven the Macedonians out of Jerusalem, you understand."

George had never heard of the event that seemed near as yesterday to the Jew. That didn't matter. What mattered was the fire. He'd always taken fire for granted, except when he worried about its getting out of control. Now he realized—he had been forcibly made to realize—how precious it was.

Bowing a little, Benjamin handed him the lamp. "Carry it back to your own home. Use it as you need it." When he saw George's hand going to his beltpouch, the Jew shook his head. "No need for that. If I give a starving man food, do I ask him for payment? Take it, I say."

"God bless you," George answered, to which the Jew bowed again.

Carrying the lamp as carefully as he had held Theodore when his firstborn was laid in his arms, George left the bronzeworker's shop. The little flame burning at the end of the wick flickered in the breeze outside, but did not go out. Dactylius said, "I think that will keep burning till you get back to your home."

"I think you're right," George said. "God wouldn't have given it to us only to snatch it away again." Dactylius nodded. George listened to himself in some surprise. Who was he, to expound on what God would or wouldn't do? He pursed his lips thoughtfully. Whoever he was, he had fire when the rest of Thessalonica—save its Jews—did without.

People saw he had fire, too, and came running up with candles and lamps and sometimes just twigs, to get some of their own from him. Remembering what Benjamin had said, he gave it to them and took nothing in return, even when they tried to pay him.

"You could be rich by the time you get back," Dactylius said.

"Wouldn't be worth it," George answered. "And do you know what? If I took money, what do you bet the next little breeze would blow out the flame here? Maybe it would blow out all the flames."

"Maybe it would." Dactylius' voice went soft with wonder.

From around a corner, someone with a big, deep voice shouted, "Fire! I need fire. I'll pay five solidi to anybody with fire!"

"I have fire," George called. "I'll give it to you for nothing."

"What?" The owner of the voice came trotting into sight. George stared with no small dismay at Menas. The noble looked ready to take fire by force if he could get it no other way: he had a candle in his left hand and a long-handled war hammer, its iron head chased with shining silver, a weapon intended more for show than for use, in his right. Seeing George, Menas looked as unhappy as the shoemaker. "You? *You* have fire? What are *you* doing with fire?" By the way he spoke, he didn't think the shoemaker deserved to have fire even on an ordinary day.

"I have it, that's all." George thrust the lamp at the noble. "Take what you need. I don't want your money."

Menas' gaze looked burning enough to start a fire by itself. "Think yourself above me, do you? Think you're too good for me, eh?" People were staring at him and George. He went on, "Don't want your hands to touch my filthy money, is that it?" The diatribe, George noticed, did not keep him from lighting the candle he clutched from the lamp's flame.

George said, "I haven't taken money from anyone else, either."

"Likely tell," Menas said. "Well, you can vaunt and preen and strut now, but the day will come when you'll wish you hadn't." Off he went, the hammer stuffed into his belt so he could shield from the wind with his hand the fire he'd got.

Looking after him, George let out a long sigh. "I could save his life, and he'd curse me for doing it."

"A man like that, he means trouble," Dactylius said, as a good many others had before him.

"Really? I never would have noticed," George said. The hurt look in Dactylius' large brown eyes made him feel as if he'd kicked a puppy. Sighing again, he said, "I'm sorry. It's not your fault I've fallen foul of him. As far as I can see, it's not my fault, either, but it takes only one to start a quarrel."

When they got to the jeweler's house and shop, Dactylius ran inside. He came back with a lamp, pursued by Claudia's raucous questions. Ignoring those, he started the lamp at the one George was carrying. Once the flame caught, he carried it inside. Claudia, for a wonder, fell silent.

George carried Benjamin's lamp into his own workshop. His wife and children were all wearing two or three tunics, with woolen mantles or blankets draped over their shoulders. Instead of falling silent as Claudia had done, they all started talking at once. George had to try several times before he could tell them the whole story.

"That Jew came in handy," Theodore said, speaking of Benjamin as he might have of an awl or a punch.

"Twice now, magic from outside the city hasn't bitten

on the Jews when it hit everyone else," George observed. "I wonder if God is trying to tell us something."

"Are you going to stop eating pork and have them do" —Theodore glanced at his mother and sister and chose his words carefully— "what they do to a man?"

The mere thought of being circumcised made George wince and want to cover himself with his hands. "Not likely," he said, to his son's evident relief. He went on, "But I don't think I'm going to sneer at them the way I sometimes have, either."

"Never mind the Jews now, for heaven's sake," Irene said with brisk feminine pragmatism. "Let's get the braziers lighted and put a little heat back into this place. And while we're at it, let's thank God for not letting the Slavs and Avars freeze us out of our homes, no matter how He chose to do that."

"Amen," George said with no hesitation at all.

"If you were the khagan of the Avars," Paul said in musing tones, "and your wizards kept promising that you'd be able to get into Thessalonica and then not delivering, what would you do?"

"I wouldn't be very happy," George admitted, looking out from the wall toward the camp of the Slavs and Avars. "But then, I don't even know whether the khagan is here right now. There's a lot of fighting south of the Danube these days."

"That's not the point," the taverner said. "You don't have anybody who works for you, do you? Besides your family, I mean?—that's different. If you have somebody who's not doing the job you pay him to do, you fling him out the door and you get somebody else."

"I don't think the khagan would fling his wizards out the door," George said. "He might see how well they do without their heads, though—barbarian princes are supposed to do things like that." He paused to think for a moment. "Been a few Roman Emperors like that, too, haven't there?"

"So they say." Paul's shrug expressed the limits of both his interest and his knowledge of the subject. "But he'll do *something* new, because what he's been trying hasn't worked."

Such conversations went on every hour of every day up on the wall, and in the taverns, and throughout Thessalonica—being besieged, the people of the city, and most of all the militiamen defending it, spent a lot of ingenuity wondering and arguing about what the besiegers would try next. Among so many speculations, some, by the nature of things, had to be correct.

George understood that—by his own nature, he understood it better than most (and he'd been right himself, once or twice). Understanding didn't keep him from boasting afterwards when, less than an hour after he said, "Well, they've tried magic, and that hasn't worked, and they've tried rams, and those haven't worked, and they've tried tortoises, and those haven't worked, either, so they'll likely get around to using the catapults they made when they started the siege," the Slavs and Avars did exactly as he'd foretold.

Someone out there beyond the wall blew a raucous horn. The noise, which bore no closer resemblance to music than a vulture to a peacock, spurred the barbarian soldiers into action. Avars rode around on horseback, screaming at the much more numerous Slavs. Some of the Slavs picked up their bows and started shooting at the militiamen on the wall. Others picked up chunks of stone and loaded them into the catapults, which, kicking like mules, flung them not only at the militiamen but also at the walls themselves.

One of those stones, luckily or cleverly aimed, hit a man less than fifty feet from George. Red sprayed out of the fellow. He dropped to the walkway, dead, without a word, without a sound, without a twitch. Having seen how hard human beings were to kill, let alone to kill cleanly, George viewed that with no small astonishment.

More stones, of course, slammed into the wall than into

the people on top of it. To George's frightened eyes, a lot of them looked big as islands. Every time one struck, the wall shivered under his feet, as if in pain. The shiverings ran together into what felt like an earthquake that would not stop. "What can we do?" Paul shouted in between the smashing of stone missiles on stone fortifications.

"I don't know," George answered helplessly. "Those catapults are out past arrow range."

Thessalonica's walls bore catapults of their own. After a bit of hesitation, the militiamen began shooting back at the ones the Slavs and Avars had built. They did not fling rocks at the foe, but jars of pitch and naphtha the men lighted as they launched them. When one of those jars hit the ground, it smashed and spilled fire over ten or fifteen feet.

But few of the enemy's catapults burned. They were covered in hides to keep flame from sticking to them. Not even the inflammable mix the Romans hurled was enough to make the hides catch fire. Only when the hellbrew splashed onto a wooden casting-arm would the engine of which it formed a part begin to blaze.

A big stone stuck about ten feet below where George was standing. The wall shuddered. He shuddered, too. How many impacts like that would it take till the wall no longer shuddered but collapsed?

Heaped here and there along the wall, along with stones for hurling down on the foe (not enough stones, not after the assault with the tortoises) and cauldrons for heating water, lay mats and horse blankets roughly basted together: padding to protect the gray stone fortifications from the worst the stones might do. George and Paul, along with many other militiamen on the works, began lowering the mats and blankets, draping them over the outside of the wall, and weighting them in place with some of the stones they would otherwise have dropped on the Slavs' heads.

They quickly discovered there was more wall than matting with which to cover it. They also discovered that covering it did only so much good, as the cloth they were using could not absorb all the force from the rocks the enemy's catapults threw. But, as George said, "Now we've done what we can do. The rest is up to God."

"And to the Slavs and Avars," Paul added, to which the shoemaker had to nod, feeling more helpless than he had before the taverner spoke.

The bombardment went on for what seemed like forever but could not have been more than a couple of hours. Men on the wall were hurt. Some of them were killed. The wall itself took a fearful pounding: certainly a pounding that made George fearful. Here and there, stones shattered.

But, in the end, the Roman engineers and masons who'd designed and built the wall were vindicated. It did not collapse, as had in his alarmed imagination seemed likely. That must have seemed likely to the Slavs, too, for their archers kept drawing ever nearer, to rush into the city if the catapults forced a breach.

When the crews manning those catapults stopped shooting—perhaps because they ran out of stones, perhaps merely because they saw they were doing no good—George and Paul the tavern-keeper solemnly clasped hands. "First mug of wine is free if you come to my place tonight," Paul said, which struck George as a fitting enough tribute to what they'd been through together.

The aftermath put him in mind of nothing so much as what happened after a bad storm: he and his comrades on the wall looked around exclaiming at the damage that had been done and sharing one common refrain: "It could have been worse." The disappointed bearing of the Slavs out beyond the wall gave mute testimony to how bad it could have been. They kept right on shooting arrows after the catapults left off trying to smash down the fortifications.

Paul shot back at the Slavs. "As long as they're just sending arrows our way, I'm not going to worry," he said.

"Neither will I," George agreed. "They won't get anywhere that way."

They looked at each other. "We never would have talked like this before the siege started," Paul said.

"I sure wouldn't," George replied, "never in my life. I remember what it felt like the first time a Slav shot at me. No one had ever done that before. But now—you're right, arrows aren't worth getting excited about."

Rufus, for once, had not been up on the wall when trouble started. He got there a little while after the catapults had stopped flinging stones at the city. "Busy time you had, looks like," he said, with which George could hardly disagree. The veteran peered down at the stones at the base of the wall. He let out a loud whistle. "Looks like they cut the tips off some mountains and tossed 'em this way," he remarked.

"That's what it felt like," George said, and Paul nodded.

"I believe it," Rufus said. "I've been bombarded. It's not what I'd care to do for fun, thank you very much." He raised his voice so the militiamen along a big stretch of Thessalonica's wall could hear him: "Let's get this matting pulled up and stacked again. We may need it again, you know."

As George hauled the lengths of thick cloth back over the wall, he said, "I didn't see it helped very much."

"It doesn't help very much," Rufus agreed. "But it does help some. You can't know beforehand whether putting it down or not putting it down will make the difference between a wall that stays up and one that doesn't, for no one hit makes a wall fall down. Since you can't say beforehand, you don't take the chance. You didn't take the chance, and you were right."

George knew Rufus wasn't praising him personally, but praise from the veteran, even if aimed at all the defenders, felt good. Raising an eyebrow, the shoemaker asked, "Where were you, anyway? Hardly seemed like a proper fight without you running around up here screaming at us."

"You'll pay for that," Rufus said, though he didn't sound angry. "Where was I?" He peered this way and that. "I'll tell you and Paul, but I don't want it all over the city. I was closeted with Bishop Eusebius, is where I was. We're trying to figure out how we're doing."

"All right, that makes sense," George said, and then, as Rufus didn't say anything more, "Well, how *are* we doing?"

"Fair," the veteran answered. "I'd say fair would be a . . . fair way to put it." Ignoring George's groan and Paul's sour look, he went on, "We're low on a lot of things. We don't have as much food or firewood as we ought to, and we aren't as good with what we do have as we might be. Food and firewood and other things, I mean." He pointed to the heaps of stones on the walkway. "We haven't replenished those the way we should, for instance. The Slavs and Avars might try tortoises again, but nobody's worrying about it. We have so many things to worry about, we can't keep track of all of them at once, even if that's what we need to do most. And it is."

"We need a real general," Paul observed. "You've worked wonders, Rufus, don't take me wrong, but you never tried keeping track of a whole city before. Eusebius is used to doing that, but he doesn't know what all soldiers need to keep track of."

"You're not as foolish as you look," Rufus said, to which Paul, one of the least foolish-looking men in Thessalonica, responded with a dry chuckle. Rufus continued, "A lot of what we talked about was just that: what all needed doing and who would take charge of doing it."

"What was the rest?" George asked. Again, Rufus did not appear forthcoming. George said, "Come on, you just told us not to gossip. Now out with it."

Rufus let out a long sigh. Then he said, "Well, it's not anything you haven't seen for yourselves, and it's not anything you couldn't figure out for yourselves, either. The bishop's not happy about how strong the powers of the Slavs and Avars have turned out to be."

"He's not happy?" Paul exclaimed. "I'm not happy, either. If they were mild little powers, the way everybody hoped, the Slavs and Avars would have given up on the siege a long time ago."

"I tried to tell him," George said. "Before we saw even a single Slav around the city, I tried to tell him. He was polite to me, and made as if he believed what I was saying, but it must not have sunk in till he saw it for himself."

"Life is like that," Rufus said. "If we really learned things from what other people told us, we'd all be smarter and richer than we are right now, and fathers wouldn't want to clout their sons over the head with rocks about the time the brats started shaving."

"Amen to that," George said with a laugh. "And speaking of brats who haven't been shaving long, I think I'm going to bring Theodore up onto the wall with me next time it's my shift. He knows how to shoot a bow, so he won't be altogether useless up here, and it's about time he has a look at the way this particular part of the world works."

"Aye, go ahead and do that," Rufus told him. "First battle, first brothel—those are the memories that'll stick with you, even when you get old. I ought to know about that, eh?"

"If I'm as hale as you are when I have your years, I won't be doing too bad," George said. He hoped he managed to pile on as many years as Rufus had, in whatever shape he might be at that time. The veteran had to be getting close to his threescore and ten, but George had seen again and again how much vitality he still had in him. George caught himself in a yawn. He didn't have all that much vitality himself these days.

Theodore flew up the stairs to the top of the wall. George plodded after him. The shoemaker was still feeling anything but vital. Maybe Rufus should have taken Theodore up on the wall, not the youth's tired old father.

When George got to the top and looked out toward the encampment of the Slavs and Avars, Theodore was already taking aim at the first Slav he saw who wasn't impossibly far out of arrow range. George made him turn the bow aside before any of the other militiamen had to come rushing over and do it for him.

"But, Father!" Theodore exclaimed, aghast. "That's the enemy!" By the way he spoke, the skinny, draggled-looking Slav at whom he wanted to shoot might have been the general commanding the barbarians, not a tired soldier who looked to want nothing so much as a mug of wine and a place close by the fire to sleep.

"When the Slavs shoot at us, we shoot at them," George said patiently. "When they don't shoot, we don't do much shooting, either. For one thing, it wastes arrows. For another, if we start shooting at them, they'll start shooting at us, and more of us are liable to get hurt. If they're quiet, we're happy enough to let 'em stay that way."

Everyone within earshot nodded. Theodore proved the point Rufus had made a couple of days before, saying, "But if they're the enemy, we need to kill them. How can we kill them if we don't shoot at them?"

"All we need to do is keep them out of Thessalonica," George said. "We don't have to kill them. If they can't get in, sooner or later they'll go away."

Dactylius came up onto the wall then. He beamed at Theodore, and failed to notice Theodore wasn't beaming back. "Young blood," the little jeweler said. "Young blood. Makes me feel old and useless."

"You know what young blood was going to do?" one of the nearby militiamen said. "He was going to start shooting at the first Slav he saw, and probably go right on shooting after that. *Christe eleison*, we'd have been ducking for days if George here hadn't stopped him."

Theodore looked and sounded ready to burst. "This isn't fighting!" he said. "This is all make-believe and cowardice!"

A couple of militiamen laughed, which only made matters worse. But before Theodore could do or say anything irrevocable, George looked out from the wall. "Hello," he said, and then, to Theodore, "Son, if you want fighting, I'm afraid you may get it." He pointed toward the troop of Avars riding out of their encampment toward Thessalonica.

As they did whenever he saw them, the Avars alarmed him. Part of that was their gear: not only did they armor themselves in scalemail from head to foot, they armored their horses the same way. Part of it was their horsemanship: they might almost have been centaurs, attached to their mounts from birth. And part of it was the arrogance that flowed off them in waves, the feeling that they were convinced they were the toughest people in the world.

Their powers were convinced they were the toughest powers in the world, too. George also got that feeling from the Avars, and very strongly, as strongly as the churches of Christian saints reflected their special traits.

He wasn't the only one who got that feeling, either. Dactylius said, "They give you the chills just looking at them, don't they? I'm glad they let the Slavs do so much of the dirty work for them."

"Yes," George said, warily watching the Avars shake themselves out from a column to a line paralleling the wall. They were, he thought, still out of arrow range of the militiamen on the wall. They did not share his opinion. Instead of quivers, they carried cases holding both bow and arrows. As if inspired by a single will, they took out the bows and started shooting.

Those bows must have been better than the ones the Slavs used—better than the ones the militiamen on the walls of Thessalonica used, too. The fellow who'd been mocking Theodore's aggressive inexperience made a hideous gobbling noise and toppled over onto his side. His hands clutched at the arrow that had suddenly sprouted from his neck. Bright red blood streamed out between his fingers and puddled on the walkway. It steamed in the chill air of early morning. The militiaman's feet drummed and were still.

Theodore stared, eyes wide. George set a hand on his shoulder. "We're going to get some fighting whether we want it or not," he said. "The Avars aren't going to care whether we and the Slavs spend the next week shooting at each other. You've got that bow. You'd better use it now."

Before Theodore could, an arrow hissed between him and his father. He jumped, coming to the same horrible realization George had at the start of the siege: people out there were trying to kill him. Then he shouted several words George had never heard him use at home, yanked an arrow from his quiver, and let fly at the Avars.

George thought that a healthy reaction. But after Theodore had sent a couple of more arrows after the first, the shoemaker said, "Take it easy, son. They have better bows than we do, so they can reach the wall and we probably can't hit them."

Theodore stared at him as if he'd started speaking Slavic. George realized the youth hadn't had the slightest idea where his arrows were going, except that he was shooting at the foe. He said, "You're right, Father. I see that. But what keeps them from—?"

Before he could finish the question, an Avar arrow pierced another militiaman not far away. The fellow howled like a wolf, then started cursing in such a manner as to leave Theodore's earlier bad language in the shade. "Christ's stinking foreskin, I'm bleeding like a stuck hog!" he shouted. "Hold a bowl under me, and you can make blood sausage tomorrow." He plainly wasn't on the point of death, but as plainly wasn't happy with what life had just given him, either.

Theodore tried again: "What keeps the Avars from doing what they're doing: shooting at us from so far away we can't shoot back?"

"Our bows can't reach them," George answered. "Our catapults can."

Now the engines on top of the walls of Thessalonica were not engaging the stone-throwers the Avars had built. They were taking on the Avars themselves, and throwing stones themselves, not fire. Theodore cheered when a flying rock knocked a horse and rider flat. But he watched thoughtfully as the animal and the man writhed about, with neither one of them showing any sign of being able to get up.

The Avars' scalemail turned ordinary arrows at long range (Dactylius told Theodore the story of the Avar he'd hit but hadn't hurt, and then for good measure told it over again). No matter how far away the nomad horsemen were, though, when a dart hit them, it struck home. An Avar let out a shriek clearly audible from the wall when one of those darts pinned his leg to the horse he was riding. The horse shrieked, too, and galloped madly away, but soon went crashing down. Again, George didn't think it or its rider would be of much use after that.

With the Romans' catapults in the fight, the Avars moved even farther from the wall than they had been. Their arrows began falling short. Seeing that, they abandoned their effort as abruptly as they had started it, trotting back toward their encampment with hardly a backward glance.

"We did it, Father!" Theodore burst out. "We drove them away!"

"That's true," George said. "We did." He didn't say anything about the militiaman who had caught the arrow in the neck and who now lay dead only a few feet away. Nor did he look in the direction of the dead man. Somehow he contrived, by not saying and not looking, to allude to the man as loudly as if he'd shouted.

Loudly himself, at least at the outset, Theodore said, "That wouldn't happen to me. There's no way in the world that could . . ." His voice, which had been fading, trailed away altogether as he obviously remembered the arrow that hadn't missed him by much.

"He did well," Dactylius said. "He did very well." Without children of his own, Dactylius didn't have to worry about raising them. He would, in fact, have made a splendid indulgent grandfather.

But he wasn't altogether wrong, either, not here. George nodded. "Aye, he'll do," he said. "He kept shooting at the Avars—even if he wanted to start too bloody soon—and he didn't start puking when people got hurt around him."

"You sound like Rufus." Theodore laughed.

George didn't. "Rufus may be old and crude, but I'll tell you this, son: if there's one thing in the world he knows, it's what makes a soldier and what doesn't. When I'm talking about soldiers, I don't mind at all if I sound like him."

He waited for Theodore or Dactylius to argue with him. Neither of them did. Dactylius nodded. Theodore changed the subject: "Why do you suppose the Avars started shooting at us like that? You said the Slavs and we were happy enough to live and let live."

"I don't think the Avars are happy letting anything live that they don't rule," George answered. "Maybe they thought the Slavs have been getting too soft and they needed to make the fight livelier. Maybe some general of theirs came by and they were showing off for him. Maybe they just felt mean and wanted to kill themselves some Romans."

"Does it matter?" Dactylius added.

"It might," Theodore said. "If we knew why they did what they do, we might be able to keep them from doing it."

Dactylius looked over toward George. "Anyone would think he was your son," he said.

"I can't imagine why," the shoemaker answered, his voice dry but a sparkle in his eye. Theodore scowled at both of them. He didn't think he sounded like his father. He didn't think he thought like his father, either. All that proved, as far as George was concerned, was that he remained very young.

"Another blow with weapons," Dactylius said musingly. "I suppose that means they'll try something magical next."

"They don't seem willing or able to do both at once, do they?" George said. "I wouldn't mind rattling them again with our own power. That sickness Eusebius called down on them left them this far" —he held thumb and forefinger close together— "from having to up and go."

"I thought the nature of the plague was that they had to up and go, Father," Theodore said, so innocently that George had no more than a momentary temptation to pitch him off the wall onto his head.

"Anyone would think . . ." Dactylius repeated.

"My jokes aren't that bad," George said, his voice full of affronted dignity. "He couldn't possibly be John's son. John wasn't anywhere near Thessalonica nine months before he was born."

Theodore turned red. Soldiers chaffed one another harder than his friends did. And George, ever so slightly, was chaffing his mother, too. "Father!" he said, and his voice betrayed him, sliding up into a boyish treble for the second syllable of the word.

"Don't worry about it, boy; I'm joking. Your mother would hit me if she heard me, but not very hard," George said, adding, "If you're worried about what she's thinking, go home and show her you're all right. She was convinced the only reason I'd taken you up here was to get you killed." That was another joke, but less so than Theodore probably thought.

"Will it be all right?" the youth asked doubtfully.

"Go ahead," George told him. "I let Rufus know I was going to bring you up here today, to see how you'd do. But you're not on any official list. I expect you can be by this time tomorrow, though, if that's what you'd like— all I've got to do is ask him to put you there. You fought well enough; no one can say you don't deserve it."

"All right, Father. If that's what you think, that's what we should do," Theodore answered, a more subdued response than the whoop of ecstatic glee George had expected. Maybe a firsthand look at war had sobered his son after all. With a nod, Theodore descended from the wall.

"He's a good boy, George. You should be proud of him," Dactylius said.

Just outside the wall fluttered one of those batlike spirits that had startled George and Dactylius on their first night patrol together. Its ugly little face twisted into a nasty leer as it echoed Dactylius' words in a high, squeaky voice: "He's a good boy, George. You should be very proud of him." Whether it was meant for mockery or not, it sounded scornful.

"Begone, foul flying sprite!" George exclaimed, and made the sign of the cross at it.

It bared its teeth and flapped a few feet farther away, but seemed unharmed by the gesture that would have sent one of the powers of the pagan days of Greece fleeing in abject terror. "You should be very proud," it squeaked at the shoemaker. Was that an echo? A mocking warning? He couldn't tell.

He drew his bow and let fly at the spirit. Maybe his arrow missed. Maybe it passed right through the thing without causing it undue harm. It did upset the spirit, which shrilled "Very proud!" and flew away, darting and dodging like a beast made of flesh and blood.

"That bat's gone," George said in some satisfaction.

"It was spying on us!" Dactylius said.

"Yes, I think you're right," George answered; that darting, dodging flight had taken the batlike spirit back toward the tents of the Slavic wizards who associated with the Avar priest. In spite of where it had gone, the shoemaker laughed. "If the Slavs think they're going to learn how to take Thessalonica from the likes of you and me, they'll be disappointed."

"Oh!" Dactylius blinked. "I hadn't thought of that. You're right, aren't you?"

"Unless you know more about the secrets of the city than I do, I am," George said. He looked out toward the wizards' tents once more. "They *are* strong: the Slavs, I mean. They aren't very bright, though, or they're not very good at using the power they do have. Otherwise, one of those little bat things would have been listening to Rufus and Eusebius, not to us."

"How do you know one wasn't?" Dactylius asked.

He stood there small and smug and proud of his own cleverness. And George demolished it, not taking malicious glee in the doing as John would have but doing it anyhow, hardly noticing he was doing it, not thinking of anything but going after the truth wherever it happened to be hiding this particular day: "If the Slavs and Avars were listening to what our leaders said to one another, they've have a better idea of where we're weak than they really do, and they'd do a better job of hurting us in those places."

Dactylius stared at him. Pride leaked out of him like water from a squeezed sponge. Even with pride gone, though, integrity remained. "You're right," he said, a sentence he'd used twice lately but one many men would sooner have been tortured than utter. "That makes better sense than my notion."

"It does only stand to reason," George said, trying by his tone to imply that his friend would surely have seen the same thing had he but waited a moment longer before he spoke. He waved up and down the length of the wall. "See? We still don't have as many stones up here as we did before the Slavs attacked the foundations with their tortoises, for instance. If they knew that, they might try again."

"Good thing none of those little bat spirits was flying near you then," Dactylius said. He and George both looked around anxiously to make sure that was so. George didn't see any of the ugly little things, so he supposed it was.

The supposition cheered him less than it might have. "Sooner or later," he said slowly, "those things are going to hear something important for no better reason than luck. If they come around often enough, they have to. And if the Slavs and Avars can figure out what to do with it—"

"We're in trouble," Dactylius finished for him.

"We're in worse trouble," George corrected him. "We've been in plain trouble for a while now."

Dactylius looked out toward the enemy encampment. "Well, yes," he said.

VIII

A barmaid sidled up to George, smiling a bright, professional smile. "More salted olives?" she asked. Partly, that was to help make him thirsty. Partly, it was pride that Paul's tavern still had salted olives to sell. Whatever it was, George had already gone through one bowl of them, and a fresh mug of wine sat in front of him. He shook his head.

A kithara gently wept, accompanying the singer's plaintive song of lost love. Across the table from George, John made a face. "If I had to listen to this fellow all day long, I'd have left him, too," the comic said.

"Practice for your act?" George asked: his friend wore the intent look he donned whenever he was about to perform.

But John shook his head. "Paul told me he'd throw me out on my ear if I ever badmouthed any of the other people he brought up onstage to make the customers forget how lousy his wine is." His flexible features displayed great gobs of scorn. "As if anybody needs me to tell him what a bad mouth this singer has." He wasn't on the platform yet, but his quips drew blood even so.

Before long, the kithara player mercifully finished his

last song. He got a tepid round of applause, half praise, half relief that he was done. Paul shouted, "And now—here's John!" The comic bounded up onto the little stage. The kithara player gave him a fanfare he looked as if he could have done without.

"I thought I was going to have good news for everybody tonight," John said. "I thought the siege would be over by now. When I was out on the wall a couple of weeks ago, one of the Avars told me their women were getting pretty tired of how long this whole business is taking, and they said they wouldn't sleep with their men unless they gave up and made peace with us Romans."

"You're stealing that from Aristophanes!" yelled a heckler with an education in the classics.

"The frogs are loud tonight," observed John, who also had one. "*Koax! Koax!* But that's from the wrong play, and besides, anybody see the siege ending? Nope, the Avars are still here, all right, and what's more, half their sheep are pregnant."

Somebody threw an olive at him. He caught it out of the air and ate it. "It's not a tough crowd if they don't throw things from the swordsmith's shop," he remarked. Maybe that was supposed to be a joke. Maybe it was just how a tavern comic went about gauging his audience.

John said, "One thing this siege has done is make me glad I'm a Christian. I have enough trouble keeping one God happy. Try and keep all the gods the Slavs and Avars have happy and you end up as worn out as an old man trying to keep a young harem happy." He pantomimed limp exhaustion—limp in every sense of the word.

After exactly the right pause, he recovered as if by magic and started counting on his fingers. "How many gods have we seen? Water god, thunder gods, fire god—I expect any minute now they're going to sic the god of shrunken tunics on us." Again, he let his body get his laughs for him, twisting and jerking as he tried to handle an imaginary bow in a tunic that was squeezing his arms like a serpent.

"And somebody," he said, sitting down on his stool

once more, "told the chief tax collector the Slavs have so many gods, they even have one who inflicts high interest on delinquent returns. From what I hear, the tax man jumped over the wall and converted day before yesterday."

That got a loud laugh. Every tax collector George had ever known would have worshiped a god like that. He watched the men in the taverns looking around at one another. Half of them would have worshiped a god like that, too. Enough people owed George money that he might have been tempted into a brief bit of fiscal paganism himself.

"That same god went down into the Jews' quarter," John added. "They told him to come back once he had some experience." No one was safe from John. That was a lot of what made him funny. It was also what made the people whose vanity he flicked hate him.

A barmaid carrying a wooden tray filled with empty mugs stumbled over somebody's outstretched foot. She squealed and managed to stay upright, but several of the mugs flew off the tray. Being the cheapest of cheap crockery, they shattered.

"Pick up the pieces, Verina," Paul said wearily when the noise stopped. "That'll come out of your pay, you know."

"What a kind and generous host we have," John exclaimed—not sarcasm, as George first thought, but the lead-in to a joke, for the comic continued, "Puts me in mind of the two fellows who owned a slave in common. One day one of them came into their shop and found the other one whacking the slave with a stick. 'What are you doing?' he asked his partner. And the other fellow told him, 'I'm beating my half.' "

As Verina swept up the shards of the broken mugs, John said, "Like I told you, Paul's a good fellow. Instead of taking it out of Verina's pay, he could have taken it out some other way." He leered at the barmaid. The largely male crowd whooped. Verina looked ready to throw the pieces of crockery at him. Again, though, he'd only used the situation to help set up a story: "I remember the poor fool who was talking with a good-looking woman, and he said to her, 'I wonder whether you or my wife tastes better.' " He leered again, and ran his tongue lewdly over his lips. "And the woman said, 'Why don't you ask my husband? He's tasted us both.' "

He got his laugh, but George, listening to it, thought it had a certain nervous undertone. Not everyone had as much confidence in his wife as he did with Irene, and everyone there, no doubt, had been devastated by an unexpected answer at one time or another, even if not by that particular unexpected answer. When John's jokes worked well, they touched a central core of humanity all his listeners shared.

"Then," said the comic, "there was the fellow who went to Maurice and wanted to be named Augustal prefect of Egypt. 'I already have one,' Maurice told him. 'Well, all right, you're the Emperor—make me governor of Thrace,' the man said. And Maurice answered, 'I can't do that, either—I like the job the man there now is doing.' And the fellow said, 'In that case, give me twenty solidi.' So Maurice did. As the fellow was walking out of the palace with his gold pieces, his friend asked, 'Aren't you disappointed you got so little?' And the fellow said, 'Are you crazy? I never would have got this much if I hadn't asked for all the other stuff.' "

That got a laugh, too, both for the sake of the joke and, again, for the obvious truth it contained: Maurice, among the most parsimonious Roman Emperors of all time, never parted with a copper if he could help it.

John got down from the platform, went over to the bar, and spoke to Paul in a loud, wheedling voice: "How about giving me half an interest in this tavern, my good and wise friend?"

"What?" Paul jerked as if a wasp had stung him. "Are you out of your mind, John? Go away."

"Well, if you won't do that, how about letting me have all the roast pork I can eat for the next year?" John asked.

"Are you crazy?" said the taverner, who obviously hadn't been paying attention to the routine. "Go back there and be funny."

"Give me a mug of wine, then."

Paul dipped it out for him. "There. Go on, now."

John turned to the crowd. "You see?" he said with an enormous grin. People laughed and cheered as he finally went back to the platform, and Paul never did figure out where the joke lay. John knocked back the wine in one long draught, then ruefully shook his head. " 'Go back there and be funny,' the man says. I'll tell you people what's funny. *That's* funny. Our beloved host thinks he can tell somebody to be funny and have it happen, just like that."

"You'd better be funny," said Paul, who was listening now.

John ignored him. Now the comic's face bore a wistful expression: maybe a true one, maybe only a trick of the light. "I wish it were that easy. I wish you could walk into a shop and say, 'I'd like a pound of funny, please,' and put it in a sack and take it home with you. Wouldn't that be fine, if you could buy funny the way you buy a loaf of bread from Justin the baker or a pair of shoes from George here?"

Now George jumped. John hadn't been in the habit of including him in his routines, and he would have been as well pleased had his friend left him out of this one, too.

And, sure enough, John sent a sardonic stare his way as he went on, "Come to think of it, you can buy some pretty funny shoes from George, all right."

"I'll remember *you* in my nightmares," George called.

"Your nightmares are ugly enough without me," John retorted; he wasn't shy about mocking himself, either. He went on, "Besides, it's hard to be funny in Thessalonica these days. God is punishing us for our sins. The Slavs and Avars are outside the wall, there's not enough food inside the wall, and He gave Menas back his legs so he could go around shouting at everybody."

Some people laughed. Others looked alarmed, either because God might have been insulted or because Menas had been. George put his elbows down on the tabletop and buried his face in his hands. Sure as sure, that crack would get back to Menas. And, sure as sure, Menas would think George had said it, not anyone else. Fourteen people might tell him it had come from John's lips; he would hear *George* every time.

The shoemaker didn't really listen to the rest of John's routine. People laughed every so often, so he suspected his friend was doing well. And, when John finally came back to the table, the bowl he brought with him was nicely full of coins. He sorted them with his usual quick dexterity.

George said, "I do wish you wouldn't tell jokes on Menas so often."

"Why, in God's name?" John didn't look up from what he was doing. "He's funny, is what he is. I can't think of anybody funnier in the whole world, him swaggering around like he's got God's hand in his drawers."

"The trouble is, he does—or he did, anyhow—have God's hand in his drawers," George said uncomfortably.

"Yes, but God didn't put it there to play Menas' trumpet for him," John answered, setting a silver miliaresion off by itself with a pleased grunt. "Menas still hasn't figured that out, even though it's been months. He's pretty stupid, too; he may never get the idea."

"Regardless of how stupid he is" —a sentiment with which George heartily concurred— "he's rich, too, and he'll get you in trouble if you keep making jokes about him." *He'll get* me *in trouble if you keep making jokes about him*. But George remained too stubborn to tell John about that.

"What's he going to do?" the comic asked. "Make me leave town? I can't go by land, and if he puts me on a ship he does me a favor."

"He can make your life miserable while you're here," George said. "Believe me, I know." That was as close as he would come to revealing the trouble to which his friend had contributed.

"My life is already miserable while I'm here," John said. "A little less miserable," he amended, "because the night's take is pretty good. And if Verina's in the right kind of mood—" He raised his voice and called to the barmaid: "Hello, sweetheart! What do you say you and I—"

"I say no, whatever it is," Verina answered. "All those broken cups I was cleaning up, I wish I'd broken them over your head." George didn't know what John had done to her, or what she thought he'd done to her, but she didn't want to have anything to do with him now, stalking off nose in air.

If he was embarrassed, he didn't show it. Going up in front of an audience to tell jokes for a living had no doubt hardened him against embarrassment. "It doesn't matter," he said lightly. "She's no good in bed, anyhow."

That, for once, hadn't been pitched to carry to Verina's ears, but she heard it and came storming back. "For one thing, you're a liar," she snapped. "For another, you've never had the chance to find out whether you're a liar. And for one more, you're never *going* to have the chance." Off she went again.

John got more laughs than he had through his whole routine, all of them aimed at him. Had George been publicly humiliated like that, he wouldn't have dared show his face on the street for weeks afterwards. John took it all in stride. By the calculating look on his face, he was figuring out the jokes he'd tell about it the next time he got up in front of a crowd.

Having gone to Paul's tavern, George was glad he had an afternoon shift on the wall the next day. He was less glad about staring into the westering sun; the day was cold but brilliantly clear. The glare in his face made it hard for him to keep an eye on whatever the Slavs and Avars might be doing.

John didn't worry about that, and had some reason

not to worry: the barbarians' encampment seemed as quiet as it ever had since the siege began. The comic said, "They're probably all out with their sheep."

"You told that one last night, John," George said patiently.

"Go on, complain about every little thing," John said. "I think—"

George didn't find out what John thought. Up farther north along the wall, someone started shouting in a very loud, unpleasant voice: "Call yourself a fighting man, do you? A fighting man is supposed to be alert in the presence of danger. He is supposed to—"

Had Rufus been giving that dressing-down, neither George nor John would have thought anything of it. As it was, John's face gave the impression that he'd smelled some meat several days later than it should have been smelled. George's lip also curled. "Menas," he said.

Menas it was, and he was, to George's dismay, heading in the direction of the Litaean Gate, spreading joy and good cheer in front of him. John glanced his way and said, "What's that thing he's carrying? Besides his big, ugly belly, I mean."

"His war hammer—is that what you're talking about?" George said. "I've seen him lugging that around before. It's a rich man's toy, if you ask me—something that makes him feel like a soldier even if he's not."

He wasn't a soldier himself, as any member of Thessalonica's regular garrison would have told him in as much detail as he could stand. But he'd done real fighting since the Slavs and Avars infested the city, which was more than Menas could have said. George checked himself. No: it was more than Menas could *truthfully* have said.

And here came the noble, twirling the hammer around by the leather strap attached to the end of the handle. He glared at George as if at a moldy spot on a chunk of bread. "Haven't I told you to stop insulting me?" he growled. "Haven't I warned you I'll get my own back if it's the last thing I do?"

"You've done all those things, sir," George answered. "What I haven't done is insult you."

"Liar!" Menas shouted, loud enough to make militiamen within a bowshot of him turn their heads his way. "The latest is, you say God cured me so I could go around shouting at people."

Whoever had reported John's joke to him had got the words right, but Menas had got the source wrong, as George had known would happen. The shoemaker wondered if John would own up to having said it, and if Menas would believe him if he did. Since John kept quiet, the latter didn't become an issue. George said, "I did not say that about you, sir."

"Liar!" Menas shouted again.

"I did not say that," George repeated. "If you keep doing the things that someone said about you, though, I will start saying them myself. I'll have to start saying them myself, because you'll have made them true."

Menas stared at him. Being a rich and prominent man, being a man to whom God had granted a miracle (for what reason, George could not imagine, and he'd tried—how he'd tried!), the noble was not accustomed to having anyone speak so pointedly to him. He raised the hammer, as if to strike George down.

George sprang backwards. He had an arrow on the string and the bow down almost as soon as his feet hit the walkway again. The point of the arrow—a bronze point, perhaps made by Benjamin—was aimed at a spot a palm's breadth above Menas' navel.

As nothing George said had ever managed to do, that made Menas thoughtful. He lowered the silver-chased hammer. George lowered the bow so the arrow pointed toward the walkway rather than Menas' brisket. He held it at full draw, though, ready to bring it up in a hurry if the noble was only pretending to back away from a fight.

"How you'll pay!" Menas snarled. "You'll wish the Slavs and Avars had got hold of you by the time I'm done." He stamped south along the walkway. George resisted the temptation to put the arrow in his bow straight through Menas' left kidney. It wasn't easy. He had to make himself replace the arrow in the quiver one motion at a time.

"Getting credit for my lines, are you?" John said when Menas started bellowing at some other luckless militiaman farther down the wall. "That's a trouble you could probably do without."

"Now that you mention it, yes," George answered. John was bolder with his insults when the target wasn't standing right there in front of him. George tried to get angry at that, but found he couldn't. Most men were made the same way.

"*That's* why you've been after me not to tell jokes about him anymore," John said, with the air of a man for whom a dark corner of the world has suddenly become bright.

"In a manner of speaking," George said.

"Well, I won't," John promised. And then, an instant later, he backtracked: "I don't think I will, anyhow. But if something comes to me while I'm up there in front of a bunch of people, who knows what I'll do?"

"No one," George said sadly. "Not a single, solitary soul. Not even you. You'd be better off if you did."

"Maybe," John said. "But if I knew ahead of time everything I'd do when I got up on a platform, and if I did just what I'd thought beforehand I was going to do . . . I wouldn't be me. Like you say, I might be better off. But I might not be able to perform at all."

George thought about that. He'd made shoes all his life, learning the trade from his father. But if, for some reason, he couldn't make shoes anymore, he was sure he'd be happy enough as a potter or a miller instead, once he'd learned one of those businesses. If, however, a man had in his makeup something that had to come out if he was to be happy, he couldn't very well go through life denying it was there.

"I will try," John said, which, as a pledge, left something to be desired.

"Do the best you can." George sounded weary, even

to himself. "The damage is probably done by now, any which way."

A man whom George needed a moment to recognize was in the shop when he came back from the wall: a burly fellow of about his own age, with rather heavy features pitted by scars from either a light case of smallpox or a bad set of pimples as a youth. The latter, George thought, and that let him figure out who the visitor was a moment before Irene said, "Dear, of course you know Leo the potter."

"Yes, of course," George said, and clasped Leo's hand. The potter had a firm grip, and very smooth skin on his palm from using it to shape clay: a great contrast to the scars and punctures that marked a shoemaker's hands. "A pleasure to see you. Will you drink some wine with me?"

"Your lady already gave me a cup," Leo answered, holding it up. "I got here myself not two minutes ago, matter of fact." Irene poured a cup for her husband, who took it with a word of thanks. He looked around for Sophia and Theodore, both of whom seemed to have vanished. But no: shadows at the top of the stairway said they were lingering as discreetly as they could, no doubt with hands cupped to their ears to hear the better.

As much to annoy them as for any other reason, George stretched small talk longer than he might have done. But small talk was also a way of getting acquainted with Leo, whom he did not know well. After a while, casually, George said, "You're Constantine's father, aren't you?" Had Leo still had his youthful pimples, he and Constantine might have been two brothers, not father and son. George stretched a point: "Fine-looking boy."

Irene frowned at him. He nodded, very slightly, to let her know he'd seen. Had he been buying a donkey, he wouldn't have praised anything about the animal till it was his. A marriage dicker, though, was a different sort of business—or so he thought.

"He's a good lad, if I do say so my own self," Leo answered, "and, since he's not here, there's nobody but me to say it for him. Helen—my wife, you know—she didn't come through the plague a couple of years ago." Absentmindedly, he scratched himself. "I hate fleas."

"They are a nuisance," George agreed. "Yes, the plague was a hard time for all of us. This siege is another hard time. I hadn't intended speaking to you till it was over and done, and things were back to normal again."

"Yes, I can see that," Leo said. "But I drew a different lesson from the plague, and that is, *don't wait*. Things may never be—what was that word you used?—normal, that's it, normal again. No telling what'll happen tomorrow, I say, so we'd better arrange today the best we can. And on account of that, I didn't figure I ought to wait before I came to see you."

George hesitated before replying. As far as he was concerned, Leo's lesson was absolutely the wrong one. *Festina lente* ran through his mind: *make haste slowly*. But the fact that Leo did draw lessons, even mistaken lessons, from what went on around him bumped the potter up a notch in George's estimation. Most people, he was convinced, went through life without a clue it might hold patterns they could use.

Irene said, "Your brother is a potter, too, isn't he?"

"Zeno? That's right, though his shop is over by the other side of St. Demetrius' church." Leo smiled at Irene. "Either you have a right fine memory, or you've been asking questions about me."

"Everyone in this family has a very good memory," Irene said primly. That was on the whole true, even if Theodore sometimes showed a maddening inability to remember what George had told him to do five minutes earlier.

"That's nice," Leo said, willing to pretend to believe Irene hadn't been investigating his family. He'd also been doing some investigating, for he went on, "I'm sorry God didn't give either of you sibs who lived."

"I had an older brother," George said. "I don't even remember him; he died when I was a baby."

"I had an older sister and a younger brother." Irene's eyes were sad as she looked into the past. "God's will." She grew brisk once more. "But you didn't come here to talk about old sorrows, but the chance for new joys."

"The chance, yes." Leo scratched his nose. "You do keep a clean shop, George, I'll say that for you. Hardly any stink of leather in the air."

Though George bristled, he made a point of not letting Leo notice. Making and repairing shoes was a perfectly respectable trade, but not one of high class. By implying as much, Leo was making a bid for a bigger dowry to accompany Sophia if she married Constantine: it was astonishing how a fatter bride portion could balance social stigma in the scales.

But George in turn remarked, "You and your son are lucky fellows, not to be melted to tallow standing in front of your kilns day after day." He had no intention of conceding that potters stood any higher on the social scale than did shoemakers.

Leo grunted. "Well, when we talk about Sophia's dowry, what are we talking about? Twenty solidi, something like that?"

George stared at him, admiring the effrontery of such a forthright thief. "You're going to lose this girl if you go on that way," he said. "We aren't nobility, and neither are you."

Sulkily, Leo said, "How much, then? It would have to be a pretty price, I'll tell you. Constantine has his admirers, yes he does."

Irene said, "When you married Helen, Leo, her bride portion was what? Two solidi and a little silver, wasn't it?"

"How did you know that?" Leo turned red as the fire under one of his kilns. George wondered the same thing, although his wife's skill at ferreting out such tidbits roused respect in him, not the horror Leo obviously felt. By that horror, George judged Irene had the straight goods.

"Never mind how I know," she said crisply. "That hasn't got anything to do with anything. What matters is, it's true. Are you so much richer than your father that you think people want to beggar themselves to join your family? And I hear Zeno's wife brought a smaller dowry than yours."

"Did she?" Leo exclaimed. "She puts on airs she doesn't deserve, then." Now he sounded indignant. He also sounded as if he hadn't known what his sister-in-law's bride portion had been. George wondered from whom Irene had pried that little nugget.

"If you're going to be unreasonable about these things, there's no point in us even talking," George said. "In fact, I probably wouldn't even be talking with you now if I didn't know how sweet Constantine was on Sophia." He didn't know that, but had a feeling it was so from the way the youth had glanced back at him when they passed on the street.

And, for a wonder, his shot proved as effective as Irene's had been. Leo turned red again, this time from annoyance rather than embarrassment. He said, "I told him not to show that on the sleeve of his tunic."

"I have nothing against love matches," George said. "A lot of times, they work out as well as the other sort. But I don't see any reason a bride should pay a fancy price so she and the groom can end up doing what they've wanted to do anyhow."

"If she brings a small portion, that makes your family and mine both look bad," Leo said. "People will find out about it and gossip." He sent Irene a glance filled with anything but delight unalloyed.

"I don't gossip," she said sweetly. "But I will say you have a point, since I know people who do."

Leo got to his feet. "I thank you for the wine. Maybe you were right after all, and we shouldn't talk this all the way through till we know Thessalonica is safe. After this, I don't know as I want to talk with anybody else, either.

Good day to you both." He edged out of the shop and fled.

No sooner had he gone than Sophia and Theodore hurried downstairs. Angrily, Sophia said, "Now look what you did! You scared him away. He won't come back anymore, and my life is ruined. Ruined!" She burst into tears.

George and Irene, by contrast, burst into laughter. That made Sophia cry harder than ever. She glared at them from red, wet eyes. George said, "He will be back, little one—I promise. The only thing your mother and I did was show him the two of us weren't fools."

Sophia stared at him doubtfully. "Do you really think so?" She wanted to believe him, that was plain.

"No doubt about it," Irene said. "He thought we'd dower you with everything we own, just for the sake of joining his snooty family. Now that he knows better, we should get on well enough."

"He wants this match, too," George added. "Otherwise, he would have waited till the siege was over before he started talking about it, the way we were going to do."

"Oh," Sophia said in a small voice. Her smile was like the sun coming out from behind rain clouds. "I hope you're right." It was evident she wanted the match at least as much as Constantine did. George resolved not to let Leo know that; it would make the dickering harder.

Theodore asked, "Mother, how did you know what bride portions Constantine's mother and aunt brought with them?"

"From Claudia, of all people," Irene answered. Before George could say anything worried, she went on, "It didn't have anything to do with this match, either. I forget whether it was last year or the year before—last year, I guess, because it was after the plague—and Claudia was complaining about people who pretended they were finer than they really were, and she mentioned Helen and her dowry, and her sister-in-law, too. I thought it was in poor taste myself, poor Helen being dead and all, but I didn't forget it, either. And when I turned out to need it, there it was."

"Your mother," George told Theodore, not joking at all, "never forgets anything."

"Me?" Irene said. "Me? Who was it, about the time we got married, who could tell which team had won the chariot races at every running for the past fifty years before then, and which rider had the most wins for each team, and how this one bald driver hadn't missed a running for fifteen years—"

George maintained a dignified silence. That was how he thought of it, at any rate. Its chief effect was making his wife and both his children laugh at him. Seeing that, he tried the opposite course: "That bald fellow had a brother who was a driver, too, and their father trained their horses, same as he'd been doing for twenty-three years before that, and . . ."

Such arcana proved every bit as risible as dignified silence. George gave up and started repairing a sandal. Sophia, having swung from sad to furious to eager and hopeful in the course of a couple of minutes, came over and kissed him on the cheek. "Thank you, Papa," she said.

"For what?" George asked, confused now.

"For a bald charioteer," his daughter answered, which confused him worse than ever. But he'd just started talking about marrying her off, and she didn't hate him for it. Confused or not, he didn't suppose he was doing too badly there.

"Magic," Rufus said decisively, peering out toward the encampment of the Slavs and Avars.

"I think you're right." George nodded. "That's what they'll hit us with next." He sniffed. The wind was out of the west, and swept the savory odors of roasting mutton and beef from the enemy's camp into the city. Sighing, he said, "They're still eating well. I wish we were."

"We've got enough to get us through," Rufus answered, which lifted George's spirits: if anyone knew how Thessalonica stood for food, the veteran was the man.

He went on, "What surprises me is that the barbarians are keeping their army so well fed. They must have dragged in all the livestock for miles around, the bastards. Even after they go, the countryside'll be bare as a sheared sheep for years."

"I hadn't thought about that," George said, an admission that bothered him: he was the sort of man who tried to think as far ahead as he could. "Meat will be expensive for a long time to come."

"We can always eat old Avars," Rufus said, "except I think they'd be tougher than your shoeleather."

"Shoeleather!" George exclaimed. "If they're slaughtering all the cattle and sheep, what will I use for shoeleather?"

"Don't know that one, either," Rufus said, if not cheerfully than with a good deal less concern than George had for the question. "What we've got to do is, we've got to get the siege over with so we can worry about things like shoeleather again."

Things like deciding whether I want to see Sophia marry Constantine, George thought. But the veteran was right. "What sort of magic do you think they'll throw at us?" he asked.

"The bishop and I have been talking about that," Rufus answered. George had a hard time gauging his tone: was he proud of having become part of the city's inner circle or scornful of the man with whom he was conferring? A bit of both, the shoemaker judged. Rufus continued, "Eusebius thinks we're going to come up against it before too long, that they're going to throw all the magic they have at us to try and break in. If they don't make it, they'll likely give up and go away."

"That sounds sensible," George said.

"It may be true anyway." Rufus' smile was crooked. "The bishop kept giving me all sorts of reasons out of the Holy Scriptures why he thought it was so. After a while, I started to doze off."

"You don't think he's right?" the shoemaker asked.

"Oh, I think he's right, but not for any of the reasons

he was going on about," Rufus said. "You look at what's left for the Slavs and Avars to eat out there, you look at the really bad weather that's bound to come, and you can't see them besieging us forever. The only thing about the cold I don't like is that it makes pestilences spread slower—but their magic for that sort of thing is pretty good anyhow. We've found out about that."

"We've found out their magic for a lot of different things is pretty good," George said. "I tried telling that to Eusebius, but—"

Rufus held up his hand. "I've heard that story, you know, George. And do you know what Bishop Eusebius said to me? He said, 'Rufus, if I'd only listened to that shoemaker, what's-his-name, we'd all be better off now, because he sure knew how strong the Slavs' magic was.' "

"Really?" George's eyes widened. He didn't even mind being called what's-his-name. "Did he really say that?"

Rufus leered evilly. "No."

The gesture George used invited Rufus to perform an act so vile, and so anatomically unlikely, that God, when He was writing the Holy Scriptures, hadn't thought to condemn it. The veteran laughed till he held his sides. "If you could have seen the look on your face . . ." He dissolved again.

"Funny," George said. "I laugh."

"Sorry," Rufus said, sounded about a quarter sincere. "I couldn't resist."

"You didn't try," George said. Rufus did not deny it. By the nature of things, Rufus hardly could have denied it. George thought for a bit. He could either stay angry at the veteran or he could forget about it. He forgot about it, suffusing himself in a warmly Christian glow of virtue. Besides, forgetting about it let him keep on questioning Rufus instead of cursing him. His relentless curiosity insisted that was the better choice. He asked, "What kind of magic *does* Bishop Eusebius think will be in the next big push from the Slavs and Avars? You never quite answered."

"Earth, most likely," Rufus said. "They've tried air and fire and water more. I don't know whether they can make the wall come down that way, but that's what the bishop thinks they'll try."

"It does make sense, I suppose." George kicked at the walkway. "I don't want the wall to crumble under my feet."

"Neither do I," Rufus said. "They've come too cursed close to managing that without using any magic at all. If they have some gods whose special province is earthquakes, say . . ."

"That could be very bad," George agreed. "Are there any special prayers we can use to keep earthquakes from happening?"

"Eusebius is looking for some," Rufus answered. "Me, I have my doubts. If there really were prayers like that, everybody would know them and use them, and we wouldn't have earthquakes anymore."

"Something to that, I shouldn't wonder." It was, in fact, the sort of logical look at a problem George might have used himself. He said, "If we can't pray to stop a quake, what can we do?"

"Pray that the gods of the Slavs and Avars can't start one that wouldn't have happened without them, I suppose," Rufus said. "That's better than nothing, and it lets us fight them on our own ground." George grimaced. Rufus grinned. "Relax, pal. I'm not smart enough to do that on purpose."

"If you say so," George answered, which won him a dirty look from the veteran. He held up a placating hand. "If you were stupid, Rufus, you would have done something that got you killed years ago."

Rufus laughed. "Ah, there's a deal of truth in that, I tell you. A soldier starting out, he's all balls and no brains." He laughed again, on a different note this time. "Maybe it's a good thing I came to the trade with Narses for my first general. He didn't have any balls at all—first eunuch I ever heard of who wanted to be a fighting man, and oh! wasn't he a fine one—but brains? That man had more brains than any five I've met since." After looking around, he lowered his voice. "And that includes Eusebius, too."

Also quietly, George said, "I've always thought the bishop's pretty smart."

"Oh, he is, he is," Rufus said. "That's what he is, sure enough: pretty smart. If we had Narses here in Thessalonica, now, if we had Narses, the Slavs and Avars would have gone away weeks ago, and they would have thought it was their idea, and they would have been proud of it."

"He sounds like quite a leader," George said, thinking he sounded like Rufus' beloved first commander, seen across most of a lifetime through a warm haze of memory.

"He was," Rufus said. "Remember, he's the fellow who finished the job of conquering Italy from the Goths after Belisarius marched up and down and up and down till his feet got flat but couldn't make those shaggy bastards lie down and quit. And Narses only had dribs and drabs of money and men to work with, too, on account of most everything got sent to the frontier with the Persians when the war started up there."

"That's so," George said slowly. Maybe Rufus knew what he was talking about after all. He had a way of knowing what he was talking about. But— "Isn't Italy full of Lombards nowadays?"

"It sure is," Rufus said. "And do you know what? That's Narses' doing, too. After Justinian finally upped and dropped dead, Sophia—his nephew Justin's wife, you know: the new Empress—heard how Narses had booted all the Goths and Franks out of Italy, and you know what she did?"

"What?" George asked, willing to oblige the veteran.

He needn't have bothered; Rufus talked right through him: "She sent him a distaff so he could spin thread. He was a eunuch, after all, so she figured she could insult him no matter what he'd done for the Roman Empire. But he had his revenge. He'd had Lombard mercenaries on his side fighting in Italy, and he invited the whole cursed tribe down. They were plenty glad to come, too, I'll bet. The country next door to theirs was filling up with Avars about then."

George thought about that. His shiver had nothing to do with the weather. "Any country next door to the Avars is a good one to get out of, you ask me."

"You mean, like this one?" Rufus asked, which was such a good question, George didn't answer it.

At first, George thought the service at St. Demetrius' basilica convened for prayer against earthquakes a coincidence. Then he reminded himself that Rufus and Eusebius had been putting their heads together. If they thought the Slavs and Avars liable to try working earth magic, the bishop would naturally do his best to forestall it.

"Why *does* the earth quake, Father?" Sophia asked as they walked toward the basilica.

"Because God is angry with us," Irene said before George could answer.

"I know *that*," Sophia said impatiently. "What I mean is, *how* does He make the earth shake? Or how do the gods of the Slavs and Avars do that, so He can stop them?"

"They jump up and down inside the earth, and when their feet hit, everything in there shakes, and so do we," Theodore said.

"Let's say that's true," George said. "What is there for their feet to land on that's any harder than anything else? And if there isn't any one part inside the earth that's harder than another, how can they jump up and down at all?"

"They're gods," Theodore said, "or demons, anyhow. Who knows what they can or can't do? Besides that Avar wizard, I mean."

George chewed on that. "Of course God—and demons, I suppose—can break natural laws now and then. That's what miracles are. But if natural laws got broken all the time, we wouldn't have any natural laws."

"Earthquakes only happen every now and then," Sophia said.

"Thank God," Irene added, and made the sign of the cross.

Theodore, being of the age where he constantly had to challenge his father, did so: "If demons jumping up and down inside the earth don't make earthquakes, what does?"

"My father said that his father said he once heard a philosopher traveling to Athens say—" George began.

Irene's loud and pointed sniff interrupted him. "Philosophers followed the pagan gods," she reminded him, "and God proved the stronger. So why should anyone care what the philosophers said?"

"Why should anyone care if I get a word in edgewise?" George said. "I don't think anyone *does* care if I get a word in edgewise." Having won a small space of silence with that outburst, he proceeded to fill it: "What this fellow said, if I have it right, didn't have anything to do with God or demons at all. He said the earth is full of caves and caverns that go deep, deep, deep underground, and when air rumbles through them in underground storms, that's what makes earthquakes."

Theodore delightedly clapped his hands together. "Earthfarts!" he cried, hopping in the air with glee. "Let's all pray that God can keep the Slavic demons from farting underground. Amen!"

"I get asked a serious question, I give a serious answer, and what thanks do I get for it?" George asked the air. "This. Straighten up, you foolish loon," he growled at Theodore, who had doubled over in laughter. He was having a hard time not laughing himself, but he would have given himself over to the city torturer before admitting it.

He was not the only one who knew their son well, either. In tones suggesting the Last Judgment, Irene said, "Theodore, before you think of breaking wind in the middle of Bishop Eusebius' prayer, imagine what your father will do to you after you come out of the church."

Theodore did imagine it. George could see him weighing whether the disaster to follow would be worth the entertainment during. What he could not see, and what worried him, was which way his son would decide.

When they got to the basilica, Irene and Sophia went upstairs to the women's gallery. George and Theodore made their way toward the altar. Along with keeping his elbows up to move other men out of the way, George kept looking around to see where Menas was. When he spotted the rich nobleman, he made a point of staying away from him. It wasn't fear: more on the order of not borrowing trouble, since every time the two of them came anywhere near each other, things only got worse.

People muttered back and forth while they waited for Bishop Eusebius. Not everyone knew why the bishop had summoned the folk of Thessalonica. Theodore made himself look wise and well connected by explaining to anyone who would listen. George kept his own counsel. Being thought close to the powerful was nothing he deemed important. Besides, Eusebius would do his own explaining soon enough.

Here came the bishop, behind a couple of muscular deacons swinging thuribles from which came the incense George often thought of as the odor of piety. Eusebius, his clever face more deeply lined than it had been when the siege began, took his place behind the altar. He raised his hands in a gesture of benediction that was at the same time a request for silence. When that silence proved slow in coming, the deacons stared out at the congregation so sternly, they soon obtained it.

"*Kyrie eleison*—Lord, have mercy," Eusebius said. "*Christe eleison*—Christ, have mercy." George echoed those prayers. So did everyone else in the basilica, the women in their gallery along with the men below. Eusebius said, "Servants of Christ, brethren, my friends: I have not bid you come to any ordinary divine liturgy. We are indeed here to beg God to have mercy on us in our struggle against the barbarians' vicious onslaughts."

In spite of the fiercely scowling deacons, a low murmur ran through the basilica from people who hadn't heard why Eusebius wanted them there or had got a garbled account that needed correcting.

Eusebius went on, "We have reason to believe the Slavs and Avars are wickedly consorting with the demons who, in their pride, reckon themselves gods, and seek to inspire those demons, whose province is the infernal regions, to overthrow the fortifications of this great and God-guarded city—fortifications the aforementioned barbarians have proved unable to overcome—by causing the ground to tremble and shake in the horrors of an earthquake, thereby transforming Thessalonica in the wink of an eye from town to tomb."

He brought out the sentence all in one breath, without the slightest hesitation. George admired that as much as he resigned himself to yet another dose of Eusebius' mortuary rhetoric.

The bishop went on, "We pray Thee, God, all of us here, individually and collectively, to spare Thy city and thwart and bind the powers of the demons, in accordance with the greatness of Thine own power. Let us live as we have lived, secure in Thy bosom and that of the Roman Empire Thou lovest. Preserve the calm Thou hast ordained in the bowels of the earth."

Theodore's face assumed a look of intense concentration. Acting with the reflexive speed he'd acquired in combat on the walls of Thessalonica, George stepped on his son's foot, hard enough to make Theodore grimace in pain. Whatever might have happened, didn't.

After that, assuming a properly reverential attitude, one that might persuade God to pay some small attention to his prayer, wasn't easy for George. He did his best, and had to hope it was good enough. He suspected the only prayer Theodore had offered up to the Lord was one for timely flatulence, and George had managed to keep that one from being granted.

Fortunately, Theodore hadn't howled when George stepped on him. That meant the reverence of the rest of the congregation remained undisturbed all the way up to Eusebius' final "Amen." People filed out of the basilica of St. Demetrius chattering approvingly about what a moving prayer service it had been.

"And when they say 'moving,' " George told his son, "they aren't talking about their bowels."

"Bishop Eusebius was," Theodore retorted, whereupon George trod upon his toes again. This time, it didn't help. Theodore dissolved into giggles, from which occasional mumbles of "bowels" and "earthfarts" emerged.

He and his father met Irene and Sophia across the street from the church. "I see you didn't have to kill him—quite," Irene said to George, again proving she knew their son as well as he did.

"I didn't do *anything*," Theodore protested, a cry that would have resounded with greater sincerity had he not still been snickering from time to time.

"Yes, and it wasn't for lack of effort that you didn't, either," George said, which singularly failed to abash his son.

Sophia gasped. George whirled, expecting some Slavic or Avar demigod to be menacing his daughter or someone else close by. Pointing, Sophia said, "Look—there's Constantine. Isn't he *splendid*?"

As far as George could see, the splendid one was still hulking, rather surly-looking, and pimple-besplotched. He knew Sophia was looking at the youth as much with her heart as with her eyes. Instead of examining Constantine (to his way of thinking, an unprofitable exercise), George nodded politely to Leo the potter. The father of Sophia's object of affection nodded back. He studied Sophia and then, warily, Irene. The smile she gave Leo showed good teeth; George was sure he'd imagined fangs in her mouth. Almost sure.

"God will provide," Irene said. Her husband wondered whether she was talking about Constantine or freedom from earthquakes. Probably both, he decided.

Several Avars on horseback stared in at Thessalonica. "They don't look very happy, do they?" Dactylius said, sounding happy himself at the Avars' appearance of unhappiness.

"No," George said, and then, more sharply, "Uh-oh. Here comes that priest or wizard of theirs. I'd almost sooner pray never to see him again than for no more earthquakes for a while."

"Amen to that," Rufus said. "He's caused us as much trouble as all their soldiers rolled together—throw in the Slavic wizards with him, I mean."

"That's so," George agreed. "But it looks like the other Avars aren't any happier to see him than they are to look at us, doesn't it?"

"Good," Rufus said with considerable relish.

One of the mounted men pointed toward Thessalonica. The priest shook his head and spread his hands in regret. Whatever the horseman wanted him to do, he couldn't do it.

"No earthquake today?" Rufus' voice oozed false regret. "Can't make the walls fall down? Oh, poor ducks. What a shame they had to go up against the power of God. When you do that, you come off second best." Realism replaced sarcasm for a moment. "Well, most of the time you do. The powers out there, they're pretty tough."

The Avar cuffed at the priest. George stared. Knowing how much power the man who wore furs and fringes controlled, he waited for the wizard to turn the horseman into a grub, or possibly even into a Roman scribe. But nothing happened, save that the Avar priest brought up a hand to keep the captain from hitting him more than once.

"Dissension in their ranks!" someone with a big, deep voice shouted from not far away: Menas. There he stood, atop the Litaean Gate. He'd been quiet till that moment, something so unusual it had kept George from noticing him. Now he went on, loudly obvious, "If they quarrel among themselves, our victory is assured."

"Why doesn't he keep still?" Dactylius asked.

"I don't think he knows how," George answered. "If he stops talking for long, he forgets he exists."

"That's no way to talk about a noble," Rufus said in stern tones, then added, "But I won't tell you you're wrong, either."

Menas waved his big, expensive, ostentatious war hammer. "We shall slaughter them, hip and thigh, root and branch."

"Is he a wrestler, a gardener, or a soldier?" George asked.

"He's a blowhard, that's what he is," Rufus said. "Haven't seen him up on the wall for a bit. He must have heard that the truth gets told here, and the truth about him is that—"

"Hush," Dactylius said. "He's liable to hear you, and then you'll have the same troubles with him that George does."

"Not me." Rufus' hand dropped to the hilt of his sword. "He tries getting wise with me, he'll regret it to the end of his days—and that'll be soon."

Out beyond the wall, the Avar captain was finally getting it through his head that the wizard couldn't give him what he wanted. He shouted to his companions. One of them produced a horn of polished brass that shone like gold even on a cloudy day. The fellow raised it to his lips and blew a long, unmelodious blast.

"Uh-oh," George said, as he had a little while before on spying the wizard.

"Oh, dear," Dactylius added. Rufus said something that expressed the same opinion a good deal more pungently. Slavs started tumbling out of the tents and little wooden shacks in which they sheltered from the elements. And, all along the wall, more horn blasts were presumably calling more Slavs out of more encampments.

"Something's going on," Rufus said, as good a statement of the obvious as George had heard in a long time. A moment later, the veteran added, "Here come the Slavs, all right."

Almost indignantly, George said, "I thought we decided the Slavs and Avars would try magic against us next."

"Maybe they did try it and it didn't work, thanks to the prayers we sent up to God the other day," Rufus answered. "Or maybe we were just flat-out wrong. Wouldn't be the first time that's happened to me, and I expect not to you, either, eh?"

George didn't answer. He was watching the Slavs, who were indeed issuing from their encampments in large numbers. Most of the barbarians were clutching bows. They trotted toward the wall of Thessalonica and started loosing great flights of arrows.

Crouching behind a battlement, Dactylius said, "This must be what they mean when they talk about shooting so many arrows, they darken the sun as they come."

"If one of 'em hits you square, it'll darken the sun for you, all right, and you can take that to church," Rufus said.

As if to underscore his words, men up and down the length of the wall shouted and screamed as they were wounded. George heard Menas say, "Here, my good fellow, lean on me. I'll get you down to safety and the help of a physician." The shoemaker's lip curled. Menas had found a way to get out of the dangerous part of the fighting, and to look good while he did it.

George popped up long enough to shoot at the Slavs, then ducked back down again. Up, shoot, duck . . . up, shoot, duck . . . "They haven't tried anything like this for a while," he said, nocking another arrow.

"Sure haven't," agreed Rufus, who was also grabbing for a new shaft. "Whatever they're doing, they're bloody serious about it."

"Of course they're serious," a newcomer said. "Have you ever seen anybody tell jokes while he was shooting a bow?"

"Hullo, John," George said without looking up. "Till you did it just now, no, I hadn't seen anybody do that."

"He did, didn't he?" Dactylius said. "Is it time to change shifts already? I mean, would it be time? If I'm not there when I'm supposed to be, it will make Claudia very unhappy."

"She'll be even more unhappy if the Slavs take the city," Paul pointed out; the taverner had come up onto the wall with the comic. He shot at the Slavs. "Got one there, I think."

"There are enough of them, I'll say that," Rufus said. "They haven't brought the whole army forward like this since . . ." His brow, already wrinkled, furrowed still more as he thought. "Since that time they used those tortoises to try and undermine the walls."

After George let fly with another arrow, he stayed upright longer than he had been doing. "I see more of them, getting ready to use those big shields they had then."

"Let me have a look." Rufus stood up beside him, ignoring the arrows humming by as if they were so many gnats. George pointed. The veteran let out a grunt. "Aye, that's what they're doing. Didn't know whether they'd try the same stunt twice, but I always figured they might. And don't the Scriptures talk about a dog coming back to its vomit?"

"That means coming back to a bad idea," George said, loosing another shaft at the advancing Slavs. "For them, this is liable to be coming back to a good idea." He shot again. The arrow ricocheted from one of the large, heavy shields. He cursed.

So did Rufus. "Aye, it's liable to be," he agreed. After he looked around at the piles of stones on the walkway, his curses put George's to shame. "I've been screaming at everybody who might listen, but we still haven't put back as many rocks as we dropped on the Slavs the last time they tried tortoises against us." He raised his voice to a great bellow: "Water and fuel for the cauldrons!" In more conversational tones, he said to George, "We'll never get stones up here quick enough to do much good. Dropping boiling water on the whoresons will still help, though."

"It had better," George said. The tortoise crews moved steadily forward. The shoemaker pointed to them. "They've learned from what went wrong the first time. Now they've got the shields up to make their shells right from the start."

"Only way to do it," Rufus said absently, and then, "I wish they were as stupid as those Goths and Franks and Lombards over in Italy. The German tribes didn't know how to do anything except bash and slash, and they didn't want to learn, either."

Under George's feet, the wall shivered. The first tortoise had reached it and, under cover of the iron-faced shields, the Slavs were using pry bars and hammers and chisels to try to pull stones out of the base and send the whole thing tumbling down. George set down his bow, picked up a stone, and dropped it down toward the attackers. It landed with a dull thud, not a clatter, telling him he'd missed.

Dactylius threw a stone down on the Slavs, too. He cheered when he heard a crash, but the barbarians kept chipping away at the wall, which meant the shields above them had turned the stone.

John said, "If this goes on much longer, it could get very boring." After a moment, he added, "Running out of rocks up here could be boring, too." *Boring*, as he used it, seemed to mean *getting everyone on the wall killed*.

Rufus lifted a stone. It was not one of the enormous boulders he'd picked up the first time the Slavs tried tortoises, but of more ordinary size and weight. Even so, it was enough to make him stagger. George decided God really had been helping him then. He also decided God wasn't helping Rufus now. When the veteran dropped the stone, he missed the tortoise, as George had.

The vibration underfoot got worse as more and more

Slavic crews got to work at the base of the wall. "We aren't going to have enough rocks to smash all of them," Paul said. "I don't know how else we're going to stop them, either." George had been thinking the same thing. He'd kept quiet, hoping it wouldn't be true if he didn't say it. Now Paul had said it. It was true.

Rufus' face was haggard, for once showing every one of his years. "We're in trouble," he said, each word dragged from him.

"A sally?" George asked, as he had before.

He saw how much Rufus wanted to say no, to keep fighting from the top of Thessalonica's wall, the wall that had for so long warded the Romans within from the barbarians outside. But the wall trembled beneath their feet, and might crumble beneath those feet at any moment. Looking as if every word tasted bad, Rufus said, "Aye, a sally." The decision made, he wasted no time wondering whether he should change his mind. Instead, he shouted, "Come on, you lugs! Grab your swords and shields and get down to the gate. If we can't make the Slavs leave the wall alone any other way, we'll have to chase 'em off!"

Having set down all his arms but his bow and arrow when he got up to the walkway, George had to snatch them up in a hurry now. Several of his comrades were doing the same thing. Rufus had already started down the stairway toward the Litaean Gate. John, Paul, George, and Dactylius hurried after him, along with a couple of dozen other militiamen from farther away.

Down on the ground, Rufus was shoving every able-bodied man he could find in the direction of the gate. "Here, what are you doing?" Menas shouted in anger and alarm. "Do you know who I am?"

Rufus kept shoving. "You're not much more than half my age, and you've got that big, fancy hammer in your hand," he answered. "Past that, pal, I don't care who you are."

This time, the soldier at the postern gate gave Rufus

no argument when he ordered it open. "Doesn't this look like fun!" John exclaimed. But the tavern comic was the first one through the gate, out into the hostile world beyond the wall.

George followed a moment later. He let out the loudest shout he could, both to frighten the Slavs and to try to make himself believe he wasn't frightened. He didn't know how he did on the first count. On the second, he failed miserably.

He ran toward the tortoise closest to the Litaean Gate. Arrows hissed past, bouncing back from the wall or shattering against it. To his relief, the Slavic archers didn't come rushing forward to engage his comrades and him in hand-to-hand combat. There were enough of them that they might have overwhelmed the militiamen by force of numbers alone.

Behind their shields, the Slavs in the tortoise saw the Romans running at them and shouted in alarm. John pulled one of the shields aside and slashed at the men it sheltered. Suddenly, the tortoise broke up as the warriors inside realized they had to fight for their lives. Their pry bars and hammers were better weapons against stone than against soldiers. The big, heavy shields were more suited to warding off rocks cast from above than attackers at close quarters, too.

One of the Slavs swung at George with the iron bar he held in lieu of a sword. George got his shield in front of the blow. Pain shot up his arm, all the way to the shoulder. He cut at the Slav, then circled rapidly to his left, away from that part of the barbarian the shield protected. The Slav grunted in alarm and tried to turn with him, but the iron-faced shield weighed so much, it made him slow. And, in his desperate urgency, he tripped over his own feet and sprawled on the ground.

Bang! Bang! Menas' silvered hammer came down upon his head. Had George dropped a pumpkin from the wall to the ground below, it would have made a sound like that when it hit. Blood sprayed. The Slav writhed, then lay still. Menas hit him again, to make sure that he was dead.

"Er—thank you," George said, feeling such awkwardness as he'd never known at having to be grateful to the noble.

Menas exploded that gratitude as thoroughly as he'd ruined the Slav's head. Swinging the hammer, he said, "I wish it had been you."

George wondered if he could make Menas suffer an unfortunate accident out here beyond the wall. It would make the noble's wife a widow, true, but, after being married to Menas, widowhood might look good to her.

Though such thoughts ran through the shoemaker's mind, he had not the slightest chance to do anything about them. Nor did Menas do anything to him that would have given him an excuse to make the noble suffer that unfortunate accident. Both of them, along with the rest of the militiamen who had sallied from several gates, were and stayed busy battling the Slavs who had been assaulting the wall of Thessalonica.

Some of those Slavs fought as fiercely as any men George had ever seen, in spite of their makeshift weapons and clumsy shields. One of them came within a whisker of caving in his skull with a pry bar. Only the pointed tip slid across his forehead, slicing the skin so that blood kept running down into his left eye.

That was the last swing the Slav ever took; George's sword slammed into the side of his neck a moment later. The barbarian let out a hoarse, gobbling cough; blood poured from the wound and from his mouth. Even as he began to topple, George ran past him. The shoemaker had been one of the first men out of the postern gate on the sally, and he'd come as far from it as any of his comrades. The farther he went, the more Slavs he could drive from the wall.

Not all the barbarians stood up against the unexpected Roman attack. More than a few ran away from the militiamen, some dropping their shields to flee the faster. Bowmen who'd stayed up on the wall shot several of them.

George let out a hoarse cheer every time he saw one fall.

The Slavic archers who'd been shooting at the defenders on the wall and at the sally parties kept their distance—till mounted Avars showed up behind them and started shouting what had to be threats. More afraid of their overlords than they were of the Romans (a regrettably sensible attitude, as far as George was concerned), the Slavs ran toward the militiamen, whom they badly outnumbered.

"Back!" Rufus shouted. "They aren't banging away at the wall anymore, and that's what we wanted. Come back!"

George would have been delighted to do just that, but he and a Slav were busy trying to kill each other. Finally, as if by common consent, they turned and ran away from each other. George was appalled to discover how close other Slavs were, and how far away all his comrades had got.

There went Paul, back through the postern gate. There went Sabbatius. George hadn't noticed him coming out. There went John, loping along with a bloody sword. There went Rufus. George ran harder. Not many Romans—hardly any Romans—remained outside the wall.

There went Menas. The noble turned around and looked out at George. He smiled. "I'm the last of us!" he shouted. "The very last!" He slammed the postern gate shut. The bar thudded down.

IX

From up on top of the wall, people shouted down to the men by the postern gate that somebody hadn't managed to get in. Those shouts did George no good whatever. The gate didn't open again right away, and what looked like all the Slavs in the world were bearing down on him.

George turned his face from the wall and ran for his life. Not quite so many Slavs were coming from the southwest, and the woods in that direction were fairly close. He slashed at a Slavic archer as he sprinted. The barbarian fell back with a howl of pain.

George was in among the Slavs now. No more arrows hissed past him. The archers most likely feared hitting their own comrades. If they closed with him, he was dead, and he knew it. But he was still swinging that sword, and they were armed with nothing better than bows and belt knives. That left them unenthusiastic about closing.

Breath sobbing in his throat, heart thudding as if it would burst at any moment, he got closer and closer to the woods. Now most of the Slavs were behind him, which meant they started sending arrows after him once more. He remembered they were in the habit of poisoning those arrows, and wished he could have kept on forgetting it.

Here was the brush. His boots scrunched on dry, fallen leaves. He groaned—how could he hope to go anywhere without giving himself away with every step he took? He wondered if the barbarians had let him get into the woods just to give themselves the pleasure of hunting him down. He'd watched cats playing with mice. Let the little creature think it can break free? Why not, especially when it's blocked off from its hole?

"Sometimes the mouse *does* get away," he panted, dodging between tree trunks. "Sometimes the cat ends up with a stupid look on its face." Most of the time, the mouse got eaten. He knew it. Again, he did his best not to think about it.

From right beside him, a voice spoke in Greek: "Sometimes mouse gets help." He had all he could do not to scream. He hadn't thought anyone was right beside him. Some Slavs were coming through the woods after him—much more quietly than he could—but . . .

He turned his head. A satyr looked back at him, its amber eyes wide and amused, its phallus jutting out almost as far as his sword. Was it the one he'd met when he was out hunting, that day not long before the Slavs and Avars came? He thought so, but couldn't be sure.

"Come," the satyr said. "Not stay here long." He didn't know whether that meant the creature couldn't stay so close to Christian Thessalonica for long, or whether it deemed staying so close to so many Slavs unsafe. Either way, George couldn't argue with it.

The satyr hurried away. Leaves flew up from under its hooves, but it made no noise as it moved. None—as far as George's ears could tell, it might as well not have been there. He blundered along as he always had, sounding like a herd of cattle being driven to market over a field of kettledrums, or so his racket sounded to himself.

But however appalling the racket he made, the Slavs didn't seem able to use it to track him. He heard them shouting back behind him. Some of them peeled off to the left of his true track, others to the right. Both groups, by the excitement in their voices, thought they'd seize him at any moment. Meanwhile, he got farther and farther away from them.

Realization blossomed. "You're doing this!" he said to the satyr.

"Yes. Hush. Not safe yet." On it went, silent itself and using the noise George made as a ventriloquist uses his voice: throwing it in every direction but that from which it truly came.

Something small and winged peered out at them from the branch of a sapling. It made a piping sound that had words buried in it. They were not Greek words. All at once, both groups of Slavs behind George started moving in the right direction.

Snorting with fear, the satyr grabbed for the fairy. It flitted into the air, those dragonfly wings buzzing. The satyr grabbed again and missed again. "Kill this thing!" it called to George.

"Who, me?" the shoemaker said in surprise. Without much conscious thought, he swung his sword at the fairy. He started to pray to God to help him, but swallowed the words at the last instant: the holy name would surely make the satyr flee. And maybe God was helping him *through* the satyr, or would be if George let Him.

He felt no resistance when his blade, as much by luck as by design, passed through the fairy's translucent body. But a tingle ran up his arm, as if lightning had struck close by. Light flared from the swordblade. Where the fairy had been was—nothing.

"Good!" The satyr groped for words. "That thing look, tell . . ." It ran a hand up and down its erection, as if it kept its brains there. George wouldn't have been surprised; he knew some men who did.

He gave the satyr the word it wanted: "It was a spy."

"A spy, yes!" The satyr's smile stretched across its snub-nosed face. "Not speak much, not need many names for longish time. Now need again. You give." Before George could answer that, the mercurial creature changed the subject: "You have wine? You give wine, like before?" It was the same satyr, then.

"No, I'm sorry. I have none." George hadn't bothered bringing a skin of wine up onto the wall with him. What point, when he'd be going back down again before long and could step into whatever tavern he liked? He hadn't expected to go beyond the wall, to be trapped outside of Thessalonica, or to need wine to make a thirsty satyr happy.

Its pointed ears drooped. "No wine," it said, as if summer had gone to winter in the space of two words. It trudged along with slumped shoulders. Now, for the first time, George could faintly hear its hooves moving through the leaves, as if the very aura of magic surrounding it was fading.

He knew how absurd it was to feel guilt at not having done something he couldn't possibly have known he would need to do. He felt it anyhow. "I *am* sorry," he said. "Here, how's this? When we find a village, I'll get some for you there." He didn't have more than a few folleis in his beltpouch, but they ought to serve. If they didn't, he would trade work—shoe repairs, for instance—for wine. The thought made him feel better.

It didn't seem to make the satyr happier. "Not find villages," the creature said, stroking itself again. "Not for a while, not find."

"What do you mean?" George said. "The hills around Thessalonica are full of villages. Why—" He paused, trying to work out the direction in which they'd gone. "There should be one over, over—" He started to point, then stopped. He tried again to get his bearings.

Eyes glowing, the satyr looked back at him. It looked amused. "You see now? Not for a while, not find."

"Yes," George said slowly. "Where are we, anyway?" He didn't know if that was the precise question he wanted to ask, but couldn't find a better one. As he ran through the woods, the ground on which he set his feet and the trees and bushes all around him seemed familiar enough:

he would have seen their like had he gone out from Thessalonica to hunt in quieter, more peaceful times.

Their like, yes. But whether he would have seen precisely these stones, those oaks, that set of brambles . . . with every step he took, he grew more doubtful of that. For the life of him, he could not tell where he was in relation to the city. He couldn't hear the Slavs coming after him, either. At first, he'd thought that was because he and the satyr had outdistanced them. Now . . . he didn't think that was all.

As if picking the thought from his mind, the satyr nodded. "You not in hills you know," it said. "You beyond hills you know." It went on quickly, reassuringly: "Can go back. Go back now, be hunted to death. But can go back. Mortals go back, forth many times." It hesitated then. "Not go back, forth so much now, on account of—" It could not say the name.

Despite its forced muteness, George understood. He was in the fairyland that had been receding from this country ever since men began following Father, Son, and Holy Spirit. Christian men would reckon they could not cross into that world, that plane, whatever the proper term was, without imperiling their souls. He supposed he was imperiling his soul.

"Who does go back and forth these days?" he asked.

"Men, women follow old ways. Some yet, yes," the satyr answered. "Up in hills, deep in hills, where . . . not come yet." Again, the silence implied the new dispensation. After a moment, the satyr added, "Those others, the ones with wolves and such" —George presumed he meant the powers of the Slavs— "they live in this kind of hills, too. They share with us a kind of being."

God—the God George had worshiped all his life—presumably either shared a kind of being (*essence*, the shoemaker thought, *the word is essence*—but what would a satyr know of theological terms, save perhaps for those dealing with fornication and lewdness?) with the powers of the Slavs and Avars or else altogether transcended those powers. George had always believed the latter; now he was less sure.

The farther he went, the stranger things felt. The strangeness did not lie in what he could see or hear or in the way the ground pressed his feet through the soles of his shoes. With every breath he took, though, he felt himself farther from Thessalonica, and that had nothing to do with getting away from the city stink. It suddenly occurred to him that Mt. Olympus lay only thirty or forty miles south and west of the Christian city in which he'd always dwelt.

Did the gods of whom Homer sang still live there? A few weeks before, he would have said no, and laughed at the idea. Now . . . now he wondered. He'd thought before that the epic poems might give those old gods a sort of half-life even in a Christian world.

But when he asked the satyr, it shook its head. "If up there, not come down. Pretty women no get Zeus—get me instead." It rubbed itself once more, smiled lasciviously, and rocked its hips forward and back. "How they laugh and squeal, pretty women!"

The great god was gone, conquered by God, Who was greater. The homely, earthy satyr remained, still a part, even if a hunted part, of the world George knew. He wondered how the Slavic powers would look after a couple of centuries of struggle against Christianity. Unfortunately, he did not have the luxury of waiting around to find out.

Another little wingety thing peeped out at him from behind a bush, then let out a high-pitched squeak. The satyr waved; its horselike tail came up in greeting. The fairy waved back, then flew off deeper into the woods. "Ours," the satyr said.

"Yes, I'd worked that out, thanks," George answered, as surprised by how much he was taking all this for granted as by anything else on a day he would cheerfully have traded for any other three bad days in his life. "Where are we going, exactly?"

"To a place," the satyr answered, which made George

wish to boot it in its hairy hind end. "Near a village," it amended, perhaps sensing his discontent. "To friends."

"When we get to this place near a village, what will we do?" George asked, being of the cast of mind to seek answers as far out ahead of possibly needing them as he could.

"Eat," the satyr said. "Maybe drink wine. Village has wine." He stared reproachfully at George.

Angry, the shoemaker almost cursed the satyr in the name of God. That would surely have made the creature flee, and as surely would have dropped George back into the mundane woods and hills around Thessalonica. He had no chance of getting back into the city on his own, not with the Slavs and Avars still besieging it. Finding a village would be a matter of luck; finding one the invaders hadn't wrecked would be a matter of much more luck. With autumn sliding rapidly toward winter, finding food and shelter enough in the woods to make it on his own would be more than a matter of luck. It would be a matter of divine intervention.

He kept on following the satyr, then. Surely coming across it in the woods had been a matter of divine intervention. He would have felt easier about that, though, had he had a better notion of which divinity was intervening.

"What's the name of this village?" he asked after a while.

The satyr shrugged. "The village. One of the villages." It took a few more steps, then added, "Pretty women." As far as it was concerned, that counted for more than such merely human things as names.

They came out into a small clearing. A rabbit bounded across it, *flup, flup, flup*, little black eyes wide with fear. George wished for his bow. If you could get close enough to kill a rabbit with a sword, you could get close enough to kill it with your bare hands. George knew he wasn't that kind of woodsman.

A rock hissed through the air, almost as fast as if flung by a catapult. It caught the rabbit in midbound. George heard bones shatter. The rabbit let out a shrill, startled cry. It tried to leap again after it thudded to the ground, but its hind legs didn't want to work. Bleeding, it dragged itself along with its forepaws.

Clattering hooves in the brush at the edge of the clearing made George tighten his grip on his sword and bring up his shield—had the Avars pursued him even here, as the satyr said they might?

But it was not Avars who burst from the screen of bushes. George was glad he had his hand clenched on the swordhilt; that made it harder for him to cross himself, which would have frightened the centaurs away. He watched, fascinated, awed, as they came out into the clearing. The one that had thrown the rock was a roan male; its human torso had thick red hair on the chest, while a red beard grew from its cheeks and chin. George had never imagined a bald centaur, but this one was.

Its companion was smaller, slighter, darker, and so fervently female from the navel up as to make George wish he were part stallion himself. The noise the satyr made reminded him that it *was* part stallion, even if to a lesser degree than the two centaurs. George wondered whether they had laws against such out-of-kind couplings. If they did, the satyr, by its reaction, cared not a fig for them.

George kept staring as the centaurs cantered across the field to pick up the rabbit, which had stopped moving. Not all the staring had to do with the way the female centaur's breasts bobbed as it moved, either. Satyrs were rare around Thessalonica, yes. Centaurs were more than rare. He'd thought the swelling power of the Lord had long since driven them from the world of men.

" 'Twill be fine, cony in a stew of leeks and turnips," the male centaur remarked, his voice a bass deeper than any man's, his Greek so archaic George had to think before he could be sure he understood it.

"Aye, thou hast reason, in good sooth," the female replied in the same old, old dialect. That dialect was not the only reason her voice startled the shoemaker, for it fell in the same baritone registers as his own. All the same, he couldn't help wondering whether the Biblical prohibitions against bestiality applied to creatures such as these.

Then he had another curious thought, not too far distant from the first. Along with those splendid, humanlike breasts, the female centaur also had a set of teats at the bottom of its horsy belly. When it had a baby or a foal or whatever the right word was, where did it nurse? George knew what his choice would have been, but he reminded himself he wasn't a newborn centaur.

"Hunting is so poor these days," the female said with a sigh.

"Aye, for the newcomers do most savagely chase and slay all the small deer they chance to run across, leaving but their leavings for us who have since time out of mind made these woods our home," the male said. George supposed it meant the Slavic wolves and other such powers. Had George been a wolf, he wouldn't have cared to run up against the male centaur, but a partly supernatural wolf might think differently.

When he'd seen the Avars so confidently planted on their horses, they'd put him in mind of centaurs. Now, seeing the real thing, he wondered what the Avars would make of them. Would they be jealous? Or would they assume the centaurs were meant to be their slaves, simply because they hadn't been lucky enough to be born Avars? That fit in with what he'd seen of the fierce nomads from off the distant plains.

The centaurs had their own measure of that lordly arrogance. Only after they'd finished with their own business did they deign to notice the satyr and his human companion. "Who is it that cometh with thee, Ampelus?" the male asked. That *thee*, unlike the one the female had used with the male, was patronizing, even insulting, not intimate. "A man from the city below, not so?"

"Yes, from the city, the city where they fight the new

people, the new things," the satyr—Ampelus—answered. "The city with saints inside."

That made both centaurs scowl, reminding them of the marginal life they—and the centaur—led in an ever more Christianized world. The male dipped its shiny head to George. "We welcome you to this fastness to which our . . . acquaintance hath brought you. Know that I am Crotus, and with me you see my wife Nephele."

George gave his own name, then said, "I didn't know centaurs still roamed these hills."

"They are ours," the female said, drawing itself up with formidable pride. "Not enough saints hath . . . your city" —Nephele could not speak the names of God or Christ any more than the satyr could, and had to talk around them— "to drive us hence altogether. Nor shall the savage strangers force us to flee, however fierce they be."

"They very fierce. They very many," Ampelus said. "How we stop them?" The satyr had fewer words and a far less elegant way of speaking than the centaurs, but seemed to George to have a better grasp on the way the world outside this backwoods retreat worked.

Crotus said, "Thou, satyr, art less afflicted than we by the powers we do not name, and so hast wider compass of vision"—the very thought that had just gone through George's mind. "But if one deem a difficulty impossible of solution, unsolved it shall surely be forevermore. Nor dost thou reckon our case hopeless, I warrant, else thou hadst not brought here this mortal, this George."

Ampelus shrugged. The satyr's erection jounced up and down. Nephele's reaction might have been amusement or disgust; George had no practice reading the sounds centaurs made. After a moment, Ampelus said, "He give me wine once. I save him, hoping he maybe give me wine again. But he has no wine this time." As nothing else had done, that made its phallus droop for a moment.

"As well that he have none!" Nephele exclaimed. "Wine for you satyrs is as it is for men: a little foolishness, a little sleep, a little headache, and then all in readiness to be done over again. Not so for us, whom the slightest taste of the blood of the grape inflameth to madness."

"Wine is sweet," Ampelus protested. "Wine is good."

"Aye—for thee," Crotus said. "When the scent of the fermenting vintage wafteth from the villages wherein the men trample the grapes . . ." A look of terrible longing filled the centaur's face. "I needs must hie me off deep into the woods then, lest instead I rush forward to guzzle and . . ." It fell silent again. The day was chilly. Sudden sweat sprang out on its forehead even so.

"Will someone please take me to one of these villages?" George asked. "Maybe I can find a way to get back into Thessalonica. If I can get down to the seaside, if I can find a boat . . ." He didn't think any of that was likely to happen, but it was the best his imagination had been able to do.

Satyr and centaurs ignored the request. In that disconcerting baritone, Nephele asked, "How is it, George of Thessalonica, you have no fear of our kind, and neither seek you to compel us to flee your presence with signs against which we may not stand?"

"Why would I do that?" George asked in return. If the female centaur thought he wasn't afraid, that only proved the pagan powers were a long way from omniscient. Hoping Nephele wouldn't notice he was responding to only half the question, he went on, "Ampelus saved my life. He didn't have to do that. I owe him a debt."

"Wine!" the centaur cried. "Jars and jars and jars of wine!"

"We stand in need of a better bargain than that," Crotus said stiffly.

"Is no such thing," Ampelus said, but then corrected itself: "Is maybe one, but cannot bring jars and jars and jars of pretty women."

Nephele set hands on . . . no, not on its hips, but the place where the narrowness of that human waist swelled out to meet the equine body that carried it. "Enough of japes and jests and fribbles," the female centaur declared, giving the satyr a severe look that altogether failed to dismay it. When Nephele went on, it was to George: "So many of your fellows would raise against us that which we cannot face or deny our existence altogether."

"Aye." Bitterness edged Crotus' voice. "And should the denial become universal, it becometh also sober truth: another reason for our clinging to the peaks and other lands wherein our being is more certain."

George had never wondered what the growth of Christianity looked like from the viewpoint of creatures pushed to the wall by the new faith. Along with other such abstract questions, though, that one would have to wait. He found a question anything but abstract: "If you have these weaknesses, how do you propose to come down and fight the powers of the Slavs and Avars?"

"We need help." Nephele spoke unhappily, but without hesitation. "Thus your coming is welcome, even if Ampelus aided it for reasons of his own rather than to promote the general welfare."

"I do what I do," Ampelus said. "I like to do what I do." The satyr rocked his hips forward and back again, aiming that enormous phallus at Nephele. The female centaur ignored it. George wondered whether that sprang from remarkable aplomb or standards of comparison different from those he was used to using.

"What is your craft, mortal?" Crotus asked. "Are you by any chance a priest of . . . ?" Again, the male used a pause to do what it could not.

That almost made George laugh. "No," he answered. "I'm only a shoemaker." That sounded as ordinary as any trade possibly could, till he realized none of the beings with whom he was talking had any need for what he did. He shook his head like a man caught between dream and reality; the difference of his new companion's feet brought home to him that dream *was* reality here.

" 'Tis too much to be hoped for that any priest should find our kind fit for aught but exorcisms," Nephele said. "So many woods and streams and paths barred to us on account of words from that book." It glared at George as if that were his fault.

In a way, he supposed it was. He was a Christian man. His belief gave the priests some part of their power, just as lack of belief threatened to doom centaurs and satyrs and other failing creatures of pagan days. But— He brightened. "I think I know a priest who would come here," he said.

He wondered what sort of penance Bishop Eusebius would set Father Luke for associating with these beings. He did not wonder whether Father Luke would associate with them if it meant saving Thessalonica. He was sure the priest would come. Which left the next question: how to get him to come?

"Of necessity, 'twill be you delivering word he is wanted," Crotus said. "Saints hem Nephele and me and the rest of our kind so close, it were the end for any of us to venture forth from these hills, as hath been previously intimated to you. Being of ruder substance, Ampelus and his fellows may fare farther abroad more readily, but cannot think to enter into the city where so many are of your opinion."

"Mm." George rubbed his chin. "Since it's surrounded by the Slavs and Avars, I can't think about entering it, either. Can you help me come close enough—maybe through the hills my kind don't usually travel anymore—to give me some chance of getting in?"

"It may be so," the male centaur answered. "I cannot speak with certainty, not here, not yet. But the thing must be essayed, lest all fail."

"New things in woods, things in those hills," Ampelus added fearfully. "Things with wings, to spy and see. Things with teeth and claws, to bite and kill."

"You can speak of them, can't you?" George asked. The satyr and the two centaurs nodded. Watching Nephele nod was worth the candle, even if the female's voice was as deep as his. Refusing to let himself be distracted, he went on, "I'm surprised you don't want to see those powers win at Thessalonica. They're more your kind than . . ." Now he used silence to indicate God, Whom he would not name here.

"Not so," Crotus said, "for their people lack all knowledge of and belief in our kind. Did they win, did they defeat even that which hath reduced us to our present estate, they would on the instant then proceed to hunt us to extinction: not a slow fading but a quick and bitter end."

"He hath courage, to speak on what redoundeth not to his advantage," Nephele said, tempering the compliment a moment later by adding, "Courage, or a signal want of good sense."

"How soon can you try to get me back into the city?" George asked. "My family—" He broke off, thinking of his family for the first time since Menas slammed the postern gate in his face. As far as they knew, he was probably dead. He hoped someone had seen him escape into the woods, but even if someone had, so what? The most reasonable guess was that the Slavs would have hunted him down regardless. Had he been up on the wall watching someone else run, that was what he would have believed.

Crotus and Nephele looked toward Ampelus, who could approach Thessalonica more closely than they. The satyr nervously masturbated itself. "Not be easy," it said, its rusty voice worried. "People round the city, *things* in the woods—"

George looked at the sky. The sun would soon be down, hurrying toward the southwestern horizon on this cold near-winter day. "Would it be easier" —by which he meant safer— "to travel at night?"

"No!" Ampelus spoke with great certainly, and kneaded its own tumescent flesh to emphasize the point. "*Things* worser at night. Eyes glow, they see like owls, they . . . No."

Realizing the hour made George also realize how worn and hungry he was. "Will you take me to that village, then?" he asked. "That should be safe."

"I doubt we should reach it ere the sun's chariot leaveth the sky," Crotus said. "Are you fain to pass the night with us, George who feareth not that which dwelt in this land long ago and abideth here yet?" Unlike Ampelus, the male centaur plainly did not want to go anywhere near where men dwelt. *Fear of wine,* George thought, and then, *or is it lust for wine?*

"Yes, of course. Thank you." The shoemaker bowed to the centaur. He did his best to tell himself getting back among men, even backwoods pagans who probably didn't know the Emperor's name, was better than passing his time with creatures whom Bishop Eusebius and almost all his fellow Christians back in Thessalonica reckoned fit only for exorcism. That was the right thing, the proper thing, to think. He couldn't make himself believe it. His curiosity was itching too fiercely. How many modern men got a chance like this? For that matter, how many men in ancient days had got a chance like this?

Crotus and Nephele went ahead at a pace he could not match. Ampelus led him through the woods to what might easily have been a hunters' encampment. It was almost disappointingly prosaic: several neat lean-tos (some of them outsized, to accommodate centaurs), with a fire in the middle, a large pot bubbling over it.

Little by little, strangenesses surfaced. The knife Nephele used to cut up the rabbit and add it to the stew was bronze, with a bone handle. The pot into which the female threw the pieces of meat had a delicate perfection of shape potters these days didn't even attempt, and was ornamented with capering satyrs in black on a red background. George didn't know how old that made it—Leo might have—but knew it was very old indeed.

Ampelus walked over to the pot. Nephele gave the satyr a look that warned it not to steal any stew. But that wasn't what it had had in mind. It pointed to one of the satyrs the potter had painted, then to its own chest. "Me," he said proudly.

For a moment, George thought that only an idle boast.

Then he took a closer, more careful look. The potter had labeled each dancing satyr. Beside the one at which George's guide had pointed were Greek letters: ΑΜΠΕΛΟΣ. The shoemaker stared at the ancient portrait. It was a good likeness.

Another satyr came into the encampment, carrying a couple of squirrels by the tail. "Ha, Stusippus!" Ampelus said. "Here is George, this man I tell you I meet yesterday."

It hadn't been yesterday. It had been months before. George started to say as much, then abruptly closed his mouth. Here was a creature with a picture from at least as many centuries before the Incarnation as had passed since. No wonder the recent past blurred together for it.

"Friendly man—I remember," Stusippus said. The new satyr's features were less manlike than Ampelus', its erection even larger. "Man with wine."

"I have no wine today," George said, and Stusippus' phallus drooped for a moment, as Ampelus' had done at the same sad news.

"Give thou me thy meat there," Nephele said. Stusippus handed the female the squirrels without making the bawdy comment George had expected. Nephele still had that knife in hand.

More centaurs drifted into the camp. A couple of females—Lampra and Xanthippe, their names were—brought in baskets of roots, while Lampra's mate (husband? George didn't know), Elatus, had a dead pig tied onto its back with vines. More fires were started. More delicious smells rose into the evening air.

With Xanthippe frolicked something George had never imagined, a baby centaur. Again, he wondered whether to think of it as a foal or a child. He watched, fascinated. "What's it called?" he asked the young one's mother, whose light roan coat and golden human hair and horse's tail might have given it the name Xanthippe.

"Demetrius," the female centaur answered. Its voice was deep as Nephele's.

George's jaw dropped. "After the saint?" he said. Could

the pagan creatures have been trying to gain the protection of God, Whose name they could not say?

But they knew deities of their own. "After the great mother goddess," Xanthippe said severely.

"Oh." George was relieved and disappointed at the same time. "How old is it?" he asked, wondering if centaurs grew according to the pattern of horses or men.

Xanthippe shrugged. Time meant no more to centaurs than it did to satyrs. "I don't know." Its voice was—not indifferent, but uninterested. "A few hundred years."

"Oh," George said again, and said no more. Would Demetrius be ranging these hills a thousand years from now? If the Slavs and Avars weren't driven away, the youngster wouldn't be. Otherwise . . . George tried not to think of the thirty or forty years that were the most he could expect to remain on this earth. But his soul would exist forever. Did Demetrius have a soul? One more thing George did not know and never would.

He missed bread with his supper, and he was used to drinking wine, not the clear, cold water bubbling up from a spring near the fire. Other than that, the meal was as good as any he'd ever eaten, with hunger a relish sharper than garlic.

After everyone had eaten, Xanthippe chanted Pindar's Second Pythian Ode, to Hiero of Syracuse. George did not understand why it had chosen that particular piece till he realized it spoke of the creation of its race. Crotus and Nephele, little Demetrius, and Elatus all got up and danced to the song that had been written ages before George's great-great-grandmother was born. But any one of them, save perhaps Demetrius, might have seen Pindar. The shoemaker's shiver had nothing to do with the cold.

The centaurs and satyrs had drifted fallen leaves in their shelters to serve as beds. Ampelus and Stusippus invited George in with them. The three of them crowded their lean-to, and the satyrs' phalluses kept prodding at him as he burrowed into the leaves. The pagan Greeks, he remembered uneasily, had found unnatural vice neither unnatural nor a vice, and so their powers would not, either. But the satyrs did not seek to molest him. He was glad he'd had no wine for them.

Shortly thereafter, he was glad to be in bed with the satyrs, a gladness that had nothing to do with carnality. Without them, he would have shivered the whole night through. With them, despite their phalluses and other minor annoyances such as their hooves kicking him in the shins, he was warm enough. He burrowed into the leaves and slept.

"What a strange dream," George said the next morning. He rolled over to tell it to Irene. Leaves rustling under him made him open his eyes. He was looking into Ampelus' face.

"Morning," the satyr said: more an announcement than a greeting.

"Good day," George said, wondering if it would be. He got to his feet and started brushing leaves off his tunic and out of his hair. If the satyrs and centaurs slept like this, he wondered why they weren't perpetually covered with bits of their mattresses.

He discovered the answer to that moments later. Ampelus and Stusippus had a bone comb. The first thing they did after getting out of their bed was to take turns combing each other free of dried leaves. George knew a couple of brushmakers down in Thessalonica. If they brought their wares up into the hills, they might do a good business.

Since he had less hair to fret over than any of his companions, and since he also had no one to groom him, he decided to make himself useful by stirring up the fire. His breath smoked as he built the blaze up again; the heat from the new flames was welcome.

"For this we thank you," Crotus said, coming up behind him. Where George had been warming his hands in front of the fire, the male centaur bent forward so it could heat the bare crown of its head. Brushmaker . . . hatmaker:

George added to his mental list of artisans who might be useful here among these creatures of an outworn creed.

What did creatures of an outworn creed do about breakfast? At home, George was ready to face the day after bread with olive oil and a cup of wine. His chances of getting any of those things here in this sylvan encampment didn't look good.

What he got were sun-dried apples and apricots, washed down with more water from that stream. It was cold enough to make his teeth ache, but almost as sweet as the fruit the centaurs gave him.

Once he'd eaten and drunk, he asked, "Shall we go on to one of those villages now?"

"If you be so eager to return to your own kind, we can do't for you," Crotus said, "however wary of villages we may be on account of the temptations of the vintage brewed therein. But if you would liefer bring us this holy man of whom you spoke not long ago, were it not wiser to seek to return to the town whence you came?"

"If you think you can get me back inside Thessalonica in spite of the Slavs and Avars all around, I'm game, but I don't see how you'll do it, especially since you can't come close to the city yourselves."

Crotus frowned. In a way, George knew a certain amount of intellectual pride at having perplexed the supernatural being. In another way, he wished the centaur had had an easy answer waiting. Crotus said, "We shall do all in our power to aid you, the more so as the holy man seemeth to be of the sort the situation requireth. That there may be risk in this course, both from the new-come powers and from the one against which we cannot stand—this we understand. We weigh here dangers one against another. In no direction standeth none."

"I think you're right about that," George said slowly. He thought for a little while himself, then said, "All right, if you think you can get me down to Thessalonica and into the city, we'd better try it. And the sooner, the better."

"There I deem you have bitten through the meat

straight to the bone," the male centaur said. "My kind is but rarely inclined to take quick action, the passage of time being of small import to us. Thus it was that . . . what you follow established itself in our land, we feeling no urgency toward expelling . . . it till too late. And now we are all but banished ourselves. May we prove wise enough to learn from one error and not commit a second of like sort."

"People don't often learn from their mistakes," George said. If these immortal creatures did, they deserved to be reckoned demigods.

"Nor satyrs, either, they being prisoners to their lusts," Crotus answered. "We dare hope ourselves the wiser. We are no longer wine-bibbers, having learnt from sore experience how such enrageth us."

They could have stood around for the next several days, talking about the ramifications of moving and not moving. George realized Crotus *would* talk about ramifications for the next several days, and not notice the flowing time. Harshly, the shoemaker said, "Let's get moving, then, if we're ever going to."

"I cry huzzah for mortal celerity," Crotus said. "On to Thessalonica!" It went back to the lean-to it shared with Nephele and talked with its mate for a while, then with the rest of the centaurs, and at last with the satyrs, who seemed to require less in the way of instruction and debate than its own kind. However much it tried to hurry, more than an hour went by before George, all the centaurs (even little Demetrius), and the satyrs started down from the hills toward the city.

In purely physical terms, going down was easier than coming up had been. But purely physical terms were far from the only ones that mattered. For one thing, George was not entirely certain he remained in the hills he knew. For another, after a while he began to feel as if every step he took required a distinct effort of will. When he remarked on that, Nephele tossed its head and replied in that disconcerting baritone: " 'Tis but a cantrip of the barbarians circling round the city, and hardly one of potency overwhelming." Its sniff declared the Slavs and Avars should have done better.

The spell's potency might not have been overwhelming to the female centaur, but it was of different substance from George, who found the going ever harder. And then, suddenly, he had no trouble at all setting one foot in front of the other, and went along as readily as he might have done on the street outside his shop in the city. "That's better," he said.

Only when the words were out of his mouth did he notice that his companions had stopped, as if they'd walked into Thessalonica's wall. After a moment, Ampelus and Stusippus gathered themselves and came toward him. The centaurs needed longer than the satyrs, and advanced as if pushing their way through glue, not air.

"What's wrong?" George asked. "Did that cursed Avar priest make the spell stronger? He's not to be taken lightly, that one."

"The barbarian?" Crotus had to fight to get the words out one by one. "Nay, that was naught of his doing. Meseems you are prayed for inside the city toward which we fare."

George thumped his forehead with the heel of his hand. Of course he was prayed for back in Thessalonica. His wife and children would be in St. Elias' now—if they weren't in St. Demetrius'. His friends would be in one church or another, too, if they weren't up on the wall.

And their prayers had succeeded in weakening the spells the Slavs and Avars had been using to keep him from approaching Thessalonica. The only trouble with that was, the prayers also seemed to have weakened the supernatural beings aiding him. That wasn't good. He had doubts about being able to get down from the hills with the centaurs and satyrs helping him. Without them, he had no doubts: he wouldn't make it.

He saw how vulnerable they were to the power of God. As a Christian, that made him proud. As someone trying to save his own neck, it worried him. If he was going to keep on being proud, he hoped he'd soon be able to start worrying less.

"The weakness passeth," Xanthippe said after a bit, tossing its head in an impatient gesture a horse without human excrescences might have made. "The petition, methinks, was not aimed straight against us, else the hurt had been greater."

Gaining strength with her, the other centaurs also came on. Down the game tracks they went with the satyrs and George. He was thoughtful and quiet. The prayer had surely been aimed at the Slavs and Avars. It had weakened their spell, to be sure, but he doubted it had done them the harm it had his companions. That meant those companions were weaker than the powers of the Slavs and Avars. He'd known as much, but didn't care to be reminded of it.

Little by little, the shock of God's power wore away. The satyrs took to playing with themselves again. That amused Demetrius, the immature centaur, who, having seen such things for only a few centuries, still found them funny. George didn't laugh. He took the masturbation as a sign the satyrs remained alarmed, even if at the Slavs and Avars, not at the Lord.

Smiling like a good dog, the first wolf stepped out from between two trees half a bowshot in front of George. It was, obviously, no ordinary wolf. It was bigger than a wolf had any business being, its teeth were longer and sharper, its very stance fiercer and more alert than an ordinary wolf's could have been.

Ampelus, who had been walking alongside of George, sprang nimbly back with a gasp of fright. The shoemaker gasped, too, and made the sign of the cross. He'd already done it before he remembered the company he was keeping. But the satyr had said he'd watched a Christian priest make the holy sign when confronted by a Slavic wolf-demon. It hadn't been aimed at Ampelus, and so had had no effect on him.

Nor did the satyrs and centaurs flee George now. But the sign of the cross, though it made the wolf draw back a pace and turned that doglike smile into a snarl, did not rout it. George remembered that the wolf the priest had met had killed him in short order. He yanked out his sword. This wolf would not have such an easy time. He had more defenses than the spiritual alone.

The wolf snarled again, as if angry at itself for yielding even slightly to the strength of the Christian sign. Then it sprang for him. He raised his shield. *If the wolf knocks me down*, he thought, *I have to keep the shield between those teeth and my throat. Maybe I'll be able to stab it before it bites too many chunks out of me.*

From behind him, a rock flew through the air and caught the wolf-demon on the tip of its nose. Its agonized yelp was sweet music in George's ears. It skidded to a stop and stared past him to the centaurs, as if it had never imagined they would do such a thing to it.

Another stone hit it, this one in the chest. It staggered, threw back its head, and loosed one of those horrifying howls George had heard coming out of the forest from the walls of Thessalonica.

The shoemaker crossed himself again. Growling deep in its throat, the wolf retreated a few paces. Perhaps because it was hurt, the sign of the cross had more power over it than had been true a moment before. It howled again, this time more in pain than to cause fear among its foes. George took a step toward it, and it drew back once more.

"Move aside, that we may pelt the creature according to its deserts," Crotus called.

"I don't care about its pelt," George heard himself answer: his mouth ran wild and free, disconnected from such wits as he had. "Besides, this is my fight, too." He advanced on the wolf, which backed away from him.

But now other howls rose in answer to those the creature had loosed. Other wolves came out of the woods to stand with the first, and still others made leaves rustle in the forest to either side of the path. Such creatures could surely have traveled silent as a thought, had they so chosen. But they must have wanted George and his companions to know they were there, so as to put them in fear. George stared now this way, now that. He and the satyrs and centaurs were outflanked.

"We have to go back!" George shouted.

Ampelus and Stusippus scampered away toward the encampment from which they'd set out that morning. All the centaurs, though, stared at George with blank incomprehension. That look told him more clearly than anything else could have why even the pagans of ancient Greece, without the power of God behind them, had been able to drive the powerful creatures deep into the hill country: the very notion of retreat seemed alien to them, however necessary it might be.

Only when wolves burst out at them from left and right at the same time did the centaurs suddenly seem to catch on to what George had meant. He hoped that wasn't so late, it would get them all killed—and him with them.

A wolf sprang at Xanthippe's flank. The female centaur whirled, startlingly quick, and kicked out with its hind legs. The hooves slammed into the wolf's snout. It rolled away, yowling in pain. Blood spurting from its wounds. Any natural creature, any creature of flesh and blood, would have had its head caved in.

Demetrius let out a sound half-scream, half-whinny, as a wolf raked the young—but not so young—centaur's side with its teeth. The wolf rammed the centaur, overbore it, and came darting back to tear out its throat.

Shouting, George ran to the—colt's?—aid. The first swipe of his sword lopped off a couple of digits' worth of the wolf's tail. That got its attention. It whirled away from Demetrius and toward George. The end with the teeth looked much more dangerous than the end with the tail.

The wolf-demon leaped straight for his face. He got his shield up—Rufus would have been proud of him—

and cut at the creature. He felt his blade bite into its side, but it didn't seem to mind in the least. It hit him like a boulder. Try as he would to keep his feet, he went over backwards.

He did all the things he'd reminded himself to do when the first wolf-demon had been about to attack him. He kept his shield up; the wolf's fangs scraped on the leather facing. He kept slashing with his sword. None of that would have mattered very long. The wolf was immensely stronger than he, and his sword seemed unable to do it much harm.

But then, just as it was scrabbling with paws unnaturally clever to pull down the shield so its teeth could do their deadly work, *thud! thud!*—two stones struck it blows hard enough to make it roll off him and away. If those stones hadn't broken ribs, the wolf owned none.

George scrambled to his feet. Elatus grabbed the wolf with human arms and hands, lifted it off the ground in an amazing display of strength, and then threw it down, hard. The male centaur trampled the wolf-demon with both pairs of equine hooves.

The wolf howled and twisted and then clamped its jaws on Elatus' left hindmost leg. The centaur cried out in anguish. George rushed to its aid. He stabbed the wolf-demon in the belly with his sword. It screamed; supernatural or not, it was sorely hurt. Its blood smelled hot and metallic and almost spicy: an odor much stronger and more distinctive than that of the blood of ordinary living things.

Elatus was bleeding, too. That did not keep the centaur from flailing away with its three good horse's legs at the wolf-demon, which finally broke away and fled, not just from the male centaur but from the fight as a whole.

"We can't go forward," George said. "There are still too many of them. We have to go back."

"A truth may be bitter but a truth natheless," Elatus said. The male dipped its shaggy head to George. "And I own myself in your debt, mortal. That was bravely done." It twisted so it could look at its wounded leg. Scabs were already forming over the bites. In a day or two, George supposed, Elatus would be altogether healed. And, in a day or two, the wolf-demon the shoemaker had stabbed would probably be well again, too. He sighed. Had he been a proper hero out of myth, he would have slain it.

Elatus shouted: a great sound without words George could discern, but one that must have had meaning to the other centaurs. They began to retreat down the path Ampelus and Stusippus had taken. George went with them. The wolves made as if to pursue, but gave up when the centaurs, having opened a little distance from them, bombarded them with showers of stones.

None of the centaurs had escaped without wounds, but all of them were well on the way toward healing by the time they got back to the encampment from which they'd set out. George counted himself lucky to have got away with nothing worse than cuts and scrapes and bruises; no sharp teeth had pierced his tender flesh. He ached and stung as things were. Being in the company of the supernatural beings did not make him so close to immune to hurt as they were.

"Manifest it is," Crotus said, scratching what had been a bite and was now a rough red scar, "that these folk and their powers desire not your return to the city whence you were abstracted."

"I didn't want to be abstracted from it," George said. When he thought of Menas, his hands bunched into fists. "I didn't get what I wanted. I don't see any reason the Slavs and Avars should get what they want."

"One reason doth suggest itself," Nephele observed: "namely and to wit, that they have the power to enforce that which they desire."

Ampelus came up to George. All the centaurs glared at the satyr, who had been of such little use in the fight against the wolf-demons. Sensitive to that scorn, Ampelus spoke with something like embarrassment: "Not good to go in day. Maybe good to go in night."

George clapped a hand to his forehead. "When I wanted

to do that, everyone said it would be worse than trying it in the daytime."

"What can be worse than that?" the satyr asked reasonably. "Try in day, not go. Try in night, likely not go, but maybe go."

George could see one way in which things might be worse. He'd come out of this try alive, even if unsuccessful. If things went wrong again . . .

He wondered what was happening back at Thessalonica. The sally from inside the city had driven back the Slavs undermining the walls beneath the shelter of their tortoises, but had the barbarians attacked again? Had the Avar priest or wizard found yet another set of demigods to hurl against the protective power that came from St. Demetrius and from God?

And on those questions depended the answer to the truly important one: how were Irene and Theodore and Sophia?

"We'd better try and get back, any way we possibly can," George said. "If it can't be by day, it will have to be by night." The children of Israel had traveled by night as well as by day, he reminded himself, with a pillar of fire to light their way as they went.

He did not expect God to give him a pillar of fire. Thinking of the children of Israel made him think of Benjamin the Jew, and thinking of Benjamin made him think of Dactylius and Rufus and John and drunken Sabbatius and Claudia and Paul and the rest of his friends back in Thessalonica. He also thought again of Menas back in Thessalonica. As they had before, his hands formed fists. Without Menas, he wouldn't have been in this predicament. Rich though Menas was, noble though Menas was, George resolved he would have his revenge. *One more reason to go back*, he thought.

Daylight hours were short at this season of the year. Time seemed to crawl by anyhow. The satyrs went out hunting, and came back with rabbits and roots and herbs. They presented these to the centaurs as what George took to be a peace-offering. Nephele looked as if she wanted to fling the food in Stusippus' face. But if the female did that, everyone would go hungry. Into the pot everything went.

George had seen the day before that centaurs had appetites in keeping with their size. He got only a few mouthfuls of stew, and a bit more dried fruit to go with it. After two days straight of fighting for his life, that didn't feel like enough. His stomach made noises that might have come from the throat of a Slavic wolf-demon.

When darkness finally came, the shoemaker shivered. Part of that, he was not ashamed to admit to himself, was fear. Part, too, was cold. His teeth had chattered up on the wall when he'd drawn night duty. Being out in the woods was worse. He would have welcomed the company of a couple of rampantly erect satyrs in a bed of leaves—they would have helped keep him warm.

Instead, having bolted his meager meal, he slipped out of the encampment with Ampelus. None of the centaurs accompanied them. "For," Crotus said as they were leaving, "strength having failed, stealth needs must serve. There the lustful ones surpass us, they being every inclined to sneak up on mortal women and so debauch themselves." The male's lip curled in scorn. "Mayhap their skulking habits shall this once prove of advantage to us."

"Huh," Ampelus said. "He not so smart as he think he is. One of these days, I climb up on rock back of Nephele, show that mare what loving can be." The satyr's hips twitched in lewd anticipation. George noted, however, that for all of Ampelus' bravado, it made sure it was well out of earshot of the encampment before making a boast like that.

They walked quietly through the woods, down toward Thessalonica. All George heard were their footfalls, scuffing through fallen leaves. Or rather, all he heard were his own footfalls scuffing through fallen leaves.

Ampelus paced along beside him, silent as a shadow. No insects chirped: too late in the year. No nightjars called, no owls hooted.

Bare-branched trees raised their boughs to the sky, as if surrendering to robbers. Those boughs passed black in front of the nearly full moon that poured pale radiance over the hillside. Normally, George would have been delighted to have all the light he could if he was crazy enough to go through the forest at night. Now— Now he said, "Won't the moon make it easier for the wolves and whatever else is out there to find us?"

"Easier, yes." The satyr played with itself for a little while, as it did whenever it was worried. "But they not need much light to see. Maybe they not need to see at all. Maybe they . . . know."

"What will you do if they *know*?" George pronounced the word as portentously as Ampelus had done. "Run away again?"

"This" —the satyr gripped its swollen phallus with both hands— "this is no sword. Can't kick like donkey, like stupid centaurs do. Can maybe throw rocks. Maybe. What good in fight, I? Made to be lover" —that hip-rocking motion again— "not fighter."

"Well, even so—" George began, admitting to himself if not to the satyr that it had a point.

Ampelus cut him off. "Shut up, mortal George, or see how mortal you be. Not get through by fighting anyhow. Get through by sneaking. Sneaking, you be quiet."

The satyr had another point there, even if it had been doing more talking than George. The shoemaker trudged along. Most of the time, he and Ampelus headed downhill toward their goal, pushing through the spell of resistance the Slavs and Avars had established against such ventures. Every so often, they climbed rises lying athwart their path, Ampelus judging that quicker than walking around. From one of those bits of higher ground, George caught a glimpse of Thessalonica, lamps and torches bravely burning inside the wall. The city hadn't fallen, then. Relief made him feel as if he'd walked fewer miles on more food than was really so.

That remained true despite his also having seen the campfires of the Slavs and Avars around the besieged city. He hadn't expected the barbarians to have cleared out since he was locked away from Thessalonica. As long as they were outside the wall, not within it, something might yet be done.

Ampelus suddenly grabbed George's arm and pulled him to one side, ever so carefully skirting what looked to the shoemaker like a stretch of ground no different from any other. "What's wrong?" George whispered. "Did you see a wolf?"

"Worse," the satyr answered with a fearful shudder. "Saint do something holy there, who knows when? Ground hurt to go on."

"St. Demetrius?" George asked.

Ampelus turned to stare at him. The satyr's eyes flashed. The light, George thought, was their own, not reflected moonlight. "Who cares St. Who?" the creature burst out. "Is saint. Is holyfied ground. Is hurt. We go different way."

"If we did go through the hallowed ground," George said thoughtfully, "we would be doing something the Slavs and Avars and their powers don't expect. It might gain us an edge."

"I do not go through holyfied ground," Ampelus insisted. "Hurt me too much. And like I tell you, I watch wolf eat one of your priests. Wolf not care about ground like I do."

That was true. It was also depressing. And standing around in the woods arguing did not strike George as a good idea. Standing around in the woods for any reason did not strike George as a good idea. *Being* in the woods did not strike him as a good idea. But when all the other ideas looked worse . . . All the other ideas' looking worse did not make this a good one. Of that the shoemaker was convinced.

He and the satyr pressed on toward Thessalonica. How

they were going to get through the encirclement the Slavs and Avars had round the city bulked larger and larger in his mind. He had, at the moment, no idea. He decided to worry about it when the time came. He had plenty of other things to worry about till the time came.

An old man stepped out into the path ahead of George and Ampelus. His long beard and bushy eyebrows were green, and glowed brighter than Ampelus' eyes had flashed. "Well," George said, "it's a good bet *he's* not a wandering peasant, isn't it?" He drew his sword.

"I am Vucji Pastir," the old man said, his voice sounding in George's mind rather than his ears: "the shepherd of the wolves." His eyes, which shone almost as brightly as his beard and eyebrows, seemed ready to pop from his head. Though he stood in the moonlight, he cast no shadow.

"I am a good Christian man," George said. "Begone, evil spirit!" He made the sign of the cross.

That had pained the wolf-demon at the start of the daylight fight, even if it hadn't routed the creature. Vucji Pastir smiled. When he did, he showed his teeth, which were as sharp and pointed as any wolf's. The holy sign did him no harm. He raised his right hand. Off in the distance, howling rose. "My sheep, they come for you," he said.

George was not inclined to wait for them. He rushed at the shepherd of the wolves, slashing as he came. His blade shortened the Slavic demigod's beard by several inches. The severed hairs glowed as brightly as they had while still attached to their master.

Vucji Pastir bellowed in surprise and anger and—fear? He vanished, leaving behind the results of George's impromptu barbering. "Bravely did!" Ampelus cried. "Now we can get away."

"No," George said. "Now we can go on." He snatched up the tuft of shining green hairs. "And now we have a holy relic—no, an unholy relic, I suppose—of our own. If that ugly thing is the shepherd of the wolves, they should pay attention to his beard."

"Yes—when they eat you, they not eat the beard," the satyr said gloomily. But it went on with George instead of turning back as it plainly would rather have done.

They had not gone far before a wolf-demon snarled at them. Instead of slashing at it with his sword, George thrust the fragment of Vucji Pastir's beard in its face. It let out a startled yip, then a doglike yelp of greeting. Having the bit of beard in his possession made George a shepherd of wolves in his own right.

"See, I told you so," he said to Ampelus—a privilege he would not have taken with Irene. But—God be praised!—he wasn't married to the satyr. The wolf-demon rolled onto its belly, then placed itself at George's left heel, exactly as a well-trained dog would have done if it was going for a walk. In the moonlight, the shoemaker grinned at Ampelus. "Come on—we've got our own escort."

Warily, the satyr moved closer to the wolf. The wolf accepted Ampelus as a friend of George's. "Strange business," the satyr said, and stroked itself for reassurance.

They had not gone far before another fierce wolf-demon tried to bar their way. Before George could thrust his fluffy talisman at it, the first wolf, the one he'd tamed with Vucji Pastir's whiskers, snarled—but at the newcomer, not at him. The second wolf-demon whined appeasingly and fell into place beside the one that had warned it.

"Maybe I'll have the whole pack of them by the time we get to Thessalonica," George said gaily. Ampelus didn't answer, but he didn't run away or masturbate, either, which meant he was happy enough.

And then, without warning, Vucji Pastir reappeared right beside George. The wolves stared at the Slavic demigod and the shoemaker, as if realizing they might have made a mistake. Vucji Pastir snatched back the bit of beard George had trimmed from him. He set it against the rest of his green whiskers; it grew fast to them almost at once. "Mine," he said, and disappeared again.

George thought he was a dead man. By the way

Ampelus moaned, the satyr expected the wolves to tear them to pieces in the next instant, too. But they didn't. Some small part of Vucji Pastir's glamour still clung to George. The wolves, however, did whine and growl when he tried to go forward. When he turned around and started uphill, the way he had come, they were silent.

"I think," he said carefully, "we'd better head back."

"See?" Ampelus said. "I told you so."

"You'll make someone a fine wife one day," George snapped. The satyr laughed at him. He looked over his shoulder. The wolves were not tagging along at his heels, as they had before. That made him more glad than otherwise: sooner or later, they were going to figure out that he'd duped them. He didn't want them anywhere near his heels then.

As things happened, he'd put most of a mile between himself and the wolves before a furious howling broke out at his back. They didn't catch up with him and Ampelus before the two of them had returned to the encampment from which they'd set out. Nor did they prove willing to attack the centaurs there. After more hideous howls, they went away.

"I can't go to Thessalonica in the daytime," George muttered, "and I can't go at night, either. What does that leave?" He didn't think it left anything, but there had to be a way into the city. No—he wanted a way into the city. There was, unfortunately, all too often a difference between what he wanted and what there was.

X

A satyr named Ithys, whom George hadn't met before, came into the camp the next morning. Where the satyrs and centaurs there moped, Ithys bounced and sparkled. "Tell me why," Ampelus said, scowling, "or I throw something at you."

"I tell you why." Ithys leaped in the air from sheer high spirits. "Find woman in village—Lete. Give her all my loving. *All* my loving, I give to her." He leaped again, like a happy billy goat.

That instantly raised the satyrs' spirits, and their phalluses, though the centaurs stayed glum. "Tell me, tell me," Stusippus exclaimed.

"I want to tell you," Ithys said. "Yesterday, I see—"

"Tell me what you see," Stusippus broke in.

"I try. I try. I tell the word" —*logos,* in Greek, could mean almost anything connected with speech and thought— "if you not interrupting. You wait. Otherwise, I looking through you." Ithys stood on its dignity, which was even more absurd than a dog standing on its hind legs. "First, I just see a face—"

"Then what?" This time Stusippus and Ampelus interrupted together.

"I get you, I think. I wave to her." What Ithys waved was not a hand. "She want me." The satyr preened. "I see her standing there. She set down her washering. She leaving home, her home. She not want to do it in road, but come out into trees. 'Love me,' I say. 'Do. Please please me.' She no ask me why. She hold me tight. We do and do and do." Ithys panted at the memory. Ampelus and Stusippus panted, too. "Not a second time, not a third, not a fourth, not a fifth," Ithys boasted. "She never say, 'You can't do that,' like women sometimes do. When she finally have to go, 'Any time at all,' she say. She say, 'I need you.' I'll be back, yes, yes, yes."

Ampelus and Stusippus both sighed, jealousy and admiration perfectly mixed. "Nice someone happy," Ampelus said. Stusippus nodded.

"Why all so gloomish here?" Ithys asked. "All you need is love." The word the satyr used was related to *love*, anyhow.

"Need something different," Ampelus answered, and went on to explain what George was doing in the camp and how the shoemaker and the satyrs and centaurs had tried and failed to reach Thessalonica.

Ithys stayed cheerful. "You not know lovely Lete well, no. You come in, I show you this, too. Maybe even show you maid." The second part of the offer raised the satyrs' . . . interest. The first part made the centaurs pay attention at last.

"What meanest thou?" Nephele demanded.

The satyr talked for some time. If not explicit, it was interesting. Finally, it said, "You come with me. I show." It started off, presumably toward the village. George, Crotus and Nephele, and the two other satyrs followed.

Lete, as far as George was concerned, might as well have been called Lethe, or Forgetfulness. Till he walked down its narrow, muddy, twisting main street, he would not have believed any such hamlet still existed in the

Roman Empire in these modern, enlightened times.

He had known paganism still survived in the hills above Thessalonica. He had always taken that to mean, though, that in some of those isolated villages pagans still lived side by side with their Christian neighbors.

But he might well have been the first Christian ever to set foot in Lete. That he walked into the village with Ithys and Ampelus and Stusippus, with Crotus and Nephele, argued that he was. Had Christians dwelt in Lete, their crosses and relics and icons would have forced the satyrs and centaurs to stay away.

The villagers stared at the centaurs, but only in surprise, not in superstitious dread. They took the satyrs utterly for granted, nodding and waving to them and calling greetings to Ithys, who was evidently a frequent visitor. Oh, a couple of matrons hustled young daughters presumably maidens off the streets when Ampelus and Ithys strolled by fondling themselves, but that was the sort of motherly precaution Irene would have taken with Sophia had they dwelt here rather than down in the city.

George got a much more careful scrutiny than satyrs or centaurs. The people of Lete were familiar with his companions. *He* was a stranger, and therefore an object of suspicion till proved otherwise.

He wondered what Bishop Eusebius would have made of a place like this. The short answer, he thought, was *hash*.

He understood why the good and holy bishop of Thessalonica left Lete alone. The good and holy bishop undoubtedly hadn't the slightest idea the village existed. Ithys, leading the way, had found it without trouble, but George doubted whether he himself could have come back unaided. Folds in the hills hid a good many villages, but none so well as this one.

"What can they have here?" he asked Crotus.

"Means for your ingress into Thessalonica, an we be fortunate and the cockproud satyr speak sooth," the male centaur answered.

That was more of a response than any George had dragged out of the creature till now. "What sort of means?" he demanded.

"I know not, not with certainty," Crotus said. "I had not thought such means yet lay under the sun."

"If you don't know what and you don't know whether, what in" —he almost said *God's holy name*, which would have forced his companions to flight— "do you know?"

"I know we have hitherto failed, which doth vex me, as it doth you, in no small measure," Crotus said.

George walked along fuming. The male made no more sense than if it had suddenly started speaking Slavic. Seeing his anger and confusion, Ampelus said, "All sorts old things here: old things, strong things. Strong things, but not strong enough out there."

That didn't make any sense, either. And then, after a moment, it did, or maybe it did. Christianity was too strong for the old paganism of Greece. As the old faith and old powers fell back, naturally they would bring their talismans with them. Could winged slippers fly without a god in them? Or maybe the satyr meant something else altogether. George would find out.

In the midst of strangeness, one thing was familiar: the grapevine painted outside a building near the center of the village. George said, "Shall we go in and have some wine?"

Ampelus and the other satyrs nodded. As their heads happily bobbed up and down, so did their phalluses. But Crotus and Nephele drew back in something like horror. "This is why we come not into villages," Nephele said. "Did you not hear, foolish mortal, that wine doth madden and enrage us?"

That deep voice coming from such a lushly female form never failed to disconcert George. At the moment, his own embarrassment disconcerted him more. "I'm sorry," he mumbled. "I forgot."

"Fortunate it is that the folk of Lete have memories better trained to retention," Crotus said. "They know better than to serve us of the drink that inflameth us—and that, by its sweet savor, tempteth us to inflammation." The male's left forehoof took a quarter of a step toward the tavern. When it noticed, it stood very still indeed.

"I want wine," Ampelus said.

"Wait," George told the satyr. Pouting, it obeyed. George spoke to satyrs and centaurs both: "Who here is best able to tell us how we can use whatever is in this village against the Slavs and Avars?"

"The taverner," Ampelus exclaimed.

Crotus and Nephele both loomed over the satyr. "Enough of this japery and nonsense," the male centaur rumbled.

"It is Gorgonius the carpenter," Ithys said. "He has this—thing."

"I pray he hath a tongue that scoffeth not," Nephele said. "Lead on."

Ithys led. George followed, not without a regretful glance at the wineshop as they passed it. He also came with a certain amount of relief that Menas had locked him and not Sabbatius out of Thessalonica. Sabbatius would have headed for the wineshop regardless of what that might do to the centaurs.

Along with the pleasant smells of new-cut wood and sawdust, Gorgonius' establishment smelled of leather, an odor with which George was intimately familiar—and which made him wish he were back in his own city. The carpenter was repairing the webbing of a bedframe when George and his companions came in. "Good day, friend," Ithys said.

"Good day, good day," Gorgonius answered, with a broad smile that grew broader when he saw the centaurs. "A good day indeed!" he exclaimed. "Welcome, welcome, thrice welcome. Your kind but seldom honors us."

"Wine," Crotus said. "We fear it."

"Aye, aye." Gorgonius nodded. He was near or past his threescore and ten; his hair and beard were the silvery white that seems to shine even indoors, and his voice sounded a little mushy because he had only a few teeth left in his head. But his eyes were still sharp, and nothing was wrong with his wits. "Satyrs and centaurs together, eh? Centaurs here in Lete at all, eh? Something is curious, sure as sure. And who's this fellow you have with you?"

"George cometh out of Thessalonica," Nephele said, sounding portentous in lieu of identifying him as a Christian, which the centaur could not do.

"Is that so?" Gorgonius said. "Is that so? Isn't that interesting? What are you doing *here*, George out of Thessalonica?"

"Trying to stay alive." George did his best to put things in order, from most immediately urgent to long-term goals. "Trying to keep the Slavs and Avars from sacking my city and murdering my family. Trying to drive them away from here for good."

"That won't be bad if you can do it," the old carpenter said, nodding. "These new people and their new powers, I don't fancy 'em a bit. Not a bit. They change things around till they aren't the way they used to be. So how do you propose to go about it?"

"I know a priest, a man who believes as I do." George picked his words with care, trying to convey to Gorgonius what he meant without naming names that would drive off Ampelus and Ithys and Stusippus, Crotus and Nephele. "Put his power together with the powers that still live in these hills" —he pointed to centaurs and satyrs— "and we ought to be able to beat the barbarians."

"A priest, eh? One of your kind of priests?" Gorgonius might not have been a Christian, might hardly have seen any Christians, but he had a good notion of how Christian priests, most Christian priests, thought. "Wouldn't he sooner exorcise our friends here—isn't that what they call it?—than work alongside 'em?"

"I don't think so," George answered. "He's—different from most priests." *And he's doing penance because of it*, the shoemaker thought. He didn't mention that to Gorgonius.

"Well, maybe so, maybe so. It would surprise me, but maybe so." Gorgonius pointed down toward Thessalonica. "What are you doing here in Lete instead of there?"

"I can't get back to the city," George said. "The Slavs and Avars and their powers are between here and there. The band of centaurs and satyrs tried to get me through yesterday during the day, and Ampelus and I tried to sneak through last night. Didn't work, either way."

"Wolves," Ampelus added.

"Ah, those. Yes, I've seen those. Nasty things, aren't they?" Absentmindedly, Gorgonius began stropping a knife on one of the leather straps that would support the mattress. "Well, well. What am I supposed to be able to do to help you?"

"I haven't the faintest idea," George answered. "Ithys thought coming to you was a good idea. All I can do is hope it was right."

The carpenter didn't say anything to that. He silently studied George for a while, then turned his gaze on Ithys. The satyr said, "You are Gorgonius. You know of what clan you spring, and why you have that name. I knew the man who founded your clan. You in the later days of your life look like him in the later days of his. I say this to you before."

"Yes, and every time you've said it, I've told you what daft nonsense it is," Gorgonius said. "He was a hero. I make tables. He killed monsters and rescued maidens. I got a cat out of a tree once, if that counts for anything, and I stepped on a cockroach the other day."

"The satyr hath reason," Nephele said. "Your foresire had wit and wisdom and knew both how to give and how to receive good counsel, than which few things are rarer among mankind."

"Wait a minute," George said. Everyone, aging carpenter and ageless immortal creatures alike, looked at him. "Wait just a minute." Everyone did indeed seem willing enough to wait. Hesitantly, wondering whether he'd heard what he thought he'd heard and whether he ought to believe it if he had, he pointed to Gorgonius. He didn't speak to the carpenter, though, but to Ithys and to Nephele. "You're saying he's from Perseus' family."

"Aye, in good sooth, we are," Nephele said. "We knew Perseus. Perseus was our friend. Doth surprise you this, mayfly man?"

"A bit," George said, trying not to show how much more than a bit it surprised him. He remembered thinking, when he'd first met Ampelus, how the satyr had been up in these hills when Paul was writing to the Thessalonicans, and for hundreds of years before that. He hadn't realized how many hundreds of years, though. He didn't know how long ago Perseus had lived, but it was back before the Trojan War, which was, by definition, antiquity immeasurable—except that Ithys and Nephele measured it.

"We have reckoned his descendants, even unto the hundred and fifteenth generation," Nephele said, measuring antiquity most precisely indeed.

"That and a few folleis will get you some wine—well, not you, but the man here," said Gorgonius, who seemed unimpressed with his illustrious ancestor. "But now I understand why Ithys brought you to me, George."

George made the sort of intuitive leap that had given him a reputation for cleverness in Thessalonica—among those who cared whether a shoemaker was clever, at any rate. He stabbed out a finger at Gorgonius. "You've got Medusa's head stowed away here somewhere, don't you, so we can turn the Slavs and Avars to stone with it."

"Are you out of your bloody mind?" Gorgonius exclaimed. "If the family had kept that horrible thing, they'd have been turned to stone themselves, some of 'em, anyhow, and I wouldn't be standing here talking with you. The whole village would be stone, too, and we could fortify it with our cousins and uncles. Daft!" He shook his head.

"Oh," George said in a very small voice. When a clever man was stupid, he was stupid in a way a man who was stupid all the time could never hope to match, for the clever man's stupidity, drawing as it did on so much more knowledge, had a breadth and depth to it the run-of-the-mill fool found impossible to duplicate.

Gorgonius took pity on him. "What I do have, pal," he said, "is the cap Perseus wore when he got up close to Medusa and her sisters."

For a moment, that cap meant nothing more to George than that it was the pagan equivalent of, say, a saint's shinbone in a reliquary in a church. But a saint's shinbone might work miracles, and so might this cap. "The Gorgons couldn't see Perseus when he came up to them," George said.

"That's right," Gorgonius said encouragingly, as if George might not be an idiot after all. "Very good."

"Does it still work?" the shoemaker asked. "Perseus wore it a long time ago."

"It works." Gorgonius' leer rivaled anything Ampelus could produce. "I've seen more pretty girls, and more of 'em, than you'll ever dream about, pal, even if you live in that big city. Oh, it works, all right."

Nephele let out a noise half giggle, half horsy snort. The satyrs' interest in the conversation, which had been small, visibly swelled. George was all at once convinced Gorgonius was telling the truth. He didn't know whether to be awed or appalled that Gorgonius had figured out a use for the cap so far removed from that originally intended for it.

After a moment, though, he doubted the old carpenter was the one who had only just begun that use. A lot of men's lives lay between Perseus and Gorgonius. Surely one of the carpenter's multiple great-grandsires had had that same inspiration. Probably a good many of them had had it.

Gorgonius walked out of the room in which they'd been talking. Instead of having his living quarters above his shop, as George did, Gorgonius lived behind his work-room: Lete was less crowded than Thessalonica and, so far as George could recall, had no buildings taller than one story.

When Gorgonius didn't come back right away, Crotus rumbled, "Whither is the fellow gone, and for what purpose?"

"An I be not much mistaken, he hath not gone, or rather, he is returned among us," Nephele answered.

Gorgonius said, "See what a clever lady you are." His voice came from a point halfway between George and Nephele. His voice was there, but he wasn't—not so far as the eye could tell, at any rate.

Then he lifted a nondescript leather cap from his head and abruptly became visible once more. "You see," he said, and George did see. Then he put the cap on again, and George saw no more. He was tempted to cross himself, to learn whether the power of the holy sign was stronger than that of the cap which had befooled Medusa and her sisters in ancient days and, evidently, other, more attractive females since.

He held his hand still. The holy sign might destroy all the power the cap contained. It would surely rout the centaurs and satyrs, who had done so much to help him.

"Come back to our eyes, Gorgonius," Nephele said. "Come back, that we may all take counsel together, each judging the probity of the others by examining their countenances."

"All right." Between speaking one word and the next, Gorgonius reappeared. "You're saying you want me to let this fellow" —he pointed to George— "borrow my cap here. Who's to say I'll ever see it again?"

"You can't see it now, half the time," George pointed out.

"That's true," the carpenter said. "Aye, that's true." He smiled at George, who thought he'd won a point. But even if he had, a point was not the game. Gorgonius said, "Why should I risk something that's been in the family for so long, to help a stack of people who have no use for it, don't believe it's any good, and would destroy it if they could?"

He sent the question toward Nephele, but the female, Crotus, and the satyrs looked with one accord at George. "Why?" he said. "I can give you only one answer: whatever you think of the folk of Thessalonica, having the Slavs and Avars sack the city would be worse—for us and for you, too."

"In the old days," Gorgonius said meditatively, "I could have gone down into Thessalonica, and so could they." He nodded toward the centaurs and satyrs. "Oh, Crotus and Nephele might not have wanted to, on account of the wine, but they could have. Now, though, one of those priests'd be on me like a fox on a rabbit. And my friends, they can't go at all, not with all the saints and such who've been through there one time or another. Is that better than not having any Thessalonica at all? I wonder, George. I do wonder."

"They think so," George answered. Now he nodded at Ithys and Ampelus and Stusippus, at Crotus and Nephele. "They wouldn't have brought me here if they didn't. And they've seen more of the Slavs and Avars than you have."

"You think so, do you?" Gorgonius touched the cap that had come down from Perseus. "With this, I can see what I like. I told you that already." He clicked his tongue against the roof of his mouth. "I didn't much like what I saw, I will say that. But to save arrogant Thessalonica with something the town's too proud to believe in . . . it gravels me, that it does."

"If I get down there, if I can get into the city, I'll be bringing back a priest, don't forget," George said. "The old powers can't fight the Slavs and Avars and their gods and demons, not alone. We know that. What I believe in" —he had to keep coming up with circumlocutions for Christianity— "may not be strong enough by itself, either. Together . . . we can hope, anyway."

"Hope came out of the box last of all," Gorgonius

said. He made that clicking noise again and stood very still, taking his own time to make up his mind. When Crotus started to say something, the carpenter tossed his head in negation. "I've heard all I want." The centaur did not try to speak again. The satyrs masturbated nervously.

Outside, far off in the distance, a wolf howled. But it was not an ordinary wolf; George had grown too well acquainted with the horrible howls of the Slavic wolf-demons to mistake them for anything but what they were. Very slightly, Nephele shuddered.

Maybe that howl helped Gorgonius decide. Maybe, concentrating as he was, he didn't even hear it. But he came out of his brown study only moments after its last echoes had died away. Holding out the cap to George, he growled, "You'd better bring this back, or I'll be angry at you."

"If I don't bring it back," the shoemaker answered, "odds are I'll be too dead to care."

The first thing George discovered about being invisible was that he wasn't invisible to himself. That came as something of a relief. Not being the most graceful man ever born, he had trouble planting his feet even when he could see exactly where he was putting them. Had he not known where they were going, his best guess was that he would have broken his leg, or maybe his neck, long before he got close to Thessalonica.

The next thing he discovered was that, when he was invisible, people didn't notice him. That made perfect logical sense, of course—it was why he needed Perseus' cap in the first place. It brought problems, too, though, problems he hadn't expected. As he walked up and down Lete's narrow streets, people didn't get out of the way for him. Why should they have done so? They had no idea he was there. All the dodging was up to him. Once he had to say "Excuse me" out of thin air, which startled the man who'd collided with him.

Something else occurred to him after he bumped into the villager. He asked Gorgonius about it when he got back to the carpenter's place. "Took me years to wonder about that," Gorgonius said, "but, seeing what you're going to be doing, I can understand how it would be on your mind. Best I can tell, dogs don't take my scent when I have the cap on, and nobody and nothing hears you unless you speak out loud."

"Oh, good," George said. "By everything I've heard, wolves use their noses more than their eyes, but if dogs don't notice your odor, I'm going to hope the wolf-demons won't notice mine."

"I don't know anything about demons," Gorgonius said. "If their power is strong enough, they might be able to beat the strength in the cap."

"The power inhering in them is not to be despised," Nephele said.

George didn't despise the wolf-demons, or any of the other powers the Slavs and Avars controlled—if the control didn't run in the other direction. They frightened him out of his wits. "I don't see that I have much choice," he said. "This cap is my best chance—probably my only chance—to get back to Thessalonica. I'm going to use it. I'll be back here with Father Luke two or three days after I set out—I hope."

"May Fortune favor you," Nephele said. She spoke of Fortune as a power in its own right. As a Christian, George knew he wasn't supposed to think of it that way. As a man who sat down with some friends to roll dice every now and then, he couldn't help thinking of it so.

He slept in the straw in Gorgonius' barn that night; it made a better bed than the one of dry leaves he'd shared with Ampelus and Stusippus, and not only because he didn't have a couple of satyrs in it with him. When he woke up, he didn't look like a young forest anymore: he wasn't covered with leaves. Being covered with straw instead, he looked like a young unmowed field instead.

Gorgonius gave him a slab of bread and a stoppered jug that almost surely contained wine. Nephele and Crotus both made an elaborate pretense of not looking at it. Though they turned their heads away, their eyes had minds of their own, and kept sliding back toward the jug. The satyrs, more than humanly fond of wine, made no bones about watching the jar.

As soon as George could see his feet and the path they would take, he left Lete. His breath smoked in the chilly air. He told himself firmly that he would presume no one but he could see it. Had the truth been otherwise, Gorgonius would have mentioned it . . . wouldn't he?

George knew the direction in which he'd have to go. He'd traveled part of that road already. He wished he'd been able to travel all of it. Then he wouldn't have had to involve himself with such potent pagan powers as Perseus' cap. Even if he was less devout than many in Thessalonica, he did believe.

"Well," he murmured, "if Eusebius wants to impose a penance on me after all this is over, I'll observe it. I just want this to *be* all over."

He hadn't been walking for more than half an hour before he spotted Xanthippe and Demetrius out on a meadow. The female centaur and the young one (young enough, perhaps, *not* to have been in a position to know St. Paul when he'd traveled through this land more than five centuries before) both moved easily, showing no signs of the wounds they'd taken from the Slavic wolf-demons, wounds that would have laid George up for weeks or killed him.

They also showed no sign of having any idea he was around. He did not call out to them. No telling who—or what—might be listening. *Good thing Ampelus didn't rescue John*, the shoemaker thought. *He wouldn't be able to keep his mouth shut long enough to get full good from this cap*.

Even that uncharitable judgment of his friend reminded George how much he missed Thessalonica and all its people. He shook his head, revising that thought as soon as he had it. He didn't miss Menas even a little.

He drank some wine. Between that and the steady exercise of tramping through the hill country, he felt warm enough, though the early-morning air still had a chilly edge to it. The right side of his mouth twisted up into an ironic smile. He'd had more exercise lately than he'd ever wanted.

The morning was still young when he saw his first wolf. It wasn't far from the place where he and the centaurs and satyrs had fought the Slavic demons, and stood by the side of the path, as if waiting for him to come past so it could finish him for good instead of just driving him back into the hills.

He stopped in his tracks. Knowing he was invisible was one thing. Believing it when his life depended on its being so proved something else again. The wolf-demon's tongue lolled out, impossibly red against its dark gray fur. Its eyes glittered with alertness. Its head turned this way and that. For a moment, it looked straight at him. Dared he believe it could not see him, could not sense him?

If he didn't dare believe that, what point to going any farther? He walked past the wolf, close enough so that he could have kicked it in the ribs. As he moved past, the wolf-demon let out a puzzled whine, as if it had the feeling it should have been noticing something it was missing. George reached up and touched the leather cap. Now he believed.

He went almost jauntily after that. He caught himself just before he started whistling a happy little tune. That would have been stupid—odds were, fatally stupid.

More wolves than the first one guarded the trails down to Thessalonica. He passed them all. Some seemed to have no notion he was anywhere nearby. Others, like the first, looked and sounded discontented, but could not understand why they dimly suspected something was wrong.

And then George approached Vucji Pastir. The Slavic demigod who shepherded wolves had a couple of his charges close by; he was talking to them in a language made up of yips and growls. His glowing green beard, George saw, had grown out to its full magnificence once more: the barbering his own sword had done proved as impermanent as the wounds the centaurs had taken.

Vucji Pastir knew he was coming. That was the impression he got, anyhow, from the demigod's demeanor. Vucji Pastir urged his wolves out onto the trail as a man hunting boar would have urged on his hounds. The wolf-demons whined and lashed their tails.

They were, George realized joyfully, trying to tell their master they could find no sign of any impertinent Christian shoemaker. Vucji Pastir peered this way and that. Once, as the wolves had done before, the demigod looked right at George—and, evidently, saw nothing.

Or perhaps, as the wolves had also done, Vucji Pastir saw next to nothing. He frowned, scratched at the roots of his green hair—and then looked in another direction. George let out a silent sigh of relief. He didn't think Perseus' cap would get a harder test till he drew far closer to Thessalonica.

He was soon proved wrong. He hadn't gone more than another couple of furlongs before he encountered Vucji Pastir again, this time with a different pack of wolf-demons. Again the Slavic demigod almost spotted him. Again the demigod apparently could not believe his own eyes.

As George hurried on toward the city, he wondered how Vucji Pastir had been behind him and then in front of him without, so far as an impertinent Christian shoemaker could tell, crossing the intervening space. Had the shepherd of the wolves been first in one place and then in the other? Or had he manifested himself in both at once? Would he show up again and again, on the lookout for George, all the way down to the city wall?

Sure enough, George saw him and he did not see

George several more times, there in the hill country. Toward the end of the day—and also a good deal of the way toward Thessalonica—the shepherd of the wolves looked so upset at having failed to spot George that the shoemaker was tempted to go up to him, tap him on the shoulder, and say, "Excuse me there, friend, but can I help you find somebody?"

He convinced himself, after some silent argument, that that was not a good idea, no matter how he would have enjoyed watching a demigod jump.

Despite Vucji Pastir, despite the wolf-demons, George made better time down toward Thessalonica than he'd expected, approaching the city before the sun had sunk in the west. That was not what he wanted. If he went up to a postern gate in the dead of night, he could slip off Perseus' cap and claim no one had noticed him till he got there. If he tried that in the afternoon, the guards would see him materialize out of thin air. So would the Slavs, with results liable to be unpleasant.

Waiting for nightfall proved harder than he'd expected. The woods near Thessalonica were full of Slavs, some hunting, others taking axes to trees and bushes to fuel their fires. They had no notion he was there but, like the fellow back in Lete, kept doing their best to blunder into his invisible but not incorporeal form. If one of them did chance to trip over his foot, he did not think a simple, friendly "Excuse me" would set matters right.

Carefully, he worked his way around the wall till he neared the Litaean Gate. The men on the wall there would be likeliest to know him and to recognize his voice when he came up to the gate. So would the men at the postern gate by the main gateway. If he presented himself and they wouldn't let him into the city . . . he didn't want to think about that.

By the time he'd found a position from which he could keep an eye on the gate, twilight was falling. The Slavs built up the fires in their encampments and started cooking their supper. The odors of roasted meat and bubbling porridge made George's stomach growl. He'd long since finished the bread and wine Gorgonius had given him.

Night quickly swallowed twilight. George waited for the campfires to die back to embers, and for most of the Slavs to shelter under blankets and furs and whatever else they used to ward off the cold of night. George wasn't using anything to ward off the cold of night. His teeth chattered. If he froze to death out here in the woods, would his corpse stay invisible till a storm knocked the cap off his head?

"One more thing I don't want to find out," he muttered.

By what he judged to be the fourth hour of the night, the encampments were about as quiet as they ever got. He started picking his way between a couple of disorderly clumps of huts and tents. One hand held the cap tight on his head, the other was on his swordhilt. If by some mischance he did run into a Slav, he thought his best bet was to kill the fellow quickly, giving him no chance to cry out.

Instead of a Slav, he almost ran into the Avar wizard. The fellow loomed up before him, outline distorted by the fringes and furs of his costume. George froze: metaphorically, to go with the literal cold that had afflicted him. From everything Gorgonius had said, from everything George himself had seen, the Avar should have had no idea he was there.

But the wizard was as wary as the wolves and as Vucji Pastir. He murmured something in his incomprehensible language and stared right at—right through—George. He took a step forward, one hand outstretched, as if to seize the shoemaker.

Heart pounding, George jumped to one side. If the Avar priest had pursued him, he would have run for the gate with every bit of strength he had left. But the Avar kept on walking toward his own tent, which, George saw, lay not far away. Maybe he hadn't sensed George at all. The shoemaker could not make himself believe it.

He looked up to the wall, wondering which of his friends were on it now. When Menas locked him out of Thessalonica and the Slavs bore down on him, he hadn't thought such things would matter again. How glad he was to discover they did.

He was within bowshot of the wall now, in the empty area the Slavs and Avars entered only when they were attacking. There was the iron-plated bulk of the Litaean Gate ahead, and there, inset into the wall, the postern gate beside it. That postern gate drew him like a lodestone.

Once there, he found a new question: how hard to rap on it. Too softly, and the guards wouldn't notice. Too hard, and the Slavs would. His first tap was too tentative. His second was so loud, it frightened him. He looked anxiously back toward the barbarians' encampment. No shouts rose there. He knocked again.

A tiny grill in the center of the gate opened. "Who's there?" a guard demanded. "Stand and be recognized."

"It's me—George," George said. "For the love of—" He cut that off, not knowing what God's name would do to the cap. "I managed to get away from the Slavs and Avars and make it back here. Let me in."

Through the iron grill, he saw one of the guard's eyes and part of his cheek. "Stand and be recognized," the fellow repeated. "If you're really a Slav who speaks Latin, you're going to be a dead Slav who used to speak Latin."

"But I'm in front of— Oh." Again, George broke off. He was glad the guard couldn't see him blush. The guard couldn't see him at all, because he was still wearing the cap he hadn't wanted to test with God's name. He'd remembered it in that context, but not in the context of making him invisible. Feeling a fool once more, he took it from his head.

The guard recoiled. "*Kyrie eleison!*" he exclaimed. "It *is* you, George. How in Christ's holy name did you just spring out of thin air like that? I'd have sworn nobody was there."

"Let me in," George said. If the cap couldn't bear holy

names, it wouldn't be much good in Thessalonica, or maybe ever after. George hoped that wasn't so; otherwise, he'd have a much harder time getting Father Luke out to Lete. "Open the gate, curse it, before the Slavs figure out I'm here."

Wood scraped on wood as the guard unbarred the postern gate. It swung open. George darted back into the city. The guard closed the gate after him and set the bars back in place. George allowed himself the luxury of a long, heartfelt sigh of relief.

"Don't know how you managed to stay in one piece out there, but I'm glad you did," the guard said. He turned away, continuing over his shoulder. "Come along with me. Tell the rest of the crew how you did it."

George didn't want to tell anybody how he'd done it. He also didn't want to return to his normal routine, which would make slipping out of Thessalonica again all the harder. And so, wondering what would happen, he set the leather cap back on his head.

"I want to tell you, George, you frightened me out of—" The guard noticed George hadn't answered. He turned around to look for the man he'd admitted. "George?" His eyes got big. He crossed himself. "George? Where in the devil's name did you go?" He scratched his head. "Were you ever here at all, or am I daydreaming—nightdreaming? I've got to get more sleep, that's all there is to it." He yawned.

"What's going on there?" one of the other guards called from the main gate. Since the fellow who had admitted George didn't know what was going on, his explanation was fumbling at best. While he stuttered and mumbled, George slipped past him, heading home.

He was glad he could do so still cloaked in invisibility. When the guard signed himself, he'd again feared the magic in Perseus' cap would dissolve. He wondered why it hadn't: perhaps because the guard had made the sign of the cross to protect himself, not to lash out at that which had startled him.

Thessalonica's streets were dark and quiet and cold. George wished for a torch to light his way—and then, after a moment, he didn't. No one could see him, but everyone would be able to see the torch. That just might cause talk in the city.

Here came a fellow swaggering along as if he owned the street. The stout bludgeon he carried in his right hand was doubtless intended to persuade anyone who might doubt his view of the situation. George reached up to make sure the cap was firmly on his head. This was a fellow Thessalonican he had no interest in knowing better.

Away from the main avenues, which formed a grid, Thessalonica's streets wandered crazily. Without a torch, George got lost a couple of times and had to backtrack. If the Slavs and Avars broke into the city, he suspected some houses would go unplundered simply because the barbarians couldn't find them.

Shouts told him he was getting close to home. They weren't shouts from anyone who'd seen him. They were Claudia's shouts, aimed at Dactylius. In the nocturnal stillness, they carried a long way. Anybody who cared to listen could get an earful of Claudia's views of her husband's shortcomings. Anyone who didn't care to listen was liable to be awakened.

You could throw a rock or an old shoe at a cat. George had no idea how to make Claudia shut up.

Partly guided by her abuse, he found his own front door. He tried the latch. The door was barred. He knocked on it. The same problem applied here as it had at the postern gate: he wanted to wake his family, but not the neighbors. He knocked again, louder, and hoped he wasn't being too loud.

After a while, he heard someone moving inside. Theodore's sleepy voice came through the door: "Who's there?"

"I am," George said.

"Father?" Theodore undid the bar. Before his son

opened the door, George remembered to snatch the cap off his head. He didn't want Theodore thinking he was a ghost.

He took off the cap just in time. The little lamp Theodore held in his left hand seemed dazzlingly bright. In Theodore's right hand was the longest, sharpest awl in the shop, in case George had turned out to be somebody else. Theodore dropped the awl with a clatter, set down the lamp, and embraced his father, bursting into tears as he did.

Somehow, George got into the shop and closed the door before Irene and Sophia dashed downstairs and added their embraces and tears to Theodore's. "Thank God you're safe," Irene said, over and over. "Thank God you're here to stay."

"I'm not here to stay," George said. His wife stiffened against him. He had to drag his words out one at a time: "I have to leave the city again, or else, I think, it will fall."

"How can you leave the city?" Sophia demanded. "Stay here with us. You'll . . . you'll . . . Something bad will happen if you don't." She'd probably been trying to say something like, *You'll get killed if you don't*, but hadn't been able to do it.

"I don't think so." As George spoke, he set Perseus' cap on his head. His wife and children cried out in astonishment as he disappeared. He took off the cap and became visible once more. "You see? The Slavs won't even know I'm anywhere around." He knew he was making it sound easier than it would be, but he didn't want his family worried.

Irene pointed to the cap. "Where did you get that? Who gave it to you? Who—or what?"

Quick as he could, he explained what it was and where he'd got it. Irene's disapproval grew with every word he said. He tried to forestall her: "Could you get me something to eat, please? I've been tramping all over everywhere on not very much, believe me." Bread and honey and olives and wine put new heart in him.

But no sooner had he taken the last swallow than Irene said, "Now—why did these pagans and these, these creatures send you into Thessalonica and expect you to come back out again?"

"They want me to bring Father Luke to them," George said.

He'd thought that would startle his wife, and it did. "But they're satyrs and centaurs and fairies and pagans," Irene protested. "What do they think a man of God will do for them?"

"Help drive back the Slavs and Avars and their powers," George said. "They aren't strong enough to do it by themselves. We may not be strong enough to do it by ourselves. Together, God willing . . ."

"Would Father Luke go?" Sophia asked. "I can't believe a priest of God would hobnob with these, these *things*." She shivered.

"I think he will," George answered. He explained the penance Eusebius had set on Father Luke for manipulating the Avars' thunder gods. "I'm going to ask him, anyhow. He's not so set in his ways as most of the other priests I know."

"What if he won't go, Father?" Theodore said. "Will you stay here then?"

"Yes, then I will stay," George said. "If we come through the siege, I'll have to go up into the hills afterwards and give the cap back to Gorgonius. But for now, I'll stay." He held up a hand. "But if I do go with Father Luke, don't let anyone know I've come back into the city now. Just say you hope I'm all right and you think you'll see me again."

"What I hope," Irene said fiercely, "is that Father Luke tells you he wants nothing to do with this scheme, and that it's mad, pagan wickedness. And I hope you listen to him, too."

"If he says that, I will listen to him," George promised. "If he says that, I'll be back here in an hour or so, and we'll go on about our business and hope for the best. I don't know what else we can do."

"We'll wait up for you," Irene said. Sophia and Theodore nodded.

"All right." George would sooner have told them to go back to bed, but he knew they wouldn't listen. He said, "In case I don't come back here, remember, *don't* let anyone know I was in the city. If people are gossiping up on the wall, the Slavs and Avars are liable to hear them and find some way to stop Father Luke and me."

His son and daughter nodded again. At last, reluctantly, so did Irene. George embraced her, knowing he was using up a marriage's worth of faith in a night, and going into debt besides. If it didn't come out right—if it didn't come out right, he doubted he'd be in any position to apologize.

He hugged Theodore again, and then Sophia. "Everything will be fine," he said. Words had power. They were magical things. Saying that made it likelier to come true. After a last awkward nod, he set Perseus' cap on his head. His wife and children exclaimed again, so he knew he'd vanished. He opened the door and went back out into the night.

St. Elias' church was only a few blocks away. Its doors stood open, as they always did. It was dim and dark inside, though, with but a handful of candles burning. George's shadow flickered and swooped like an owl after mice as he walked down the aisle toward the altar, in front of which Father Luke stood praying. *Probably still at his penance*, George thought.

At the sound of George's footsteps, the priest turned. Even in the semidarkness, Father Luke's smile glowed. "George!" he exclaimed. "Thank God you're safe!"

"Yes, I—" George stopped in confusion as he realized he was still wearing the cap. "You can see me?"

"Of course I can." Now Father Luke gave him a quizzical look. "Shouldn't I be able to?"

"This is hallowed ground," George muttered, reminding himself. He hoped that meant nothing more than that the magic in Perseus' cap was overcome by a stronger power here, not gone for good. Only one way to find out. "Your Reverence, will you please not think I'm a crazy man if I ask you to step outside with me for a minute or two?"

"George, I could think you were a great many things," the priest answered, "but I'm hard-pressed to imagine you crazy. I'll come with you."

George couldn't feel anything different happen when he left the holy precinct. Father Luke, though, suddenly jerked in surprise. George let out a sigh of relief. He took off the cap. His reappearance startled Father Luke again. "You see, Your Reverence," George said.

"Yes, I see," Father Luke said. "Or rather, I didn't see you for a little while there. I suppose you're going to tell me there's a story attached to this, this—vanishing trick."

"There certainly is," George said, and proceeded to tell it. Only the faintest light leaked out of the church. Shrouded in darkness and shadow, Father Luke's face was unreadable as the shoemaker went through the strange things that had happened to him since Menas slammed the postern gate in his face.

When he'd finished, Father Luke stood silent for a while, then said, "This village of Lete and others like it up in the hills, they sound as if they're ripe for evangelizing one day soon."

"That may be so, Your Reverence," George said in some alarm, "but—"

The priest held up a hand and laughed quietly. "But one day soon isn't quite yet," he said. George nodded. Father Luke stood in thought for another little while, then said, "Well, let's go."

"Just like that?" George said in surprise.

"Just like that," Father Luke agreed. "That's what you wanted, isn't it?"

"Well, yes, but—" Only a couple of days before, George had been thinking about the difference between what he wanted and what life commonly handed him. Something else crossed his mind, too: "What will Bishop Eusebius do to you after you come back from consorting with pagan powers again?"

"I don't know," the priest answered. "Whatever it is, he will do it and I will accept it. If we save the city, he'll be able to do it. If Thessalonica falls to the Slavs and Avars, what Bishop Eusebius might want to do to me becomes a bit less important, wouldn't you say?"

Since that was exactly what George would have said, he didn't say it. Instead, he nodded again. "Thank you, Your Reverence."

"For what?" Now Father Luke sounded startled. "You've been risking your life, and maybe your soul as well, for the sake of the city. Wouldn't you call me mean-spirited if I did anything less?" Without giving George a chance to reply, he started west along the street on which St. Elias' church lay. "You did say you came in at the Litaean Gate?"

"That's right." George hurried after him. If the priest was worried about traveling through Thessalonica by night without even a torch to light his way, he showed no sign of it. George said, "Uh, Your Reverence, the one thing I haven't been able to figure out is how to get you out of the city and past the Slavs and Avars without them spotting you."

"God will provide," Father Luke said serenely. "His plans are hidden from mortal eyes, but never from His own thought. Now, I suggest you put on that extraordinary headgear you borrowed. You won't want to leave the fellow at the postern gate any more confused than he is already."

"You're right about that," George said. He and Father Luke were walking past the cistern where the priest had defeated the Slavic water-demigod. Seeing it reminded George how urgent their mission was. He set the leather cap on his head. He'd carried it till then, out of a vague sense that vanishing in front of Father Luke would be rude.

"Extraordinary," the priest repeated when he did disappear.

No footpads came leaping out of deep shadow to assail Father Luke. That was as well for them, since he now had more unseen protection than the power of the Lord alone. On a cosmic scale, George supposed his using Perseus' cap to baffle robbers would be only slightly more important than Gorgonius' using it to spy on good-looking women, but, as a mere man, the shoemaker found the cosmic scale too large to worry about anyhow.

When he and Father Luke got to the Litaean Gate, he discovered a new crew of guards had come on duty since he'd entered Thessalonica. He was glad of that; as things were, the fellow who'd admitted him wouldn't be faced with the improbability of Father Luke's wanting to go out along with the flat impossibility of his own arrival.

The new man at the postern gate was surprised enough as things were. "Why on earth do you need to go out there, Your Reverence?" he asked Father Luke.

"Because I have reason to believe the Slavs and Avars are planning something particularly devilish, and I have the chance to forestall it," the priest answered: all true, but none of it very informative. Father Luke put some snap in his voice, saying, "Are you going to listen to me, or shall we send for Bishop Eusebius to tell you what he thinks?"

George knew sending for the bishop was the last thing Father Luke wanted. The guard didn't. Hastily, he said, "All right, Your Reverence. You know what you're doing, I'm sure." He unbarred the postern gate and pulled it open. Perhaps because it had been opened not long before to admit George, the hinges did not squeak much.

Father Luke got between the guard and the open gate for a moment. That let George slip out ahead of the priest. The postern gate shut behind Father Luke. "Well, well," he murmured, peering this way and that. "How best to get past the Slavs and into the woods?"

"Would you like to wear the cap yourself, Your Reverence?" George asked. "I got past them once in the daylight. I expect I can do it again."

"No, don't worry about it." Father Luke stepped away from the sheltering shadow of the wall. "We'll just go on and trust in God."

In every church in Thessalonica, in every church in the Roman Empire, in every church in Christendom, priests preached sermons on the glory of martyrs. St. Demetrius was a martyr for the faith. George felt horribly certain Father Luke was about to become another one.

As Father Luke had stood between the guard and the postern gate, so now George stood between the priest and the encampment of the Slavs and Avars. He told himself that was useless: if he was invisible, the barbarians would see right through him and spot Father Luke. He kept on doing it anyhow, on the notion that it couldn't hurt and might possibly do a little good. He didn't know exactly how the invisibility worked. If it made people see around him instead of turning him transparent, maybe it would make the barbarians see around Father Luke, too.

With every step he took, he expected a hoarse shout from a Slavic sentry. He glanced back at Father Luke. The priest's lips were moving in prayer. Maybe that was why the Slavs and Avars failed to spot him as he walked across the open ground toward the woods. Maybe George—and Perseus' cap—did help shield him. Whatever the reason, no outcry came.

In among first brush and then trees, George murmured, "Thank God." Father Luke heard that. The shoemaker thought he smiled, though in the darkness he had trouble being sure. "Did I not say the Lord would provide?" the priest said quietly. "If He sent a chariot and horses all for fire for Elijah, surely He could manage something rather less dramatic for me."

George wondered what sort of miracle God had worked. Had He cloaked Father Luke in a separate bit of invisibility, or had He used Perseus' cap to His own ends? Could He do that with magic not His own? George had no answers, but those were intriguing questions.

He wondered what Father Luke thought. If he ever had the chance in a place where making noise mattered less, he resolved to ask him. Of one thing he was certain: this was not the moment.

Having been this way before, he guided Father Luke north. He did not think, though, that he could find the hills beyond those he knew without help from Ampelus or one of the other creatures out of legend. He would have to get to the encampment of the centaurs and satyrs on his own.

Somewhere ahead in the woods, a wolf-demon howled. George knew the creature could not sense him, not when he wore the cap. The Slavs and Avars hadn't been able to sense Father Luke's presence, but they were only men. He wondered what the wolf-demon would do, and remembered what Ampelus had said of the one that encountered a priest in the woods.

No sooner had he whispered a prayer that none of the wolf-demons would find Father Luke and him than one of them, eyes glowing even in forested night, strode out onto the game track the two men from Thessalonica were using. It snarled—it knew the priest was there.

George drew his sword and started to advance on the wolf. If it could not see him, he might hurt it badly—that was how Perseus had slain Medusa. But before he got close enough to slash, Father Luke made the sign of the cross and said, "Depart, in the name of God."

The wolf howled. It sat back on its haunches in absurd surprise, as if the priest had hit it in the muzzle with a stick. Then, awkwardly, it turned and ran, tail between its legs—again, for all the world like a beaten dog.

"How—how did you do that, Your Reverence?" George asked in a low voice. "These creatures, they—"

"I have faith," Father Luke said calmly. "I need nothing more."

Remembering Father Gregory, whom the water-demigod had killed, George slowly nodded. The other priest, the one Ampelus had watched, must have been uncertain or arrogant, too. Father Luke, as far as the shoemaker could tell, had neither arrogance nor uncertainty in him.

They went on, stumbling through the undergrowth. More wolf-demons gave cry, but none came near. *He's put the fear of God in them*, George thought. Most of the time, that was only a phrase. Not here. Not now.

And then, instead of the wolf-demon Father Luke had routed, Vucji Pastir blocked his way through the woods. As he had with the wolf, the priest crossed himself and said, "Depart, in the name of God."

Vucji Pastir's eyes, always protuberant, almost popped out of his head. Their glow, and that of his hair and beard, dimmed a little. But he did not depart, nor even retreat. "You are strong, priest," he said, "but not strong enough to defeat the shepherd of the wolves." As it had in George's earlier meeting with him, his voice sounded directly in the shoemaker's mind, and no doubt in that of Father Luke as well.

"Depart," Father Luke repeated. "In the name of Father, Son, and Holy Spirit, and the name of the holy Virgin Mother of God, in the name of St. Demetrius the chief martyr, in the name of gentle St. Catherine, in the name of St. Elias whom I serve—depart, depart, depart!"

Now Vucji Pastir's eyes blazed. He opened his mouth wide, showing his own fierce teeth. A great laugh burst from him. "Are you deaf, foolish priest? You have not the strength to make me do your will. I shall not leave if you tell me once, if you tell me three times, or if you tell me three hundred. Flee now, I tell you in the name of great Vucji Pastir—flee or be my meat."

As had been true when George came down to Thessalonica with Perseus' cap on his head, the shepherd of the wolves could not tell he was there. If anything, Vucji Pastir was less concerned now than he had been before, for George's presence on the way down had troubled him. Now, intent on making Father Luke his victim, he heeded nothing less.

The priest stood his ground, defiant but weak. George wondered what he thought he could do against an angry demigod his spiritual force had proved unable to rout. Whatever it was, Father Luke never got the chance to try it. Vucji Pastir had come within a couple of paces of the priest when George drove his sword into the small of the Slavic demigod's back.

Vucji Pastir screamed, a great bellow of mingled astonishment and anguish. George pulled out the sword and stabbed the demigod again, this time in the side. He said nothing, not wanting to give the shepherd of the wolves any clue about where or what he was beyond the wounds themselves.

He stabbed Vucji Pastir for a third time. He tried for the demigod's throat, but succeeded only in striking his shoulder. "Murder!" Vucji Pastir cried, to whom or what the shoemaker did not know. "This vile priest does murder!"

"Depart, in the name of God," Father Luke said again.

And Vucji Pastir ran, screaming still. Maybe the holy name had more effect on him once he was hurt, as had been true with the wolf-demon. Maybe he was simply afraid of the holy man who had hurt him so horribly without moving from where he stood. George did not think Vucji Pastir slain, despite his shrieks. Had he struck off the demigod's head, then—perhaps. But perhaps not, too.

Father Luke said, "He would have done better had he hearkened when I bade him leave. I would have left him in peace, other than having him gone. As it was, he suffered for his stupidity."

"What would you have done if I weren't along?" George asked.

"I don't know," Father Luke answered. "I expect I would have managed, one way or another. God provides. How He provides will differ according to the circumstances, I am sure. He is not wasteful, but uses whatever He has handy."

George thought about that. To his way of looking at the world, it was taking a long chance. Irene would have said—Irene had said—he lived too much in the world of the ordinary senses and not enough in the world of the spirit. Most of his experience with the world of the spirit since the Slavs and Avars laid siege to Thessalonica had frightened the whey out of him.

Lessons came from the world of the ordinary senses, too. He drew one now: "We'd better get going, before something else dreadful happens to us here."

"That makes excellent sense," Father Luke said. He and George moved deeper into the hills. The quiet struck at George. All the wolf-demons had left off their terrifying howling after their shepherd was hurt. Maybe that meant they'd all fled back to their lairs. But maybe not, too. George did not want to find out the hard way.

When dawn began making the hillsides go from black to gray, a large bush by the side of the path quivered. At first George, who by then was so tired he had trouble putting one foot in front of the other, thought his eyes were playing tricks on him. Then he realized another of Vucji Pastir's wolves might have found Father Luke and him after all. But from behind the bush stepped not a wolf-demon but Ampelus and Ithys.

Quickly, George spoke to Father Luke: "Don't frighten them off, Your Reverence. They're the people, uh, powers we're looking for."

"I see a mortal here." Ampelus pointed to Father Luke, who was staring back at him with frank fascination. The satyr turned and pointed in the direction from which George's voice had come. "I hear a mortal there. These are the mortals we seek, then."

If the satyrs had dared come so far down in the hills, George thought he could safely take off Perseus' cap. "Ha!" Ithys said. "Is—*are*—two mortals, for true." As Ampelus had done, he pointed to Father Luke and George in turn, but he used phallus rather than forefinger. George had seen enough of satyrs' ways not to be surprised or offended. He wondered what Father Luke thought.

Whatever it was, the priest kept it to himself. To the satyrs, he said, "Take us on to your friends, so we can all talk about how we are going to fight against the Slavs and the Avars and the powers they've brought into this country."

Ithys pointed to George again, this time with a hand: perhaps a gesture of respect. "He does what he says he does," the satyr said to Ampelus. "Not many mortals like that."

"Truth—not many," Ampelus agreed.

That made George proud. He yawned, then nodded toward Father Luke. "Here is a truly good man whose word is truly good." He introduced Father Luke and the satyrs.

"If I say a thing, I will try to do it," the priest said. "If I do not think I can do it, or if I do not think I should do it, I will not say it." He had humility in him, but no false modesty. Being around him had helped educate George to the difference.

"We go, then," Ampelus said. "Talk with centaurs." He rolled his eyes. "Centaurs like talk. Centaurs like lots of talk. Maybe, good mortal who does and not says, you make centaurs do more, not say so much."

"Redeeming a centaur, even if only from loquaciousness, would be a deed worth trying," Father Luke said with a smile. "Whether I can or not, though, remains to be seen." He waved ahead. "Lead us, and I'll find out."

Together, the satyrs and the men went deeper into the hills above Thessalonica. Ithys and Ampelus walked warily, stealing glances at Father Luke and every now and then, when they got so close it made them nervous, skipping back from him. They knew the power he held, and did not quite trust him not to loose it against them.

George could not tell whether they took a shortcut through the hills that lay beyond those he knew. For one thing, he was so tired, even a shortcut would have seemed dreadfully long. For another, having come so far in the night, he could not be sure where he and Father Luke were when the satyrs found them. Since that point was unfamiliar, everything after it seemed strange, too.

Then, without any warning, almost as if a wolf-demon, Nephele stepped out into the path in front of them. The female centaur nodded to George and asked, "This is the cleric of whom you spoke?"

"Yes," he answered. Having introduced priest and satyrs, he introduced priest and centaur without a qualm.

Father Luke bowed as if Nephele were a lady high in the court at Constantinople. "I am honored to meet you," he said. "I am honored you would let me meet you." In an aside to George, he murmured, "I have, every once in a while, regretted my vows of celibacy. I never expected to do that quite like this, though."

However quietly he spoke, Nephele heard him. The female centaur threw back its head and laughed. Listening to that laugh with his eyes closed, George might have thought it came from a drinking companion in a tavern. Looking at Nephele, he did not want to close his eyes—on the contrary. To Father Luke, the centaur said, "I take't as a compliment, being sure 'twas meant so."

"Er—yes," the priest said. George could not recall having seen him flustered before. He did now.

"Onward, then." Nephele turned to lead them. Seen from behind, the centaur seemed less human than when viewed straight on.

They came to the encampment bare moments after George realized they were on the path leading to it. Stusippus spotted them first, and made a sound more like a birdcall than any speech George had ever heard. The centaurs in the camp came out of their lean-tos. Demetrius cantered up to Father Luke, who stared at him in delight. "I never thought of there being young centaurs," he said to George.

"I know what you mean," the shoemaker answered. "Neither did I."

Several centaurs whom George had not seen before

were among those crowding round him and Father Luke. He caught a couple of names—Pholus, Tachypus (a female)—but missed more.

Crotus still seemed to lead the band. The male inclined its head to Father Luke. "We are told you fear not and despise not the linking of your power and our own against that to which both stand opposed."

"If it can be done, I think we can do it," the priest replied. "We have shared this land many years now; we can live at peace."

"By share you mean your taking and our yielding," Crotus pointed out, not without bitterness. "That you be preferred to the incomers and their powers, who would slaughter us for sport, meaneth not you are belovèd."

"I understand as much," Father Luke said. "For the time being, though, the enemy of my enemy is my friend."

Xanthippe said, "Reasoning thus, we may cooperate, one side with the other. And afterwards, remembering our aid, it may be that you prove more inclined to leave us in peace."

"For myself, I am willing," Father Luke said. "I must tell you, though, for I would not lie to you, that my superior, Eusebius, will remain set in his ways. To expect him to change is as foredoomed a hope for you as for him to expect you to become a member of my faith."

"For the honesty, we are grateful," Crotus said. The other centaurs and satyrs nodded. The male went on, "For the sentiment, we would it were otherwise." The nods came again. Sighing, Crotus observed, "Necessity driveth all; we can but yield to it."

George wondered how much that attitude had to do with the failure of the old gods against Christianity. Bishop Eusebius and, no doubt, Father Luke, too, in his gentler way, were convinced their faith would triumph, regardless of the adversities it faced. That was their notion of necessity: not yielding to whatever the passage of time might bring against them.

Nephele set hands on the narrowing of human waist

above the outswelling into horse's body. "Very well, priest: you say you are fain to make alliance with us. How then, this being so, shall we best combine against the foe tormenting us both?"

"How?" Father Luke looked straight at the female centaur, which impressed George. The priest smiled, but not altogether happily. "My dear, at the moment I have no idea."

XI

The first thing George did was sleep till the sun, which had been low in the east, was low in the west. He was relieved to find some stew in the pot. "Aye," Nephele said, "the world waggeth on, seek to stay it as we may."

George ate and yawned, realizing he would have no trouble going back to sleep not long after nightfall. He set a hand on Perseus' cap, which lay beside him on the boulder on which he was sitting. "I want to go into Lete," he said, "and give this back to Gorgonius. I don't want him to think I'm a thief."

"We cannot do't today," Nephele answered, "the sun's chariot, as you see, having drawn too near the western horizon to permit the journey."

"Tomorrow, then," George said.

"It could be," Nephele said, "but then again, perhaps not. Surely we shall be undertaking many matters most urgent on that day, conferring with your priest, and—"

"Someone mention me?" Father Luke came up.

"They want to talk with you instead of taking me to Lete to give Gorgonius back his cap," George said, his voice a little sour. "If I understand right, *all* the centaurs want to talk with you, and *none* wants to go to Lete."

"That is good sooth," Nephele said.

"But why?" Father Luke asked.

"Why? Because we but seldom venture among the habitations of mankind for any reason, and have held to this rule for a time that seemeth long even to ourselves," Nephele replied. "If George be fain to return the cap, doubtless a satyr will guide him, they being eager to have as much to do with mankind, or rather womankind, as we are needful of holding to our sylvan fastness."

"You went with me before." George would not have argued so with the immortal had he not failed so completely of understanding. "Why not now?"

"We went, aye, but with greatest reluctance, as you must have seen. Gaining the cap of Perseus held an urgency returning it lacketh," Nephele said, an answer that was not an answer. The female centaur saw George and Father Luke recognize that it was not an answer. A very human-sounding sigh came forth. "Are the two of you blind and deaf? What, as is proved by experience bitter, must my kind avoid at all costs?"

Father Luke, with only a day's acquaintance with the centaurs, looked blank. George thought the answer was on the tip of his tongue and, thinking that, found it: "Wine!" he exclaimed.

Gravely, Nephele nodded. "Even so," the female centaur said. "Even so. Being of the mortal kind that prepareth and drinketh the blood of the grape with no further ado than that it should be a vintage you favor, you have no notion of the longing for it we know, a longing we also know we dare not sate."

"All right," George said. He had seen the hunger on Crotus' face when they went into Lete: seen it but evidently underestimated its power. "If it's as bad as that, I'll let Ampelus or Ithys or Stusippus take me to the village."

"For which you have my thanks." Nephele looked at him from under heavy-lidded, long-lashed eyes. No, even that disconcerting baritone wasn't always disconcerting enough to keep the female's almost human and more than human beauty from stirring him and making him think how he might want to have those thanks shown.

"Wait." Father Luke spoke only the one word, but with such authority that both George and Nephele turned their heads toward him. He paid no attention to George, for which the shoemaker could hardly blame him: had he had to choose between Nephele and himself, he would have chosen the centaur, too. The priest said, "Perhaps it would be for the best, Nephele, if, this once, you and all your kind drink yourselves full of wine to the very point of bursting."

Those splendid eyes were heavy-lidded no more, but wide and staring. "Priest of the new, you know not what you say. Wine looseth in us a blazing madness oft satisfied only by blood. It is the curse of my folk, against which we have no power of resistance."

"I don't want you to resist," Father Luke said. "I want you to yield to it, to revel in it."

With each shake of the female centaur's head, black, curly hair flew around its face. "You know not what you say. Even to suggest such a thing is madness, nothing less. Aye, madness: akin to that madness we knew in the far-off days when the world was young and nothing had stolen from us the greatest part of the land that is ours. Not since the disaster of the supper with the Lapiths have we taken wine, for fear of what it will do to us. Nay. I say again, nay." The last word was almost a horse's ringing neigh.

"But don't you understand?" Father Luke, by contrast, sounded calm and rational: so calm and rational that George, who aspired to those conditions, wondered if the priest had lost his wits, or perhaps did not fully appreciate even yet the depth of the centaurs' revulsion. Unperturbed, Father Luke went on, "You should be mad with wine—you need to be mad with wine—if you are to stand against the Slavs and Avars and their powers. When you remain your sober selves, they have more strength than you, not so?"

"That is so," Nephele admitted. "It is so, but it hath no significance, not set against our dire need to fight shy of the lovely, deadly stuff."

"If you will not set the arrow in your bow, you'll never know how well you might shoot," Father Luke said. "And if you refuse to use the arrow, will you go down to defeat wondering till you perish whether it might have done you some good?"

Nephele studied him. "The satyrs are fain to seduce us," the female centaur said slowly, "but they seek no more than the use of our bodies, which, while no small thing, also is not a matter of greatest consequence. Some have even yielded to them, for a romp. Not I, but some. You, now, you would seduce our minds to do as you will, not as custom ancient and long-established teacheth: in my view, a stronger seduction."

Father Luke shrugged. "After George brought me here, I was asked how I could help rally the strength of your kind and mine together. I didn't know then. I still don't know, but this is far and away the best idea I've had."

Hearing George's name reminded Nephele he was there. The centaur rounded on him, demanding, "What think you of this crackbrained scheme?"

"Me?" George said. "I think that, if you haven't got any better ideas yourself, you'd be foolish not to pay attention when somebody else does."

Nephele's shoulders sagged, as if the answer he'd given was exactly the opposite of the one the female wanted to hear. "Even you, too?" The centaur sighed, a wintry sound. "Very well, then: I shall broach the matter to my fellows. What may come of it, I do not presume to say. This prohibition your friend is eager for us to break hath almost the status among us of a law of nature. But we shall see." The centaur turned and trotted away.

"Isn't this interesting?" Father Luke said with a broad smile.

"Very interesting," George replied. "If it's all the same to you, Your Reverence, I'd sooner be bored."

✧ ✧ ✧

After Nephele left, George expected the female or Crotus or one of the other centaurs would be back with an answer, yea or nay, in short order. That didn't happen. George remembered what the satyrs had said about centaurs and discussion, and also his own experience with Crotus. He wondered if he and Father Luke would have a response before spring.

While he waited and the centaurs debated, he asked Ithys to take him to Lete. Father Luke stayed behind, operating under what George was convinced to be the delusion that the centaurs would decide anything soon. "I shall have to be ready to cooperate when the critical moment comes," the priest insisted.

"I understand that," George said. "You understand that. The centaurs don't understand that, though. And they don't understand that they don't understand—they think they're in a hurry. And you, Your Reverence, I don't think you understand that they don't understand they don't understand."

"I don't think I understand *you*," Father Luke said, laughing. George listened again in his mind to what he'd just said, no longer sure he understood himself. But, after a little thought, he decided he'd—probably—said what he'd meant to say.

A little thought was all he got, because Ithys kept plucking at the sleeve of his tunic. "We go," the satyr said. "Come. We go." Having found a willing woman in the village, he was comically eager to get back there: not only to see if she was willing again, but also to learn whether he could find another one.

George carried Perseus' cap. Now that he was out of Thessalonica, he wished he'd used it to pay a visit to Menas. He hadn't thought of it while he was in the city, having been more worried about his family's knowing he was alive and about getting Father Luke. He wondered if that single-minded concern for duty made him an exceptionally virtuous man or an exceptionally stupid one.

He and Ithys drew near Lete without seeing any women of any sort, lecherously inclined or otherwise. The satyr grumbled: "This bad time of year. Spring, summer—women bathe in streams. Wintertime, no."

"It's cold in the winter," George pointed out. "Do *you* go into a stream in the middle of winter?"

"Bad time of year," Ithys repeated. Where centaurs seemed given to endless arguments, satyrs hardly argued at all. They knew what they knew (regardless of whether what they knew had anything to do with the truth), and had no interest in anyone else's opinions.

Lete occupied only a small hole in the woods, even with fields all around the village. One moment, Ithys was leading George down a game track; the next, they were staring at the village across those fields. Crossing the open ground, Ithys nodded familiarly to the now bare grape vines. He had nothing against wine—on the contrary.

To his annoyance, he got nothing more than giggles from the few women walking through Lete's narrow, twisting streets. "Not right." He gave George a dirty look. "Must be your fault."

George wondered how many times, over the centuries, Ithys had failed to find female companionship coming into Lete alone. Thousands, no doubt. Of course, he'd had only himself to blame then, which was sure to mean he'd blamed nobody.

Gorgonius was pounding a wooden peg into the end of a table leg when George came into his shop. "Good day," the carpenter said, setting down his mallet. "I'm glad to see you back, and that's the truth. You seemed a good fellow, but nobody can tell for certain till the deeds are done, if you know what I mean." He suddenly looked anxious. "I don't aim to offend, of course."

"I'm not offended," George said. "I understand what you mean. You did me a large favor that you didn't have to do, and I'm grateful for it."

"You looked to be a chap who needed a large favor," Gorgonius answered. "Not even the oldest old wife in town remembers hearing from her granny about the last time centaurs came into Lete. Centaurs! If they think you're important, do you suppose I'm going to argue very hard?"

"I do thank you," George said, "and here's your cap back." He set it down on Gorgonius' workbench.

"You're sure you've done everything with it you wanted?" the carpenter asked.

"Everything I needed," George answered. Again, a vision of the visit he hadn't paid on Menas flashed through his mind.

Gorgonius was no fool. He caught the difference between his question and George's answer. Walking over to the bench, he picked up the cap and thrust it at the shoemaker. "If you're not done with it, friend, take it back. You've come up here once to return it to me. I expect you'll come again."

"Are you sure?" George said. "That thing is a temptation, and no mistake."

"If you came once, you'll come again," Gorgonius repeated. "As long as you have come all this way, would you like some wine and olives before you go back? And you, too, Ithys, of course," he added politely for the satyr's benefit.

George nodded. Ithys said, "Yes, I take some some wine and olives. Just you leave out the olives." Laughter set the satyr's phallus bobbing up and down. The two men laughed, too. Gorgonius went off to get the food and drink. Ithys pointed to the cap. "He let you keep that longer, eh?"

"It seems so, yes," George answered.

"Then we come all this way for nothing? No need to give back hat. No pretty women for me to take." But Ithys could not quite manage a full-blown scowl, especially not after Gorgonius came back with a bowl of olives and three cups. "Wine," the satyr said, as if reminding itself. "Wine. No, this walk not for nothing after all."

⟡ ⟡ ⟡

On the way back to the encampment where the centaurs and satyrs dwelt, George stumbled several times. His feet did not want to go where he meant to put them. Ithys, normally as graceful as any of the supernatural kind, also had trouble. "Wine," the satyr said, and giggled, a surprisingly high-pitched, squeaky sound to come from such a large, shaggy creature.

"Maybe." But George, though he didn't argue, wasn't so sure. He'd had only a couple of cups in Lete, not nearly enough to make him too tiddly to walk straight. On the other hand, if the problem wasn't wine, what was it?

When he reached the encampment, he found Father Luke looking worried. "I wish the centaurs would make up their minds," the priest said. He pointed down toward Thessalonica. "Can't you feel the trouble in the air— and the power?"

Maybe there was a reason George had been so clumsy. "Is *that* what I'm feeling?" he said. "You deal with powers all the time, Your Reverence, so you'd know better than I do. Something's wrong, I think, but I don't know what."

"Something enormous is building, down by the city," Father Luke said. "I can't tell what it is, only that it is— and that I don't like it."

"I don't think the Slavs and Avars ever really turned their strongest gods loose against Thessalonica," George said. "They've tried to get into the city without doing that, unless I'm wrong. I don't quite understand why, but that's the way it's looked to me."

"You may have made a very good guess there," Father Luke said. "I think the Slavs and Avars have been using their demigods and lesser deities for the same reason we often ask saints or the Virgin to intercede for us with God. Facing too much raw power, trying to turn that power to your own ends, can burn out a mere man."

"That makes sense," George agreed thoughtfully. "But if the Slavs and Avars are changing what they're doing now . . ."

"I can think of only one reason why they would change,"

Father Luke said. "And that is that everything they've tried up till now has failed. If they're going to take Thessalonica, they'll need everything they can possibly bring to bear against it." The priest nodded. "That fits well with what I'm feeling. Do you know what their great gods are like?"

George shook his head. "I haven't the faintest notion, Your Reverence. We're going to find out, though, aren't we?"

"I wish I were back at St. Elias'," Father Luke said, but then, immediately, he shook his head. "No, I'm wrong. Inside Thessalonica, with faith so strong all around me, I might not have noticed this till too late."

"What can you do here that you wouldn't be able to do there?" George asked.

"Pray, of course." Father Luke looked surprised that he should need to put the question. Then the priest looked surprised again, in a different way. "And I can also pray that the centaurs will decide to do whatever they decide to do soon enough for them and us to draw some benefit from it, whatever it turns out to be."

"That would be good." George peered in the direction of Thessalonica. He was no holy man, to feel subtle disturbances in the relationship of powers and the material world in which those powers—and he—dwelt. But what was coming up from out of the south wasn't subtle. His shiver had nothing to do with the chilly day. "How long do you think we have?" he asked.

"I don't know," Father Luke said. "It's like a cloudburst hanging over us. The rain will come, but when? And when it does, will it wash us away? The one thing I will say is, I don't think we have very long."

"What do we do, then?" George turned to Ithys. The satyr had been ignoring him and Father Luke. "How do you go about making the centaurs move faster?" the shoemaker asked.

"Is no way," Ithys answered.

Ampelus, who was sitting close by the fire, shook its

shaggy head. "Is maybe a way." The satyr got to its feet and silently vanished into the woods.

"What's he going to do?" Father Luke asked.

Ithys shrugged, as if to say it couldn't possibly make any difference, whatever it was. George answered, "If I knew, I'd try it myself."

Not much later and not very far away, a loud baritone shout rose from the woods. George needed a little while to remember male centaurs all had bass voices. That wasn't a shout, then. It was a scream.

Ampelus came back into the encampment laughing and staggering a little and rubbing at what George first took to be a bruise on the hairy flesh of the satyr's chest. Then the shoemaker saw that it *was* a bruise, all right, a bruise in the shape of a hoofprint. Ampelus said, "Centaurs here soon. Minds made up. Not know which way, but made up."

"How did you manage that?" George exclaimed.

Ampelus laughed some more, though the laughter looked as if it hurt. "Went up in back of filly Nephele, tried to screw. If I do it, I think I have good time. If I don't do it, I make Nephele, all the centaurs so mad, they give over talk talk talk."

"You get it in?" Ithys demanded.

By way of reply, Ampelus sadly rubbed at that hoof-shaped bruise. Though the satyr healed with the speed characteristic of immortals, George suspected it would wear that mark for a good long while.

Sure enough, though, Nephele burst out of the woods a few minutes later. The glance the female centaur aimed at Ampelus should have annihilated the satyr more thoroughly than any kick, no matter how ferocious. Ampelus, however, only leered back, which made Nephele more furious than ever.

Father Luke spoke quickly: "Have you decided, then, whether you will drink the wine to try to save Thessalonica?"

Distracted, Nephele turned away from Ampelus. "Oh,"

the female centaur said. "That." Anger cooled somewhat, it spoke now with more than a little hesitation. "Aye," it said at last. "We are decided. Let it be as you say, priest of the new. We shall do this thing, and run wild upon the earth, and madness shall overtake us, and, if it be fated, we shall overfall the folk and powers that have come down into this land."

"In the name of—" Father Luke checked himself before he named the Name the centaur could not bear to hear. "In my name, and in the name of Thessalonica my city, I thank you."

"And while we run mad," Nephele went on as if the priest had not spoken, "if it be fated, mayhap I shall run across a certain wretch with horse's tail and billy goat's nature, and mayhap tear the said wretch limb from limb beyond any hope of healing, even though that wretch belong to a race said to be undying. Mayhap this too shall come to pass."

George would not have wanted to be on the receiving end of a threat like that, not when Nephele so obviously looked forward to the prospect. If it bothered Ampelus, the satyr didn't show it. "Maybe you just get drunk and happy. Maybe we go someplace and—"

Nephele flung a stone. Ampelus' dodge was, and needed to be, supernaturally quick. The satyr darted in among the trees. A volley of well-hurled stones followed. George didn't think any of them hit.

Lete was overrun with centaurs. The townsfolk, pagan though they were, had stared when Crotus and Nephele accompanied George and the satyrs to Gorgonius' shop. Now George would not have been surprised if the centaurs here outnumbered the human population of Lete.

From where had all the creatures come? How had they gathered here so quickly, when the shoemaker had seen but few signs of them up till now? He'd tried asking Nephele, but the female centaur gave him no answer he could understand. His own best guess was that her kin had traveled by way of the hills beyond those he knew, and that paths long in his own mundane world might prove shorter there. He did not know that for a fact. He did not know whether any humanly graspable facts were there to be known.

Lete might not have seen centaurs for a long time. Lete might never before have seen centaurs in profusion. But, when those centaurs began gathering around the couple of taverns in the town, the people of Lete, pagans as they were, knew what that was liable to mean. A lot of those people expressed their opinion of what was about to happen, or was liable to happen, by fleeing for their lives.

The proprietor of one of the taverns, a dour little man who looked better suited to be a gravedigger, came out of his establishment to look at the centaurs, who stared hungrily back at him. Seeing Father Luke in the front ranks of the creatures alongside Crotus and Nephele, the taverner called to him: "Do you know what will happen when these centaurs get themselves a bellyful of wine?"

"No," the priest answered cheerfully, "not in any great detail. Do you?"

"Detail?" The fellow stared at him. "I don't care anything about the details. You crazy—" He might have said, *You crazy Christian*, which would have routed the centaurs and ruined Father Luke's plan on the spot. Instead, he backed up and tried again: "You crazy bugger, they get wine in 'em, they'll tear up everything they can get their hands on."

"That's the idea," Father Luke said, cheerful still. "How would you like to be a Slav or an Avar and have a pack of drunken centaurs come thundering down on you when you didn't expect it?"

"Oh." The taverner started to say something else, but again checked himself. He very visibly did try to imagine himself a barbarian caught by surprise under such circumstances. The expression he donned after making that mental effort was merely dyspeptic, a considerable improvement on the way he'd looked before. "They won't be happy, will they?"

"We hope not," George said. "That's the idea: to make them unhappy, I mean. Why don't you bring some wine jars and dippers out here? Your place looks crowded for centaurs, you don't mind my saying so."

Dour glowering returned to the taverner's face. "They'll drink me dry. Who's going to pay me for all this?"

"If you don't bring out the jars and dippers, they'll go into your tavern, drink you dry, and probably wreck the place, too," George noted. "Wouldn't you say keeping the building and furniture in one piece counts for something?"

The taverner's lips moved. George could not make out what he was saying. That was liable to be just as well. The fellow went back into his shop. George worried. If no wine was forthcoming, the centaurs were liable to storm and sack the place.

But then the taverner reemerged, carrying a large jar. He stabbed the pointed end into the ground so it stood upright. By the look he gave George, he would sooner have stabbed him. George felt a certain amount of sympathy; he wouldn't have wanted to give away all the shoes he'd made over several months, either. Nor was the taverner saving his own town; the Slavs and Avars had shown no interest in Lete. If, however, the other choices were worse . . .

Out came the taverner again, with another jar of wine. Seeing him give up, his colleague also began bringing out jars of wine. Behind George, the centaurs leaned forward, like a forest with the wind blowing through it. They might not have tasted wine since the long-ago days, but they remembered—and they hungered.

George turned to Father Luke. "Once they start drinking, how will we turn them toward Thessalonica? If they go mad or do whatever they do here, that doesn't help us much."

"I don't quite know." The priest's face was drawn and

worried. "One way or another, we'll manage. We'll have to manage. Can't you feel how close the Slavs and Avars are to doing whatever they're about to do?"

"I can't feel anything but how close we are to getting trampled when the creatures decide they're not going to wait anymore," George said. Father Luke smiled at him, but wanly.

Crotus started shouting in a dialect even more archaic than the one the male and the other centaurs used when talking with mortals. George could catch a word here and there, but, while he was getting that one, three or four more would go by that had no meaning for him. They meant something to the centaurs, though. Several large, burly males pushed their way through the crowd and took up stations by the growing rows of wine jars.

To Father Luke and George, Crotus said, "They are pledged to resist the lure of the wine as best they can, to aid others in drinking whilst abstaining themselves. So far as it may be prevented, the madness shall not lay hold of all of us at once."

George and the priest beamed at each other. The sober centaurs could send the rest of their kind in the required direction—if they stayed sober, and if the others, once drunk, paid any attention to them. George was glad they were there. Of one thing he was certain: drunk, the mob of centaurs would have paid no attention to him.

At last, everything was to Crotus' satisfaction. "Let us taste the wine!" the male cried, a sentence that had not changed much over time. The rest of the centaurs did not cheer, as George had expected them to do at that welcome exhortation. Instead, a deep sigh ran through them, as when a lover spied his beloved after the two of them had spent a long time apart.

Crotus was the first to fill a dipper. Instead of also being the first to drink, the male centaur, oddly ceremonious, passed the dipper to Nephele. The female savored the bouquet of the wine for a moment, then poured the dipper down. A shudder ran through both the human and the equine halves of the centaur's body. Its eyes slid almost shut. A low, soft sigh escaped its lips. If that wasn't ecstasy, George had never seen ecstasy.

And, when Nephele's eyes opened again, they had fire in them. The transformation was abrupt, and a little terrifying. All the planes and angles of the centaur's face were different. Every one of them screamed *danger!* Something wild and terrible, something not seen in these hills for many long ages, had slipped its bonds and was running free.

Father Luke saw that, too. He did his brave best not to seem alarmed. In a conversational tone of voice, he asked, "Do you know the writer on magic named Philotechnus, George?" When George shook his head, the priest went on, "One of the bits of advice he gives is, *Do not call up that which you cannot put down*. I think that may have been good advice indeed."

Nephele roughly flung the dipper back to Crotus. The male centaur refilled it and drank. George watched in astonishment: the change in Crotus was even greater than that in Nephele had been. The male centaur seemed large and more . . . predatory than had been true only a moment before. If it turned that fearsome gaze on George, he told himself he would make the sign of the cross at the creature—better to drive it off than be torn limb from limb.

And then George wondered if the sign of the cross would do any good against a centaur maddened by wine. He could see Father Luke wondering the same thing. All at once, he understood in his belly what Philotechnus' maxim meant.

More and more centaurs drank. More and more centaurs underwent that transformation, awe-inspiring and terrifying at the same time. Hoarse shouts rose into the sky. The more drunken centaurs there were, the more the horse shouts gained in volume and ferocity.

Even Demetrius, still the only centaur colt George had seen, took a dipper of wine and was remade in the savage image of its elders. Demetrius put the shoemaker in mind of a fox cub worrying at a bone too big for it, but that didn't mean, or didn't have to mean, the small centaur wasn't dangerous in its own right.

"How do we go down toward Thessalonica?" Luke asked.

"I think we'd better have the males who aren't drunk tell the rest to get going," George said. He wasn't anxious to draw to him the notice of the centaurs who had been drinking.

"That isn't what I meant," the priest said. "How do *we* go down to Thessalonica? I may be needed there, to bring the power of . . ." —he didn't speak God's name, not wanting to find out whether or not the centaurs could bear it in their present condition— "to bear against the Slavs and Avars and their powers."

"Oh," George said, and then, "Well, how do you feel about being cavalry, Your Reverence?"

"Riding a centaur, do you mean?" Father Luke said. George nodded. The priest went on, "Riding a drunken centaur? Riding a maddened drunken centaur? Of all the things in the world, the only one I'd less rather do, I think, is stay up here in Lete."

George nodded again. He started to go up to Nephele, to ask if the female centaur would bear him down the long and winding road that led back to Thessalonica. Then, remembering what Ampelus had tried to do to Nephele, he sheered off. He could think of only one way to hold on as he rode, and feared the female centaur would take it as an undue liberty.

He went up to Crotus instead. "Will you carry me to Thessalonica?" he asked. "Will one of your friends carry Father Luke?"

Crotus' eyes were tracked with red. Slowly, slowly, they focused on George. "Thessalonica," the centaur said, one thick syllable at a time, as if it had never heard the word before. Then its head went up and down. "Oh, aye, the new town." George did not think of it as a new town, but George did not personally remember its founding, as Crotus no doubt did. The male went on, "And you, mortal, you are . . . ah, who you are returneth to me: the follower of the new." The centaur looked ready to tear him to pieces for being a follower of the new. But then more memory seemed to make its way through the haze of wine. "And we are . . . we are in alliance. Alliance with bad against worse. A hard path, but the only one left to us."

Without another word, Crotus squatted down on all fours (or rather, on four out of six). George scrambled onto the centaur's back. Crotus shouted for Elatus; the other male stood nearby. Elatus squatted, too. Father Luke hurried over and mounted his unorthodox—in both the literal and theological senses of the word—steed.

"Thessalonica!" Crotus shouted in a huge voice. "Thessalonica! The foe awaiteth. Thessalonica!"

In a moment, the whole great band of centaurs had taken up the cry, baying like so many wolves: "Thessalonica!" Down the hillside they poured, a drunken mob of supernatural creatures. Beneath George's fundament, Crotus' muscles heaved and rippled. The shoemaker clung to the centaur's human torso with one hand and to Perseus' cap with the other. If he needed to draw his sword and fight . . . he wouldn't be able to hold on then. He hoped—how he hoped!—it wouldn't matter.

He looked around to see where in the band Father Luke was. Riding behind Elatus' torso as George rode behind Crotus', the priest made his centaur look as if it boasted two upthrust human parts rather than the standard one. George and Crotus no doubt made the same absurd picture.

"Thessalonica!" the centaurs shouted, urging one another on and, George suspected, reminding themselves where they were going.

"Hurry!" Father Luke called to them. "In the name of whatever you hold dear, hurry! The foe ariseth in his might." He imitated the old-fashioned Greek they spoke, which made them heed him almost as if he were one of their own. George, who could not have done the same, wished he had hands free with which to applaud.

Now, despite being in among the band of centaurs, he too could feel the gathering of power to the south. He'd known that sort of feeling in the churches of Thessalonica, but the power rising here had nothing to do with the God he worshiped. Whether it was—or could be, if fully manifested—more powerful than his God, he did not know.

That frightened him worse than anything.

"On the way home," he murmured, trying to reassure himself. But the way home was, as it had been, blocked by the Slavs and Avars and by the powers that had already accompanied them into this part of the world.

A shout from the front-runners among the centaurs said they'd spotted one of those powers. Peering forward over Crotus' shoulder, George spied a Slavic wolf-demon. The creature's howl, this once, brought no terror with it; had it burst from a human throat, it would have been an exclamation of surprise and dismay.

The wolf turned and tried to flee, as if to take news of what it had just seen back to those with more power than it possessed. Since it was heading down toward Thessalonica, the drunken centaurs ran after it. In short order, they ran over it: the whole band, or at least as many of them as its battered body happened to pass beneath. George felt it go under Crotus' trampling, pounding hooves. With four legs on which to stand, the centaur had no trouble keeping its balance and delivering a good stomping at the same time.

Once the band had passed over the wolf, George turned and looked back over his shoulder at it. It didn't look as if it had ever been alive; far from seeming immortal, it didn't look as if it would ever be alive again, either. He might have been wrong: things from beyond the hills he knew were often next to impossible to slay. Not many of them, though, endured what the wolf-demon had just suffered.

Before long, the centaurs came upon more wolves. A few peeled off from the main band to chase them. The wolf-demons, more used to chasing centaurs, ran away from their numbers and their ferocity, baying as they went. But a lot of the centaurs went on yelling "Thessalonica!" at the top of their lungs. For whatever reason they did it, it helped keep most of them together.

George kept looking for Vucji Pastir. The shepherd of the wolves would be a more dangerous foe than the creatures he herded. But of Vucji Pastir there was no sign. George remembered the swordwork he had done while invisible. He still did not think he had slain the demigod; to think that, on the basis of what little he knew, would have made him both more stupid and more heroic than he actually was.

Disturbed by the centaurs' thundering hooves and by their cries, bats rose in chittering swarms. Remembering that bats had spied on Thessalonica, George shouted a warning. The centaurs were already flinging volleys of stones and branches at the creatures. They brought down a good many, and trampled them as they had trampled that first wolf. Again, George wondered if any creature, supernatural or not, could survive such treatment.

"Close now," Father Luke called through the din the centaurs made. "When will the Slavs and Avars notice what's bearing down on them?"

"If we're lucky, they'll take one look at the centaurs and run screaming," George answered, punctuating that with a sharp "oof!" as he came down awkwardly on Crotus' back after the male took a particularly long bound. "Of course, if we were lucky, God wouldn't have inflicted the Slavs and Avars on us in the first place, would He? I expect we'll have a fight on our hands."

Bishop Eusebius would sure have droned out some pious platitudes on the topic of all mankind's being able to live together in peace and understanding and everyone's worshiping God—in, of course, the orthodox fashion. That would have been wonderful, except that the Slavs and Avars had no interest in peace, understanding, or, for that matter, God.

And Father Luke, unlike most clergymen of George's acquaintance, had little use for pious platitudes: not that he wasn't pious—far from it—but he expressed his piety more through his life than through his talk. Now he nodded, and said, "That's what I think, too." He looked worried again. "I hope we aren't too late."

Off to one side of the main band of centaurs, a scream rose in the woods. It was not the sort of scream that might have come from the throat of one of the Slavic demons or demigods: it was a simple scream of human terror. The Slavs had had men hunting in the woods since before their assault on Thessalonica, as George knew full well. No doubt Slavs still roamed the woods, trying to keep their larders full. One of the small groups of centaurs that had peeled off from the main band in pursuit of a wolf-demon must have come upon a hunter instead. By the sounds the fellow had made, he wouldn't be making any more sounds in the near future—or in the distant future, either.

A few minutes later, a centaur let out a screech filled with both fury and pain. An arrow sprouted from the creature's right hindmost leg. Another centaur tore the shaft out, which caused the wounded male to screech again. Its bleeding slowed as quickly as George had seen to be commonplace among immortal beings. He hoped the Slav hadn't poisoned the arrow, as his kind were known to do. If the Slav had poisoned it, he hoped the venom was not of a sort to harm supernatural creatures.

The male centaur ran on as if not badly hurt, so George supposed the arrow was either unpoisoned or harmless to the centaur regardless of poison. He did not have long to contemplate such things, for several centaurs, both males and females, galloped in the direction from which the arrow had come. Shouts rang out, some theirs, others from a man. When they rejoined the main band, blood dappled their human arms and torsos.

Before long, as they drew nearer to the encampments of the Slavs and Avars, more and more arrows began coming their way. "Keep on!" George shouted to Crotus. "If you waste your time chasing down a few archers, you won't get to the main body of the foe till too late."

More and more, as power built in the air around him, he got the feeling they had very little time. Whatever the Slavs and Avars were going to do, it was on the point of being done. "So that we slay them, what boots it an we slay them individually or collectively?" Crotus shouted back.

That was, George realized, the wine raging in the centaur. Sober, Crotus liked nothing better than to deliberate, to choose with great care the best possible course. Drunk, none of that mattered. All the male wanted to do was kick and stamp and tear and kill. Hows and whys and wherefores concerned it not at all.

"We have to get down to the city and break up the magic they're working," George said desperately. "Can't you feel it? Can't you sense it? If their gods fully come through into the hills we know—" He broke off. If that happened, God would have to intervene, perhaps through St. Demetrius, to save Thessalonica—if He chose to save it, if He was strong enough to save it. But Crotus cared nothing about God and little about Thessalonica. George tried a different explanation: "If they manifest themselves in these hills, they'll be too strong for you."

Crotus bounded along, seemingly tireless. But after a few more strides, the male let out a great rumbling bellow: "Thessalonica! To Thessalonica! Straight on to Thessalonica!"

The centaur sprang out ahead of the rest of the band, leading not just by shouts but by example. Straight on they went. They did not turn aside for holy ground of any sort. Maybe, in their drunken madness, the power in patches of holy ground had less effect on them than had been so while they were sober. Maybe, too, they simply happened not to run across any. George was too busy trying to stay on Crotus' back to be sure.

The woods thinned. Followed close by the other centaurs, Crotus burst into the open ground around Thessalonica. The male shouted once more when he came out into that open country, for the Slavs and a large troop of Avar cavalry were drawn up in battle array against the city. So intent on Thessalonica were they, they did not turn against the centaurs till the drumroll of hoofbeats bearing down on them drew them away from the attack they had been about to begin on the wall.

Indeed, it might not even have been the hoofbeats from behind, but rather the shouts from the defenders of Thessalonica, that made the Slavs and Avars realize the centaurs were there. The shouts were joy, not amazement: at that distance, the defenders must have taken the centaurs for regular cavalry coming to their rescue. The surprise—even the horror—on the faces of the barbarians, who knew better, was marvelous to behold. Till then, their powers not only held their own against the Christian God, but had routed the supernatural beings native to these hills and valleys.

Perhaps the centaurs were, in true terms of strength, still overmatched. If they were, they neither knew nor cared. Maddened with wine, all they wanted was to close with the folk whose demons and demigods had done so much to them up till then. Being afraid never crossed their minds.

It crossed George's mind. It also crossed the minds of whole troops of Slavs, who turned and fled from the raging band. But not all the barbarians fled. Some of them began shooting arrows at the centaurs. They cried out in dismay when, even after they scored hits, their foes would not fall. Seeing that sent more of them running.

The Avars were made of sterner stuff. They shot arrows at the centaurs, too, arrows from their heavier bows. They also wheeled their armored horses around and rode into battle, some with swords, some with spears. They might never have seen these supernatural creatures before, but they showed hardly more alarm than the beings galloping at Crotus' heels.

Here and there, one of those centaurs, shot through the chest or perhaps the eye, crashed to the ground and thrashed toward death. Not even their marvelous flesh was proof against an arrow lodged in the heart or in the brain.

George knew too well that his own flesh, marvelous only to him, was proof against very little. Not wanting the Avars to take any special notice of him, he clapped Perseus' cap onto his head. He held it with his left hand. With a great many misgivings, he drew his sword with his right. That left no hands with which to hold on to Crotus' human torso. Clenching the centaur's equine barrel with legs inexperienced at horsemanship, he hoped he would not fall off and be trampled like a wolf-demon.

While a few centaurs went down, most of them, even those who were wounded, stormed on toward the Avars. As the Slavs had before them, the mounted men lost spirit when their most telling shots availed them little. And the stones the centaurs flung smote as if they came from the hurling arms of the siege engines on the walls of Thessalonica. When one of those stones struck home, an Avar pitched from his saddle or, despite armor of iron, a horse staggered, limbs half unstrung.

And then it was no longer a fight of arrows and stones. The onrushing centaurs were in among the Avars, wrenching the spears from their hands, wrenching riders off the backs of their horses, and throwing them to the ground. The Avars remained brave. They also retained the arrogance that made them believe they had the right to rule everything they could reach. When confronted by immortal madmen who also could and did kick like mules, none of that did them much good.

George slashed away with his sword. Every so often, edge or point would find a gap in an Avar's scalemail. The barbarian would howl with pain and look around wildly to see who had wounded him. He would discover that he, like Polyphemus in the *Odyssey*, had apparently been hurt by Nobody.

Remembering that Father Luke lacked the option of invisibility, George looked around to see how the priest fared. He was glad to find he had a lot of trouble picking Father Luke's human torso out from those of the centaurs in whose midst the holy man rode. He would have had more trouble still had Father Luke divested himself of his robes, but, while the priest's piety was more flexible than that of Bishop Eusebius, George was certain it would not bend so far as that.

An Avar in a gilded helmet shouted something that sounded incendiary even if George couldn't understand a word of it. Crotus struck the man with a powerful fist. The Avar's iron armor warded him against the blow. George hit him, too: in the face, with the edge of his blade. Blood spurted. The Avar screamed. He clutched at himself. George wished he'd served Menas the same way.

Losing the officer's steadying hand helped unsettle the Avars. So did their foes' furious, unyielding attack. The nomads found themselves moving back instead of forward. That unsettled them more. Now men began to break away from the fight instead of rushing toward it.

The centaurs seemed oblivious to the way their foes fought. *They* fought hard, no matter what. Some of the regular soldiers who had left Thessalonica for the wars to the north and east owned warhorses that would strike out with their hooves at a rider's command. George had thought that marvelous till he saw the centaurs in action. At close quarters, one of them, unarmored and unarmed except for what nature had provided, was far more than a match for Avars trained to horsemanship and war since childhood.

And the centaurs did not stay unarmed long. Many of them—those, George thought, rather less maddened by wine than some of the others—not only wrested spears and swords from the men they were fighting, they used them and weapons picked up from the ground with wicked effect.

George reveled in his own invisible deadliness. Whenever the melee brought Crotus close enough to an Avar, the shoemaker on the centaur's back struck and struck hard. The nomads did not know why Crotus was a particularly dangerous enemy, but soon figured out the male was such, and did their best to stay away from it. In the press of battle, that best was too often not nearly good enough.

Quite suddenly, the press loosened. With a small shock, George saw that the centaurs had fought their way through the entire troop of Avars. Some of the nomads rode away from them, urging their horses to the best turn of speed they could. More were down on the ground behind Crotus, dead or wounded. More than a few riderless horses were mixed among the centaurs. Seeing the horses in that company, George thought they looked oddly incomplete, which only proved how used to centaurs he had grown over the past few days.

Only a few warriors—some stubborn Avars, some Slavs rushing up to try to plug the gap in the line their overlords' overthrow had created—remained between the centaurs and . . . what? Though seeing it from an unfamiliar angle, George recognized the tent of the Avar priest or wizard, and the satellite tents of the Slavic sorcerers nearby. The sorcerers were not in their tents, but capered around an immense bonfire not far from them.

At first, George thought it was waves of heat that were beating against him from the bonfire. Then he realized that, large as it was, it wasn't large enough for that. It wasn't heat—or rather wasn't heat exclusively—coming from the fire. It was sorcerous power.

"That way!" He leaned forward to shout in Crotus' ear. He pointed toward the great blaze, forgetting he was as invisible to the centaur as to the Avars and to everyone else. But his words did what his outflung arm could not:

"We have to get rid of those wizards before—" He didn't know just what they would or could do, but, from what Father Luke had said . . . "I've already asked you once—do you want their great gods fully in this world with you?"

That did the trick. Drunk as the centaur was, supernaturally wild with wine as it was, Crotus somehow kept some semblance of sense far down at the bottom of its mind. "Thither!" the male roared to the rest of the centaurs, and pointed toward the bonfire. Its arm, unlike George's, was perfectly visible.

Had George got an order like "thither," he would have spent the next half hour trying to figure out whether it meant *this way* or *that way*, regardless of any gestures accompanying it. He was sure the same held true for all his comrades in the militia, and for Thessalonica's regular garrison as well. The centaurs, though, had no trouble with it.

Now that they had broken free of the Avar cavalry, they were in plain sight from the wall. Distantly, George heard the cries of astonishment that rang out from the militiamen there. He hoped none of those shouts had God's name, or Christ's, in them, or that, like arrows, such names had only a limited range. Otherwise, some of Thessalonica's defenders were liable to rout the rest before the latter had done all they could do.

What would he have done, had he been up on the wall instead of up on Crotus' back? What would his friends up there do, seeing a horde of centaurs? Sabbatius, now, Sabbatius would think he was drunk and seeing things that weren't there. But the rest? What would they do? One answer that crossed George's mind was, *holler for Bishop Eusebius*.

And what would Eusebius do when he saw centaurs? Being who and what he was, he would start praying them away. Since he was a holy man, his prayers would have more power behind them than those of ordinary militiamen. George murmured a small prayer of his own, to keep Eusebius off the wall as long as possible.

An arrow hummed past George's head. The Slav who shot it had no idea he was riding Crotus. That mattered only a little. The arrow might have pierced him only accidentally, but would have caused every bit as much anguish as if aimed by a clever archer.

A thrown stone caught the Slav in the ribs. He dropped his bow and folded double, clutching at himself. Another Slav nearby threw down his spear and fled the field. That struck George as an eminently sensible thing to do. He might have done it himself, had he been in a position where it was practical, or even possible. Atop Crotus, he had no choice.

As if recalled from other business he had thought more urgent, the Avar priest suddenly seemed to spy the centaurs. Moving with obvious reluctance, he pulled several Slavic sorcerers away from their wild dance. He and they stared at the onrushing supernatural creatures hardly more than a bowshot away.

Crotus' hooves came down in thick ooze. The male centaur had to yank each foot from the ground to go forward. Angry cries said other centaurs were similarly mired. The shouts from the walls of Thessalonica, loud before, suddenly seemed weak, distant. George glanced toward the city—and stared. All at once, it looked very far away.

"We're not in the hills we know," he called to Crotus. They weren't in hills at all, but rather in a muddy marsh. The Slavic wizards acted perfectly at home in the new environment. The Slavs were people of forests and marshlands. The Avar who led them had got them to make their foes try to fight on terrain unsuited for any kind of quick movement.

"Natheless, we go on," Crotus answered. The centaur no longer sounded so fierce nor so sure of what it was about as had been true a little while before—the wine, George guessed, was beginning to wear off. But, step by slow, frustrating step, the advance did go on.

The Slavic wizards' magic went on, too. Seeming

satisfied the centaurs would not be able to interrupt till too late, the Avar released the sorcerers he had called on to help him slow them. The wizards went back to their dance. He held the smaller magic by himself, while they built the greater. The hair stood straight up on George's arms, as if lightning was about to strike.

And so perhaps it was. Clouds boiled into being out of nothingness, though somehow they avoided covering both the sun and the nearby crescent moon. A harsh chant rose from the wizards. George ground his teeth. This was the moment. He and the centaurs had come so far, dared so much . . . and fallen just short.

As clouds will, these formed vast shapes in the sky—or rather, one vast shape, the shape of a middle-aged man of bull-like power, his arms and the cloak draped over them flung out wide. "Perun!" the Slavic wizards cried, and thunder and lightning roared. The Avar priest had called up thunder gods, too, but they were playful little things next to this brooding majesty.

After a moment, as if they had paused to make sure their first summons was a success, the sorcerers called out another name: "Svarozhits!" More motion in the sky drew George's glance. Suddenly the moon was not only the moon, but also the blade of an axe borne by a heavenly warrior taller than the treetops. If the moon god brought down that shiny-bladed axe, surely it would cleave the whole world.

Along with their Avar overlord, the Slavic wizards capered in delight. They cried out yet again: "Svarog!" Where the moon had become Svarozhits' axe, now the sun was also the blazing eye of a god enough like the other to be brother or father. George bowed his head against Crotus' back. If that burning gaze fell on him, he would be nothing but ash blowing in the breeze.

And the Slavic wizards summoned yet another god to their aid, bellowing out his name: "Triglav! Triglav! Triglav!" Unlike his comrades, Triglav was rooted to the earth, and seemed strong with a boulder's great strength. He had three conjoined heads on a single neck, which perhaps accounted for the wizards' summoning him three times. He looked in all directions at the same time, and carried a great sword.

Had the great gods of the Slavs fallen on the centaurs, the fight, such as it was, would have been over in moments. But the wizards had not summoned them into the world to deal with a minor annoyance, but rather to crush the great city that had resisted the Slavs and Avars for so long. And so Perun and Triglav, Svarog and Svarozhits swung their ponderous attention toward Thessalonica.

Not only did the walls of the city seem distant to George, but also tiny. The advancing gods would crush those walls underfoot, as a careless man might crush a child's toy. "God, help Thy city!" George groaned.

He forgot all about the centaurs. Since the holy name was not aimed against them, it did them no harm. As a man will, George had sent up a great many prayers in his life, some to get this or that, some to avoid that or the other thing. As is God's will, some were answered, some not. He had never had a prayer answered so spectacularly as this one.

From the walls of Thessalonica—and also, at the same time, from Father Luke on Elatus' back, among the band of centaurs—shone a clear, white light, dispelling the gloom the clouds that were Perun had cast over the landscape. Having seen the Slavic gods manifest themselves on earth, the shoemaker expected he would also see God the Father, probably in the guise of an angry old man, appear to stand against them. Bishop Eusebius, Father Luke, and every other priest to whom he'd ever listened insisted God was uncircumscribable in that fashion, but, to George, *uncircumscribable* had been nothing but a big word. Now he began to understand.

In that glorious light, Svarozhits and Svarog all at once seemed pale, attenuated, like men stricken with consumption. Perun drew back his cloak of clouds, as if to protect himself from the divine radiance. Triglav paused, seeming frozen in his tracks.

But neither the gods nor the wizards of the Slavs were to be despised, nor, for that matter, was the Avar priest who led them as Bishop Eusebius led the Christian hierarchs of Thessalonica. The Avar shouted angrily to the wizards. The wizards screamed at their gods. And the gods regained a measure of the strength and purpose they had lost in the first fierce glow of God's power.

Triglav stumped forward once more, sword held high. Perun unveiled his features, to show his furious face. Lightnings rippled round the edges of his cloud-cloak. Svarog's solar eye cast a fierce light of its own. Svarozhits swung his axe, and the heavens seemed to tremble as the moon moved.

The Litaean Gate opened. Out rode a horseman, gorgeous in the parade armor of a bygone era. The Roman cavalrymen carved on the arch of pagan Galerius had gear rather like his. But he was no pagan: he glowed with the same light as had given the Slavic gods pause. "St. Demetrius!" George shouted joyfully.

As if naming the saint had given him fresh force, he lowered his lance and rode straight for Triglav. The Slavic god did not give back a step, but swung his savage sword and bellowed harsh defiance from three throats at once. Demetrius' lance was aimed straight at his broad chest. The hooves of the saint's horse thundered like—*like those of a centaur*, George thought. Though he rode one, he had almost forgotten the centaurs, transfixed as he was by the clash of greater powers.

But the centaurs were still very much in the fray. Crotus hurled a fist-sized stone at the Avar wizard's head. It hit the sorcerer just above his left ear. He crumpled, limp as a sack of barley. The centaurs roared with delight. The Slavic wizards also cried out, in horror. Stones started falling among them—and striking home, too.

All at once, the marshy ground to which the fight had been transferred faded, returning it—and George, and the centaurs, and the wizards—to the lands the shoemaker knew. It was, he thought, at last a good day. Sunshine streamed down from a sky free of Slavic gods. No divine radiance shone forth from Thessalonica's wall (where George could see Bishop Eusebius' bright robes) or from Father Luke, but that was a fair trade. George looked around. No sign of St. Demetrius, but no sign of three-headed Triglav, either. That was a fair trade, too.

Now the centaurs were on solid ground once more. Where they had wallowed forward through mud to get close enough to the Avar priest and Slavic wizards to do them any harm, now they could gallop once more. They might have been an avalanche rolling down on the sorcerers. The Slavs fled from the fire, screaming. It did them no good. The centaurs thundered after them (trampling the unconscious Avar underfoot), flinging stones, seizing with hands, kicking out with hooves. From Crotus' back, George slashed till his arm was sore.

The massacre took bare moments to finish. George looked around to see what the centaurs might do next. With some astonishment, he realized they didn't have to do anything more. The wizards must have promised the Slavs and Avars that this last push, with their great gods brought forth to back them, would surely let them break into Thessalonica.

And now, with success promised, they and their warriors had failed. Having failed, and having failed so unexpectedly, the barbarians must have decided nothing could make their siege succeed. Avars in scalemail and Slavs in hides and linen began streaming away from Thessalonica. Here and there, a chieftain from one people or the other tried to persuade his men to hold fast. It did no good. Nothing did any good now, not in holding the siege together. George watched a band of Slavs mob a chief who tried once too often to hold them to the fighting.

"We did it!" the shoemaker shouted, and pounded on Crotus' back with a hand he detached for a moment from

Perseus' cap. "We did it!" He let out a great ringing shout of joy.

Great ringing shouts of joy rose from the walls of Thessalonica, too, as the defenders of the city watched the siege break up before their eyes. Gates opened. Militiamen came forth to harry the Slavs and Avars as they withdrew. A few of the militiamen stared in wonder at the still-rampaging centaurs and tried to approach them. More, though, paid them no attention whatever, as if doing their best to pretend, perhaps even to themselves, that the creatures from a bygone era did not, could not, exist in modern, Christian times.

From the wall, faint but unmistakable, came Bishop Eusebius' voice: "In the name of God, in the name of Jesus Christ, in the name of the holy martyr St. Demetrius, let all pagan powers depart this land. May it henceforth be free of them forevermore!"

Beneath George, Crotus shuddered as if an arrow had pierced its vitals. Behind him, all the centaurs cried out. They began to move away from Thessalonica. Even mad with wine, they could not bear the power of holy names directed specifically against them. The last thing George wanted was to be taken away from Thessalonica when he'd gone through so much to get back there. As carefully as he could, he slid from Crotus' back to the ground.

That turned out not to be carefully enough. He couldn't keep his feet, but went down onto his backside. Perseus' cap fell off his head. He grabbed it and started to put it back on, but then, when a centaur dodged around him, realized that might not be a good idea right away. If the centaurs saw him, they could avoid him. If they didn't see him, they'd trample him without knowing he was there.

Impelled by the name of God, the band of centaurs fled back up into the hills with amazing speed. Not a bowshot away from George, Father Luke stood staring back at their retreating hindquarters. He waved to the shoemaker. George waved, too, and walked toward him.

Father Luke clapped him on the back when he came up. "Thank you," the priest said. "I want to tell you, this has been, I think, the most astonishing day of my life, and I wouldn't have had the chance to take part in these great events if not for you."

"If that's how you look at things, Your Reverence, you're welcome," said George, who would have been as happy—happier—to have had no part whatever in these great events. "And will you thank me tomorrow? When you go back into the city, you'll have to explain to Bishop Eusebius what you've been doing."

"He will set me a penance, I will accept and perform it, and we'll go on as we did before," the priest answered. "With the siege broken and Thessalonica delivered from the Slavs and Avars, he may not be too harsh."

"I hope you're right," George said.

Father Luke looked concerned. "But what of you, George? You still have troubles with Menas. I will do all I can for you, but I do not know how much that will be. Menas is a powerful man. He had a will of his own even before God gave him back the use of his legs, and now—"

By way of answer, George did put Perseus' cap on again. He patted Father Luke on the back. Then, when the priest turned one way, he went around and tapped him on the other shoulder. Father Luke turned again. George patted him on the head. A moment later, he poked him in the ribs. A grin stretched across the shoemaker's face. Father Luke could not see that grin, which was exactly the point.

"I think I can manage," George said out of thin air.

"I think you may be right," Father Luke admitted, fortunately not angry at the cavalier way the shoemaker had treated him. "Try not to be so ferocious in your rejoinder that you make a new martyr."

"I'll—try," George said grudgingly. Menas hadn't shown any such restraint toward him. Menas had done his level best to get him killed, and the rich noble's best had almost been good enough.

"Good." Father Luke started walking toward Thessalonica. George followed invisibly. The gates remained open. Some militiamen were still coming out to pursue the Slavs and Avars. Others, many with light wounds, came back into the city. No one paid much attention to Father Luke as he walked toward the Litaean Gate. No one paid any attention to George at all. Invisibility had its advantages.

On the other hand, he might have painted himself orange with green stripes and got into Thessalonica unchallenged right then. So long as the men coming in didn't look like Slavs or Avars, the guards who stayed at the gates weren't bothering them. The guards were not in a bothering mood. They were passing a jar of wine back and forth. He wondered what Rufus would say about that. *Give me some*, most likely. George walked past the guards into the city.

XII

People packed the narrow, winding streets. They pounded one another on the back. They shouted out bits of song, generally off-key. Men and women kissed in doorways or sometimes out in the middle of the street, blocking other traffic. Nobody showered them with abuse, not now. George would have bet anything anyone cared to name that not all, or even most, of the couples embracing were married to each other. Nobody cared, not now.

He spied a familiar tall, thin figure. The Thessalonicans were so overjoyed at being delivered from the Slavs and Avars, they even included Benjamin the Jew in their celebration. No one showered him with abuse either, not now. He looked absurdly confused. He had no idea how to cope with acceptance. It wasn't anything he'd ever had to worry about before.

Then he spotted George. He smiled, waved, and picked his way through the crowd toward the shoemaker. He clasped his hand. "Praise the Lord, to see you here and well," he exclaimed. "I had heard you were lost beyond the wall, which grieved me greatly."

"I *was* lost beyond the wall," George said. "I managed to get back."

"God must think well of you," Benjamin said.

George wondered about that. If God thought so well of him, why had He put him through so much trouble and danger? Why had He inflicted Menas on him? Why, for that matter, had He cured Menas, so the noble had a fresh chance to inflict himself not just on George but also on the rest of Thessalonica?

Before George could come up with answers for any of those questions, a different, more obvious one occurred to him. "You can see me!" he exclaimed. Of itself, his hand went to his head. Yes, he was still wearing Perseus' cap. "How is it you can see me?"

"With my eyes?" Benjamin suggested, which was, George supposed, about as near as the sobersided Jew came to making a joke. Before either of them could take the question further, the crowd separated them. Someone stepped on George's toes. In the crush, whether that fellow saw him or not was irrelevant.

Under the rim of Perseus' cap, George scratched his head. The Slavic demons and demigods hadn't plagued the Jewish district of Thessalonica, and now Benjamin not only penetrated the pagan Greek enchantment that lay over George, he didn't even seem to notice there was an enchantment to penetrate. George didn't know exactly what that meant. Whatever it was, he had the strong feeling Bishop Eusebius would not approve.

He got stepped on several more times before he finally reached his own street, and elbowed, and kneed, and poked. In close quarters, invisibility had its disadvantages, too. When he did get to his own street, the first thing he found was Claudia arguing with the woman who lived next door to her and Dactylius. Between them was a pile of garbage someone—George didn't know who—had thrown into the street right between the two houses. If the two women knew the Slavs and Avars had been routed and the siege of Thessalonica broken, they didn't care. George smiled. Some things didn't change.

But if Claudia and her neighbor remained intent on

their own private quarrel, the rest of the street celebrated along with the rest of the city. People passed jars of wine back and forth. Those who still had salt meat or candied fruit stored away brought them out and shared them with friends—and sometimes with passersby, too—confident they could replace them now.

And, everywhere, people were embracing. George almost walked past a young couple in a doorway three or four doors down from his house and shop. They didn't seem any different from scores of other happy pairs he'd seen . . . till he noticed that one of them was Constantine the potter's son and the other his daughter Sophia.

He coughed. At the same time, he took off Perseus' cap, returning to visibility. Constantine and Sophia jumped in the air, then flew apart from each other as if he'd dumped a pail of water over them.

"Father!" Sophia exclaimed. She managed to pack a multitude of meanings into the one word: joy at having him come back again, along with something that wasn't joy at all at having him come back at that particular moment.

"Uh, we didn't see you, sir," Constantine added.

"I know. I noticed," George said. Constantine and Sophia both turned red. The cap of invisibility wasn't why they hadn't seen him. They'd been otherwise occupied. If he'd kept quiet, he might have stood there for an hour before they noticed him. "Maybe you won't see me the next time, either," he went on. "Maybe I'll be more annoyed about it the next time, too. Go on home, Constantine. Sophia, you come with me."

Constantine went, without a murmur. Only later did George realize that, with a sword on his belt and with his right arm and tunic splashed with blood obviously not his own, he looked well able to enforce any orders he might give. Even Sophia followed him without arguing.

In his own doorway, he found Theodore kissing the plump daughter—plump despite the siege—of Dalmatius the oil-seller, who lived in the next street over. He hadn't known the two of them cared about each other (for that matter, he didn't know whether they would care about each other tomorrow, or in an hour). An evenhanded man, he coughed as loudly as he had with Sophia and Constantine.

Theodore and his friend—her name, George remembered, was Lucretia—sprang apart, as Sophia and Constantine had done. "Hello, Father," Theodore said, sounding a little less reproachful than Sophia had.

"Hello," George answered mildly. Lucretia headed for home without George's suggesting it. He wondered how many more she'd kiss before she got there. Then he wondered if Theodore was wondering the same thing.

A moment later, such abstractions stopped troubling his mind, for Irene came running out of the shop and threw herself into his arms. He tilted her face up and kissed her, doing a good and thorough job of it. Sophia and Theodore both coughed. They sounded downright consumptive as each tried to outdo the other.

Irene ignored them. Her lips were urgent against her husband's. George ignored his children, too, till he started to laugh. That ruined the kiss. "We're married," he growled at Sophia and Theodore, and returned to what he'd been doing when he was so rudely interrupted.

Except for his son and daughter, no one paid one more kissing couple any mind. Claudia and her next-door neighbor, by contrast, had drawn a fair-sized crowd. A quarrel in Thessalonica, just then, was remarkable for its rarity.

"Thank God you're safe!" Irene exclaimed when her lips separated from George's again. She dragged him into the shop. A couple of braziers made it a little warmer in there than it had been outside. If Theodore and Sophia hadn't followed them in, George got the idea his wife might have dragged him down onto the floor of the shop, too. Before he got in there, he doubted whether he would have been able to do anything in response to that. Just when he decided he would, he found he didn't have the chance.

"Were there really centaurs out there, Father?" Sophia asked. "People are saying so, but people are always saying all sorts of things that aren't true, so they can make a better story out of them."

"There really were centaurs," George said solemnly. He could feel the truth of that on the insides of his thighs. He wasn't used to riding a donkey, let alone a horse, let alone a supernatural being with a mind of its own—a mind, when he was aboard Crotus, full of mad, drunken fury.

"And those other things?" Irene asked. She shivered against George and crossed herself. "I didn't want to look up in the sky, for fear I'd believe what I was seeing."

Only Irene, George thought with a smile, *would put it like that*. But the smile quickly faded. "Those other things were there, too. I'm glad they're gone."

"God overcame them," Irene said.

George wondered about that. The Slavic thunder god and gods of sun and moon had paled before the power of the Lord, but they hadn't vanished. And the struggle between Triglav and St. Demetrius had barely begun before the centaurs distracted and then overwhelmed the Slavic wizards and their Avar leader, thus returning the conflict, at least as George perceived it, to the mundane plane.

"However it happened, the siege is over," he said, "and that's what matters."

Nobody argued with him. "The Slavs and Avars won't be back here any time soon, either," Theodore said. "We taught 'em a proper lesson, we did." To listen to him, he'd beaten back the barbarians single-handedly during his brief stretch of duty on the wall.

"You still have that cap," Irene said, pointing to it. By the way she spoke, it might have been Joseph's coat of many colors soaked in blood.

"Yes, and glad of it, too," George said. "Without it, we wouldn't have had the centaurs in front of the city, or Father Luke with 'em, and who knows what would have happened?

I've got to go up into the hills and give it back, but I want to use it one more time before I do."

"I don't want you to do that," Irene said.

"Well, I'm going to," George answered in a tone that brooked no argument. Irene stared at him. He wasn't the sort of man who commonly ignored what his wife wanted. Maybe that was what let him get away with it this once.

Even after midnight, revelers remained on the streets of Thessalonica. In a way, George liked that. The people of the poor, beleaguered city deserved to celebrate their victory over the Slavs and Avars. In another way, noisy roisterers on the street were a nuisance to the shoemaker. He would have preferred everything around him to be dead quiet. That would have made what he was doing more impressive.

Maybe I should have waited, he thought. *What if he's out celebrating? What do I do then?* He shook his head. He couldn't afford to wait, not if he wanted to keep the peace in his own home. At the moment, Irene wasn't arguing with him. If Perseus' cap stayed in his home for several days before he got around to using it, that would change. He knew his wife. She would come up with a reason why he shouldn't use it, and likely reasons why he ought to get rid of it, too. And they would be good reasons—he was sure of it. If he turned them down, he would have a quarrel on his hands. He didn't want that.

And so, instead of a quarrel on his hands, he had Perseus' cap on his head. He slipped through Thessalonica's streets unnoticed, unremarked upon. Some of the things he noticed while slipping through the streets were themselves remarkable, but he kept quiet.

The district by the citadel, up in the northeastern part of the city, was where the rich people lived. One of the privileges of being rich was taking shelter in the citadel if the city wall was breached. George went slowly; he seldom came to that part of town. From the outside, the house he was looking for wouldn't be much different from its neighbors. And, in the darkness, the differences were next to impossible to make out.

"I don't want to knock on the wrong door," the shoemaker muttered. "I *really* don't want to knock on the wrong door."

At last, he found what he thought was the right door. He tried it, gently, so as not to disturb anyone inside. It was barred. He muttered again. He'd known it would be, but had hoped that, just this once, life would make things easy for him. No such luck. He rapped loudly on the door, as if he had every right in the world to go straight in. When nothing happened, he rapped again, even louder.

A tiny window with a metal grate was set into the timbers of the door. After a little while, a small part of a face, dimly lit by a lamp or taper, appeared on the other side of the window. "Who disturbs Menas' rest at this ungodly hour?" asked a voice presumably connected to the face.

"I am an angel," George announced. He stood very close to the door, so the servant inside could tell where his voice was coming from—and could note that he was hearing it without being able to see anyone speaking. "I am come to test both you and your master. Open at once, or you will share his fate."

In a way, this was the weak part of his plan, and he knew it. If Menas' servant liked the rich noble and was loyal to him, he would leave the door closed, and George wouldn't be able to get in. The only thing invisibility would be good for then was to keep anyone from seeing how foolish he looked.

Coming to Menas' home, though, he'd pinned his hopes on the idea that no one who knew Menas and had to work for him was likely to like him. And so it proved. The door flew open. The servant said, "If you want Menas, you can bloody well have him!"

"You have passed your test," George said, and squeezed past the fellow, careful not to touch him as he did so.

Lamps set in wall niches lighted the halls of Menas' home; George wished he could have afforded to use oil so prodigally. There were a lot of corridors, too—he wandered for a bit before finding the one that led to Menas' bedchamber The noble's own snores guided the shoemaker down the corridor to the proper room.

There, dim shadows, lay Menas and his wife. She snored, too. George took a deep breath, then shouted at the top of his lungs: "Injustice!"

Both shapes sat up in bed and looked around wildly. Menas started to cry out. George whacked him with the flat of his blade. The rich noble tried to reach down under the bed, where he likely kept a sword of his own. George stepped on his hand.

About then, Menas realized that, while he could hear and feel whoever was in the chamber with him, he couldn't see anyone but his wife. "Injustice!" George shouted again. Menas' wife opened her mouth to scream. George yelled once more: "Silence!"

Menas' wife didn't scream. The noble did: "Ho! My men! Help! To me! A murder! To me!"

George whacked him again. He howled. Down the hall, George heard the servants stirring. That was liable to be trouble. If they came after him, they could trap him in these narrow halls without having to see him. Then, if he wanted to escape, he'd have to cut his way through them, which he hadn't intended to do.

But the servants did not come to Menas' rescue. Instead, one after another, they ran outside, into the chilly night. Maybe the doorman had told them what sort of visitor the household had. Maybe they weren't interested in rescuing Menas any which way. George wouldn't have been.

He laughed, unpleasantly. "You see what the wages of injustice are," he boomed, trying to sound as impressive—and as much unlike George the shoemaker—as he could.

"Who—who—who are you?" Menas, now, Menas sounded like an owl.

His wife had a different question: "What are you?"

"I am an angel," George declared, as he had for the servant. Menas' wife crossed herself. George had already seen—and was very glad—that that did not destroy the power in Perseus' cap. He went on, speaking to Menas: "Wretch, God did not give you back your legs so that you could use your regained bodily vigor to wrong those who have done you no harm. The grave awaits such wickedness, the grave and eternal torment."

He *didn't* sound like himself. After a moment, he realized he *did* sound like Bishop Eusebius. That was all right, he supposed; angels could reasonably sound like churchmen. Churchmen certainly thought they sounded like angels.

"But—I've never done anything like that." This was not the angry, blustering Menas George had come to know and loathe. This was a frightened Menas. But it was also an utterly bewildered Menas. With no small shock, George realized the noble had no idea he'd done anything wrong or reprehensible.

Hesitantly, Menas' wife spoke up: "Maybe, dear, maybe the angel means that shoemaker who was persecuting you."

George felt like kissing her, though that wouldn't have done his impersonation any good. If he'd had to mention himself, Menas was liable to have put two and two together.

On the other hand, maybe he wouldn't have. Menas seemed to have trouble putting one and one together. "That Gregory or George or whatever his name was?" he exclaimed. "Not likely! He deserved whatever happened to him, the way he spread lies about me through the city."

He never knew how close he came to having his big belly ripped open by a sword he never saw. "Fool!" George shouted. "Arrogant idiot!" He whacked Menas with the flat of the blade again. The temptation to let it turn in his hand, to slash instead of whacking, was as strong in his mouth as the maddening taste of wine in a centaur's. Menas cringed. Fighting down the urge to murder, George went on, "Being a liar and a cheat yourself, you reckon all men possessed of a like mean-spiritedness." He knew he was stealing that phrase from Father Luke, but did not think the priest would mind. "The shoemaker told you the truth: he did not slander you."

Menas hadn't even bothered to remember his name. That infuriated him more than almost anything else.

"Really?" The rich noble sounded astonished. "Everyone said he did."

"And you believed gossips and liars, not the man himself," George said scornfully. "Know you not what rumor and gossip are worth?" He still thought Menas hadn't listened very well to what "everybody" said, too, but kept quiet about that, not wanting to escape trouble by putting John into it.

"What must he do to be saved?" Menas' wife asked the question, perhaps because she thought her husband wouldn't.

Stirred by that, Menas spoke up, in a petulant voice: "I suppose you're going to tell me I have to pay him ten pounds of gold, or something outrageous like that." He stuck out his chin and looked stubborn.

Did he suspect George was George, and not an angel at all? Or had he been visited by a veritable angel before, and made to pay compensation for whatever he'd done to prompt the visit? George wasn't sure he wanted to know. He answered, "Leave the man at peace and trouble him no more. That will suffice. Obey me not, and the grave and the pangs of hell await you."

"I'll obey," Menas said quickly. "I will." Now he sounded perfectly tractable. George wondered why. It occurred to him that, if Menas were an angel (an unlikely thought), he would have demanded money in exchange for good behavior. George's not doing so must have struck the noble as particularly holy, even downright angelic.

He didn't mind Menas' thinking him holy. He didn't want Menas thinking him soft. He walloped the noble with the flat of the blade again, and shouted, "Obey!"

By then, Menas' head was probably ringing like a gong. George hoped he hadn't broken that head, although his own heart wouldn't have broken if it turned out he had.

Deciding the wisest thing he could do was not overstay his welcome, he left the bedchamber then. For good measure, he slammed the door shut behind him, which made Menas' wife scream. George didn't mind that; if she was impressed with him as an angel, she would help hold her husband to the straight and narrow.

As things were, George discovered he'd almost stayed too long. After fleeing the house, a couple of servants had nerved themselves to go back inside. "We'd better see if there's anything left of the boss," the one in front said to the other, who seemed to be doing his best to walk in his footprints.

"Hope not," the one behind him said—but he said it quietly, in case Menas should have disappointed his hopes.

George flattened himself against the wall of the corridor. That just gave the servants room to squeeze past without touching him. As soon as they *were* past, he shouted "Beware!" and ran for the door. Their frightened shouts rang most enjoyably in his ears as he dashed out into the night.

More servants were coming toward the house. So were a couple of neighbors. So was a priest; the church of the Archangels wasn't far away, and somebody must have run and fetched him. George wasn't sure the power in Perseus' cap could survive an exorcism aimed directly at it. Then again, he didn't have to put it to the test, and he didn't. Hoping—and praying a little, too—the lesson he'd given Menas would stick, he dodged around the people cautiously approaching and headed home.

John said, "Let me make sure I understand this. You hung around in the woods until the Slavs and Avars got driven away. Then you came back into Thessalonica through one of the gates we opened to come out and chase 'em."

"That's right," George said. And it *was* right. It omitted a good deal—and all the most interesting parts—but it was the essence of what had happened. George was as well pleased to have the interesting parts omitted.

John rolled his eyes. "There's only two problems with it. The first one is, I don't believe a word of it. How come nobody saw you coming in?"

"I don't know," George answered stolidly. He'd said the same thing whenever any of his friends asked him that question. Even more stolidly, he went on, "I suppose everybody was too busy staring at the herd of centaurs to pay any attention to one ordinary shoemaker."

The tavern comic grunted. "If I hadn't seen them with my own eyes, I wouldn't believe that, either. I'm still not sure I do."

"Fine. Don't believe it, then. Believe we're still under siege," George said. "Me, I'm going to go out there and do some hunting." The Litaean Gate loomed up ahead of the two men.

"That's the other reason I don't believe the story you're telling," John said. "If I'd been dodging Slavs for however long it was, I wouldn't want to stick my nose outside the wall now. There are still barbarians skulking through the woods, you know. You remind me of the clever fellow during the storm at sea. He saw everybody else on the ship grab something to save himself with, so he took hold of the anchor."

"Heh," George said. "Have you used that one at Paul's place yet, or are you trying it out on me first?"

"I'm trying to keep you from getting killed," John said with some asperity. "I thought you'd gone and done it once, with a little help from your friend Menas, but then you came back again—however you came back again." He gave George a dark look. "And now you want to go out there some more. You used to be such a sensible fellow."

"I'm sensible enough to know when I need to do some hunting," George said. Someone else went out of the

Litaean Gate. George pointed. "See? I'm not the only one, either. Why don't you nag him for a while?"

"I'm not his mother—I'm your mother," John said, which startled a grunt of laughter out of George. John threw his hands in the air. "All right, go ahead. See if I care. But if you come back dead, don't run crying to me saying I didn't warn you."

George contemplated following that through to its logical conclusion, but his own logical conclusion was that it didn't have one. He walked out through the gate. When he looked back, John was still framed in the gateway, staring out after him. The tavern comic shook his head and turned back toward the center of the city. George headed out to the woods.

Once trees and brush screened him from view, he took Perseus' cap out of the large leather wallet he was wearing on his belt in place of the more usual pouch. John had assumed he'd be bringing small game back to Thessalonica in it. He would, too, if he caught any. Meanwhile, though, the pouch let him take the cap out unnoticed. As soon as he put the cap on his head, he was unnoticed, too.

He headed north, toward Lete. When he got farther up into the hills, he intended to take off the cap, in the hope that a centaur or satyr would find him then and guide him to the pagan village, which he was still unsure of finding without such aid. In the meantime, he killed several rabbits that, thanks to Perseus' cap, never knew he was there. It wasn't sporting, but he wasn't hunting for sport—he was hunting for the pot.

He spent the night in a chilly bed of leaves and boughs. Early the next morning, noises from beyond the brush ahead made him move forward cautiously. He had seen a couple of small bands of Slavs in the woods: poor, hungry-looking fellows for whom he would have felt more sympathy had he not known they would have cut his throat if he were visible. If he was coming up on another such, he wanted to make sure they had no idea he was anywhere close by.

These noises, though, weren't quite like the ones the barbarians had made. As George drew closer, he realized they weren't like any noises he'd ever heard in the woods. As he drew closer still, he realized that didn't mean they were altogether unfamiliar.

Thanks to the cap, he made no noise working his way through the undergrowth. He bit down hard on his lower lip to keep from exclaiming, which would have been heard. He'd found a satyr, all right: there on the stump of a toppled forest giant stood Ampelus. And there, back to the satyr, golden tail in the air, stood Xanthippe the centaur. Nephele hadn't been interested—which was putting it mildly—but the female had said other centaurs would sometimes sport with satyrs.

And some sport it was, too. Ampelus had both equipment and stamina to make George acutely aware of his merely human shortcomings (a most appropriate word) in those regards. At the end, when Xanthippe let out a sound half moan, half whinny, what George felt—as opposed to what the female centaur felt—was closer to awe than to excitement.

And, even afterwards, Ampelus tried to persuade Xanthippe to stay for another round. The centaur laughed. "One—and in especial one of that sort—sufficeth."

"Not for me," Ampelus said grumpily. Sure enough, the satyr's body showed how ready it was for another go.

Xanthippe laughed. "Then thou mayest sate thyself." Centaurs habitually used the familiar second-person pronoun when speaking to satyrs. Was it, here, the familiarity of insult or intimacy? *A bit of each*, George thought.

Laughing still, Xanthippe cantered away. Ampelus took a few trotting steps after the female centaur, then seemed to realize the game truly was over. The satyr stroked its own flesh. If what had gone before failed to satisfy it . . . it was, George supposed, true to its own nature.

With Xanthippe gone, the shoemaker thought he could reveal his own presence without embarrassing anyone—

not that Ampelus was liable to embarrassment under any circumstances. As soon as George took off Perseus' cap, Ampelus stiffened, now with wariness rather than lust. Before the satyr could flee, George stepped out into the clearing.

"Oh. Is you." Ampelus relaxed. An enormous grin stretched over the satyr's not-quite-human features. "You know what I do?"

George knew exactly what the satyr had done. He shook his head anyhow. "Could you tell me on the way to Lete?" he asked.

"All right, I do," Ampelus said. "Sooner tell you than other satyrs. They talk too much in front of centaurs, and I get a kicking like you don't believe." The bruise Nephele's hoof had given the satyr was gone from its flesh by now, but evidently not from its memory.

Ampelus bragged all the way up to the pagan village hidden in the hills. George had heard much the same from men. The satyr, by what he'd seen, boasted only of what it had truly done. As much as its incredible performance, that served to set it apart from mankind.

As they approached Lete, a woman who had been spreading tunics and cloaks on the branches of a tree to dry paused in her work and stared at Ampelus. The satyr leaped in the air with glee. "Maybe this the one Ithys get," it said. "You go to village yourself now, George. I have to find this out." It trotted toward the woman. She didn't run for her life, so maybe she *was* the one with whom Ithys had frolicked—which meant Ithys' bragging hadn't been a pack of lies, either.

When George got to Gorgonius' shop, the carpenter nodded as if he'd been expecting him just then. "See, I knew you'd be back," Gorgonius said. "Is everything well down in the city?"

"Yes, the siege is broken," George answered. A moment later, he realized Gorgonius might have meant something else. "And everything's well with me, too—I think." He set Perseus' cap on a table. "Thank you."

"You're welcome," the carpenter said. "You're a good fellow, even if you are a Christian." George jumped to hear the name. Gorgonius laughed. "I can say it. No centaurs or satyrs to frighten now, so why not? I'm willing enough to let you go your way. Your bishops down in the city, though, they wouldn't be willing to let me go mine."

"When there were only a few Christians, pagans persecuted them," George said with a shrug. "Now it's the other way around, that's all."

It was Gorgonius' turn to look surprised. "I hadn't thought of it like that," he admitted. "Shall we drink some wine on it?" When George nodded, he went on, "I've got some chicken left over from yesterday, too, if you'd like that."

George nodded again. He reached into the wallet, took out a rabbit, and laid it by the ancient leather cap. "Why don't you take this, then? You can use it tomorrow, or it'll keep a couple of days more if you leave it out in the cold."

"You're a gentleman," Gorgonius said. "Don't go away. I'll be back with the wine and the food."

He brought everything in on a fancy wooden tray he must have made himself. Along with the chicken, he had bread and sun-dried apples. One cup of wine became several. George taught him a couple of tavern songs from Thessalonica that hadn't made their way up into the hills before. In turn, Gorgonius sang a couple so old they'd been forgotten down in the city. They might have been old, but they weren't bad. George hoped he'd remember them.

After a while, Gorgonius said, "You'll spend the night in my barn again. Better that than finding some place to lie up in the woods, I expect."

"I should be all right, as long as I have—" George stopped and stared suspiciously at his winecup. Once he left Lete, he wouldn't have Perseus' cap anymore. He covered his mistake as best he could, saying, "Thanks again."

"Any time, any time." Maybe Gorgonius hadn't noticed the error anyhow; he sounded pretty vague himself. He held out the dipper. "More wine?"

"Why not?" George said.

As he had the last time he slept in Lete, George spent a little while brushing wisps of hay out of his hair and off his tunic when he woke up in the morning. Gorgonius gave him a flat loaf of barley bread and a small flask of wine. "You want to have a care going home, you know," he said seriously. "You won't be wearing the cap, mind you."

"Yes, I understand that," George answered. No, the carpenter hadn't noticed his flub the night before. "I'll keep my eyes open."

"Come up here again," Gorgonius said as the shoemaker stepped out into the street. "You'll be welcome."

"Why don't you come down to Thessalonica?" George said. "I won't tell Bishop Eusebius you're there." He realized Irene would have some detailed opinions to express about the prospect of a visit from a pagan. But, since Perseus' cap had saved not only George but also, very possibly, Thessalonica itself, the shoemaker had some opinions of his own, too.

"Who knows?" Gorgonius said. "Maybe I'll even do that. You never can tell." He sounded as if he might have meant it, and was surprised to discover as much.

As George headed out of Lete and down toward Thessalonica, he looked around for Ampelus and for the woman who'd been hanging out her wash. He didn't see either one of them. The laundry she'd hung out was still draped in the tree. George wondered what that meant. She and Ampelus couldn't still be at it . . . could they? He supposed satyrs wouldn't be satyrs if anything along those lines were impossible for them.

When he got into the woods, he moved as quietly and cautiously as he could. He'd come to take for granted the protection Perseus' cap gave him. Now that he was without it once more, he knew how vulnerable to his foes he was. If a band of roving Slavs found him, he was in trouble. If a Slavic wolf-demon found him, he was in bigger trouble.

Perhaps because he was so cautious, he had another good day hunting. He got a couple of rabbits, and also got a squirrel he caught on the ground before it could scramble up into a tree. If he found a place where he thought it safe to build a fire, he'd eat well. If he didn't, he'd bring the meat home to Irene, who could do tasty things with it beyond toasting chunks of it on a stick over the fire or baking it in clay.

He was, he supposed, somewhere a little more than halfway to Thessalonica when he came across the Slav. Each of them stepped into the same small clearing at the same time. George's sword was in his hand. The Slav carried a heavy javelin or light spear. If he threw it and hit George, he'd win the fight straightaway. If he threw it and missed, all he had left with which to defend himself was a short dagger.

He didn't throw the spear. Instead, he darted back in among the trees. So did George. The shoemaker began a cautious sidle to his right, hoping—praying—the Slav was alone. He'd gone more than halfway round to the other side of the clearing before he called to mind the expression on the barbarian's face at seeing him. The Slav had been at least as horrified as he was. That argued the fellow was alone, too, and hoping George wasn't part of a band of Romans.

When George got to the point from which the Slav had emerged, he stepped into the clearing and looked around. At almost the same moment, the barbarian poked his head out from the spot George had occupied. They stared at each other again, then both went back into the forest once more.

This time, George kept on heading south. He paused every little while, listening to make sure the Slav wasn't stalking him. He never heard anything, and the barbarian didn't leap out at him from behind with a savage shout. After he'd gone a few furlongs, he had a sudden mental picture of the Slav nervously traveling north, pausing every little while to make sure the fearsome Roman wasn't on his trail.

George laughed. He knew he wasn't particularly fearsome. If the Slav didn't know that, he wasn't about to tell him. Even so, George walked a bit more confidently after that.

He got back to Thessalonica a few minutes after sunset, with the last of the evening twilight still staining the sky. "You have a good day out there?" a militiaman at the Litaean Gate asked.

"Pretty good." George patted the wallet so the guard could see how nicely fat it was. Nodding, the fellow waved him into the city.

A few minutes later, he was back on his own street. People waved to him there, too. He was something of a hero to his neighbors, not for anything he'd actually done while he was trapped outside the city—he had said very little about that, thinking the fewer who knew, the better—but simply because he'd come back after being given up for lost. Even Claudia called, "God loves you, George," as he walked by. George wondered how much God had had to do with it, and how much the pagan powers had accomplished. He didn't argue with Claudia, though. Arguing with Claudia was a losing proposition.

Constantine, Leo's son, nodded warily to George as they passed on the street. George nodded back. He remembered giving that same sort of wary nod to Irene's father, back in the days when they were courting and their families were dickering. He supposed that meant Constantine was likely to end up his son-in-law. He sighed. He still thought Sophia might have done better. But then, Irene's father had thought the same thing about him.

He walked into his shop. Sophia and Theodore let out squeals inconsistent with the adult dignity they usually affected. He hugged them both. Irene came downstairs.

He hugged her, too, and showed her the carcasses of the animals he'd caught on the way to and from Lete.

She ignored them. "That thing you had" —she would not dignify Perseus' cap by its proper name— "it's gone?"

"Yes, it's gone," George said.

"You went to and from that place" —Irene would not dignify Lete by its proper name, either— "safely?"

George decided on the instant that she did not need to know about the Slav he'd met in the woods. "Yes," he answered.

He thought he'd spoken without hesitation. Irene's face told him he was wrong. But she didn't press the point, saying instead, "And now that you're back, you'll stay here with your own family for a while?"

By *a while*, he knew she meant something like, *the next thirty or forty years*. Nevertheless, he said "Yes" again.

This time, he really must have spoken without hesitation. His wife smiled and said "Good" and kissed him. Right then, staying in Thessalonica struck him as a pretty good idea after all.

As if Rufus were making a command decision in the middle of a battle, he grabbed three of the rickety little tables in Paul's tavern and pulled them into a line. "There," he declared. "Now we can all sit together."

Along with Dactylius, Sabbatius, and John, George slid stools over behind the tables. John kept his at one end of the new formation. "I'll be going on in a while," he said. "This way, none of you can trip me as I head up to the stage."

"That's true," Rufus said. "We'll just beat on you when you come back." He spoke as if he might have been joking—but he might not have been, too.

Paul stepped out from behind the bar and walked over to his fellow militiamen. "First cup's free tonight, boys," he said, as he'd been doing since the Slavs and Avars abandoned the siege. George wondered how long such generosity would last. Not much longer, if he knew Paul.

John sipped the wine and made a sour face. "If it weren't free, it'd be cheap, I can tell you that," he said.

"That's good, John." George made as if to applaud. "Go ahead—bite the hand that feeds you."

"Good to see *you* back, George," Paul said. "You always pay your scot, you drink enough so you don't just fill up a stool, and you don't get rowdy and tear the place apart. And you don't soak your tongue in vinegar before you come in, either." He gave John a hard look.

The tavern comic, who had seen a lifetime of them, did not seem unduly damaged. "Behold perfection," he said with a mocking bow to George.

"Well, *I* like the wine," Sabbatius said. That, however, was a recommendation not even Paul could view with pride. Sabbatius liked the wine because it was wine, not because it was good wine. As if to prove as much, he held out his cup. "Fill me up again. I don't care with what."

"Sawdust might be good," John said musingly. "Or maybe rocks."

Sabbatius folded his right hand into a fist. "Here's one rock." He closed his left hand, too. "And here's another one. How would you like to meet up with the two of them?"

"Any time," John jeered. "Any time you're awake, anyhow."

Sabbatius started to surge up off his stool. Rufus grabbed him by the shoulders and slammed him down. "Too early to start brawling—didn't you hear Paul?" Sabbatius was bigger and stronger than the veteran, and less than half as old. He obeyed him without question anyhow. That was what made Rufus a man to lead men.

"Don't start on your friends," George advised John, "or after a while you'll go around wondering why you haven't got any."

"I don't wonder," John said. "I know." He held out his cup to Paul for a refill, too. When the taverner gave it to him, he gulped it down.

Dactylius said, "If you know your jokes annoy people, why do you keep making them?" The little jeweler plainly did not aim to be annoying; as usual, he sounded serious and sincere.

John's eye glinted. With one more cup of wine in him, he would have wondered aloud why Dactylius stayed with Claudia if he knew she was a harridan. George could see that. He shifted so he could kick John in the ankle if he began to ask the question. Rather to his surprise, John kept quiet. Maybe he'd listened to George. George wasn't used to having people listen to him, but understood why: he spent most of his time talking to his children.

The tavern filled up fast. Since the Slavs and Avars broke off the siege, the people of Thessalonica had been in a mood to have a good time. Sooner than he might otherwise have done, Paul called, "And now, to make you laugh, to take your troubles away, and maybe to give you new ones, here's John."

"Ha!" John said as he got to his feet and hurried to the platform with a sort of boneless lope. "He knows me too well." He paused and looked out over the crowd, then shook his head. "You're a bloody poor lot if you've come *here* for a good time. You should all be home with your wives." He paused again, as if contemplating what he'd just said. "Well, that explains *that*."

"What does he mean?" asked Sabbatius, who was not only unwed but already drunk. Without waiting for an answer, he laughed anyhow, a loud, empty bray.

"Here we are, all safe and sound," John said thoughtfully. "There were times when I wouldn't have believed it, not during the siege I wouldn't." He pointed to the table from which he'd come. "There are the valiant militiamen who defended the wall near here. Would *you* think they could keep out a pack of howling barbarians?"

"Thank you, John," George and Dactylius called out together, one in Latin, the other in Greek. They grinned at each other.

"Hey, I'm a militiaman, too," John said. "Would you

think *I* could keep out a pack of howling barbarians?"

"If they understood what you were calling 'em, yes," somebody said loudly.

John didn't annihilate him, as he did most critics. The remark fit too well with the way his routine was heading. "Maybe," he said. "It all worked out, thanks be to God. You even see rich people over on this side of town, and you didn't hardly do that during the siege, did you? No. Most of them stayed over on the east side, where they could duck into the citadel in a hurry if they needed to."

George listened with wary attention. After the putatively angelic visit, Menas had left him alone. If John started poking fun at him—for he was one of the rich men who had been on the western wall of Thessalonica—George knew he was liable to get blamed for whatever the comic said. That might mean the immunity he'd won would unravel.

But John chose a different tack, saying, "During the siege, those rich people hardly even knew they were living in the same city with us. Somebody told one of them that there was an assault going on, and he said, 'Well, no need to panic. It's only the Litaean Gate the Slavs and Avars are attacking.' "

"Why is that funny?" Sabbatius demanded. He hadn't fallen asleep yet, as he usually did sooner than this.

Patiently, George explained: "Because the rich fool thinks that what happens over at the Litaean Gate couldn't matter to his part of the city."

"Oh." After a bit, Sabbatius let out that braying laugh again.

By explaining, George had missed some of John's routine. The comic was saying, "—and the fellow's son promised to come back from the sally with a Slav's head. 'Oh, that's all right,' the fellow answered. 'I don't care if you come back without a head.' "

Somebody threw a roll at him. He caught it and ate it. "That's one way to get something to eat around this place," he said pointedly, and stared over toward Paul.

After a moment, the taverner had a barmaid bring over a plate of olives. John made as if to grab the girl instead of the plate, and stared out at his audience in mock indignation after she escaped. "How did she know what I wanted to eat?" he said. The barmaid threw a roll at him. He caught that one, too.

"We all had a hard time," he said. "No two ways around that. What I want to know is, why didn't the barbarians have the decency to besiege us in the summertime, when we wouldn't have had to stay up on the wall in such miserable weather? I know one fellow" —he pointed to Sabbatius, who had started to snore by then— "who stood out in the rain so long, he jumped in the river to get dry."

"Christ!" Rufus said. "They were telling that joke in Italy when I was a lad."

"They were telling that joke in Italy when Caesar was a lad," George said, and couldn't resist adding, "and he's only a little younger than you."

"God will punish you for that," Rufus growled, convincingly angry, "and if He doesn't, I will." They laughed together, as old friends will. Why not? The siege was over.

George laughed at John's jokes, too: at some more than others, as is the way of such things. What pleased him best about the comic's routine was that John did not mention Menas even once. Maybe, however late in life, he'd learned the beginnings of discretion. Or maybe, and perhaps more likely, events of the past few weeks had given him so much new material that, for the time being, he didn't need to bait the rich noble.

John ran a hand through his hair and said, "I suppose you're wondering why I don't have so much up here these days." His hair was cut a little shorter than it had been before George got locked out of Thessalonica, but only a little. He went on, "I have to tell you, it's Rufus' fault."

"Just because you have to tell it, that doesn't make it so," Rufus exclaimed.

John ignored him. "There at the end of the siege, he was throwing us up onto the wall with anybody who was still healthy, not just with men from our own company." Because George had been out of the city, he didn't know whether that was so or not. John continued, "Me, one night I was up there doing a shift with old bald Basil and with Victor the barber. Sometimes, when nothing much is happening, you'll doze up there instead of tramping back and forth all the damn time."

"You'd better not!" Another exclamation from Rufus, this one in an altogether different tone of voice.

John kept right on ignoring him, saying, "So that's what I did, and Basil, too. I told Victor to wake me in an hour's time, and then I'd do the same for him. I fell asleep, good and hard. So did Basil. Well, Victor got bored while we were snoring away. He got out his little razor and shaved my head for a joke. When he finally shook me, I thought it was colder than it should have been, and I rubbed my head and found out I didn't have any hair left. 'What a fool you are,' I told Victor. 'You've gone and woke Baldy there instead of me.' "

"Here," somebody called. "I'll give you a miliaresion *not* to tell that one again."

John leered at him. "And how much will you give me not to tell the next one on you?" He looked over the crowd and held out his bowl. "Or on *you*? Or on you there, with the ugly tunic. Yes, you. You know who I mean."

He was grinning when he came back to the table, the bowl nicely heavy with money. "Not a bad take," he said. "Not a bad take at all." He started separating the coins with his usual quick dexterity, then looked up from his work. "Where are you going, George?"

"Home," the shoemaker answered with a yawn. "I'm not like Sabbatius"—who was still snoring away—"I don't sleep in taverns."

"And besides," Dactylius put in, "you don't want to wake up bald, the way John says he did."

"Everybody thinks he can do my job," John muttered

darkly. Then he brightened. "Ha! Justus really did give me silver. *Now* you can go home, George."

"I don't take orders from you," George said. "I take orders from Rufus."

"Go home, George," Rufus said. Laughing, George did.

George said, "Dear, I think we really have to dicker with Leo now."

Irene let out a sigh. "I wish we didn't. Constantine's not a bad lad, mind you, but I think we can do better for Sophia."

"I don't think Sophia wants better. She wants Constantine, and I think she's going to get him no matter what we say about it." George told how the two of them had been kissing when he came back into Thessalonica after the Slavs and Avars gave up the siege.

"And what did you do about that?" his wife asked.

"I coughed. They jumped apart," George answered. "They were embarrassed. But they'll do it again whenever they find the chance. You don't take one kiss like that without wanting another. If they find the chance, they'll do more than kiss."

He expected Irene to be affronted at the way he'd impugned Sophia's care about guarding her virtue. Instead, his wife sighed and laughed a laugh half wry, half genuinely amused. "All right, we'd better talk with Leo," she said.

"You pick the oddest times to be sensible," George remarked. Irene, luckily for him, was already intent on the dickering that lay ahead, and so paid less attention to him than she might have done.

Rain pattered down outside. Some of it turned to ice when it struck the ground. George didn't mind. He was under a roof that didn't leak too badly, a couple of braziers spread heat, and woodcutters could go out into the forest again, even if they did go with armed guards to make sure no lurking Slavs picked them off. Some of the woodcutters wanted armed guards against the centaurs and satyrs. George knew that was foolish for any number of reasons, but said nothing. He was not a man to whom people listened on such matters.

"The one thing we have to do," Irene said, her mind running ahead on its own road, "is make certain Sophia doesn't do anything out of the way" —a euphemism George hadn't heard before, but clear enough— "till the dickering is done. When I tell her it would hurt the bargain we're striking, she'll understand that." She looked sidelong at her husband. "My mother told me the same thing about you."

"Did she?" George said. "You never mentioned that before."

"A time for everything, and everything in its season," Irene answered: not quite the language of the Holy Scriptures, but close. She grew brisk again. "Now—how do we approach Leo without making it too obvious we're approaching him?"

"Why don't you go buy a pot from him?" George said. "If you like, you can break one over my head, so the story will get round that we need a new one."

"I usually get them from old grouchy Antonius, but that will do, I think." Irene gave him a kiss for coming up with a good idea. Musingly, she went on, "I don't think I have to break one on you. Maybe I don't even want people to think I did that. I'm not Claudia, after all."

George kissed her this time. "And a good thing, too, says I."

Irene came back with a fine new pot—George was ready to admit (though he never would have done so to Leo's face) it was better than any they already had. She also came back with a triumphant smile lighting her features. "I didn't even have to start the dickering," she told her husband. "Leo did that, as soon as I walked through the door. Constantine must be giving him some heat."

"That's very good," George said equably. "Do we have a bargain? Do we have a bride-price set? Do we have a day for the wedding?"

"Of course not," Irene said. "There's no hurry to these

things—well, not too much of a hurry, anyhow, provided Sophia and Constantine don't give us a reason for one. But we have a bargain that there will be a bargain, if you know what I mean."

"All right. Nice to have that settled, or on the way to being settled." George paused, then said, "Come to think of it, we may be doing some more bargaining one of these days before too long." He told how, coming back into Thessalonica, he'd found not only Sophia kissing Constantine but also Theodore kissing Lucretia.

"Lucretia?" Irene said in some dismay. "She's so heavy." Her eyes glinted dangerously. "And why didn't you see fit to mention this until now? I might have been caught unawares, you know."

"It slipped my mind," George answered with a shrug. "We have had rather a lot of things going on lately, you know. And I don't have any idea how much she means to Theodore—if she means anything. He hasn't talked about her, you'll notice. Maybe that just means he's shy about it, I admit. But maybe it means—"

Irene finished that for him: "Maybe it means the whole town was going crazy because the Slavs and Avars were leaving, and he decided to see what he could get. Yes. That sounds like a man."

"Oh, I don't know," George said, not about to let his half of the human race be slandered so. "Who came out of this shop and kissed me a lot harder than either of our children was kissing right then?"

"Hmm," Irene said, and George thought he'd won the exchange. But then she said "Ha!" and pointed at him, and he knew he hadn't. She said, "I kissed *you*, my husband, not the first man I saw on the street." She drew herself up in triumph.

"Well, so you did," George admitted. But he had a finger to wag at her, too: "Theodore's not married, so that isn't fair."

"Hmm," Irene said again. This time, she didn't go, "Ha!" She seemed content to leave it a draw. So was

George. They both started laughing at about the same time, most likely because they both realized leaving such things as draws was the best way to get through life together and stay friends doing it.

George was coming back from Benjamin the Jew's with a sack full of jingling bronze buckles—Benjamin had gone back to his regular line of work once the siege ended—when he ran into Father Luke. That was literally true; each was hurrying around a corner. They both said, "Oof!" Father Luke, who was the lighter of the two, staggered back a couple of paces.

"I crave your pardon, Your Reverence," George said, steadying him.

"No harm done," the priest said with a smile. Most people in Thessalonica, by then, had lost some of their siege-induced gauntness. Grain and livestock had come in from several towns to the east, easing hunger. Father Luke's skin, though, seemed more tightly drawn over his cheekbones than ever. He looked as if a strong wind would blow him away.

"Are you all right?" George asked. He'd gone to St. Elias' for the divine liturgy each Sabbath after the deliverance of the city, but hadn't had a chance to talk with the priest since then.

Father Luke nodded. "Yes, I'm very well, thank you."

"You don't mind my saying so, Your Reverence, you don't *look* very well," George said bluntly.

"The well-being of the flesh and that of the spirit are not always one and the same," the priest replied. If he wasn't contented, his voice didn't know it.

"If you haven't got any flesh left—" George began.

Father Luke cut him off. "If I haven't got any flesh left," he said, "my spirit will have been translated into a world better than this one, as I pray it shall be one day in any case." He set a hand on George's shoulder. "You needn't worry about me. Bishop Eusebius is not so angry as to require me to give up the ghost, I assure you."

"You couldn't prove it by looking at you," George said. "In a high wind, you'd be gone, near as I can tell. Look—there's a place." He pointed to Paul's tavern. "Why don't you let me buy you some bread and sausage and a mug of wine? You'll be better off for it—and happier, by the look of you."

"I'll break bread with you, if you like," the priest answered, "but I am forbidden flesh, and likewise I am forbidden strong drink."

"Drinking water all the time's not healthy!" George exclaimed. Father Luke shrugged. "You are the most exasperating man!" the shoemaker burst out, and Father Luke shrugged again. George rubbed his chin. "Suppose I get you some bread, and some cheese to go with it?"

Now Father Luke looked thoughtful. "I was forbidden meat and wine, but I was not ordered to subsist on bread and water alone. Now, this may well have been an oversight on the bishop's part, but he cannot in justice claim I have violated the terms of his penance if I start eating cheese before Lent." With that, he started toward the tavern, leaving George to hurry to catch up.

George almost ran into someone else who was hurrying around a corner: a big, burly fellow with an expression that warned anyone in his way to get out of it. He recoiled from George, however, as much as George recoiled from him. They gave each other a wide, silent berth as they went their separate ways.

"That was Menas, wasn't it?" Father Luke asked when George came up to him. "He left you alone."

"Yes, he did," the shoemaker agreed. "I hope he goes right on doing it, too."

"I've prayed he would." Father Luke's eyes twinkled. "Whatever the agency of his change, I am glad to see he has made it." The priest did not ask what George had done with Perseus' cap before going back up to Lete with it. What he did not know, he did not have to notice in his official capacity.

George got him bread and honey and cheese and onions

and olives and mushrooms fried in olive oil. "There you go, Your Reverence," he said. "No flesh, no wine, but food that'll put some meat on your ribs."

Looking at what was set before him, Father Luke murmured, "The most holy bishop would *not* approve." Then, louder, he went on, "But you won't see me turn it down, either." He ate every little thing on the platter, down to the last fried mushroom. When he was done, he still looked hungry. But, when George waved for the barmaid to bring him more food, he shook his head. "I've already committed gluttony. Don't make me compound the sin."

"Eating a meal that keeps you from starving a digit at a time is not gluttony," George declared, as if daring the priest to argue with him.

All Father Luke said, though, was, "Eating two such meals in the space of half an hour surely is."

When the priest seemed mildest and most gentle, he was hardest to move. George had seen that a good many times already. If Father Luke didn't yield, the shoemaker would have to, and he did: "All right, Your Reverence. I was only trying to help you through the worst of it."

"I understand that, and I'm grateful," Father Luke answered. "But this is not the worst of it. This is only the aftermath. The worst of it was galloping down through the hills on centaurback, fearing at every bound we would be too late."

Compared to that, George supposed going hungry for a while wasn't the end of the world. He'd come too close to seeing the end of the world himself, or of that part of the world that mattered most to him. "I think the worst of it for me—just for myself, mind you, not for Thessalonica—was when Menas slammed the postern gate in my face."

"Even Menas has a place in God's plan," Father Luke said serenely.

George's hackles rose. "I'll tell you where I'd like to place Menas," he growled. "If you dropped him off the highest part of the wall into a really ripe midden heap, he might go deep enough to suit me. Yes, sir, he just might."

Father Luke held up a hand. "The two of you are quits. I have seen it is so, and I am glad it is so. Very well, then: let it be so. And let us speak of happier matters: do I hear rightly that your lovely daughter is to marry the son of Leo the potter? I know you were asking me about Constantine not so long ago, and I regret having been unable to tell you more. I gather you and your clever wife finally judged the young man adequate?"

"Adequate. Yes." George knew he should have spoken with more warmth, more enthusiasm. He couldn't do it. What father ever truly believes any young man this side of a prince—and sometimes *that* side of a prince, too—adequate to marry his precious daughter?

Maybe, somewhere not far away, Dalmatius the oil-seller was at that moment wondering if Theodore could possibly be adequate for Lucretia. If so, he was a fool, and shamefully ignorant of Theodore's myriad sterling qualities. Anyone who knew Theodore would think the same. Theodore, after all, was George's son.

"I pray they will be happy together, and enjoy many prosperous and fruitful years," Father Luke said.

"Well, Your Reverence, if anything can make that likelier, I expect your prayers will do the job," George answered. Father Luke dipped his head, acknowledging the compliment.

"More bread? More olives? More cheese?" the barmaid asked. "Some wine? Neither one of you is drinking any wine." *What are you doing here if you're not drinking wine?* she seemed to be saying.

George shook his head. Father Luke set a hand on the shoemaker's arm. "Because I may not," he said, "does not mean you should not."

"One cup," George said, and the barmaid went off to pour it. Father Luke beamed, pleased to have been taken at his word. George had long since found that taking the priest at anything less than his word was a mistake.

When the woman brought back the wine, Father Luke

asked, "May I propose a toast? If you consider that rude because I am not drinking, by all means say so." George made haste to wave for him to go on. Smiling, the priest said, "Drink to Nephele and Crotus and the rest of the centaurs for me, then. They went without wine rather longer than Bishop Eusebius has enjoined such abstinence for me." Half to himself, he murmured, "Abstinence," again, and then, very quietly, "Nephele." If the thoughts going through his mind at that moment were ecclesiastical, George would have been amazed.

"I'm glad to drink to that one," the shoemaker said, and did. "If it hadn't been for the centaurs—and for you to persuade them to get roaring drunk—we'd all be worse off than we are now." He raised a quizzical eyebrow. "Didn't the bishop tell you not to have anything more to do with them, though?"

"That he did." Father Luke grinned. "He did not, however, forbid me to drink their health, at least vicariously." The grin got wider. George recognized it: it was the one Theodore had given him when, as a small boy, he'd found a way around some instruction of George's. Laughing, George finished the wine.

But he didn't laugh long. After a little while, he said, "I'm afraid we're not rid of the Slavs and Avars for good."

That sobered Father Luke, too. "If the Emperor Maurice can drive the barbarians back beyond the Danube—which I pray he succeeds in doing—then we may be free of them for a long time to come," he said. "If he is less fortunate on the battlefield—"

"Heaven forbid!" George exclaimed. "What I wouldn't have given to see our garrison of regulars come galloping to the rescue, there at the end of the siege."

"And I," the priest agreed. "But they served the Roman Empire elsewhere, as was God's will. And so we, and Thessalonica, made do with centaurs. Centaurs fit into the divine plan, too."

"They would tell you otherwise, if they could speak the name of God," George said.

"I know they would." Father Luke was unruffled. "They are undying, and wise, and lovely." Was he thinking of Nephele again? Before George could nerve himself to ask, the priest went on, "But they are also faded, defeated by the new dispensation, and in any case only creatures of local power seeking to judge the one universal and almighty God. They may no more comprehend Him in fullness than may you or I."

"They would tell you otherwise there, too," George said.

"I know," Father Luke repeated, unruffled still. "If you like, I'll say my say all over again, so we can have the argument at yet another remove."

"No, thanks." George tried another tack: "If we'd been late coming down from the hills, the gods of the Slavs might have overthrown Thessalonica before we could do anything to the wizards who brought them forth."

"So they might have," Father Luke said. "But we were in good time, if barely in good time, the reason being that God did not allow us to be late."

"You've got all the answers," George said, chuckling.

The priest shook his head. "No. Only one." He rose from the table and clasped George's hand. "I was heading back toward St. Elias' when you waylaid me and dragged me in here. If you can stay a bit longer, drink another cup of wine for me." Off he went, a man who knew where he was going and why.

"Do you want that cup of wine or not?" the barmaid asked when George sat for a minute or two without calling for it.

He stared at her. She stared back, altogether unembarrassed about eavesdropping. "Yes, I'll take it," he said at last. She brought it over to him and hovered till he set coins on the tabletop. By the way she scooped them up, she might have suspected they were counterfeit. Thus encouraged, George gulped down the wine and left.

It had started to snow while he was in the tavern. Snowflakes danced in the air. A thin layer of white lay over everything, not yet streaked with soot, not yet trampled into slush. George stood outside the doorway for a moment: the falling snow was beautiful.

It was also cold. He wrapped his tunic more tightly around himself and hurried off toward his own home and shop. The snow crunched under his boots. Every time he exhaled, he breathed out fog.

As he walked along, shivering, he thought about what Father Luke had said. Crotus and Nephele thought differently: he'd said as much himself. The Avar priest had thought differently, too, till the centaurs put paid to him. Who had the right of it?

"Menas, a part of God's plan?" George snorted. The notion was absurd on the face of it.

He walked a few steps farther. Then, despite snow, despite cold, he stopped. *Was* it absurd? Or was the pattern of events larger and more complex than George had perceived till this moment? Had God cured Menas' paralysis so that the rich noble, having become George's enemy, could, by shutting him out of the city, force him up into the hills to meet the centaurs, to gain Perseus' cap, to bring Father Luke up into the hills to get the centaurs drunk so they would have the spirit to attack the Slavs and Avars besieging Thessalonica and help save it?

He looked up into the gray sky. Was that God's will he saw, or only his own imagination running away with him after a couple of cups of wine? Either way, how was he supposed to tell?

A snowflake landed on the tip of his nose. He brushed it off and started walking again. He was only a couple of blocks from home.